Thinly Veiled

Eliza Modiste

Book Cover Design by Mitxeran

ISBN: 979-8-3772-0201-1

www.elizamodiste.com

Contents

Chapter One

E scape. It was always a word that daunted me, but I supposed that was because it's more of a relative term than anything. For some, it meant feet pounding against pavement. Running. Gasping for breath. A pulse that rattled one's ribcage from within as they prayed for release from a hellscape that was unknown to others. For many, it meant a far-off land where they could bury their toes in the sand as they listened to waves crashing against a shore in the distance.

For me, escape had brought me to Salem, Virginia.

There was no rhyme or reason to the choice of the town itself. Once my mind was willing to accept the idea that I desperately needed to relocate, I had eyeballed a radius from my hometown of Ogden, North Carolina and scoped out the potential locations with a pen, paper, and a very, *very* poorly drawn map. Salem, for whatever reason, called to me. Perhaps it was because it was so far across state lines that I could deem myself as unfindable...or, rather, invisible. Perhaps it was because I could break free from the coastal air that I was so accustomed to and breathing in the cold of the Appalachia's sounded invigorating. Or, perhaps, it just sounded...*right*.

I didn't know, really. All that *was* known was that we were here, and the constraints that used to consistently bind my chest like a vice had loosened to the point that I was able to take a deep breath and sigh as I took in the sight before me.

The space was nice enough. The floors were a light cherry wood, though they weren't visible at the moment as they were obscured by the mass amount of boxes that we had yet to unpack. Countertops in the kitchen were a pristine white, spanning across a small island and cabinets edging the wall. I dragged my tired legs past the kitchen, bypassing the rectangular dining table that was holding too many boxes to count, and walked straight to the living area to rest our last box on the coffee table. Spent, I sank onto our grey couch which I considered to be remarkably plush for its age. My phone, which had at some point been haphazardly tossed onto the chair adjacent to me, dinged with a text message. Before I could even pick it up to respond, my best friend-turned-roommate, Zoey Sheffield, snatched it away from me.

I mumbled, "Fuck, you're fast for how small you are."

Zoey stretched all five feet of her height upward as she crossed her arms and tucked my phone by her waist in a defensive maneuver. Her emerald eyes narrowed at me as she tilted her short, blonde pixie cut to the side in a way that conveyed, *I'll beg your pardon?* I chuckled under my breath—she wasn't always this predictable, but this was par for the course with Zoey. Back in high school when I tried nicknaming her *Tink,* I had quickly realized that she's a bit sensitive about her height.

"And you have a dirty fucking mouth," she retorted.

Oh, the irony.

"You know, Claire," Zoey continued, "you don't have to respond to every text. It's just going to rile you up. And sitting on your ass eating an entire carton of ice cream again isn't a great idea."

She had a point. Even though Zoey was still holding my cell, I knew with about ninety-nine percent certainty that it was my ex-boyfriend, Colton Langdon—and the ice cream moment that Zoey referred to was not quite as cliché as it seemed. I wasn't a girl in pain, mourning an unreciprocated love. I was the one who ended it, after all. Our relationship had been, if I had to sum it up in a word, tolerable. Or, perhaps, necessary. I cared for Colton as a person, of course—I'm not a monster by any means, but when I decided that we needed to part ways, the process of doing so was difficult. Difficult in the fact that Colton and I had a relationship of mutual convenience. We could have called it love if we wanted to, and we actually did for quite a while. But I don't think I even knew what *love* was—and neither did Colton, but the point was that he was having trouble letting me go. And to say the least, he hadn't taken too kindly to the fact that Zoey and I decided to up and move to Virginia.

Though the move in my mind was necessary, to describe it as hasty would be, well, apt. I remembered how vividly his icy blue eyes bored into mine when I told him.

"Virginia? Really, Claire? Virginia? What are you expecting to find there? How are you going to get by?"

I continued calmly packing my clothes into boxes.

"First of all," I replied, "you know I've been saving money for a while. I can use that while I try to find work. Besides that, I don't really know what I'll find...a new life?"

His gaze softened.

"Babe—" he said the word with a gentle caress of my hand.

I yanked it away.

"Don't Babe me!" I didn't mean to yell. It just automatically came out that way. I assumed that this was how it felt to be truly at the end of one's rope. It felt like fire ran through my veins, boiling my blood until my entire being was ready to spill over. I breathed in quickly once, and then out. "Just stop, okay? We were barely even a couple!"

"Bare—barely even a couple? For an entire year? Really?"

His face contorted in a way that made me wonder if he really did care about me, but I decided that it was best for my sanity to cut that thought short. That point was neither here nor there—I didn't need to try to delve into whether or not my now ex-boyfriend harbored any love for me at all.

"You tried to use me, Colt." I paused for a moment before rephrasing, "Actually—you did use me. Multiple times."

I held up a frilly pink blouse in front of my face and shriveled up my nose at the sight of it, tossing it into a Goodwill pile that I had been steadily adding to. 'New clothes, new start, new me' played like a mantra in my mind. Was it a cliché? Yes, yes it was. Did I care? It made me feel better about picking up my shit show of a life, so no. In fact, I couldn't find it in me to give a single fuck about clichés in this moment.

Colt murmured, "I liked that shirt."

I snorted. "Like that matters."

He quietly noted, "It made you look innocent."

"Yeah," I replied. "Bringing me full circle to the—" I held up my hands to use my fingers as quotation marks, "—using me for my innocent looks thing."

"Which. I. Apologized. For," he argued. "I'm fucking sorry, Claire, okay?!" I allowed myself to glance at him, feeling exhausted by his one-hundredth half-assed apology. He huffed out a short breath and looked back at me with an air of desperation. "We can do so much more," he started. "This is—this is just the beginning—"

"That's exactly the point," I interjected, holding up a hand to stop him. "I don't want..." I hesitated, gesturing between us vaguely in a circular motion. "I don't want this."

His face fell. His arms hung limply at his sides and I damn near almost backtracked, but I reminded myself of the type of man that he is and steadied my resolve. I squared my shoulders and faced him fully, steeling myself for my next words.

"You were a manipulative shit, Colt."

His eyebrows raised, his buzzed head bobbed up and down, and I questioned if I stunned him into silence. His shocked face did little to deter me from my original mission, though—which was getting the hell out of dodge. If anything, it spurred me on further as I thought back to what he had dragged me through. I had been Colton's doormat for a year, and any time I had the inkling to better myself—to start anew—to not follow him on every path, especially the damning ones—he would guilt me. It was all, 'Oh baby, I love you,' and playing with my easily deceived heart until I would come around and do whatever he asked. Honestly, it felt like everything we had been through was eating at my soul. All of it deprived me of my own individuality, not to mention the massive amounts of danger he put me in on a daily basis. If I didn't leave now while I still had the motivation to do so, I would fall right back into it all. I let out a slow breath and picked up a dark pair of jeans, folding them gently and placing them into my suitcase.

"I need distance," I told him plainly. "I need a new life."

His light blue eyes searched my face, holding a trace of astonishment.

"And you think you can achieve that?"

His tone degraded me as if I was no better than staying in the life that we had. He didn't mean that, though—I knew he didn't. He just wanted me here. The thought made me close my eyes tightly, clenching a fist so hard that I felt my nails make deep indentations into my palm. As I let my hand relax, I turned my gaze back to Colton.

I shook my head and said, "This conversation's over, Colt."

"Claire—"

"Get the fuck out and let me pack!"

"Claire!" Zoey broke me out of my reverie, snapping her delicate fingers in front of my face. "Seriously. Stop thinking about it...about him." She knew me too well. Handing back my phone, she stated, "It's not worth it."

I agreed with her, really, I did. It was just a little too difficult to stop obsessing sometimes. I exhaled, blowing a strawberry-blonde strand of hair away from my face.

"I know," I replied. "Thanks."

Zoey looked over at me with her all-too-knowing gaze.

"Come on," she goaded me, grabbing my hand to pull me up and toward the door. In my exhausted haze, I followed her, placing one foot in front of the other blindly as she continued, "There's a dive-looking bar a block away. Let's go out!" She practically jumped up with excitement, her eyes glowing.

I groaned, throwing my head back and slouching my shoulders as I pulled my hand out of hers.

"*Zoey,*" I whined. "I'm tired. This place is a wreck. My mattress doesn't even have sheets on it." I mumbled to myself, "Oh no, did I even pack sheets?"

She sighed audibly. "If you didn't, I have an extra set—and I know you're tired. I am too, but we're *here!*" She flashed a wide smile at me. If she *was* tired, she didn't look it in the least. "Let's go walk down the street, take a breath, and toast a gigantic *fuck you* to your past!" As she spoke the last few words, she flipped the bird with both of her hands and wiggled them in my direction.

I broke and let out a small giggle. "Fine," I said sarcastically, "twist my arm, will ya."

"Okay, come on, let's go then," she announced quickly, taking the few steps to the exit and placing one of her tiny hands on the doorknob.

I exclaimed, "Good God, woman, wait a minute!"

I scanned her from head to toe. I didn't know how, but she looked remarkably put together for having been stuck in a car and then moving boxes with me all day. There may have been a hair or two out of place on her blonde head, but she somehow was pulling it off with ease. I also wasn't sure exactly when, but at some point, she had changed out of her ratty moving attire and into black jeans and a tight red t-shirt.

"Let me at least try to look decent." I held up my hand, spreading my fingers. "Give me five minutes, okay?"

She rolled her eyes, crossing her arms across her chest. "Fine. Five minutes. Only five."

I all but sprinted to the bathroom, for I knew that her gentle threat was one that was very, *very* real. If I didn't hurry, I'd be dragged out of here by my hair with mascara on only one eye. I took a brief moment to look in the mirror. Wide, blue eyes looked back at me. The smattering of freckles that were on my nose and cheeks were a feature that I'd grown to love. My light red hair that I also typically adored, however, looked like a bird's nest sitting on my head.

"Oh, dear lord," I muttered, pulling my hair down and running a brush through it hastily. I finished putting on a little makeup and threw on a tighter fitting shirt rather than the old hoodie I was wearing all day when I heard Zoey call for me from the hallway.

"Time's up, bitch! Don't make me come in there!"

I slipped on my converse and walked into the hallway. She eyed me up and down.

"You'll do. Now let's go! I'm dying of thirst over here!"

The air was crisp as we walked down the street. Trees lined both sides of the pathway, our feet crunching through their fallen orange and yellow leaves that littered the cobblestone sidewalk. Fall was definitely upon us. The chill in the air was just starting to make the goosebumps rise along my arms when we halted our steps to take in the entrance that we approached. A wooden sign hung above our heads that simply read, *'Henry's.'* The weathered letters were probably once a vibrant red but had faded over time to a lighter, sun-bleached pink.

I looked down at Zoey. "Is this it?"

She nodded emphatically. "Yup. Close and convenient, right?"

I hummed in agreement. The walk was short. Probably too short. The type of short that made me idly wonder if I was going to be at this establishment far too often. I was just beginning to think that we should have found an apartment that was further away from a local watering hole—for my liver's sake, at the very least—when I was pushing the door open. Zoey followed me, and just as I heard a bell chime above us, I found myself standing stock-still.

There was little that was extraordinary about the bar. It was dimly lit and small—approximately ten chairs sat at the counter and five tables were against the wall with additional seating. An older man sat on a stool furthest from the door we walked through, silently enjoying what looked to be whiskey, and a handful of other patrons were scattered amongst the tables. The countertop of the bar ran perpendicular to the entrance that we walked through, the backsplash of the wall behind it ordained with shelving that held various liquors that were lit up with a light yellowish glow. Aside from the signs and posters illuminated with a neon light, the walls were covered with wood paneling. It wasn't the appearance of the bar that caught my eye, though. It was the bartender.

He had light brown hair, cut short on the sides and left a little longer on top. My eyes traced over his slim nose to his stubble-covered face. The dark facial hair failed to obscure his jawline which was, to say the least, angular. It could have been etched with a pencil, ruler, and a protractor—though I was unsure if protractors were available to those who were responsible for drawing the Greek Gods. Either way, the man before us looked to be a portrait of one come to life.

Zoey ran smack into me, waking me to the reality of my standing and gawking at the gorgeous man behind the counter, and she grumbled, "What are you do—*oh.*"

I shook my head quickly. *"Nothing—"*

"Oh, *he* does not look like nothing," she returned. "In fact, he looks like something—something you would enjoy *very much.*" I protested wordlessly, and she held up a hand to stop my incoherent stammering. She rhetorically asked, "Sit at the bar, yes?" and began to lead the way, slinking into a seat and beckoning me to follow her.

I sat next to her, easing into my stool and trying not to blush at the man who I was ogling. Steel grey eyes met mine and a smirk appeared on his lips as he greeted us.

"Well, hello red," he drawled. "Blondie."

I chortled a bit at his lame greeting and asked him playfully, "Are we characters in a western?"

Amused, his smile widened, and he quipped, "No, but I can pretend, right?"

I returned his toothy grin.

"Whatever gets you through the day, erm—" I hesitated, waiting for him to introduce himself.

"Luke." He stuck his hand out for me to shake. "Ah, Turner. Luke Turner."

"Claire Branson." I grasped his hand, cocking my head to the side in mild surprise as I realized how smooth it was. He turned to Zoey, shaking her hand as well as she introduced herself, and I couldn't stop myself from remarking, "You have *really* soft hands."

He shrugged. "Self-care is important. What'll it be, ladies?"

"Vodka soda," I replied.

"No sugar, no calories, no flavor, no fun," Zoey stated with a grimace before adding, "Appletini, please."

"Says the girl who gets hangovers from hell, sure," I told her.

Luke's eyebrows raised as he let out a chuckle and went about to prepare our drinks. He stayed well within earshot, scooping ice into a martini shaker.

"You know what they say about soft hands," Zoey joked, bringing up my prior comment as she looked at me with a side-eye that I knew far too well.

I twisted in my seat to look at her, held up an index finger in warning, and muttered, "If you say something about penises, I swear to God."

I noticed Luke's shoulders shake gently with a laugh at my retort, but he said nothing.

Zoey's gaze shot skyward. "I would *never.*"

I chuckled. "Hoe."

"I was just saying that they use a lot of *lotion,*" she replied. Her perfectly manicured brows bobbled up and down as Luke slid a martini glass filled with bright green liquid her way.

I glanced at him apologetically. "You can ignore her, really."

He reached for a lowball glass under the counter and set it in front of me, preparing my drink as he spoke mockingly, "Oh, she's not wrong, I use *loads* of lotion." His grey eyes danced with humor as he added, "Has nothing to do with my penis, but thanks for trying to defend it for me."

I felt my face flush a bit from his comment and cast my eyes downward as he pushed the glass toward me. He ambled his way to the other end of the bar to check on the man whose whiskey glass had since been drained and I shook my head, hoping that my hair shielded my reddening face as I peeked at him. Zoey elbowed me in the ribs and I redirected my attention to her, picking up my drink in the process and taking a large sip.

I smiled at her sweetly. "Yes?"

"Cute bartender's flirting with you, you blushing fiend."

I rolled my eyes heavily. "Oh please, no he's not."

"Sure, he's not—"

"Tips, Zoey. He lives off of tips. Of course, he's gonna flirt if he has the chance."

"Mhm," she voiced disbelievingly.

"Regardless," I reminded her, "I need another boyfriend like I need a hole in my head."

"Who said anything about a boyfriend?" She set her martini glass down gently on the wooden bar top. "Everyone needs a little *wham, bam, thank you, ma'am."* She pointed an index finger at me, speaking far too loudly as she said, "After everything you've been through, you need to get *laid—"*

"Zoey!" I chastised her with a quiet hiss as I noticed Luke in my peripheral vision making his way back to us. I whispered to her, "For the love of God, *chill."*

"You should take the stick out of your ass," she muttered back, "lighten up a little." Her eyes lit up. "Actually, take the stick out of your ass, replace it with his cock—"

"Christ, *Zoey!"*

I thanked my lucky stars that I didn't have any of my drink in my mouth, for it would have been sprayed all over the counter.

"So," Luke announced his presence as he approached our vicinity once again, "where are you guys from? I know I haven't seen you in here before."

"As a matter of fact," Zoey replied in what I could only describe as her wing-woman voice. "Claire and I just moved into town today!" She beamed a bit too brightly at me. "Didn't we, Claire?"

I slouched my shoulders as I looked back at her with a fake smile plastered on my face. I hummed through my teeth, "Mhm," and brought my drink to my lips once more.

"Here in Salem?" Luke asked. Zoey and I both nodded, and he smiled, simpering, "Well lucky us, then."

"What about you?" I asked. "Are you local?"

"Grew up closer to Roanoke—not far from here. I just never left, I guess." He shrugged, adding, "It's a good place to be though, I like it here. I'm sure you both will too." Just as he was offering me a genuine grin, the ice clinked together loudly in my glass as I pulled it away from my face. "Ah," he pointed at my now empty beverage, "another one?"

I nodded.

Luke picked up the vodka bottle from beneath the bar and held it up, tipping it at a 45-degree angle above his head, observing the lack of spirit within.

"Er," he tapped the glass, holding up a finger, "be right back."

I tilted my head to the side as I watched him walk away to grab a new bottle, finding myself increasingly interested in the design on the back pockets of his jeans as he moved. By the time he got to the other end of the room and disappeared into what I could only assume was the kitchen area, I had nearly forgotten that Zoey was sitting next to me.

"And you said you didn't want to go out," she said.

Well, I think that was what she said. All that reached my ears was a dull murmur as my mind was elsewhere. Perhaps slurping down my first vodka soda like it was the essence of life itself was a bad idea, but I was a tad bit distracted.

All that came out of my mouth in response was, "Hmm?"

Zoey reached her hand out and gently pushed upward on my chin until my teeth clacked together. *"There* we go."

I swatted away her hand as she chuckled at me.

"I'm allowed to *look,*" I replied.

"Coincidentally," she stated, slinging the remainder of her drink back, "if he likes ya, you're allowed to touch too. It's a free country, dear."

"I don't *need* that," I reiterated yet again.

"Right," she responded quickly, waving me away with a flick of her wrist. "Hole in your head, yeah, I know. *But,*" she stuck her finger towards my face, "he's *rather* good looking."

"Then *you* hit on him," I countered.

"First of all—he's too pretty-boy for me."

"Oh, you actually have a type?" I joked, "I couldn't tell."

Zoey had always been...open to any and all men that threw themselves her way.

"Secondly," Zoey laughed, "fuck you." She held up three fingers in front of me. *"Thirdly,* and lastly, *why* must you punish your vagina so?"

I snorted. *"My vagina,"* I nearly whispered back to her, "is perfectly fine, thank you very much."

Someone tapped me gently on my shoulder. I turned around to see a woman who was, to say the least, stereotypically beautiful. She was tan, blonde-haired and blue-eyed, had a body most women would kill themselves to get, and was looking at me with what I could only describe as sympathy.

"Hey there," Zoey greeted her none too politely considering the odd look on her face. "How can we help you?"

"Ah—wasn't trying to eavesdrop," she noted, "but I figured I'd catch you before he came back—don't bother." She smiled, though it didn't quite reach her eyes, and she tipped her head towards the opening to the kitchen. I followed her gaze and as if on cue, Luke reappeared, brand new vodka bottle in tow. The blonde lowered her voice to a murmur and quickly told me, "I tried to jump on that train years ago. He's gay." Zoey's smile faded off of her face as if she was a child and someone had stolen her candy, and the mystery woman remarked, "Don't tell him I told you, though. He gets kind of sensitive when people know."

With a flip of her golden hair, she turned away from us, leaving with a strut that screamed, *'There—good deed done.'* Truthfully, I felt bad for her. If her idea of a good deed was outing a man—a man who she admitted did not want this information to be public—to complete strangers, then I would hate to see what the rest of her personality had to offer.

I shifted my attention back to Zoey, and though I wouldn't want to admit it, I was wearing a slight frown. Everything I had said about not needing attention from men right now was certainly true, but dammit if the flattery of flirtation didn't boost my ego a little bit. I sighed softly.

Zoey shook her head. "You know, it's always the hot ones—"

I elbowed her in the ribs swiftly in an attempt to get her to shut her mouth because Luke was, once again, within hearing distance.

"Gah, bitch," she griped, rubbing her side gingerly.

Luke halted his steps in front of us.

"Sorry about that, oh—" His brow pinched together as he took in the scene in front of him, absentmindedly repeating the steps of making my second drink. Not a question asked, he looked to Zoey as he slid my glass to me. "Another for you too?"

She nodded, asking me, "And shots?" One of her eyebrows peaked up high again to ask if I was interested. The intensity in her questioning eyes told me that I had no choice in the matter. Without an answer from me, Zoey deduced, "Shots."

With that, it was determined that the night had only just begun.

I woke in a daze with sunlight peeking through my window and searing into my eyes. Our walk home from the bar, which we later learned was named Henry's because—you guessed it—the owner's name was Henry, was incredibly hazy. It was past midnight by the time we left and when we got back to the apartment, I all but fell into bed and immediately went to sleep.

Rubbing the sleep out of my eyes, I grabbed my phone from my bedside table and unlocked the screen to reveal five missed calls and ten missed texts, all of which were from Colton, as predicted. They ranged from, *'Claire, please come home,'* to, *'You can't just run away from your problems, you'll get that eventually.'* I laughed sardonically, closing my phone thinking that I can, and did, run away from my problems, thank you very much.

I rose from my bed, willing myself to clear my mind of Colton, and winced. Hangovers *were* real after all, and I decided that Advil, coffee, and bacon were a must. I padded through the apartment, feeling like I was walking amongst the clouds as my head bobbled on my shoulders, to find Zoey sitting at the kitchen table. Her head hung in her hands and a mug that appeared to be untouched sat in front of her.

"Mornin' sunshine!" I spoke in the cheeriest, loudest voice I could manage.

She looked at me through half-lidded eyes, emitting a sound that I could only describe as alcohol-induced misery.

"I made coffee," she stated with a groan. "Also, we're out of Advil and I may be dying."

I snorted at her expression. "Don't you worry your pretty little head, I'll go grab some at the market down the street. How about some breakfast burritos too?" She moaned almost sexually, and I deadpanned, "Please never make that noise in my vicinity again."

Zoey finally lifted her head, her eyebrows dancing up and down in my direction, and quipped, "You know you like it." Her vocal cords still sounded like they were rubbed raw, but the thought of greasy food must have sparked some sort of life back into her body as she said, "Give me two seconds; I'll go with you."

We walked the few blocks to the store in our pajama bottoms and loose sweatshirts for there was no point in changing. We decided that today would be nothing more than laying around and watching movies considering that tomorrow we were going to start job hunting. I happily breathed in the crisp air around me as we made our way back home with burritos, an Advil container that had already been opened and contained four fewer pills, and Starbucks in hand. Sure, we had a pot already brewed at home, but Zoey was the one who made it—and she makes *really* shit coffee. I silently praised myself for successfully avoiding the concoction as we rounded the corner to our apartment. As the complex came into our line of sight, Zoey grabbed my arm, pulling my caffeine fix away from my mouth abruptly.

"Oh, my God!" She exclaimed. "Look!"

A certain clean-cut bartender who I couldn't help myself from chatting to all night was leaving our building.

I felt my eyebrows raise as Zoey and I slowed our steps, taking in the situation from afar. The curious thing about the scene that made Zoey squeal out in the first place was that Luke wasn't alone. Another man trailed behind him as they walked down the sidewalk away from us.

"*Hello*, tattoos," Zoey cooed quietly enough so he wouldn't hear.

The man in question was facing the opposite direction and I couldn't get that great of a view of him, but I was on par with Zoey with the first thing that I noticed about him being the dark ink that spanned over both of his rather large arms. He had similar colored hair to Luke, but it was longer, almost chin length, and tucked behind his ears. He shivered against the cold of the morning considering he was only wearing a black t-shirt and jeans.

I whispered to Zoey, "Where the hell did we just move?"

"I don't know," she replied, "but I *like* it. Do you think it's something in the water here that makes the men ridiculously attractive?"

I snickered. They stopped walking as they approached a grey car and when they did, Luke turned around and gave the tattooed man a tight hug. As he pulled away, Luke was saying a few choice words. He clapped him on the shoulder and the man walked around the car, sliding himself into the driver's seat.

Zoey muttered, *"Hot.* If they live here, can we figure out a way to watch? For real, I'd pay good money—"

I had to shove her to make her stop talking. Without the other man obscuring his view, Luke had seen us, waved hello, and was now making a beeline toward us. By the time our paths were about to cross, we were situated right at the stoop of our apartment complex.

"Hey, Claire!" He smiled. "Zoey. How are your heads this morning?"

"I'm operating at a solid 90%," I told him with a grin, "so I'm getting there. I think Zoey has seen better days, though."

He let out a deep laugh. "Serves you right for ordering that many Fireball shots," he said. "Didn't you hear that shit has antifreeze ingredients in it? You've got to have a hell of a headache."

"Okay, first of all," she began her ramble, the pep seemingly back in her step, "the antifreeze thing was disproven. Or it was fixed—whatever. It doesn't have antifreeze in it. Secondly, it's delicious. I regret nothing."

"Yeah, well," he responded, "I can't touch that stuff with a ten-foot pole. Not since the incident I had with it anyway."

I was sure that I looked like a dog that was about to be given a bone. It was natural to be intrigued after a sentence like that—or at least that's what I had to tell myself.

I questioned, "Oh, the incident, you say? It sounds like you have a story to tell."

"It sounds like you have a reason to come back to the bar, then." He winked.

All I could do was laugh, for the action had made my head swim. The term 'panty-dropper' came to mind.

"All right, you're on," I replied. "We'll be back, but give us at least a day to recover. Oh, and probably not tomorrow, we'll be busy job hunting."

"You guys both need a job?" He spoke while he fiddled with his car keys, "Henry's is hiring if either of you are interested. I mean, we'd prefer someone with at least a little experience, but—"

Zoey cut him off. "No way, this is perfect!" She placed her green eyes on mine. "Claire used to bartend! Didn't you, Claire?"

"Oh, um, yeah," I stammered.

Not only had I not expected where this conversation had gone, but I wasn't sure if my past experiences technically counted as bartending. Sure, I was *tending to a bar*...but I was neither compensated nor working in an actual establishment...*nor* was I of age to be serving alcohol.

"She's damn good at it too," Zoey added. I thanked her with a quick glance. I was never very good at singing my own praises, not to mention that I wasn't sure if these praises should be sung at all. But Zoey—well, Zoey could be a walking billboard for anything if she put her mind to it. It was the extroverted streak in her. She continued, "I'd take the position, but I've never been great at that...I can't get the ratios right in any drink." Her coffee-making skills came to mind, and I smirked. "Anyway," she circled around to her original point, "Claire's your girl. Really."

Luke's gaze turned towards me as I pondered everything. "Well," he asked, "do you want the job? We've been having a hard time finding someone. If you want it, it's yours."

I initially considered turning him down, but I wasn't sure how many choices I realistically had for my employment. I didn't go to college, and I didn't exactly have a respectable looking resume—okay, I didn't have a resume at *all* and I was in my mid-twenties. I cringed even thinking of the response I would have if someone asked me what I'd done with my life so far. *Oh, just following my ex-boyfriend around like a lost puppy dog* doesn't exactly come across very well in an interview—and my pre-Colton years could have been just as hard to explain away, if not worse.

"I mean, you can think about it, of course," Luke announced, backtracking a bit.

I suddenly realized that in getting lost in weighing my options, I had remained silent for quite a while.

"Oh, um." I shook my head quickly. "No, sorry there was erm—something else on my mind there for a bit. That actually sounds great!"

"Yeah, you'll take it?" His silvery eyes sparkled.

I nodded vigorously as I agreed, "Yeah, I'll take it!"

"Awesome!" He smiled so brightly that I wondered if I had been briefly blinded. "Henry'll be stoked, we've been shorthanded for a while now." Luke reached into his pocket to pull his phone from it, unlocking it with a swipe of his finger. He extended it out to me and said, "Give me your number and I can get back to you once I talk to Henry, but I think I'll have you start tomorrow if you want—maybe 6:00?"

I typed my digits into his cell quickly and placed the phone back in his palm.

"That soon?" I asked curiously.

"I don't know—never hired anyone before." He flashed me a crooked smile. "Like I said, I'll just talk with Henry and make sure."

"And how do you know that I'm not *absolutely* insane?" I countered with a smirk.

"Okay first of all," he replied, mockingly whining, *"stop it!* Don't make me all nervous about hiring you! If it doesn't work out, it'll look bad on me, right?"

"Okay, okay, I'm sorry," I relented.

"And," he added, "I just have a feeling, I guess."

I squinted my eyes at him, having already forgotten my previous joke. "A feeling?"

"That you're not insane."

"Ah, right," I responded, shifting my eyes to the ground for a moment as I smiled at his candor.

"Anyway..." he rubbed the back of his neck in almost a shy manner, "tomorrow. I'll text you."

"Got it," I said. "Thank you, really."

He shrugged off my thank you and smiled softly, pointing his car keys at me that he still held in his hand. "I gotta go. Zoey," he jingled the keys in her direction, "good to see you."

She gave him a tight-lipped smile. "Luke."

He waved yet again at both of us and as he turned to walk away, Zoey and I began to ascend the staircase to our new home on the second floor. In my peripheral vision, I saw Luke's head tilt to the side in surprise.

"Wait a minute," he called out. "Do you both live here?" We nodded in unison. Luke shook his head and looked skyward for a moment. "Well damn," he remarked, "I guess we really will be seeing a lot of each other, then."

Luke backed away, waving goodbye again with another soft chime of his keys.

It only took her three steps upward for Zoey to pipe up and say, *"You're welcome."*

I nearly chanted, "Thank-you-thank-you-thank-you!"

The relief of finding a job so *remarkably* quickly had left me elated. My legs attempted to do some sort of a celebration dance as we made our way, but my uncoordinated self and slightly dizzy head had other plans. I tripped on the concrete loudly, choking out a laugh as I did so, and held my left hand up high to save my coffee from spilling on the ground below. In my actions, I had spun and landed flat on my backside, staring directly toward Luke. Naturally, after I had fallen and yelped in laughter, he turned around out of curiosity.

His eyebrows pinched together, and he called out, "You good?"

I smacked my right hand over my mouth to keep from cackling maniacally.

"Good God, get it together you klutz," Zoey mumbled. She reached down to help me to my feet and yelled back to Luke, "Don't mind her! Like a baby giraffe trying to learn how to walk sometimes, this one!"

It looked like he just pressed his lips together tightly to hold back his laughter and bid us an additional silent adieu.

"So, you're a mess," Zoey commented as she righted me.

I exhaled as I stood and took a deep sip of my coffee.

"Just excited," I said, forcing myself to hold back a squeal. "I got a job!"

"Happy for you," she replied with a genuine smile.

We finally began to officially make it up the staircase and I inquired, "Where do you think you're going to look tomorrow?"

"There's that cute boutique down the way that had a help wanted sign out front," she said. "I think I'll start there. God knows I have enough experience with that."

Zoey had always worked in retail. It was a good fit for her. She's sassy and hard-headed enough to handle rude customers, but bubbly enough to still give great customer service.

"That sounds perfect for you." I added, "I'm sure they'll love you and hire you immediately."

Zoey smiled as she unlocked our apartment. "Uh huh, I'm sure they will. So—movie night?"

"It's only eleven in the morning," I reminded her.

"Er," she corrected herself as she placed her belongings on our kitchen table. "Movie *day*. And night."

I shut the door behind me, feeling like a fifty-pound weight had been lifted off of my shoulders.

"Sounds perfect," I replied.

Chapter Two

It was nearing 3:00 in the morning when I let out a blood curdling scream.

No—I wasn't getting murdered in my new home. Neither was Zoey, but at this point, I was seriously considering killing her anyway. We had burned right through all of the romantic comedies that I had requested to watch when Zoey, the hopeless romantic that she is *not*, firmly alerted me that it was now her turn to choose the movie. She decided to take us for a 180-degree tailspin and pop in a film in which people are being hunted down by a murderer wielding a chainsaw. Now, I had gotten through the majority of the movie just fine. I was hiding behind a pillow and trying to shove my face full of popcorn and chocolate to distract myself—but I was fine, nonetheless. However, when the grinding noise of a chainsaw rang through the television at a moment in which I *so* did not expect it, I screamed. Loudly. So, here we were.

Zoey laughed, pausing the movie before throwing popcorn at my head.

"You're such a wuss," she muttered, rolling her eyes.

I let out a loud breath, feeling my heart rate attempt to return to normal as it jack-hammered my insides.

"I did not agree to this," I said, pointing at the television. "I did *not* agree to watch this."

She retorted, "Well, I didn't agree to watch people make googly eyes at each other for hours on end either!"

"You seemed perfectly fine for those hours on end," I argued. *"This is torture for me."*

"Well, I was being tortured on the inside and I didn't say shit about it," she noted. "We have one television, Claire. You wanna stay up with me when it's my choice, you have to deal with people getting brutally murdered on screen for entertainment." I groaned, and Zoey added, *"And* you don't get to complain."

She had a point—I just didn't want to agree to it. Regardless, my train of thought was cut short when a knock sounded at the door.

"Not the best introduction to the new neighbors," Zoey chuckled. "You're the one that screamed, you get it."

I griped under my breath and shuffled toward the entryway, not excited to feel the wrath of the neighbor that I had most likely woken up. I opened the door hesitantly to see warm, brown eyes, a mess of blonde hair, and muscular hands wrapped around a worn-looking aluminum bat. The man seemed taken aback, mouth agape as he looked me up and down none too subtly. I followed his eyes, remembered what I had chosen to dress myself in for the evening, and whipped my hands up to cross them over my chest. My snug white shirt sans bra combined with the cold outside air had caused me to be a bit more *at attention* than I normally was, and I felt my blush heat my face.

"Oh...um...hi," he stuttered, snapping his eyes to mine. "Everything okay in there?" He tried to peek around the corner as if he was looking for some sort of intruder.

I cast my eyes to the floor. My laid-back attire practically announced, *'Hello, new neighbor. Sorry I woke you up with my screaming—wanna take a good look at my nipples?'*

"Hi," I cringed. "I'm, um—I'm so sorry if I woke you up. My room-mate and I are having a movie night and she likes scary movies and I...definitely do not."

"Oh." He let out a soft laugh. "That's not what I was thinkin' was going on but, um—glad everything's okay."

"What exactly were you anticipating?" I asked the question, tipping my head in a gesture toward the bat that now hung loosely from his fist.

"I'm not really sure," he stated. "A break-in? Or...I dunno, a guy trying to hit his wife? I would have *happily* used this in both cases." He nudged the bat with his red sneaker and shook his head. "Anyway, I don't mean to keep you away from the movie you're clearly enjoying." He smirked a lopsided grin, making me notice a faint white scar that resided over the left side of his upper lip. A single dimple appeared in his lightly freckled cheeks as he turned his brown eyes to mine. "I'm Liam Cohen." He threw a thumb over his shoulder. "I live across the hall in 2B if you ever need anything. Ya know—cold beer, shoulder to cry on, baseball bat to kick some guy's ass."

He was cute. Really cute—and it *could* have been the ridiculous number of romantic movies that we had just finished watching, but I was feeling remarkably bold.

"Claire Branson." I introduced myself and followed up with, "I might have to take you up on that, Liam Cohen from across the hall with a baseball bat."

His lips pulled up to one side. "Claire Branson from 2A who hates scary movies—sounds good. Maybe you'd want to take me up on that cold beer tomorrow night?"

The smile fell off my face. During our third movie, Luke had texted me to confirm that I could start working tomorrow night and, obvi-ously, I had accepted.

"Actually," I replied, "I just got a job at Henry's down the street. I'll be working; it's my first day tomorrow. Rain check, though?"

"Sure thing...so—working at Henry's, eh?" I nodded, and he noted, "I take it you're not their new chef."

"Ah, bartender," I clarified. "Do they even serve food there?"

"Hell if I know; I don't exactly go there for the food...wait, you guys just moved in, didn't you?"

"We did, yeah—yesterday."

"Wasting no time with starting to work, I see."

I found myself playing with a lock of my hair for absolutely no reason. "It's been kind of a whirlwind since we got here and it just fell in my lap, honestly. No rest for the wicked, I guess."

"Sure, sure," he replied. "So, where'd you move from anyway—"

"Claire!" Zoey called to me from inside the apartment.

I sighed, shooting Liam an apologetic glance before I turned my head on a swivel and peeked back at Zoey. I clenched my teeth together and jerked my head towards Liam, feeling my eyeballs bulge out of my head in an attempt to silently communicate. The message that I was thoroughly occupied was, unfortunately, not received.

"What?" She asked, her brow pinching together in confusion.

I decided not to respond, just looking back to Liam and stating, "I should probably get back. Sorry, again—"

He waved me off, responding, "Nah, you're good. It was a nice surprise." I raised my eyebrows, making him reiterate, "Ah—I mean *after* I found out you weren't getting killed or somethin'."

"Well, thanks anyway—you know, for the almost-rescue," I said.

"Any time," he stated, showing his dimples again. "See you later, Claire."

"Liam."

I backed away, smile still written on my face, and closed the door. Zoey looked at me incredulously as I strolled back to the couch.

Acting as aloof as I could, I asked, "Did we say something about the water here?"

Zoey stammered, "Were...were you flirting with one of our new neighbors?"

I shrugged and her eyebrows shot up as I giggled out, "What?"

"What happened to the hole in your head that you don't need?"

"I dunno," I replied. "He's all...cute...and *straight.*"

"Based on the look on your face," she started, "I give you about three months before you're head over heels, moving in across the hall, and planning on getting married and popping out two-point-five children."

Okay, maybe I *did* watch too many romantic movies today. I rolled my eyes heavily and scrunched up my face in disapproval.

"I'm not planning the rest of my *life,*" I explained. "I'm just having a drink with him at some point."

"Pick a side, Claire. You either want a relationship right now or you don't," she mentioned casually, tossing a handful of popcorn in her mouth.

"*It's just a drink,* but point taken," I grumbled, falling backward on the couch with a sigh. "Maybe he doesn't even want to date," I pondered aloud. "Maybe he just wants to get to know the new neighbors."

Zoey's laugh hitched in her throat.

"*Yeah,*" she voiced disbelievingly, "because the guy asking to get together later when you're dressed like *that* is just looking for fun conversation."

"Dressed like *what?*" I challenged.

"You know what I'm talking about, hard nips," she retorted with a grin, dropping her eyes to my chest. She moved her head from side to side. "Jesus, you could cut glass right now, for real."

I rolled my eyes again. "Whatever."

She must have sensed my mild annoyance because she dropped the subject at hand and pointed at the television once again, asking, "You ready to start this again?"

"Do we have to?" I complained.

"*How* many of your movies did I watch, huh?" She thought to herself silently for a moment before her eyes widened and she exclaimed, "Seven! Oh my God, Claire, you made me watch *seven fucking romantic comedies in one day.*"

Zoey pushed herself up, holding a sarcastically disgusted look on her face.

"Okay, yes," I attempted to defend myself, "we watched a lot of those. It's...getting *really late* though." She was about to argue further, but I added, "Actually, it's so late that it's early morning." I stretched my arms over my head and pretended to yawn loudly. "We should *really* get to bed, right?"

Zoey exhaled loudly, her eyelids falling halfway over her gaze.

"Bitch," she grumbled. "One day, *I* will control our movie nights." A wistful expression appeared on her face. "It will be glorious."

"One day," I agreed, smiling at her before standing back up and waltzing to my room. "Night, Zoey."

"Yeah, yeah, good night," she muttered, pointing the remote back to the screen.

The noise of a chainsaw vibrated my eardrum briefly before I reached my bedroom, closing the door behind me and muffling the sound that I was so happily escaping.

My eyes didn't even attempt to open until well after noon. I would have been mad at myself for sleeping in so late, but assuming that I'd be working night shifts in the upcoming days, I figured I would have to adjust my sleeping schedule anyway. In reality, I unknowingly made tonight easier on myself—the hours at Henry's stretched until 2 A.M. and whether there were patrons there or not, I'd be on the clock. On the clock and *awake.* I stretched my well-rested limbs and ambled into the kitchen.

The sight before me was strikingly similar to the one that I had seen yesterday morning, save for the fact that neither of us were horrifically hungover. Zoey sat in the exact same seat, in the same exact outfit. Her black rimmed glasses sat on her face to aid her vision before she put in her contacts, and she was swathed in comfort with a loose grey hoodie and pale blue pajama bottoms. She even drank from the exact same coffee mug as the day prior, a beige mug painted with red roses. It was a gift I had given her years ago when we attended a pottery class—there was a negative percent chance that Zoey would ever buy anything with flowers on it willingly. Flowers equal love and romance and therefore, she avoided them like the plague. Despite the romantic connotations, she drank from the mug almost daily. The thought brought a smile to my face as I made my way to the cupboard that held our drinkware. I reached for the mug that Zoey had gifted me in turn—a bright white all over with red stitching stripes that resembled that of a baseball—and filled it with the mud-like coffee that she had brewed earlier. I added a dash more milk than I usually take and sat with her at the table. Her eyes glanced at me as she noticed my presence, lowering the ceramic and offering me a slight grin.

"Good morning," she said. "I was about to check if you were alive."

"Morning," I replied, picking up my mug by gripping the side with my palm rather than attempting to use the wonky handle.

I took a sip and immediately felt my face contort as the bitter tannins pulled at the sides of my cheeks. The extra dairy had *not* helped. Unable to control myself, I voiced a quiet, "Oh, no."

"Drama queen," Zoey chuckled under her breath.

"So, when are you planning on venturing down to that boutique?" I asked.

"Actually, I called them a bit ago," she said eagerly. "Chatted a bit with the owner's sister, but the owner herself won't be in for another few hours. Regardless," she flashed a wide smile across the table, "after talking for a little bit, she asked me to come in and seemed pretty excited to have me."

"Naturally," I quipped.

"Well, you know I'm good at selling myself," she paused, "and I somehow mean that in the *least* sexual way possible."

"Right," I laughed. "I take it you're free for a little while, then?"

"Mhm. Why, what's up?"

"I wasn't sure what to wear tonight and—"

Zoey cut me off with a bright-eyed smile and raised her hand. "Say no more!"

She nearly bounced in her seat with excitement. In nearly every other way, Zoey was more of a tomboy than anything. With a mouth like a sailor, a love for action, and a mind that seemed to have a permanent home in the gutter, it would come as a surprise to many people that Zoey absolutely loved fashion. It wasn't necessarily in a *let's travel to Paris and go to a fashion show* type of way, but more of an *I could use an entire spare bedroom as a closet* kind of way. I've never been big into that type of stuff myself, so any time I turned to Zoey for clothing advice, she relished in the moment. Zoey looked toward the clock on our oven.

"You start at 6:00?"

"Yup."

She sighed. "If only we had more *time.*"

"Er—we have like four hours until I need to even *think* about showering."

She rolled her eyes. "Yes, but *I* have to leave in two," she spoke as if it was some sort of impossible task to find an outfit in that span of time. "Finish your coffee, we should *really* get going…"

Her voice rambled off into oblivion as she stood and flitted her way to my room, buzzing like a hummingbird. Not before making sure that she was well out of sight rummaging through the boxes that I had yet to unpack in my closet, I promptly stood and emptied my coffee into the kitchen sink, shivering at the recent memory of its taste.

Zoey trilled from around the corner, "Are you coming in here or what?"

"Um, yeah—coming!" I called, rushing to my bedroom and instructing her, "Do your worst."

Her worst in question lasted for an entire hour until I walked out of my closet in tall, black stiletto boots, tight black jeans, and a green halter top that showed off what little cleavage I actually possessed.

"Fucking *finally!*" Zoey exclaimed from a cross-legged position on my mattress.

I spun halfway around and back again. "Yeah?"

"Oh yeah," she replied, nodding hard. "You look so hot, *I'd* do you." I snorted, and she remarked, "Hot gay bartender may even want to do you."

"First of all, he has a name. It's Luke. You know that. Secondly," I scolded her, holding up two fingers, "you have to keep that in check if you come to the bar! He probably wouldn't appreciate being called *hot gay bartender* when he apparently doesn't like people knowing."

"The travesty of the year, honestly."

"*Zoey.*" I shot a stern eye in her direction, silently begging her to *not* get me fired by outing the guy that hired me.

"Ugh," she groaned, throwing her head back, "stop with the side eye already! I'm not gonna *say* anything, I promise. It would just be a *lot* more fun if I could play wing-woman for him or something."

I asked, "Do you not remember him leaving his apartment with another man?"

"The scruffy, muscular, tattooed guy? Are you kidding?" She smirked at me, tipping me off to her gutter-minded ways as she mentioned, "I didn't even get to see his face, but that didn't stop me from having him play the role of my vibrator in my mind last night."

"Have I mentioned today that you are absolute filth?" I cocked an eyebrow high in her direction.

Her teeth blinded me. "Filth incarnate, at your service."

"My point," I reiterated, "is that it *sure* seems like Luke is spoken for by the scruffy, muscular, tattooed man."

"You do realize that Tinder is a thing, right?" Zoey asked me. "It's not necessarily my cup of tea, but some people have that app on their phone to," she mockingly gasped, clutching at her chest dramatically as she whispered, "meet up and *get it on.*" I rolled my eyes. *"My* point," she repeated my words back to me, "is that—unbeknownst to you—*some* people don't feel the need to get wrapped up in relationships. *Some* people just—"

"Yeah, yeah."

"Anyway," she noted, "You look great—I have to shower." Zoey uncrossed her legs and bounced off of my bed.

"Wait, wait," I called to her before she left the room, holding my red strands in one hand and lifting them up. "Hair up?" I dropped my hand, displaying the alternative. "Or hair down?"

"Hair down," she replied before I even asked the latter question. "Soft waves. You can do it. I believe in you."

"Soft waves? That's gonna take *forever,*" I complained.

"Well," she retorted, turning around for the second time as she leaned against my door frame, "that's what you get for having long, beautiful locks! Don't like it? Chop it off like I did."

After Zoey had lopped off her blonde hair years ago, she'd decided to keep the style short for more than just reasons of low maintenance. It looked absolutely fantastic on her. Her dainty features and high cheekbones were accentuated in just the right way when her hair was in a boyish style. I tried not to be too envious of that fact—I *so* could not pull that off like she did.

"Uh huh," I muttered under my breath, calling out, "if I don't see you before you leave, good luck!"

She whipped around once again, this time not stopping her legs from moving as she continued to walk backward. She asked confidently, "Do I *need* luck?"

"Humble," I mocked her, failing to hold back a smile at her impeccable mood. "Nice."

Her body finally disappeared into the living room as she yelled, "I'll meet you at Henry's after!"

Time passed faster than I had anticipated and before I knew it, I was approaching the same vintage-like wooden sign that I had seen just two days prior. I pushed the door open, the familiar bell sound chiming above my head happily. There wasn't a soul except for Luke in Henry's when I walked in and I couldn't have been more thankful. The first reason being, I didn't want it to be particularly busy right from the get-go. I was a tad bit nervous seeing as how I hadn't bartended—if you could even call what I did *bartending*—in over a year. The second reason was that the moment that I saw him, I had to fight tooth and nail to try not to rake my eyes across his body. I didn't need any customers catching me behaving this way—staring at my coworker longingly from across a room was a serious no-no, but I couldn't help myself. Luke was casually leaning back against the wall behind the bar, wearing dark jeans and a charcoal t-shirt that stretched across his lean chest. Just like the last time I was here, the dim lighting did wonders for framing his stubble-covered face. I exhaled a quick breath, shaking my head quickly to clear any lingering thoughts regarding my ogling nature, and removed my jacket.

Luke's light eyes didn't turn to me until I had forced myself out of my stupor. He bobbed his head upward in a nod hello, beginning to move his attention elsewhere, when he went through the motions of a classic double-take. He stood straight, crossing his arms as he took in my appearance from toe to head. It was possible that this was the longest that someone's eyes had ever stayed on my body, and the thought made me shift my feet nervously from side to side. I questioned my bolder choice in clothing, silently cursing Zoey for telling me to, in her words, *'put my tits on display,'* and dipped my head down to allow my hair to shield my face.

My face contorted when I finally chanced a glance at Luke and shyly asked, "Too much?" I held my hands out to the side to display my outfit in its entirety.

He stammered, "Um—"

"I'll go home and change," I spoke all too quickly, spinning myself around on a single toe with a surprising amount of grace.

"No, no-no-no," Luke said, making me up my 180-degree spin to a full circle. "You look lovely," he stated in a deep voice. "Really."

His tone of sincerity made me smile softly, but I still felt the need to state my thoughts aloud. "I don't really do, er," I waved a hand in front of myself, *"this* very often. If you think I'm sticking out like a sore thumb, I *really* can go home and—"

"Claire." He interrupted my anxious meanderings and said, "Seriously, you look great."

"Not a sore thumb?" I questioned.

"Definitely not a sore thumb," he reassured me with a wide grin. "If you go home, I'll fire you, okay?"

I finally exhaled a relief-filled laugh as I strolled my way around the bar to stand on the opposite side with him. "Do you even have that power?"

"Hey!" He exclaimed, "I brought you into this world—er, this *bar.*" He pointed a finger at me in a mock-admonishing manner, finishing with, "I can just as easily kick you out of it."

"I'll keep that in mind," I chuckled, clacking my heeled boots against the wood floor. "So," I halted my movements once we were eye to eye, about an arm's length apart, "where should we start?"

"First," he said, pointing behind me, "you can turn right back around and put your things in the back wherever you want."

"Right," I replied, doing as he asked and leading myself through the opening in the wall.

I rounded the corner and, to my surprise, there was no kitchen. All that I saw was a fridge in the far right corner and a freestanding sink with a dingy white finish directly next to it. Aside from that, boxes lined the wall to my left, all labeled as different brands of booze, and in front of me, a square folding table stood with four accompanying chairs. I felt a corner of my mouth pull up, remembering Liam's offhand comment about assuming that I wasn't going to be Henry's new chef. As I set my belongings on the grey table and looked back to Luke, he had his head cocked to the side in inquisition.

"What's that look for?" He asked with a smirk.

I laughed softly. "Oh, um, nothing," I said, throwing a thumb over my shoulder as I walked back to the main area. "No kitchen?"

"Yeah," he replied, "the place never had one, Henry didn't want it—said it was too much trouble." I nodded, idly thinking that perhaps that was a good thing. If they *did* have a kitchen and needed me to sub in for any reason, it would be an absolute nightmare—I could burn a house down trying to boil water. "Anyway," Luke remarked, "let me give you a quick rundown of the place."

He went over the general do's and don'ts of Henry's briefly, and then dove into more intricate tips for being behind the bar itself. He was just showing me one of the more persnickety beer taps, saying how I would have to pull it *just so,* when he had me grab a glass to practice the motion. As I lifted my hand to mimic him, the sputtering of the tap was interrupted by Luke's questioning voice.

"Oh, I almost forgot to ask," he began, "did you hear that scream in the complex last night?" The inquiry that I wasn't expecting made my grip adjust slightly enough to make the glass I was holding fill rapidly with foam. I lowered it quickly. "Told you," he noted quietly. "Anyway—I had just gotten home from my shift when I heard it. Scared the shit out of me! I'm up on the third floor, I'm pretty sure it came from below."

Great.

I pressed my lips together and turned the glass in my hands to empty it into the drain. I was considering either lying or not answering him at all, weighing both options in my head silently as I focused on the foam sliding through the grate.

"Er—Claire?"

I cleared my throat, raising the glass yet again as I tried with all my might not to look his way, and pulled the tap. "Um...yeah, that was me," I replied as nonchalantly as I could.

I finished the pour and set it in front of him with purpose, hoping that we could blow right past this conversation and avoid any and all embarrassment on my end. I gestured towards the beer-filled glass with a flick of my wrist and finally chanced a glance at him. He crossed his arms, his expression silently conveying, *'Good job, but you're not getting out of this.'* I sighed, feeling my shoulders sag in a telepathic battle lost.

"For real?" He pressed me.

I grumbled, "Unfortunately."

"Well, obviously you're okay," he noted with a soft smile on his face.

"Oh, it's just my pride," I said sardonically, "no big deal."

Luke let out a hearty laugh. "Well, what happened? It sounded like I was about to be witness to a murder."

"This literally could *not* be more embarrassing," I muttered, feeling my cheeks heat. "How thin are the walls in that place?"

"Very," he stated bluntly.

"I'll have to keep that in mind."

"So..." he ushered me further.

"Zoey—" I paused, wondering exactly how to phrase this. "Zoey has...an affinity for scary movies."

His face scrunched up in confusion, slim nose wiggling slightly with the movement. If I weren't so mortified, I would have swooned over how adorable the action was.

"Er—*and?*"

"*And,*" I replied, "She made me watch a movie where people were practically getting sawed in half and it scared the shit out of me."

I felt the blush on my face extend all the way to my ears. Luke's mouth dropped open in understanding, amusement flooding his face as he said a quiet, "Oh." He reached for a washcloth on the counter and began wiping at it needlessly to busy his hands, a smirk still present on his lips.

"Look, time got away from us!" I practically exclaimed, my reasoning spilling out of me uncontrollably. I was uncertain as to *why* I felt the need to defend my actions from the night prior—a scream in the dead of night is far from sinful, after all. All I knew was that my embarrassment was causing me to ramble. The words nearly tied together in their desperation to exit my mouth. "I didn't realize how late it was. I mean, I would have tried to muffle myself somehow if I realized it was fucking 3 A.M.!"

Luke snickered, "Claire," as he threw the towel on the countertop, turning himself to face me again.

His attempt at an interruption did little to stop me as I directed my eyes to my black-booted feet and kept them there for the time being.

"All of this is Zoey's fucking fault anyway; she basically *forced* me to watch the fucking movie—"

"Claire—"

I waved my hands around for dramatic effect, looking skyward this time as I added, "I mean it's not like it was a hostage situation or anything, but it was close e-fucking-nough!"

"Claire!"

Luke finally raised his voice enough to convince me to shut my mouth. I huffed out an aggravated breath and tucked an errant strand of hair behind my ear hastily. He laughed softly at my behavior, and as I redirected my gaze to him, I noticed that his grey eyes were absolutely dancing with hilarity. His candor softened my stubborn exterior and I felt my eyes pinch at the corners in a small smile.

"I'm so glad you find this amusing," I remarked sarcastically.

Luke held up his arms in defense. "I hate scary movies too; I get it! No judgement here."

"I probably woke up the whole fucking complex," I said, smacking my forehead with my right palm lightly.

38

Luke barked out another laugh.

"There it is again!" He exclaimed; his index finger pointed at me briefly.

"There's *what* again?"

"Oh nothing," he almost sang. "Just your filthy mouth that erupts when you get all flustered."

I snorted at his description, remembering that I had used the word to describe Zoey mere hours ago. If he wanted to see filthy, he should talk to her a bit more.

"Filthy?" I asked with a grin, and he replied with a silent nod and a single cocked eyebrow. I said, "I'm anything but."

"You just said *fuck* five times in the past two minutes," he retorted monotonously, adding, "one of those *fucks* was actually in the middle of a word." He laughed again, his breath catching in his throat briefly. "You broke a word in half and put *fuck* in the middle of it. If that's not a filthy mouth, I don't know what is."

"Touché," I responded simply.

"Own that trait, though," Luke mentioned, drawing my eyes back to his. "It's cute."

The compliment made me flush in an entirely different way and I stood a little straighter, smiling as I asked, "Yeah?"

"Oh yeah," he replied, "very cute." I had to squash the thoughts that swam through my mind as I briefly relived the fact that he just called me cute—twice. Luke continued on with eyes full of sincerity, "You know, if I had known that was you last night, I would have checked up on you and made sure you were okay."

"Actually," I replied, happy with the distraction from my all-too-in-appropriate thoughts, "my neighbor from across the hall did come and check on me."

His light eyes narrowed fractionally as he asked, "Neighbor from across the hall, huh?"

"Yeah."

It really did seem to be a small world in this area. Luke was bound to have seen Liam before, especially considering the small size of our apartment complex. That fact aside, Liam was a pretty hard guy to miss—hell, if Luke had noticed him before, *he* could be jealous of *me.* I laughed briefly to myself at that thought and it came out like a girlish giggle.

"It's actually kind of funny," I told him. "He literally showed up at my door with a baseball bat ready to beat someone up."

Luke's eyes squinted even further into slits, his irises turning to steel. "Is that right?"

I nodded, feeling my smile dim ever so slightly at his odd reaction. "Yeah," I shrugged a shoulder. "Call it an attempted rescue, I guess? He had invited me to get a drink sometime later—"

"Which neighbor, exactly?"

"Oh, um," his curt interruption caught me off guard, making me stammer, "It was Liam, er—Liam Cohen?"

He practically spat out his next words. *"Liam Cohen?"*

Chapter Three

He blinked quickly and shook his head as if it would clear his thoughts.

"That guy..." He paused for a moment and then spoke again with disdain, "I...I just...I can't..." He couldn't seem to form the words he was trying to say, finally settling with a confirmation of, *"Liam Cohen* went to your apartment to check on you and ended up asking you out?"

He said his name as though it were an expletive.

"Umm..." I had a feeling I was missing out on a pertinent story. "Yes?"

Luke shook his head again, this time so hard that a few strands of his hair fell onto his forehead. I think I even heard a scoff when he muttered more to himself than to me:

"Fucking *Liam.*"

To say I was taken aback was an understatement. It was clear that whatever opinion Luke had of Liam, it was a bad one.

"Am I missing something here?" I tried to question him, "What's wrong with Liam?"

He scoffed. "What's *wrong* with him? He—"

Just as he was about to speak once again, an entire crowd of people entered through the front door. Luke shut his mouth promptly, glancing at the onslaught of customers as the bell chirped above their heads again and again, and he appeared to be in deep thought until I ushered him again:

"Luke?"

"We, um," he hesitated until he glanced in my direction. Upon him seeing what I assumed was an expectant, dare I say impatient, expression on my face, his teeth glinted out in a lopsided smile. "We can talk later, okay?"

He seemed oddly pleased at the intrusion, and I narrowed my eyes at him. "Mhm. Sure we can."

He smiled a bit brighter at my annoyed response. "Let's tackle this crowd," he said. "Let me know if you need help making anything."

He turned on his heel and headed straight away from me with an added pep in his step. To say I was disappointed would have been an understatement—and he knew it. I groaned quietly, resigned to my task at hand, and moved my legs underneath me in a quick shuffle to approach the opposite end of the crowd. I bounced from person to person to take their drink orders. By the time I had swung back behind the bar, Luke was grabbing several shot glasses and lining them up in front of himself. While his portion of the group desired something that appeared more complex, my end had been simple, all of them only wanting beer. I held up a large pitcher to the persnickety tap that Luke was helping me with earlier and began to pour.

"Whatcha got goin' on there?" I asked.

He emptied the remains of a Rumchata bottle into a tumbler and scrunched up his nose in distaste.

"Cinnamon Toast Crunch shots," he replied.

"Which, by the look on your face, you think are *delicious.*"

"Let's just say I'm on the same page as you when it comes to sugary liquors," he said. "I mean, I'm not a sorority girl."

I peered at the group that he was tending to, noting that they were all long legs, tanned skin, and eyes that were raking their way across Luke's body from across the bar. I felt my eyebrows raise up subconsciously from their blatant display of attraction. I didn't blame them for it, but *still*.

"Well, *those* sorority girls seem to be quite interested in you," I mentioned.

He raised the cocktail shaker and twisted his head to look at me, giving it a vigorous shake in the process, and grinned.

"Yeah, they're not exactly my type."

The ice clinked against the metal of the tumbler loudly as he glanced curiously at my group of patrons and he pressed his lips together, shaking his head slightly. I pushed the tap back into its original position.

"What's that look for?"

"Oh, nothing," he replied. "You're not doing any better over there."

"What?"

Luke popped the top off the shaker.

"Really?" he asked, bewildered.

"Yes, *really*. What?"

"Their eyes have been *glued* to your ass," he whispered just loud enough for me to hear.

I whipped my head to look over my shoulder none-too-subtly. My eyes landed upon three older men; their beer bellies as large as their heads were bald. The dim bar lighting shined off of them as all three of their lines of sight collectively snapped away from me, looking anywhere but in my direction. I tried not to visibly cringe, but failed.

"Switch me," Luke said.

I huffed out a breath. "Luke—"

"You think I want to keep getting hit on by those girls?" He returned quickly. "They're *relentless.*"

"Well, no," I replied, "but you don't need to do me any favors either."

He set down the tumbler next to the line of shot glasses behind him and approached me, grabbing the pitcher from my hands. "No favors," he stated. "Really."

I thanked him with a glance and he shimmied past me, grabbing a stack of glasses from under the bar top. I pondered about our respective situations as I finished preparing the shots, pouring a small amount into each glass. The more that I thought about it, our trade off didn't seem quite even. Sure, rumor had it that he was gay, but wouldn't beautiful women coming onto you still be a stroke to your ego? It wasn't exactly the same as me being happy to escape the dirty old men who were eyeballing my behind. Nonetheless, I maintained my appreciative demeanor and smiled as I made my way to the group of girls, setting the tray with their drinks down on the cocktail table they were standing around.

"Can I get you guys anything else for now?"

I asked the question in as bubbly of a manner as I could considering the fact that they were visibly disappointed to see me. Their collective initial cattiness dissipated quickly, however, and the brunette closest to me thanked me with a megawatt smile.

She asked the group, "Another round?"

They nodded enthusiastically at her inquisition. One of their sets of acrylic nails tapped against the wood of the table impatiently as they waited to indulge themselves in liquified boozy sugar-laced cereal.

"You got it," I noted quickly.

As I turned on my heel, I heard the clink of the glasses as the ladies downed their beverages. My next task to go straight back to make them their next round was abruptly put on hold when I heard one of the girls chirp:

"Think I could catch his attention for the night?"

I slowed myself and feigned a double take at the table next to theirs, retracing my steps as I pretended to rearrange the napkin dispenser. I took my time jiggling the aluminum contraption loudly in an attempt to make my faux-actions seem believable.

"I wish," another one of them spoke. "I heard he's gay."

General noises of scoffs and derision emitted from all of them.

"Who'd you hear that from?"

"Sarah," she spoke back in a quick whisper.

"Bet I could turn him."

I was lucky that salacious laughter had filled the air around me at that statement and distracted the rest of the table, for I couldn't hide my reaction. A mixture of amusement and revulsion made my face contort as if I were trying to identify a bad smell that I couldn't make quite make out. The girls continued to speak in a conglomeration of voices so quick that I failed to follow who spoke when.

"You think so?"

"Have yo*u seen* my tits?"

"Bev!"

"You're terrible!"

"I'd make him an offer he couldn't refuse, if you know what I mean."

"Bev!"

"I say go for it—"

"It's not like I haven't managed to...*you know.*" Their chatter died down while who I could only assume was Bev carried on with her not so modest admission. "I've turned a man or two before—*kind of* my specialty."

I stopped fiddling with the dispenser and, noting that was I facing directly away from the girls, allowed my eyes to roll backward for a brief moment. I stomped my way back to the bar, trying to erase the eavesdropped conversation from my mind. It was no wonder that Luke wanted to switch groups with me. I made it a priority to remember to steer him away from Bev and company and, thanks to that revelation, they were gone after two more drinks a piece. I pictured the door hitting Bev on her way out as they left and just like that, Henry's was remarkably empty save for Luke, myself, and the old man who I recognized from my first night here.

"Thank you." A deep, appreciative voice murmured in my ear and I jumped slightly in surprise. "Shit, sorry." The smile on Luke's face and the amusement in his eyes looked anything but apologetic.

"Don't sneak up on me!"

"Noted," he laughed back, raising his hands in a defensive maneuver.

"And why are you thanking me, anyway?"

"For helping me avoid all...*that.*"

He scrunched his nose in the same way he did when he poured Rumchata.

I shrugged casually, taking back my prior thoughts with, "Fair trade."

"Guess so," he replied, eyes crinkling at the corners happily.

I searched the room for anything or anyone I could have missed and came up empty. I crossed my arms behind my back and scuffed one of my heels against the floor loudly.

"So," I asked hesitantly, drawing out the sound of the word for as long as possible, "you were saying something about Liam?"

"I'm not sure if I remember where we were with that," he joked.

"Oh, I think you know what I'm talking about."

"Do I, really?" His grey eyes were alight with humor yet again.

I squared my shoulders, narrowing my gaze at him in a sarcastically mocking gesture when the door chimed yet again, and Zoey strolled inside. Luke glanced over his shoulder and, at the sight of her, beamed a large smile back at me.

"Saved by the bell."

"Oh, what, *her?*" I asked as Zoey slid her petite frame into a barstool in front of us.

She replied nonchalantly and to neither of us in particular, "Yes, hello, hi."

I waved at her with a flick of my wrist, my attention still high-beamed on getting Luke to talk. "Yeah, she can wait."

"*Yeah-she-can-wait* will have a cider, by the way," Zoey announced.

I crossed my arms, tilting my head at Luke as I waited for him to speak his mind.

He took a single step in my direction, presumably to grab Zoey her drink, which was situated behind me, and I held up a hand to stop him. He attempted to sidestep my upturned palm, but I planted it firmly on his chest, making him stop in his tracks.

He looked down at it and then back to me, turning his head curiously. I could feel his heartbeat underneath his shirt, tickling my hand and sending electricity down my arm with every pulse as we stared at each other.

After what felt like an eternity, Luke leaned down to murmur in my ear, "Pardon me."

The gravelly, almost sultry tone of his voice left me stunned, and I pulled my hand off of his chest as if it had shocked me. I couldn't bring myself to look at him as he walked past me with purpose, grabbing a bottle from the fridge underneath the bar top and popping the cap with a flourish. I cleared my throat, bringing my mind back to the matter at hand just when he was handing Zoey the drink she had requested.

"I take it you don't like him, then?" I asked Luke. "You know, considering that you're avoiding the subject."

Luke snorted, rolling his eyes in the process. "No, I don't *like* him."

Zoey set down her bottle quickly after taking a rather rushed sip and asked, "Oh, *who?!*"

"Luke here seems to have a problem with Liam," I noted.

Her brow furrowed as she asked, "Liam?"

"2B."

"Unashamed flirter 2B?"

"That's the one!" Luke exclaimed.

Zoey peered at him with her inquisitive emerald eyes and she questioned, "What's your problem with the hot guy across the hall?"

"Let's just say I'm not his biggest fan right now, okay?" Luke replied.

Both Zoey and I began to attempt to interrogate him further, but before either of us could get a full word out, Luke's eyes had shot from the entrance and back to us. He groaned under his breath.

"Speak of the devil," he said quietly.

He waltzed away from us and toward the man who I assumed was a regular, and the bell chimed through the bar happily once more. The chill from the air outside ran over my bare arms as Liam walked toward us. He was wearing a navy, thermal long-sleeve shirt and worn jeans. I allowed my eyes to trace over the way the pants hung from his hips and how his shirt stretched over his arms. By the time he reached the bar, he flashed me a single-dimpled smile and pulled the out stool next to Zoey for himself to sit. The legs scraped along the wooden floor loudly and he rested himself firmly in the seat, interlacing his fingers in front of himself as he placed his forearms on the bar top.

"Hey, Claire," he greeted me with a smirk. "Long time no see."

Zoey's eyebrows were starting to retreat into her bangs as her head pinged back and forth between us. After she seemed to wipe the shock off of her face, she thrust her hand in front of him, smiling at him sweetly. His face pinched together in confusion as he sat back a bit, away from her dainty fingers, and forced a smile right back.

"I believe you have me at a disadvantage," Zoey remarked.

Liam shook her hand hesitantly, fully encompassing her fingers in a quick grip, replying, "Um—I'm Liam?"

"Liam," I cooed, summoning my brightest smile. "This is my roommate, Zoey. Zoey, this is Liam, he lives across the hall."

"Ah." He nodded in understanding as he bobbed his hand up and down in hers briefly and let go. "You're the horror film freak."

"Oh, I'm a freak in many ways—"

"Zoey!" I chastised her with a hiss, but she neither seemed to hear me nor care.

"But," she continued on, "enough about *me.*" She turned her bright gaze toward me and asked, "So, this is the guy?"

Liam's smile could not have possibly been wider. "What guy am I, exactly?"

"Oh, I don't know." Zoey took it upon herself to respond, speaking slowly as she looked to the ceiling. "The guy that shamelessly flirted with my roommate at 3:00 in the morning after she made it sound like someone was going Lizzie Borden on her ass?"

"Lizzie Borden?" He asked.

Zoey responded, "You don't know Lizzie Borden? Really? Went down in infamy for murdering her family with an axe? Not ringing any bells?"

Liam moved his head from side to side. "Umm...no?"

"Well, that's your loss," she commented to Liam. "Shit's interesting! I love it."

"God, you're weird," I muttered in a mixture of disgust and awe. "You're lucky that's one of the reasons that I like you so much. Any way..."

I leaned across the counter toward Liam and rested my head on my hands, redirecting my attention to him. I vaguely heard Zoey attempt to conceal her laughter in a gulp of cider. There was about a ninety-percent chance that she was amused at my lame attempt to flirt, but I chose to ignore her.

I asked, "What are you doing here?"

It looked like it pained him to keep his eyes on mine. I wasn't an idiot—I knew I was giving him an amazing opportunity to view my chest...or what I had to offer of a chest, anyway. Rather than glancing downward as I anticipated, he leaned in on his elbows, grabbed a coaster to my left, and began to toy with it. He rotated it back and forth between his fingers lazily.

"Well," he replied, "I figured since you were too busy to meet me for a drink, I would come to you."

"In that case," I rocked back and forth on my heels, "what would you like, Liam?"

I may have even batted my eyelashes at him. The way he was looking at me, I almost expected him to say, '*You,*' but his gaze slipped away from my eyes and behind me for a split second and his demeanor seemed to cool. A prickling sensation at the back of my neck made me wonder if there was a certain silvery gaze directed at me from behind. Liam pushed himself away and darted his eyes over my shoulder once again.

"Just a beer would be great, thanks, um—the amber," he told me.

I pushed myself up and turned around to grab his drink, but almost ran right into a judgemental looking Luke. His light eyes were boring into Liam's, an amber beer already in his hand, and he reached past me to slide it over to him. I looked up at Luke quizzically, but he just shook his head and turned to walk back to the regular who seemed to be slumped over himself. My stomach sank, and I glanced apologetically at Liam. He shrugged his brawny shoulders, taking a sip of his beer. I held up a single finger, signifying for him to wait a moment, and darted my way back to where Luke was. He had a hand on the old man's shoulder and seemed to be having a serious word with him.

"Everything okay?" I inquired as I arrived within earshot.

Luke's gaze flashed to mine briefly, exasperated, and stated, "Peachy keen."

I exhaled loudly. "Really?"

He reiterated, "Everything's *great,*" His voice teetered between genuinity and annoyance as if he couldn't decide how to feel. "Just seeing how Clyde's feeling here. Right, bud?"

Clyde grumbled out a nonsensical string of words.

"Yeah, thought so," Luke grumbled.

"I'm sorry, I didn't even realize—"

He shook his head quickly. "It's fine, Claire, just—can you just help me out here?"

I nodded my head so hard that I felt my brain rattle from within. "What can I do?"

"Call a cab, an Uber, I don't know—whatever's going to get here soonest."

"Yeah, of course," I replied.

I pulled my phone out from my pocket and let my fingers dance across the glass face to unlock it. Luckily for Clyde, a quick check of my Uber app showed a ride being available just two minutes down the street. I began the process of ordering it, but a notification on the screen stopped me in my tracks.

"Oh, um," I stammered, "shit, I need his address."

"1502 Main, number 305," Luke rattled off the address with little hesitation.

I felt my eyebrows raise slightly as I entered the information. My phone pinged with the confirmation of the order.

"Done this before, I take it?" I asked him.

"Only once," he stated, showing his own cell to me before stowing it promptly in his pocket. "I was just a step ahead of you—I wrote down his address last time in my phone."

"Ah, I see."

I squirmed uncomfortably, shifting my weight from foot to foot as I watched Luke's lips purse together in agitation. Though his gaze was not directed at me, I had to assume that his thoughts were. The guilt regarding my uncharacteristically negligent behavior was washing over me in a tidal wave. I was off in my own little dreamland flirting earlier—on my first day, no less—and was none the wiser that my new coworker *really* could have used some assistance. I felt the nagging need to apologize further, but my embarrassment held me back. I was stuck in place, eyes glued to the black plastic mats beneath my feet as a rush of heat spread up my neck and across my face until the entrance announced the arrival of two more patrons.

"Got it," I mumbled in a rushed voice.

I turned around so fast that my hair fanned out behind me, and I took in the two individuals that had entered. My embarrassed blush almost immediately dissipated at the sight before me. I smirked, crossing my arms as two lanky teenage boys seated themselves just one chair down from Zoey. One had hair as dark as his eyes and skin so pale that I could have found his pulse with my eyes alone if I were so inclined. The other was his polar opposite with tanned skin that accentuated his buzzed bleach-blonde cut. His nervous, blue-eyed gaze darted around the room.

"Hello boys," I greeted them, grabbing coasters from the stack in front of Liam and tossing a single one at them both. "What'll it be?"

The dark haired one looked sideways at Liam for just a moment before announcing with a bit too much enthusiasm, "Redbull vodkas for the both of us!"

"Right," I replied. "You got your ID's on you?"

They both nodded and removed their wallets from their jeans, pulling out plastic cards that looked far from government-issued. They could have passed for real identification at first glance, but unfortunately for the boys in front of me, I was especially well-versed in this subject. I picked them up and held one in each of my hands. The plastic was stiff and brittle. So much so that if they weren't laminated, a quick stress test would snap the material in two with ease. Speaking of the laminate itself, it held an opaque finish that marred their snapshots to the point where I could barely recognize the faces. I ran my thumbs over the text and the ever so slight indentation of the lettering tickled the nerves of my fingerprint. I scrunched my face up in apology—after all, I remember being underage and skirting the law. I would like to think that we all do.

"These aren't real," I stated bluntly, dropping them back on the counter with a clack.

If it were even possible, the blonde grew even more nervous, laughing out, "What?"

"You barely even looked at them," the other one noted with diminishing confidence.

"I don't have to," I replied. "The material's all wrong, the laminate's foggy—how much did you guys pay for these?"

They snatched the cards off the counter quickly, spinning each of their bodies off of the bar stools, and scurried towards the exit in the blink of an eye. It was just then that I saw Luke trailing behind them, one of Clyde's arms slung around his shoulders.

"Need any help?" I called out.

He replied with a simple, quick, "Nope!"

I sighed loudly, hoping more than anything that I could redeem myself from my earlier actions.

"Bad day?" Zoey asked.

I gestured towards the exit that Luke had just walked through and stated, "I didn't exactly notice that Clyde over there had gone comatose on my first day." I groaned out the last word and muttered, "He could fire me."

"*Fire* you?" Liam asked incredulously. He set his beer down with a purpose and peered at me with warm eyes. "Luke gets his panties in a bunch pretty damn easily—" I chortled, cutting off his sentence and forcing one of his dimples to appear. "He's grouchy," he continued, "but hold yourself up high! Ya just went all girl-cop on those high schoolers. *Good catch.*"

Zoey snorted. "Claire, a cop—that's a good one."

"*Zoey.*"

Liam's eyebrows bobbed upwards. "Not as innocent as you look, eh?" He asked curiously.

"I'm *plenty* innocent!"

"You're plenty *prude* is what you are," Zoey retorted.

"*Zoey!*"

Liam chuckled at our back and forth, watching us with amusement as he drank his beer with delight.

"What?" She asked. "He set you up for that perfectly—*not as innocent as you look, eh?*" Zoey repeated Liam's prior words in as deep of a voice as she could manage. "You're supposed to say something back like...oh, I dunno...*not at all, wanna play good cop bad cop?*" Her second choice of voice held a husky, sex-dripping, gritty tone to it. "I got the handcuffs in the back," she purred, reaching for my hand.

I pulled it away, laughing, "Zoey!"

"I made sure to get the non-fuzzy kind," she added with a beaming smile. "I like something with a little more...*bite.*"

I scoffed, "Slut."

"You'd be fun at parties," Liam offhandedly remarked to her, a wicked grin on his face.

"Would be?" She questioned with a cocked brow and corrected him with, "I *am* fun at parties."

He laughed. I laughed. Well—we *all* laughed. We all laughed it up right up until the entrance to the bar opened again and Luke strolled inside with a grimace marring his abnormally perfect mouth.

I mumbled, "Be right back, guys."

Before I had a chance to whip my way around the bar, Zoey tipped her head back to drain the rest of her cider. She reached into the yellow clutch she had strung over her shoulder and across her chest, grabbed a very crisp looking ten-dollar bill, and placed it on the bar top. She dropped from the stool to her feet, losing a good six inches of height as she touched the ground.

"I'm outta here, actually," she noted. "See you tomorrow, good luck with the rest of your first day."

"Wait, wait," I called to her. "I didn't even ask, did you go to the boutique?"

"Yeah."

"Well?" I asked, egging her on. "Did you get an interview?"

"Of course I did, we did one on the spot."

"Oh?" She nodded, and I pressed her further with, "Erm...*and?* Do you think you'll get the job?" Zoey looked at me pointedly, and I said, "Wait—did you already get the job?"

She practically whispered, "Of course, I did."

"Why the hell didn't you say anything sooner?" I exclaimed. "Congrats!"

I was excited for Zoey, truly I was. My happiness for her was abated, however, because I knew that I had a job of my own and a relationship with a coworker to attempt to salvage. My gaze bounced from her to the back, where I knew Luke had gone.

She waved me away with a dainty hand.

"We'll talk later, it's cool."

I mouthed a quick, *'Thank you,'* and started to make my way to the back, but hesitated, seeing Liam fiddling again with a coaster. He noticed my apologetic eyes on him and smiled.

"Go, Claire," he said. "I'll be fine."

I nodded and beelined my way to Luke. As I crossed the threshold to where he was, I could already hear an annoyed grumble of curse words.

"Hey, um—Luke?"

He stood in front of the sink, facing away from me until he heard my voice. He threw a hand in the air, smacked it down angrily against his thigh, and turned around quickly.

"Yeah?"

All I could see was disappointment radiating throughout his expression.

"I, uh," I stammered, "I'm really sorry about earlier."

His brow pinched together in confusion. "What?"

"Earlier," I reiterated, looking to the floor. "I screwed up, I wasn't paying attention—"

"Claire."

"And now you're pissed at me, I can tell—"

"Claire."

"I really am grateful that you gave me this job, I'm sorry—"

"Claire!"

His exclamation bit through me, forcing me to stop my rambling. I cringed away from him, waiting for him to continue to scold me, but was only met with silence. It stretched on for a long while until I could take it no longer, and I glanced up. His light eyes had softened, and he held a hint of a grin on his face.

"Isn't this where you yell at me?" I asked.

His perfectly coiffed head bobbed backward.

"*Yell* at you?"

"Because of the fuck up," I noted.

"There's that mouth again," he said, stretching his enough to show his teeth.

"You're not mad at me?" I said the question as if it were a statement.

Luke barked out a laugh. "For what?"

"Er...well, Liam," I started to only mention him and corrected myself, adding quickly, "and Zoey—"

"What about them?"

"Well, they came in, I got distracted obviously—"

"You're a bartender, Claire," he stated bluntly.

"Yeah?"

"Yeah," he replied, "and bartenders socialize...it's practically in the job description."

"So," I drew out the word, taking in his reassurance with a relieved breath, and finished the rest of the sentence with, "you're *not* mad...nor are you going to fire me?"

"Of course not," he responded with a sigh.

Although I was elated by the fact that this was all a misunderstanding, I was still curious as to why he was acting the way he was before. The coldness towards Liam, looking all-together irritated with me whilst dealing with Clyde, and then storming into the back room after depositing him in the Uber.

"So," I began a question in a similar fashion to how I had before, "why are you...whatever you are?"

He held out his hands to the side. "Look at me, Claire."

I obliged, but other than seeming a tiny bit out of sorts, he still looked like perfection personified.

"What about you?" I asked.

"My pants."

"Uh—"

"Come on, Claire, can you really not *smell* that?"

I did a double take to look more carefully toward the hem of his jeans and saw dark streaks stained into the material. My mind filled in the blanks for me regarding the scent. I was too far away to smell it, but it was most likely just as putrid as the color. It was rather distinct—a bitter scent that a person typically doesn't want to come into contact with.

"Oh God," I said. "Clyde?"

"Right when I got him in the Uber."

"So...you're mad because—"

"Because Clyde fucking vomited on me, yes!" He exclaimed, looking at his pants in disgust. "These jeans are effectively ruined, right?" Luke squirmed in revulsion. I couldn't do anything but let out a cackle of laughter. *"Please* don't laugh," he stated, cringing. "I am *not* good with...germs—bodily fluids—"

"They're not necessarily ruined," I responded. "You want some help?"

"With cleaning vomit off of my jeans?" He asked disbelievingly.

"It's not like I haven't done it before," I noted, adding, "er—not my own puke."

"That's—really nice of you, Claire, but that's...ridiculous, honestly. We just met, I'm not about to make you clean my pants for me—*especially* considering what's on them." He sighed loudly. "I'm just going to run home, I reek."

"Wait, *home?"*

He made his way toward me, clearly intent on exiting the building at a rapid pace. I held up a hand to stop him, shifting my feet to block his path, and he ran right into my palm for the second time tonight. I looked up and into his eyes and he cocked a brow up high, glancing at my hand and back to me. He exhaled softly through his nostrils.

We looked at each other until I stated, "You can't leave me here alone—first day and all."

Luke countered, "You would rather me stay here, smelling like this?"

Our closeness in proximity and the way that I could feel his pulse through his t-shirt had thoroughly distracted me from the scent that had begun to waft its way up to my nostrils. I sniffed at the air—and I immediately regretted that decision. I groaned at the repulsive smell of bile mixed with half-digested whiskey and pulled my hand off of Luke's chest, stepping away from him abruptly as I covered my nose with my fingers.

"Right, well—at *that* reaction," Luke said as he clapped his hands together with a tone of finality, "I'm going to go find another pair of pants."

Despite agreeing with Luke desperately needing to clean himself up, anxiety flooded through me at the thought of manning the bar alone. He wouldn't be gone for long, but I wasn't sure how I would handle it all if another crowd came in. My heart raced at the idea of Luke coming back to find Henry's in disarray, unruly customers frustrated at my possible ignorance.

"No, no-no." I stopped him for the third time now with a touch to his chest.

Luke laughed out, "You *gotta* stop doing that!"

I felt the words rumble through my wrist and I yanked my hand off of him yet again.

"Gah, I'm sorry, I just—you *can't* go," I said quickly.

"Claire, come on."

"No, *you* come on!" I exclaimed, pointing a finger at him accusatorily.

He looked down at my extended digit, amused, and asked, "Seriously?"

"Yes, *seriously,*" I replied. "You'll leave, the bar'll go to shit, people will start fucking yelling at me, and then—*then*—you're *really* gonna fire me."

Rather than addressing what I had said as fact, he simply asked, "Are you always this nervous?"

I huffed out a quick breath, but it did nothing to help me collect myself. I had never been this concerned about thinking into the future domino effects of my life, but the spirit of starting anew had caused me to reevaluate that attitude. Perhaps I was overreacting, but I just wanted my new life to be put together as cleanly as possible—was that too much to ask for? Realistically, Luke leaving me to fend for myself for a while would probably do no harm, but I wasn't ready to take that chance.

"No, er," I paused before allowing myself to think aloud. "I've just been doing this new thing where I actually worry about what the future will hold for me."

"Hmm," Luke hummed. "Well, regardless...I'll be five minutes—ten at the max—"

I threw my head back and blurted out, "Oh, for the love of God, Luke, just take your fucking pants off!"

His jaw went slack, and my internal monologue chastised me with, *'Smooth, Claire—real smooth.'*

"I, er," I stuttered, "not like—in a weird, sexual way."

Luke pursed his lips in an attempt to hide a laugh. I think I even heard him whisper in a chuckle, "Oh, wow."

"Um, just to, er," I continued, looking down towards my boots to allow my hair to shield my face, "like, you know—to clean them."

"Uh huh," Luke replied, nodding his head in an exaggerated motion.

As if I had no control over my mouth, my word vomit ramble kept going on and I stated confidently with a wave of my hand through the air:

"I don't *want* to see you with your pants off."

At this point, I think my soul had wriggled out of my body and was simply watching me make a fool of myself from across the room. Floating Claire sat cross-legged, clicking her tongue at me in a disappointed manner.

"This just keeps getting better and better," Luke noted, sympathy at my nervous defense written across his face, "and I can't believe I'm saying this, but oh, dear God, *please* stop."

I softly smacked my forehead with my palm before uttering, "What I was getting to was if you use club soda on it with maybe some lemon—which we *obviously* have here—your jeans probably won't stain or smell, and you won't have to leave."

I peeked at him from between my fingers and was nearly blinded by his beaming smile. It seemed as though he was taking immense pleasure in my self-induced misery.

"Well, why didn't you say so sooner, silly?" He asked in a bubbly tone of voice.

"I'll just grab everything for you and bring it back here?" I asked, hoping we could blow right over my prior awkwardness. "I'll man the bar while you clean up."

"But, Claire," he replied in a serious tone, "if you're out there while I'm in here, you won't be able to see me pantsless."

"Uh huh, bite me—you're not gonna let me live that down any time soon, are you?"

Luke smiled brightly and replied, "Not a chance."

"Fantastic."

I grumbled in response, turning to grab the various items for him and having a hard time keeping a grin off of my face. That is, until I exited the back room and noticed that the bar was completely empty. I paused for a moment in my strides as my face fell, taking in the empty stool that Liam had sat in previously. A glass in front of the seat stood atop a few dollar bills, the inside coated in the last of his beer's foamy dredges. His payment, the frothy glass, and the coaster that he had continually fiddled with were the only evidence that he was ever here.

Chapter Four

"So," Luke spoke, letting the sound linger in the air.

We both stood behind the bar, watching the final patron stroll out the front door. Closing time had come and gone and just like that, my first shift at Henry's was over. I tore my gaze off of the exit, looking over to Luke, and saw him bobbling his eyebrows up and down in a suggestive hint.

"So?" I asked.

"I think you're forgetting something *very* important," he noted, crossing his arms across his chest.

I started to rack my brain, going through the checklist of everything I had to do before locking up, but I couldn't think of a single thing I missed. My eyes started to widen as I drew a blank and cursed myself silently. I shook my head quickly as if that would make the mystery task appear in my mind, and Luke let out a deep laugh.

"Sorry," he chuckled out, "I couldn't really help myself on that one."

I felt my eyelids fall halfway over my line of sight. "I didn't forget anything, did I?"

Luke's grin pulled up to one side as he mentioned, "You're adorable when you're confused. You know that, right?"

"I'm sure it's one of my most attractive qualities," I retorted in a bland voice.

"Uh huh," he mumbled. *"Anyhoo,* I was more talking about somet hing...not so work related."

I squinted my eyes in further bewilderment and Luke must have taken the hint from the look on my face. He shifted his eyes pointedly towards a certain sugar-filled liquor and the puzzle pieces clicked together in my mind.

"Oh, shit!" I exclaimed, remembering our conversation yesterday before he hired me. Luke's smile widened further in response, and I inquired eagerly, "Your fireball incident?"

He nodded. "How about we have a drink, and I can tell you all about it? We're going to be working together a lot, we should get to know each other better."

I suddenly felt remarkably awake despite the time. After all, I had already experienced my fair share of embarrassing moments around Luke. It was only fair that he leveled out the playing field.

"Unless you have plans," he stated. "I know plenty of people tend to make very important arrangements at this time of day."

I giggled at his sarcasm that was becoming rapidly familiar and replied, "Oddly, no plans at the moment."

"Alright," he rubbed his hands together, "what's your drink of choice? Shots?" I exhaled softly through my nose in a chuckle as he mimicked the way Zoey had spoken on the night that we had met him. He smirked at my lack of response and deduced, "Shots."

"Alright, shots." I replied, and his eyes scanned over the shelves of booze as I asked, "What are you thinking?"

"Let me guess, you're a tequila girl?" He spoke as if it was an evaluation of my personality itself.

"You're not *guessing*," I noted in an admonishing voice. "I had tequila shots with Zoey the night I met you." I pointed a finger at him in mock accusation. "Don't pretend to be all-knowing!"

His seemingly ever-present smirk grew, grey eyes twinkling in the dim lighting.

"Astute," he stated. "Alright, fine—but tequila?"

I nodded enthusiastically and confirmed, "Tequila."

Without another word, I turned and nearly jogged my way to the back room to grab a handful of fresh limes out of the fridge. By the time I returned, he had everything laid out on the bar top—a tequila bottle, along with two shot glasses and a shaker of salt—and was walking around to the other side so we could sit. I followed behind him until I reached my stool and placed the limes on the counter in front of us. He poured both of our shots with gusto and slid mine over to me. I held up the clear liquor and examined it briefly, noting that the glass was pre-rimmed with salt. I clinked my glass with Luke's and we took our shots simultaneously, playing out the typical ritual of salt, tequila, and lime. For having no alcohol in my system, it went down surprisingly smooth.

"Damn," I said, biting on my lime, "you pulled out the good stuff, didn't you?"

Taking his own piece of citrus out of his mouth, Luke let his eyes wander back to me. "Only for you, my dear." He stated further, "Actually, I take it back, I did that for myself too. This shit's good."

He immediately poured another for us, allowing the filled glasses to sit on the counter next to our juice-drained limes.

I snickered a little, feeling the effects of the alcohol begin to seep into my veins, and demanded, "Alright, spill."

"You're awfully eager," he replied.

"You're the one that said we should get to know each other better."

"Alright, fine, fine," Luke acquiesced. "It was two years ago—my twenty-third birthday. I was out with a few buddies. The first mistake I made was agreeing with them to line up 23 shots that we could all share."

I raised my eyebrows in amusement. "Please don't tell me that they were all Fireball." He hung his head in shame. "Oh my God," I laughed. "How many did you actually take?"

He winced. "See, that's the thing...I'm not exactly sure."

"Oh boy," I groaned, tossing my head back. "That bad, huh?"

"So very, very bad," he mumbled back. "All I know is, between the three of us, we finished them all within two hours *and* we were drinking beers in between."

"I'm almost impressed," I muttered.

"Oh, I can handle my liquor, that's not the issue," he said offhandedly. "My hangover wasn't even that bad."

"How?"

"I have a gift," he admitted with a slight flair of confidence.

"A gift of your liver being able to process mass amounts of alcohol?" Luke flashed me a toothy, lopsided grin, and I chuckled, "Okay, I'll believe that when I see it—but go on...what kind of trouble did you get yourself into?"

"Well," he spoke again, "the night was hazy, obviously. From what I remember, we started talking about our biggest fears. I honestly have no idea how the conversation got there, but my buddies were convinced that if I faced my fear that I would get over it."

Luke instinctually reached for one of the glasses that I had filled in front of us.

"Hey!" I exclaimed, reaching out to smack the top of his hand with mine.

He yanked his fingers backward and looked at me, grey eyes wide. "You slapped me!" He gasped as if he were in pain and smiled even wider than before, whispering, *"Feisty."*

I rolled my eyes softly. "Yeah, well...that wasn't nearly enough information to warrant a next drink."

"I have to *earn* them?" He joked.

I chose to ignore that question. "What's your biggest fear?" I asked. "Lay it on me."

Luke groaned. "It's snakes, I hate snakes," he stated rather quickly. His gaze had dipped to the counter as he refused to make eye contact with me.

I let out a surprised laugh. "Snakes? Really?"

Luke had already put salt on the back of his hand, clearly deciding that he had given enough details. His grey eyes shot to mine as he licked the salt off and followed it immediately with his tequila. My face heated as I watched his tongue graze his skin, and my imagination briefly wandered off to a place that it most certainly should not have gone. I mimicked his movements, salting my hand and allowing myself to glance at him while I licked it off. I would have wondered if the act affected him similarly to how it had affected me, but it was far too dim in the bar to tell. He looked down to break our brief eye contact and let out a gruff cough.

I chastised myself for even beginning to consider flirting with Luke and took my shot quickly, putting the thought out of my mind as much as I possibly could.

"So, snakes," I said, breaking the tension.

He nodded oh so slightly.

"Like I said," he repeated, "they were convinced that if I faced my fear, I could get over it. Everything kind of went black from there. I'm not sure how it happened, but I woke up the next morning to a terrarium on my bedside table."

"You drunkenly bought a snake for a pet," I clarified as he nodded again. "I mean, yeah that's a little weird, but it doesn't seem that bad."

"Claire," he spoke in a low voice, "I said I woke up to a terrarium. I didn't say there was a snake in it." I must have looked like I was trying to piece together the puzzle in my head, because Luke decided to spare me the trouble and continued on. "There was a note next to the terrarium that looked like it was written by a goddamn 5-year-old that said, *This is Gilbert the Snake! He likes small mice. Take care of him and you'll overcome all your fears!* I woke up honestly not believing it and thinking my friends were just fucking with me."

"Ah, I see," I said, trying not to laugh, "I take it you found Gilbert later on?"

"Um..." He fidgeted with his hands in his lap. "No, I didn't find Gilbert per se...but I did find Gilbert's shedded skin about a week later." The laugh I had been holding in burst out of my mouth and I grabbed the tequila bottle again, refilling our glasses. "Oh, come on," he pleaded. "Don't laugh. This was literally the most terrified I've been in my life!"

I put my hand to my mouth and tried to stop. "Okay, okay, I'm sorry. So...what are you saying, then?" I questioned him one last time. "Gilbert's still running rampant around your apartment, and you just have to deal with it?"

I salted my hand once again and picked up my glass, looking expectantly at Luke. He spent an abnormally long time salting his hand and picking up his drink. The only sound that interrupted his silence came from the act of him clinking his glass against mine. I tipped my drink back, and when I looked back to the counter, his was still full.

"Luke?"

He quickly said, "Yeah...I broke my lease and moved out that week," and went through the motions of his tequila shot.

"Oh my God," I exclaimed, "you're such a dork!"

Luckily, Luke seemed to regain his sense of humor and laughed along with me.

We stayed at the bar, talking and joking with each other until 4:00 A.M. When we left, I stumbled as my heel clacked against a crack in the sidewalk. Luke caught me with an arm around my shoulder before I tumbled to the ground.

"Easy, sailor!" He laughed and righted me, continuing to walk with his arm around my shoulder for support.

The feel of his light embrace around me gave me a sense of carefree happiness that I wanted to sink into and I let out a breath of air, admonishing myself inwardly.

My thoughts brought our almost-conversation back to the forefront of my mind. I stopped walking as we came to a corner and Luke looked at me with a peaceful, glassy-eyed gaze, and a lopsided smile.

"I just remembered," I said, letting out another breath and seeing it cloud the cold air in front of me, "what were you going to tell me about Liam?"

Luke's smile lowered a bit. He took his arm off of my shoulders and leaned against the lamp post next to him, thrusting his hands in his pockets.

"Look," he started, "I'm sorry I even said anything. I've never hung out with him, but he's been around the bar a *lot*. Normally, just aimlessly hitting on girls." I must have looked like I was about to interrupt because he started to talk faster. "You just seem like a cool girl and I feel like you deserve better." My drunkenness wanted to ask him what kind of guy he thought I deserved, but he spoke soon enough so I didn't embarrass myself. "Besides, you just started working at Henry's!" His smile returned and he shoved me playfully. I followed him as he began walking towards the complex. "I don't want Liam to run you off and leave me empty handed on a busy night."

I nodded without saying a word, stored my dejected feelings away in a dark corner of my mind, and we walked the rest of the way home in silence.

❧❧❧❧❧❧ ❦❦❦❦❦❦

I woke to Zoey frantically calling for me in the apartment.

I rolled out of bed, grumbling as I made my way to the doorway and yelled out, "I'm sleeping, Zoey! I didn't get to bed until like 4:30, you're killing me!"

I entered our common area and slumped on the couch, imagining that my eyes were about as bloodshot as they felt. I glanced at the time on our stove clock—it read 8:00 A.M.

Zoey eyed me warily from her seat at the dining table and said, "I texted you like a million times! I was worried. It was way past your shift, and you weren't home yet."

I peeked at her through my fingers.

"Shit, sorry," I tried to talk through the grit in my voice, "I was a little preoccupied, I had a few drinks after my shift."

Zoey grinned at me. "Ooooh!" She sang a girlish note, accusing me of what clearly did not happen last night. "Drinks with Liam?! You have to tell me all about it. Did you close down the bar with him? Oh my God, did you do it on the bar with him?! I need to know!"

I looked at her, amused. "Not drinks with Liam, Zoey. Drinks with Luke."

Her animated face fell. "Well, that's not nearly as interesting. We both know nothing can happen there."

I bitterly thought to myself that *that* fact did not need to be reiterated to me.

"No," I replied, pushing my foolish bitterness aside. "You know, it was actually really nice. We had fun."

I was nearly reminiscing in a dreamland when I heard Zoey snort.

"Okay, cool, I guess," she said in a monotone voice, clearly disinterested in the lack of sex in that conversation. "What happened to Liam?"

I fought to keep my eyes open considering my lack of sleep.

"Yeah, Liam," I yawned. "He's cute...kinda disappeared though. Got all caught up with Luke in the back and by the time I went back out there, he was gone."

"Caught up with Luke?" She asked.

"Yeah," I managed to let out a rough chuckle, "he erm—got vomited on, it was a whole thing."

"By the dude he was carrying out of the bar?"

"That's the one."

"Gross."

"Mhm," I replied, "and then *I* word-vomited and told him to take off his pants."

She blurted out, "Atta girl, I'm sure that went over well."

"As well as it could, I didn't embarrass myself to death quite yet so..."

I allowed my sentence to ramble off, the purpose of what I was saying known well enough that I didn't need to complete it. My eyes fluttered closed, each breath I took becoming longer and deeper.

"You should go back to sleep for at least another two hours." Zoey's voice chimed in my ears. "You look like shit."

I had to laugh because I knew she was right despite not even seeing a mirror yet this morning. I traipsed back to bed, silently waved goodbye to Zoey, closed my door, and laid down. My phone, which had died at some point throughout my shift, sat on my nightstand charging from the night before and hummed out two short vibration pulses, indicating missed messages. Eyes still half-closed, I felt my way around to my left until I felt my phone and unplugged it swiftly to check my messages.

Zoey, again, was right—she did text me quite a bit this morning.

3:00 A.M.: Didn't your shift end at 2:00?

3:15 A.M.: Claire?

3:32 A.M.: Okay I know you're not home, I checked your room.

3:33 A.M.: Not like in a weird trying to watch you sleep kind of way.

3:34 A.M.: Trying to make sure you didn't get murdered?

3:45 A.M.: Your radio silence is not helping my anxiety.

3:47 A.M.: If you're fucking the guy across the hall, props. But also maybe confirm you're not dead?

3:55 A.M.: Is it true that you have to wait 24 hours to report a missing person?

3:56 A.M.: Because I'll do it.

4:00 A.M.: Your phone went straight to voicemail.

4:05 A.M.: Okay, I'm gonna walk myself back off this cliff and not assume you're dead in a ditch somewhere.

4:06 A.M.: Going back to sleep, if you aren't here when I'm up I'm calling the cops, I swear.

4:07 A.M.: Charge your phone next time you're out this late, you inattentive hoe.

I called out, "Got your texts, sorry!"

I barely heard Zoey's passive aggressive, "Mhm." Not because it was too quiet, but because a distraction in the form of an additional message had just come through. I didn't recognize the number, but it read:

8:05 A.M.: Hey there. Want some coffee?

I smiled, albeit a little confused. I quickly sent:

8:06 A.M.: New phone, who dis?

I laughed quietly to myself at my terrible joke, and my phone pinged about 10 seconds later. A photo popped up of Liam, smiling lazily. His chocolate-colored eyes were hooded, traces of sleep still present within them, and his hair was going in about six different directions. I felt my smile widen, figuring that he must have not looked in a mirror yet this morning either. It suited him well, though. I messaged again:

8:08 A.M.: I'd love some coffee. Come over in 10?

I received an immediate thumbs up emoji. Despite telling myself over and over lately that I needed another significant other like I needed a hole in my head, I felt a thrum of excitement run through me. Liam seemed...nice.

My inner thoughts snidely remarked, *'Colton seemed nice at first, too.'*

I sighed loudly. He *did* seem nice. Well, he *was* nice—it didn't hurt that he had helped me in one of my darkest hours. That particular type of help was misguided, though. It took me far too long to realize that.

I got up to make sure I looked presentable, looked in the full-length mirror that was hanging on my wall, and moaned loudly, "I do look like shit!"

Zoey's laugh emanated through the walls, and I noted that they were remarkably thin, confirming what Luke had said the night prior. I darted rapidly from my closet to the common-area bathroom that Zoey and I shared and back, grabbing whatever clothing that appeared to be casual yet flattering along the way. I moved so quickly that I didn't fully comprehend what I had dressed myself in—all I knew was that I was comfortable, yet not wearing pajamas, so I marked it down as a win in my book.

I returned to the kitchen, and Zoey was still sitting at the table scrolling through her phone when she glanced up and gave me a confused look.

"Thought you were going to sleep—who the hell are you trying to impress? You look adorable, what's wrong with you?"

I smiled lightly, pleased that I had her nod of approval regarding my clothing, and whisper-yelled, "Liam's bringing me coffee, shut up!"

She snickered, and a knock sounded at the door. I skipped over to it and opened it with what I tried to portray as a casual smile.

Liam beamed down at me.

"Well, hello freckles!" His eyes crinkled at the corners as he smiled. "Do you always look this way this early in the morning? Because if so, I'm going to have to come over more often."

Zoey let out a booming laugh from the kitchen.

I muttered, "Thank you," and said, "Just ignore her. I try to." I stepped back to let him inside and closed the door behind him. "So, how exactly did you get my phone number, Liam? Not that I'm complaining."

Zoey yelled from across the room, "That would be me!"

Liam's broad shoulders shook a bit with a silent laugh and as I met him in the kitchen, he was setting a full French press coffee maker on the counter. I tried to stop myself from gawking at it but failed, hiding my surprise by turning to grab mugs out of the cabinet instead.

It wasn't that I was overly impressed with his use of the contraption—a French press is relatively simple to use, cheap to buy, and makes a pretty decent cup of coffee. The fact that Liam brought one over was just a happy coincidence considering that my previously owned French press was broken as I was packing my belongings to move to Virginia. Happy coincidence aside, his decision to bring it over instead of buying a cup from a coffee shop in town earned him major brownie points.

I set the mugs on the counter next to him as Liam pressed the plunger of the machine down swiftly.

"I'm not trying to boost your ego or anything," I spoke, motioning towards the contraption, "but damn. Nice work."

He grinned knowingly as he poured both of our mugs. "Do you take anything in your coffee?"

I had already walked to the fridge, grabbed the milk, and set it on the counter aside the steaming cups.

"Just a splash of milk," I responded. "Sweetener?"

He looked up and shook his head. "Nah, I just drink it black, nothing frilly."

"You know," I spoke again, grabbing my mug and walking towards the couch, "I like no frills."

He followed me, and as he sat beside me on the couch, he smiled at me a bit too brightly.

"Yeah, I know you do," he raised his eyebrows and took a sip of his coffee, obviously referring to himself and not the coffee.

I deflated a bit, his clearly cocky personality practically ticking away the points that he had just earned in his favor. I vaguely wondered how I would deal with this situation should Liam's personality not mesh with mine. Do I just grin and bear it until he decides to return to his humble abode? Or should I consider setting up a strike system if he *really* got under my skin, and figure out how to send him on his way if he strikes out?

I wanted to give him the benefit of the doubt. I did, truly. But I heard him chuckle, still laughing at his own joke nearly a full minute after he originally told it, and I had to hold back an eye roll.

'A swing and a miss, I suppose,' I thought to myself. *'Strike one.'*

I brought myself back to the present.

"So, Liam," I asked, crossing my legs as I sat in the green chair adjacent to the couch, "What do you do for work?"

He smiled and stretched an arm over the back of his head. "I freelance."

I took a sip of coffee to try to hide my amused disappointment at his vague, non-answer to my question. The coffee really *was* good—I needed to buy a new French press.

I tried to look back at him sweetly. "What do you mean by that, freelance?"

"Oh, you know," he sighed loudly. "I do a lot of this, that, and the other."

Zoey was vibrating with silent laughter at the kitchen table. I nearly heard her voice chirp in my ear, *'So...jobless. He's jobless. He's either jobless or sells drugs.'* The offenses that Liam presented weren't the worst things in the world by any means, but Zoey knew all my ticks just as well if not better than I did. She was probably counting the strikes right along with me the second that he laughed at his own terrible joke. I glanced over at her and mouthed, *'Help.'* She kept her mouth clamped shut and shook her head.

"Umm," I stammered, trying to fill the silence.

Christ on a cracker, it should not be this difficult to think of things to talk about.

Liam decided to finally speak. "You just moved here, right?"

I let out the breath I didn't realize I was holding out of sheer awkwardness. "We did, yeah. Just moved here from a small town in North Carolina."

"I'm from North Carolina, I moved here a few years ago! Whereabouts were ya?"

I shifted in my seat.

"Er—Wilmington. Near there, anyway."

His eyes widened and his mouth dropped open. *"Weird,"* Liam whispered. "I'm from Southport! Where were you near Wilmington?"

It was then that I wondered if I had made a gigantic mistake.

I clenched my teeth as I replied, "Ogden."

"Oh-*ho,*" he laughed in return, "not far!"

I didn't particularly want to talk about North Carolina. I left for a reason and reminiscing always had a way of reminding me of Colton and our... extracurriculars. I was tired of reliving that nightmare, but for the sake of giving Liam a last chance, I pretended to be interested.

I mentioned, "I definitely didn't think I'd be meeting anyone out here from my neck of the woods."

"Me either!" he said, excitedly. "Man, I miss it there."

That makes one of us, buddy.

He blabbered on about the high school he went to that he played sports for and the ins and outs of his hometown and I just...let him go on. I couldn't help it—the man looked so excited to be talking about his glory days and I didn't want to rain on his parade. So, instead, I sipped at my coffee and tried to focus on the taste rather than the poor choice in conversation that quickly ramped up Liam's strikes.

The fact that he was a cocky, hometown sports jock irked me, there was no doubt about that. Not to mention, the lack of desire to speak a single word about his means of employment was...concerning. I pondered if I could inevitably look past these misdemeanors because it was clear that Liam was a nice guy. His connection to a town that was a stone's throw away from the one that I had just left, however, was too much for me to handle. At that realization, the *tiny* shred of romantic interest that I still held for Liam faded into the air like smoke—and I could only distract myself with good coffee for so long. Ten minutes into his monologue and

I had *ooh'd, ahh'd, hmm'd,* and *oh really'd* more than I thought could be possible and he just. Wouldn't. Stop.

I glanced over at Zoey with pleading eyes and she finally mouthed, '*Fine,*' and cleared her throat.

"Hey, Claire," she announced, "I think I hear your phone vibrating in your room."

I made sure to act surprised. "Oh, really?"

I shot up to go grab it and feigned a conversation, speaking loudly into my silent phone. "Oh, Mom, don't cry! I'm doing just fine here!" I traipsed back into the main room and gave Liam an apologetic look, cupping my hand over the bottom of the phone, whispering, "I'm so sorry, I have to take this." Liam looked like someone just kicked his puppy as I added, "I'll see you later, okay?"

He nodded and held a forlorn look as he walked across the room to grab his coffee maker. I made my way back to my room, ensuring to continue my façade of a conversation.

"I just got here; I can't go back!" I paused for what seemed like an appropriate amount of time and spoke again. "Of course, I'm going to visit you at Christmas! What kind of daughter would I be if—"

The front door shut, and I lobbed my phone on top of my ivory comforter.

I lugged myself back into the living room and looked at Zoey pointedly as I dragged my feet to the kitchen table. The sound that the chair adjacent to her made as I dragged it along the hardwood was almost melancholy—it perfectly depicted the hopeless amusement that surrounded me, and she snorted.

"Pretending to talk with your mom of all people, really?"

I shrugged. The chances that my mom would call me out of the blue would be slim-to-none and if she *did*, it most certainly would not be laced with her concern for my well-being. It was long, long ago when she last worried about me in the slightest—to say we were estranged would be a massive understatement.

Zoey bypassed my brief silence, and said, "He's cute, but so opposite your type that I almost feel sorry for you."

I groaned and took my seat.

"I think I shouldn't even be dating at all," I remarked.

"You've said this more than a handful of times."

"Yeah, yeah," I replied, waving off her comment. "Well, anyways if you think he's so cute, he's all yours."

She scoffed and asked, "To *date?*" I shrugged again, and she began, "Not that I don't appreciate the sentiment, but I've been told that I have the emotional wingspan of a goldfish when it comes to relationships." I chuckled at her brutal honesty as she continued talking. "And those who have told me that would be absolutely right. If I did anything with Liam, it would just be for a night. For one, mind-blowing night." She began to stare off into space for so long that I had to clap in front of her eyes to get her back on track. She stuttered, "Ah—anyways...the point I'm trying to get to is that all of that aside, I *still* wouldn't allow myself to have my fun because I don't shit where I eat. Liam's clearly off limits."

There wasn't even a purpose to responding aloud to that, amusing as it was. I simply nodded and allowed my scattered thoughts to drift as we enjoyed the remainder of our morning.

Chapter Five

L uke was preoccupied when I walked in for my second ever shift, turned away from the door and serving Clyde again. I wandered to the back to put my purse away and when I returned behind the counter, Luke was ringing in Clyde's first drink.

"Hey stranger," he said. "How are ya?"

I grinned in response. "I'm good. You?"

"Oh, I'm peachy," he replied, smiling a bit wider. He paused, though, and his expression faded slightly. "How's, um—how's Liam?" He didn't seem to be able to meet my eyes as he focused on reorganizing the beer glasses.

"Liam?" I asked, narrowing my eyes and cocking my head to the side.

"I went for a run early this morning," he said, still focused on the glasses. "I saw him leaving your apartment."

I'm not sure why, but I giggled. Perhaps it was the way that he phrased the question or how it oozed with potential scandal. Luke gave me a sideways glance, clearly unsure of the reason for my amusement, which only served to make me laugh deeper.

"Oh, wow," I finally caught my breath. "I believe I have a story to tell you."

He beamed back at me, though the confused tension between his brows was still present.

"Tequila?" He asked.

I nodded in confirmation. "Definitely tequila."

The rest of my shift could not have gone fast enough. To tell the truth, my poorly spent morning with Liam wasn't even that interesting. I was simply hoping that my post-work tequila talk with Luke would be just as entertaining as last time.

Luke seemed to be working just as quickly as I was, busying himself nearly all night with a constant shuffle of patrons. Not a minute later than 2:00 in the morning, the advertised time that Henry's was to close, he was going through the motions of locking up. By the time he turned around from deadbolting the front doors, I had everything we needed splayed out on the bar top. Two shot glasses already filled with Luke's preference of chilled tequila—this time a reposado rather than the silver—were calling our names. The bottle sat atop the counter as well, along with a shaker of salt, and a bevy of sliced limes. I gestured grandly at the countertop before me, sitting in the same seat as the night prior, and Luke smiled broadly at me, looking near giddy. He jumped in the seat next to mine and salted his hand, looking at me as he grabbed the small glass filled with light amber liquid. I clinked my glass against his, and we drank.

"Alright, spill," he said, biting on the fruit.

"So eager," I simpered, mimicking our conversation from last time. Luke grinned back at me shyly, and I began my story. "Liam offered to bring me coffee, so I thought it would be a good opportunity to get to know him this morning."

Luke's jaw went slack, and his mouth perfectly formed the shape of the letter *o*.

"You're saying," he interrupted quietly, "Liam went over to your house this morning for *coffee?*"

"And what else would we be doing?"

The sideways glance and cocked brow that Luke gave me needed no further explanation. It screamed that his initial thought was sex, sex, and more sex.

I scoffed and feigned offense. "Have I no shame?!" He laughed and began to pour our next drink, relief evident on his face. I thought out loud for a moment, "You and I didn't even get back to the complex until the sun was about to rise, when would I have even had a chance to do—"

He shrugged and held up a hand in defense.

"I don't know, no judgement here!" I chuckled at his wild assumption, and he remarked, "Just rolling off of previous Liam experiences."

"Yes, he came over this morning," I reiterated.

"I'm sorry, I didn't mean to—"

"Obviously that matters to you." I joked, "Don't worry, I'm not running for the hills, you won't be short a bartender any time soon."

"Of course, it matters to me, Claire," he said softly. I could tell in the sincerity in his eyes that he meant it.

"Basically," I attempted to continue my story, "Liam's cocky. I think he expects girls to fall all over him because of his looks."

Luke snorted. "I think I tried to warn you about that."

I rolled my eyes at him heavily and began to salt my hand while he did the same.

"Oh, fuck off," I grimaced.

Luke snickered and mumbled, "I like it when you're sassy," right before he tapped my glass with his. I tried and failed to not watch him as he licked the salt off his hand and drank. I followed suit. "It can't have been that bad just because he's a cocky ass," Luke suggested as I was biting my lime.

"Hey," I chastised him. "I didn't say he was an ass! Just cocky. He's actually really nice."

He spoke with humor in his voice, "I know *you* didn't say he was an ass. I did. I regret nothing."

I teased, "I like it when you're sassy." He let out a deep laugh. "Okay, truthfully, it really wasn't that bad," I said. "He's just not really my type. He's kind of from the same area as me in North Carolina and he just wouldn't shut up about it! He was some sort of high school sports star and the whole jock vibe just...rolls off of him in waves." I took a breath and willed myself to continue. "The guy's nice to look at, but the second he opens his mouth, everything goes downhill for me. Zoey had to help me fake a phone call to get him to leave."

Luke snickered as he grabbed the tequila again and refilled the glasses. "You did a fake phone call? He *had* to have known!"

I shook my head vigorously. "Nope! Not at all. I pulled an Oscar-worthy performance out of my ass. You should have seen it."

Luke muttered, "I would have loved to." He seemed like he was pondering something silently to himself before he questioned me, "Why did you come to Salem?" I felt my eyes widen—I *really* wasn't drunk enough to talk about this with him yet. I grabbed my shot glass and took it straight up without any salt or lime. Luke flinched at my sudden motions and he mumbled a long, drawn out, "Okay," as he grabbed his drink and mimicked my actions.

"Sorry," I said, speaking my thoughts aloud, "I really need more alcohol for that."

He glanced over at me, slight concern in his eyes, and replied, "Alright, then." He filled both glasses and salted his hand once more. "Friends don't let friends drink alone."

We took three more. Our eyes locked as we simultaneously licked salt away from the back of our hands on the last drink and I felt my blush creep up my chest. My face warmed in turn. My teeth began to numb from the onset of the alcohol and though I didn't feel completely at ease speaking about Colton, I decided that this was the appropriate level of inebriated that I needed to be to begin to talk about him.

Luke was about to pour us another when I mumbled, "Okay." He looked over at me with curiosity in his eyes and put the bottle down. "I was with Colton for a year."

"Colton?"

"Ex-boyfriend," I replied. "The whole relationship was a shit show...I don't know what I was even thinking trying to start something with Liam." I mumbled, "I'm not even remotely ready for that after everything with Colt."

He asked, "So, what did the asshole do?"

"Ah, it's kind of a long story. The main thing is that we didn't have... passion." The admission felt like a white lie, for I *knew* that Colton and I had passion. In fact, near daily adrenaline rushes were proven to be a natural aphrodisiac, so my use of the word felt wrong. One look at Luke's face, which I was beginning to deem as wholesome, and I corrected my phrasing, "Or, I dunno, we were just acquaintances rather than having an actual relationship. It was comfortable, but...he ended up treating me a certain way that I did *not* appreciate." I decided inwardly that there wasn't enough tequila in the world that would allow me to delve into the details of that, yet. "It's a long story, but I took that opportunity to just...get out. I know it sounds petty, the whole *leaving the area because of your ex* thing, but—"

"You don't have to explain," he said. "He gave you your reason. You didn't leave because of him...he just broke the chain that you were tied to."

I hummed in agreement. Although I had given Luke the *highly* abridged version of my past life with Colton, I couldn't have worded it better myself. Yes, he most likely would have come to a different conclusion if I had given him all of the grisly details, but...I didn't, so I decided to skirt that line of thought for now.

Luke pressed on, "You're lucky, in a way." With that note, I almost cut him off, but he spoke quickly. "I know it probably doesn't seem like it now. Trust me, I know that more than you think."

"Oh?"

"Yeah—now you have the opportunity to be better than *just happy enough.*"

"You're insightful," I noted, unable to hold back my curiosity about his past. "What do you mean that you know that more than I think?"

His smile slowly eased off his face.

"Her name was Emma," he said.

"Emma?" I asked in a similar fashion to how he had asked of Colton.

"Mhm, an ex of mine."

"Oh."

My mind raced, focusing a bit too much on the gendered word *her*. I was too gobsmacked to say anything. I thought about the woman who approached Zoey and me on our first night here and the man we saw Luke with the night after and honestly...it was foolish. The point was moot because it was none of my goddamn business.

Luke continued to speak as honestly as I had earlier, saying, "We were together for..." He looked skyward, pausing as he thought to himself. "Two years and change. And things had been rough for...a while. We hadn't been, you know, *together* in, I dunno—three months or more? I didn't think anything of it at first, honestly. I just chalked it up to us being a long-term couple—sex ebbs and flows, yeah? That happens, right?"

"You hadn't had sex in months?" I questioned, my eyebrows up high.

Luke nodded, his face twisting as he thought back to the memory. "TMI?"

I shrugged. "Nah." What could have been an overshare considering the amount of time that we knew each other didn't bother me in the least. "So, what—you left her?"

He let out a bitter, singular, "Ha," and continued, "Um, no—not quite that simple. I was happy."

"You were happy with being in a near sexless relationship?" I blurted out, and Luke pressed his lips together tightly. "I—sorry—not judging—"

He waved me off with a hand, a corner of his lip pulling up at my frantic apology. "No, I get what you're saying. It wasn't *ideal,* obviously, I would have liked to be intimate more often. But, you know, I loved her. Erm," Luke hesitated, "I mean, I thought I did. I don't know anymore. It got *very* complicated."

"Complicated?"

"I—yeah, um." He stammered, interlacing his fingers in front of him and focusing only on them until he confessed, "She was pregnant."

"Oh."

"Yeah."

"You have a kid?"

"Ah—no." Luke leaned in to whisper the kicker into my ear. "It wasn't mine."

"Oh, fuck," I breathed, feeling my heart beat heavily in my chest.

"Yeah," he said on an exhale. "Fuck. Timing didn't add up with how far along she was—it was pretty damn obvious. So...after being *very* suspicious for a while, she eventually confessed that she had been cheating for...like *forever,* basically." I saw it coming, but I winced, nonetheless. Luke stated, *"That* was when I left her. She went to go be with the other guy and I think the kid—a little boy—think he's like two years old now."

"I—I'm sorry," I stuttered, not sure how to respond, but sure as hell that I felt the needless urge to apologize.

His eyes met mine again and he smiled softly.

"Don't be," he said. "I thought I was happy then, but the more I think back to it, the more I realize that she was...kind of terrible." I nodded, and Luke continued to speak, saying simply, "Now I can be better than *just happy enough.*"

All I could manage to reply with was an emotionally charged, "Damn."

He thought to himself for a moment before saying, "I don't just go spouting off my life story to every person I meet, you know."

"Is that right?" I cocked an eyebrow in his direction.

"I gave you way too much detail," he said offhandedly. "I, ah—I promise I'm not a crazy person. To be fair, you *did* get me drunk."

A slight flush came to his cheeks, and the need to reassure him swarmed me.

"No!" I laughed. "No, you're fine! It's nice to get to know you better. For what it's worth, I didn't need to tell you anything about Colton, either."

"Ah, drunken bonding," he sighed. "One of the easiest ways to make friends."

"It helps that you're easy to talk to," I remarked.

He threw me a lopsided grin and said, "Likewise."

The night went on, and we decided that we needed to remedy our respective depressing conversations. It began with just playing music, but with the alcohol consumed, it inevitably progressed to something that I could only describe as dancing. I wouldn't have called it dancing in the traditional sense—this wasn't two bodies gently swaying together as we listened to whatever tune we desired. After all, that would have been far too romantic. No, we had decided for whatever reason to recreate the stereotypical dances throughout the past few decades. When Luke tried to replicate *the twist,* I practically lost it.

"What are you even doing with your knees?!"

He stopped mid-twist, oblivious with one leg in the air, grey eyes twinkling in the light, and asked lightheartedly, "What?"

My cheeks ached. "You look like a confused flamingo."

"No way," he mock argued, "this is how they used to do it! The trick is you have to make sure you have your hands out like *this.*"

He splayed his hands out at his side and did one of the most flamboyant gyrating motions that I had ever seen.

"You're *such* a dork," I chuckled, moving to the nearest table as my exhaustion set in.

I sat down with a thud, and Luke exclaimed, "No, wait—don't sit!"

"Luke," I complained. "How do you have all this energy? I'm dying over here."

"I'm having *fun* with you, Claire. Come on," he ushered me, grabbing my hand and pulling me up. "One more."

"Fine," I feigned annoyance. "What's your one?"

He very seriously stated, "Dirty Dancing."

One of my brows shot sky high.

"You want to *dirty dance* with me?"

"Of *course,* I don't," he said plainly.

I couldn't help but hear, *'Well, that's a major bummer,'* ring through my mind in Zoey's voice. I smirked, agreeing with her fairy-like tone that rang in my brain.

"I'm not asking you *to* dirty dance with me," he corrected. "I'm saying the one move—from the movie. Dirty. Dancing."

A scene flashed in my head of a woman held high up above a man, her arms spreadeagle and her legs pin straight as he stared up at her.

"The—the jump thing?"

Luke nodded his head up and down, hard. So hard, in fact, that a loose strand of his typically well-coiffed hair fell limp across his brow.

"No, no," I said, "that's not happening."

"Oh, yes, it is," he retorted, blinding me with his teeth.

He turned an about-face, his steps patting across the hardwood to the other end of the room. I supposed that I could have argued that the look on his face before he turned around was alight with such excitement that I couldn't say no. If I were to retell this story to Zoey the next day, I assumed that I would describe my thought process as such. If I was being honest with myself though, my willpower around this man whom I had met mere days ago was...nonexistent. It *could* have been the tequila, or it could have been his carefree attitude, but there was something about being around him that made the air feel just a little lighter—and that was saying a lot considering what I had been through in my life.

Luke questioned me silently with a tip of his head at the other end of the bar, arms thrown out to the side. I nodded with a grin, holding up a single finger in a sign to wait for a bit.

I blew out a breath, shaking my hands out in preparation, and then I ran with all the intention in the world. I came up several feet too short, skipping to a stop as the irrational fear of falling was prevalent in my mind. This continued to happen again, and again.

By my fourth attempt, Luke had called out, "Come on!" His arms that were expecting my presence hung limp at his side and he said wryly, "You know, I'm not gonna ask how much you weigh or anything...but you're like...*tiny*, Claire. There's about a million percent chance that I can pick you up over my head." I scoffed. "Trust me!" He yelled, waving a hand towards himself and beckoning me to him yet again.

Without thinking any more about the matter, I sprinted at Luke with as much gusto as I could manage.

"Are you actually gonna—" Luke began to ask the obvious question, but when he took in the steadfast look on my face, he cut himself off with a happy, "Oh." His *oh* was immediately followed by a much less gleeful, "Oh, shit!"

My body hit him with a thud. In my determination to keep my legs moving, I was somehow unable to get them off the ground quickly enough. Instead of jumping up for Luke to catch me, I jumped straight *into* him—and bowled him over completely. He groaned loudly. We laid beside each other with our backs on the floor, catching our breath as it seemed to have been knocked out of both of our lungs.

I whined, "Sorry! I must've—"

Luke's bellowing laugh cut off my apology. "Terrible!" He announced loudly. "Zero out of ten stars—grace is *not* your strong suit, is it?"

I snorted. "No, it's not—are you okay?"

"Not a scratch on me," he returned, turning his head towards me. "You?"

"I think you broke my fall well enough."

"You're welcome," he mocked me.

It looked as though he was going to say something else, perhaps something even more sarcastic. For a fleeting second, there was a mischievous spark in his light eyes. It disappeared quickly when he glanced down to the floor, remembering where he was laying.

"Ah, we should get up," he said quickly, nearly jumping to his feet and offering me a hand. "I don't even want to know how many diseases are living on these floors."

"It's just a little dirt, Luke."

I took his hand, ignoring my urge to hold onto it for far longer than was appropriate. I let go as soon as he yanked me upwards and dusted off my jeans.

"I can guaran-fucking-tee you that it's way more than just a little dirt that's leached into these floors."

It was now my turn to laugh at him. "Nice mouth," I quipped, "am I rubbing off on you that quickly?"

He returned a wide grin to me. "Oh, I don't think that would hurt me in the least, Claire."

I tried not to focus too hard on how his voice cradled my name and made it sound like it was engulfed in velvet. Instead, I imagined the opposite of what I had just said and wondered if Luke's personality could rub off on me in the same way. Even on our walk home as we silently strolled through the cold, I considered the thought. By the time I began to drift to sleep that night, the idea had turned into a desperate hope.

Chapter Six

"**Y**ou wanted to fix all the shit with your life, right?"

    A buzzed head with icy blue eyes threw his hands in my direction, frustrated, and his demeanor made my defenses thaw. It had been approximately four weeks since I met Colton. Nearly twenty-eight days. One month—and that span of time felt oddly short. I was swept up. Inundated into his world like a language that I didn't even intend on learning. His way of life—his dialect—played on repeat in the background of my mind and, in the blink of an eye, I was fluent. My fluency was begrudging, though, as what I had been thrust into was...a lot. It was thrilling. Lucrative. It made my heart pound like none other, but still, I was hesitant.

"*Yeah, Colt—I...I need to. I guess so.*"

"*What do you mean you guess so?!*" *He grabbed me by the shoulders, ushering me to look at him.* "*When we ran into each other, you told me you needed help. Look at how far we've come already!*" *His tone was begging, and as his hands slid up to my face, I bowed into his touch. I arched toward him as he kissed me once, roughly, and asked me with a plea,* "*Don't you trust me?*"

It was a question that I didn't know the answer to, but I felt as though my hands were bound because I really, truly needed him.

"*Yeah,*" *I responded.* "*I trust you.*"

I woke feeling as if I had slipped on ice, my entire body jumping with the brace of an upcoming impact.

Where the hell did that come from?

The memory of when my life had turned on its axis stayed vivid in my mind for a few minutes. Talking about Colton with Luke must have stirred up some old mementos of the past in my brain. I moaned in misery at the thought. I felt blindly to my left, finding my phone right where I expected it, fully charged and sitting upon my nightstand.

I tapped the glass face to see that Luke had texted me twice:

9:30 A.M.: Need. Caffeine. There's a coffee place down the street if you're interested.

9:40 A.M.: I'm seriously dying. If you don't message back in five minutes, I'm assuming you're still asleep.

My phone pinged in my hand while I read the second message.

9:45 A.M.: This offer expires in 3...2...

I sat up in my bed, giddy, welcoming the distraction from my blast from the past, and messaged back:

9:45 A.M.: GOOD MORNING

It was a fight to get him to give me more than ten minutes to get ready before he was knocking on my door. My closet was an absolute mess as I had yet to fully unpack it, so I considered myself lucky to find a cream-colored sweater that I supposed was casual enough to wear for grabbing a cup of coffee. By the time I threw on a pair of jeans, the sweater in question, and had my hair in a messy bun, Luke had already arrived. I answered the door to find him tapping an imaginary wristwatch.

I met his sarcastically impatient gaze and allowed myself to glance over his appearance, albeit quickly. His hair looked like he just rolled out of bed, but I knew realistically that it took time and the perfect amount of product to look that way. He had on a red flannel shirt, jeans, and brown boots. The shadow of stubble on his face somehow made his jawline look *sharper,* and it forced me to stifle a groan as I wondered why on God's green earth he had to be *so* good looking. It was, possibly, a crime against humanity.

"Seriously? You look like you just strolled out of a magazine for new fall attire. I look like an ogre compared to you."

The words had left my mouth before I had the chance to stop them. Luke's face lit up from the compliment.

"Ogres have green skin," he joked. *"You* do not."

I snorted, pushed through the threshold and past him, and announced, "Let's go."

Our walk to the local coffee shop was short and sweet. The few minutes that it took to get there were spent in blissful silence, the soft sound of leaves falling around us the only thing that reached my ears. Upon our arrival, I mentally noted that I needed to come here every morning if my wallet allowed. The entire place was just...cozy. Chalkboards hung from the ceiling at the checkout counter, elaborate cursive text detailing the newest seasonal beverage. The slim, rectangular space had various options for seating that I could view if I stood on my toes to peek beyond the handful of individuals in line in front of us. A small table sat next to a wood fireplace in the far corner, and I itched to reserve it before anyone else did.

"Should I grab that table?" I asked Luke, pointing to the seats.

"Ooh, *yes—go.*" He ushered me. "What do you want? I'll meet you there."

"Weak, bagged breakfast tea," I deadpanned.

He scrunched his nose up adorably. "*Yeah,* about the whole *us being friends* thing—"

"I'm joking, God. Just a latte."

Luke chuckled, ordering, "Go before anyone takes that spot."

I did, rushing to sit at one of the two chairs that surrounded the small table. As I sat, I found the padding on the chair plusher than I anticipated, and I reveled in the sound of the crackling noise of the fire beside me until Luke returned.

"This is my favorite spot in here," he told me.

Luke slid a large mug across the table to me carefully so as not to ruin the latte art. He placed a plate between us that balanced both an orange-tinged slice of bread and his own coffee, which was black save for the appearance of what looked like cinnamon.

"Is that pumpkin bread?" I asked. "Please tell me it's pumpkin bread."

"With chocolate chips," he replied. "Don't worry, I actually did get it to share."

He wouldn't have needed to tell me twice. I broke off a piece and popped it into my mouth, feeling my eyes roll into my head from how good it tasted.

"I love this place," I simpered.

Luke asked, "Speaking of, how do you like Virginia so far?"

"Well," I said. "I haven't really gotten a chance to experience much. It's just nice to be somewhere different."

He nodded. "What would you want to experience?"

I shrugged. "I don't really know...I'm not the type to go out to clubs or anything. I'm more of a lay-low person. I think as long as I'm happy with the people I'm around, then I'm happy where I am."

"Totally," he said. "I get that."

"So," I asked, "what do you do for fun?"

"You know, I always hated that question." His eyes showed that he was mocking me.

"Why?"

"Because," he explained, "you never really think about how boring of a person you are until you have to answer that question or think about what you *actually* do for fun. Think about it. What would you say if I asked you that?" I hesitated for I wasn't sure of an answer, and he exclaimed, "See?! It's harder than you think. It makes you sound so boring if all you say to that is, *'Netflix and maybe some video games.'*"

It was for the best that Luke didn't find my lack of interesting hobbies strange. The extracurricular activities of the life that I had decided to leave behind were...well, they were left behind with it. The time I spent with Colton didn't leave me much availability for friends...hobbies...any sort of fun, now that I think about it. I was lucky to get away with Zoey, who stuck by me through all the shenanigans regardless of how little we saw each other.

I began to wonder if I was more of a homebody than anything else as Luke was to expect from my reaction. If I was honest with myself, I probably wouldn't have developed any thrilling hobbies even if my life was...*normal*.

So, I laughed, nodding and agreeing with him, and allowed our morning to continue on. We sat in the coffee shop for a while, at times in peaceful silence and at others, people watching through the window. I found that even idle chit-chat with Luke was pleasant. Remarkably so, to the point that I felt myself breathing a sigh of contentment when we began to approach our apartment complex once again.

When my door was within sight, he said, "Well, I'll see you in a few hours at Henry—"

It was clear that Luke intended to say more, but his voice was cut short when the door across from mine opened. A certain broad body with a mess of blonde hair appeared, and I mumbled:

"Ah, fuck."

Liam immediately saw us walking up and beamed at me, calling out, "Well, hey there!"

Luke cooed, "As much as I would *love* to stay—"

"Don't you dare leave me with him," I hissed.

Luke's grin grew wickedly crooked as the three of us met at my doorstep. He wiggled his fingers in my direction in a snarky wave goodbye and skipped up the stairs to his apartment. I was certain that I heard a muffled laugh as he rounded the corner a floor above us.

"Morning," Liam rasped.

I had to fight not to roll my eyes. I supposed that if I were more interested in him—or, rather, if I hadn't attempted to have a full conversation with him the last time we spoke—that his tone of voice would have been appealing. Sexy even, with the low and gravelly tone of a man who still had a hint of sleep in his vocal cords. I *wasn't* interested in him though, so instead, Liam's morning greeting came across as fake. He leaned against the wall that met my front door, arms crossed over his chest.

I sighed again. This time it was out of mild irritation, though by the way that Liam looked at me, it would seem as if he thought that I was excited beyond belief.

"Hey Liam, how's it going?"

"Good," he replied, drawing out the word as he smiled, showing his dimples. "You?"

Considering my morning and the night prior, I grinned and said, "Good, thanks."

"I was thinking," he began, "we got cut short the other morning...we should do it again sometime. Coffee, drink, whatever."

I frowned in response, and he must have sensed my hesitation. He stood a bit straighter, rubbing the back of his neck. The act, considering the odd smirk he now wore, made me sense that he was trying to show off his arms. The thermal shirt he wore did little to disguise his bicep, along with the ridge of muscle that ran from his underarm to his waist. The view, gratifying as it was, burned into my retinas. Seeing Liam as an attractive man damn near physically pained me. With his personality *so* not meshing with mine, it created a conflicting feeling that just made me want to cringe. I was sure I would become accustomed to it over time.

"You barely got a word in before," he added. "I'll take you out, you can tell me all about yourself and where you were in Ogden. We can get all...acquainted."

I swallowed my groan at the mention of my hometown. As nice as the intention seemed, the end result was one that I wanted to avoid with all of my being. The last thing I needed at this moment was to feel...exposed. Exposed to be the type of person I behaved as over the past year or so. I wasn't that girl—or at least, I hoped that I wasn't.

"Look, Liam," I could see his expression morphing into disappointment, "that's not going to work out."

"Aw, come on!" He goaded me; his initial dismay wiped clean as if it never existed. "We could have a good time!"

For the second time in the past twenty-four hours, Zoey's voice crooned in my head, *'Yeah, I'm sure you could.'*

"I just don't think we have much in common, Liam, I'm sorry."

Liam leaned against my door jamb yet again. "And what makes you say that?"

A laugh caught in my throat. "What makes me *not* say that?" I returned, his cockiness forcing my view on the matter to spew out of me. "I'm not into sports—like *at all.*"

"I like more things than sports—"

"I *don't* like North Carolina—"

"Probably a good thing you don't live there anymore, then—"

"And you didn't say *anything* about yourself except for things that happened when you were under eighteen years old," I reminded him. "It was all *my high school baseball team* this and *my high school football team* that but when it came to what you *actually do now,* I *kinda* got nothing. You *freelance?* What does that even *mean?*"

Sometime in the middle of my rant, Liam had stood up straight, his hands thrust into the pockets of his jeans. His jaw was clenched, but it only stayed that way for a brief moment.

"Y'know, I moved here when I was eighteen." He stated, ever-present smile returning to flash at me. "Just good memories, I guess."

I didn't anticipate that Liam would give me any further explanation for what he did on a daily basis, but the dodging of my inquisition was still a mild frustration. I exhaled a long breath through my nose.

I replied, "I'm sure they were."

Liam nodded. "I'll see you 'round, Claire."

He bounded down the stairs casually and I shook my head at his peculiar attitude.

As I allowed myself inside the apartment, I saw Zoey sitting comfortably on the far side of our couch, head resting on her hand as she idly watched television at a low volume.

Her gaze turned to me, and she ever so subtly asked, "The fuck is that look for?"

I tossed my belongings on the kitchen table and joined her on the couch, crossing my legs as I faced her. "What read do you get on Liam?"

"Big dick," she said quickly.

I chortled. "Aside from his penis size, Zoey."

Her green eyes glowed. "Fucks like an animal."

"His *personality,*" I clarified. "What do you think his deal is?"

She shrugged. "Doesn't like talking about his life in the now."

"Obviously."

"There's a reason for that, clearly."

"Don't think he's just...vapid?"

Zoey squinted her eyes as she considered that possibility. "Somehow," she spoke slowly, "no."

I hummed, knowing that Zoey's judge of character was typically spot on. Though the thought could have been intriguing, I found my mind elsewhere, for I was brought back to the night prior when Luke and I were sharing brief versions of our collective pasts.

"So, Luke almost had a kid," I told her as offhandedly as possible.

"I—*gay Luke?*" She asked, eyes wide.

"Yeah, not totally sold on that," I stated. "Long-term cheating ex-girl-friend, kid ended up not being his, yada-yada."

"Damn—and you didn't ask?"

"*Ask?* About him being gay?" I replied incredulously, and Zoey shrugged as I said, "Kinda insensitive, don't you think?"

Her head bobbed backward. "Uh—no, I don't think, *'Hey Luke—quick thing, a girl literally pulled me aside and said you were gay. Then, you told me you had a girlfriend that you thought you knocked up. Trying to get the story straight. What up?'* would be very insensitive."

"Well, I don't want to, I dunno, *offend* him or anything."

"You've known him for like two days, Claire, ya can't predict his emotions. *But,* I'll say that he doesn't seem like the most masculine-obsessed man in the world." She laughed softly. "I don't think he's some bro who's going to be up in arms throwing a fit because you heard a rumor that he's gay."

"Fair," I replied. "The thing is, I don't know if I even want to pry. Who gives a shit, right?"

"I don't, but it would be pertinent information for *you.* "

"Me?"

Zoey bobbled her eyebrows suggestively at my clarification question. "Yes, *you.* "

I scoffed, reiterating my thoughts on a new relationship with, "Hole. Head."

She smirked. *"Sure.* Hole in your head. *Right.* "

I was uncertain if time simply passed quicker in Virginia, or if my days were beginning to blend together with the monotony of them. Though it could have been seen as dull and the consistency of my routines played over and over time and again, it was...happy. Zoey and I had a standing girl's night to ensure that our friendship remained intact as we were unable to see each other the majority of the time due to our conflicting work schedules. Liam was a near permanent fixture at Henry's, our idle chit-chat slowly morphing from shameless flirting on Liam's end to friendly pleasantries that I began to genuinely look forward to. Luke and I became attached at the hip, falling into a groove that felt effortless. The habit of staying late after hours to hang out almost always led to coffee the next morning.

On our days off, there was always something—a rare bowling night, the less rare vegging and watching television, or even, upon Luke's insistence, playing video games.

The holiday season came around before I knew it, and it was near Christmas time when I was preparing myself for a cold outing. Luke and I had prior plans to go to Henry's—it wasn't often that we could go to the bar when we weren't working, and tonight was one of those infrequent nights. No matter how blistering the cold or how heavy the snow, the walk to Henry's was always short. Regardless of that, I donned an overcoat with a hat and gloves for good measure and braced myself for the cold that I would inevitably encounter.

Ice chips flecked my face. I hiked up the stairs to the left of my front door as quickly as I could, inbound for Luke's apartment so we could brave the walk together. I pounded on the door that I knew all too well, staring at the gold *3C* that was attached to it as I waited for him to greet me.

The door swung open to reveal his face, and he smiled down at me.

"What, are ya cold or something?"

I blinked the snowflakes out of my eyes. *"Yeah!* Let's *go—* "It was when I began to usher him out the door that I realized that he was, most certainly, *not* dressed for going out. A loose white t-shirt hung from his shoulders, black sweatpants low on his hips, and his feet were bare. I asked, "Are you planning on getting hypothermia?"

A gust of wind blew the icy air between us and he leaned away, scrunching his face and wrapping his arms around himself as if it would protect him from the elements. His hair, uncharacteristically free of product, hung low on his face, and he brushed it out of his eyes.

"No," he chuckled. "Wanna stay in?"

I nodded briskly, and he stepped aside to allow me in. I strutted past him and shivered off the cold, kicking off my boots and stripping myself of my winter apparel, hanging various items on the coat rack that resided in his foyer.

Luke's apartment very much expressed that he lived alone. There were two solemn, black, leather-back bar stools at the tall kitchen counter, and no dining table. The open space in his kitchen ran right into his living area, a couch in front of a television on one end, and the door to his bedroom on the other.

I sat at one of the bar stools, resting my sock-laden feet on the rungs of the chair.

"Didn't feel like going out in a blizzard?" I inquired.

"You good with that?" He returned; a single eyebrow peaked high. I sighed contentedly, the warmth from his abode melting away the snow that decorated my hair, and he laughed softly. "I take that as a yes?"

"Fucking freezing out there," I replied. "So, yes."

Luke traipsed into his kitchen, pulling the stainless-steel handle on the grey cabinet next to his fridge to gather two lowball glasses. Various types of liquor sat beneath the cabinet door, and he picked up a bottle of what I knew was tequila, holding it up to me with a questioning eye. I nodded, and he went through the process of making us both a drink—his containing something with whiskey, and mine, the tequila.

As he handed me my glass and I took a tentative sip, he suggested slowly, "I could let you kick my ass in Mario Kart?"

It wasn't my most beloved thing to do. In fact, any time we had played video games together, Luke had to practically beg me to partake. I remembered the one time I had beaten him in a game and his mock outrage that followed, and though it forced a smile to just barely begin to form on my face, I shriveled up my nose in distaste.

I suggested, "Maybe just tv instead?"

Luke sighed a long, sarcastic sigh, and he replied, "Fine—*have it your way,*" as he lugged his body towards his couch. I nearly skipped behind him, throwing myself beside him as he grabbed the remote control that sat on the side table to his left. His grey eyes rolled mockingly, and he glanced at my giddy feet tip-tapping away as he pressed the red power button. He took a singular sip from his glass and set it back down on the table beside him, feigning an admonishment with, "Don't act so pleased with yourself."

"Don't act like you don't also want to watch..." I glanced at the guide that appeared on the screen before us and pointed. "The holiday movie watch-a-thon." It was a selection of several holiday movies, all laced with romantic intent. It was a joke, of course, but the joke dissipated when I realized that the movies listed beneath the title were under a genre labeled: *Suggested Viewing*. I jovially shrieked, "Oh my *GOD,* those are recommended titles!"

Luke chuckled. "You act like you don't know that I'm a fuckin' softie."

"I mean, *yeah,*" I responded, "but *these—*"

"Are amazing?"

"Are corny," I corrected.

He looked at me with a knowing smile, holding the remote up high as he clicked a button with purpose and announced, *"And,* we're watching."

Midway through the second movie, my head was buzzing; the alcohol that I had indulged in wrapping around my body like a warm blanket. I glanced at Luke who was seated beside me, lazily watching the expected plot unfurl on the television in front of him. His eyes were hooded as they bounced across the screen, lips upturned in a soft smile. He blew out a breath through his nose in a gentle, silent laugh, and it made me repeat the action myself. I traced my gaze across his right arm that had stretched over the back of the couch, his long fingers grazing over the material back and forth.

It was a comfortable moment, and I yearned to rest myself against him—to bury my head in his chest and inhale deeply—to sleep softly against his side. It was an urge that I had experienced with Luke many a time before and for whatever reason, I felt it especially so now. The thought had begun as wholesome. They usually did, of course, but as Luke stretched further into his seat, flexing his grip on the couch, I allowed my eyes to move over the muscles of his forearms. They twitched in a way that struck me as sensual and I found myself exhaling to steady my breath.

Luke heard me and looked my way, cocking his head to the side in a silent question. He nearly whispered, "What?"

His gaze danced across my face, inspecting my expression, and his smile slowly fell away. I considered that he could read right through me. As if he knew that when he looked at me, I pictured him staring deeply into my eyes. As if he knew that when he clenched his jaw in frustration, I imagined the same flexion between my thighs as he worshipped me. As if he knew that when he took a shot of tequila and groaned as the alcohol burned his throat, the sound shot straight through me as I visualized him in the throes of passion. It certainly seemed as if all of that was true as his eyes widened fractionally and he pushed himself to sit up straight.

Rather than obsess over what his thoughts could possibly be as my eyes were raking over his body, I did what my mind was instinctually telling me to do. It was a simple movement, and far less brazen than I had envisioned moments ago—I spanned the distance between us and leaned my head against his chest. My free arm reached to wrap around his waist, and I let out a long breath.

Luke's body stiffened. His arm which had been resting casually along the back of the couch hovered in thin air above me, and though I could hear his heartbeat, I feared that he had stopped breathing. If it weren't for the tequila flooding through my veins, I would have pulled away. Maybe I would have even apologized, because his frozen stance felt uncomfortable. By the time that my mind recognized his discomfort, however, Luke had placed his arm around my shoulders and wriggled his way to a position that allowed my body to fall into the crook of his side. He let out a quiet hum of contentment, and his thumb grazed back and forth over my arm as we continued to watch the movie in silence.

Chapter Seven

I woke the next morning lazily. Slowly. Happily. At least I did at first, until realization set in. While my eyes were still closed, the final snapshots of the night prior flashed in my mind. The most vivid of the memories was Luke's touch wisping over my arm as I embraced him around his waist. I recognized the same touch now, one hand clasped over one of my wrists and the other resting in front of my stomach.

I wondered how we even managed to get ourselves into this position. I had fallen asleep on the couch, and it seemed that Luke had done the same. Our legs were entangled just as much as our arms were, and I could feel him exhaling softly on my neck, still deep in sleep. The feeling of being safe and cherished in his arms only lasted for as long as it took me to completely wake.

I wanted him. *God,* I wanted him. But the more that I thought about it in the bleakness of my current sobriety, the more that I knew that Luke's perception of me was only one of in the now. He thought I was innocent—*actually* innocent, not Colton's warped view of it. Perhaps Luke thought that I had a family. Perhaps he thought that, if we were to be together, there were parents that he could inevitably meet. Perhaps he wondered if he could eventually visit my old home in North Carolina.

The thought made my stomach twist, for the answer to all of those imaginary questionings was, undoubtedly, no. I *don't* have a family—not anymore. My parents wouldn't be there to meet him, and no—*fuck,* no—he would *not* be visiting my previous home. It would lead to too many questions about my life that I had so wanted to avoid. I wasn't ready to address my past. In fact, I would rather brush it under a rug and set it aflame. I knew that even if I *could* do that, though, it would survive the blaze and I would be left in the exact same position as I was now—and I couldn't bear that.

The truth was that I had left North Carolina for a reason. I left North Carolina to live as much of a normal life as I could. I left North Carolina to be...*happy.* And, somehow, it felt too soon to be *this* carefree. Luke had quickly become one of my favorite people and it hurt me just to think it, but I needed to distance myself from him. If I allowed myself to fall too deep, this would all become...too much. It had already begun to feel like it as I laid, far too comfortable, in his arms.

I slipped out of his hold on me and luckily, he didn't wake. I wasn't sure what I would have been able to say to him if he did. Perhaps an awkward, hurried, *'Er, gotta go, bye?'* He deserved better, and I internally scolded myself before I took a last look at him.

His hair had grown since we first met. It was splayed every which way and hanging over his forehead. Thick stubble lined his jaw, far more than a five-o-clock shadow, yet not quite able to be considered the start of a beard. Although his slumber was uninterrupted, Luke seemed to notice my absence. His eyebrows pulled together, and he let out a soft groan. It made his nose scrunch up and his face pull together. I felt like groaning myself, but kept silent out of better judgement and grabbed the blanket that was folded over the couch. I laid it over him, tiptoed to the door, and closed it quietly behind me.

I arrived back at my own apartment and Zoey was sitting on the couch, legs crossed beneath her and a steaming mug halfway lifted to her lips. She saw me and lowered it promptly, placing it on the coffee table.

"You look like shit, what gives?" She spoke to me, and I felt myself draw in a long breath through my mouth and into my lungs, letting it out in a ragged sigh. Zoey's eyebrows rose slightly, forcing her thick rimmed glasses to slide down her nose as she questioned my reaction. I moved to sit next to her, and she demanded, "Spill."

"Luke." My answer was as blunt and monotonous as I could keep it, but it failed to disguise the worry that remained.

"Oh?"

"I went over to his place last night."

"I figured," she replied. "And?"

"I slept there."

"Again," she stated, "I figured."

"It was...different."

I wasn't sure why I was having such a problem describing my night with Luke. It felt almost like...embarrassment? Or perhaps, shame? Yes, that's what it was—shame. Shame for knowing that the feelings I had for Luke were creeping up on me in the past few months. Shame for allowing myself to be vulnerable around him. Shame that I let myself feel this way when I knew my fears would hinder a relationship progressing. Just...shame. And longing—but that particular emotion needed to be buried six feet under, and I did exactly that with a shake of my head.

"Gonna have to give me more deets than that, Claire," Zoey urged me on. "Different how?" I groaned, and she asked, "You want coffee?" I nodded and pushed myself up to blindly make my way toward the kitchen. I made myself a cup, took a sip as I returned to Zoey, and grimaced, as it was watery and weak. She ignored my reaction, grabbing her own mug and taking a small taste. "So...what did he do?"

I nearly spat, "Nothing." Zoey pursed her lips, clearly dissatisfied with that answer, and I told her, "We slept together." Her eyes widened right as she began to take another drink, and she coughed loudly. I added quickly, "On his couch, literal sleeping, nothing else."

"Thanks for the clarification, you almost made me fucking choke," she croaked out, thumping her chest as she coughed a few more times to clear her lungs.

I managed a small smile and continued, "When we woke up, our bodies were like...practically *braided* together and I just—" I sighed to gather my thoughts. "I don't think Luke even realized the position we were in, I left before he could wake up. I—the lines are...blurring for me." I reconsidered the phrase. "The lines are *gone* for me."

Zoey bobbed her head up and down in thought.

"Did he have a boner?"

"Zoey," I admonished with a groan and whined, "I'm in *pain.*" She glanced at me as if to say, *'You didn't answer the question,'* and I clarified, "And God *no,* of course, he didn't."

"So, what's the problem?" She inquired.

"What's the *problem?*"

"Yeah, the guy clearly likes you, Claire."

"Uh—not sure about that and even if he did...so what?"

"So *what?*" Zoey voiced incredulously. "Go tell him ya like him too; go be happy...what's the problem with that?"

I drank my coffee and didn't even register the taste.

"Getting closer will lead to...more questions," I noted. "And I don't think I can *do* more questions."

She nodded, mulling over my words, and deduced aloud, "Look, I know I can't tell you what to do but...if ya can't be honest with him, you should *probably* cut that shit off."

"Yeah," I agreed, my throat constricting. "I know."

"Sorry," she almost whispered. "Can I do anything?" I began to shake my head no, and Zoey suggested, "Want to watch some mindless tv?"

I exhaled quickly. "So much."

The day passed slowly. Too slowly. My phone repeatedly dinged with messages from Luke as the hours ticked by, and the ache in my chest grew with each one. I looked through them the next morning as I laid in bed, feeling deprived of air.

10:15 A.M.: I woke up and you were gone...where did you go?

11:04 A.M.: You okay?

12:36 P.M.: Claire?

2:47 P.M.: Hey...did I do something wrong? Text me back.

I had ignored all of them. Luke had tried calling as well—twice—and I had silenced them both. I wanted with everything I had in me to be able to talk with him, but I didn't know what to say or where to start. I considered what my response would inevitably be as I tossed and turned in the young hours of the morning, and landed on nothing. I finally roused myself from my bed when I could see the sun beginning to peek through the window.

It was quiet. Zoey had yet to wake. I patted around the kitchen softly, gathering the things to make coffee with my recently bought French press. The strips underneath our cabinets and lamps near the couch were the only lighting that I turned on, and they left an ambient glow throughout the apartment. I sat with my fingers knit in front of me at the kitchen table, coffee grinds soaking in boiling hot water on the counter while my thoughts wandered. The scent of a dark roast filled the air. It would have been peaceful if it weren't for my inner turmoil.

I prepared my mug and just when I was finished, there was a knock at the door. I traipsed over, mug in hand, and cracked it halfway, peeking before letting it open fully.

Luke stood in the doorway, hand resting on the outer molding as he looked towards the ground. When the click of the door reached his ears, his gaze snapped to mine. The light grey of his eyes was accentuated by the dark circles that marred the skin underneath; the whites of his eyes bloodshot. He squinted at me with a peculiar emotion that appeared to be a silent questioning, but there was an edge to it that I couldn't pinpoint.

I couldn't think of anything else to say, so I just blurted out a simple, "Hi."

"*Hi?*" Luke released his grasp from my doorway and stood, limp limbed. "So, you're alive then."

"My, er—phone died?"

"Don't bother trying to lie, you're shit at it." I pressed my lips together tightly, and Luke bluntly stated, "You've been ignoring me."

"Do you, um," I stammered. "Do you want a cup of coffee? I just made some."

"That's not exactly what I came here for, but sure, let's coffee it up!" He spoke sarcastically, and I glanced awkwardly at the floor between us, stepping aside to let him in. I beelined to the kitchen and grabbed him a mug, making it how I know he likes it—sugar and a dash of cinnamon. I gave the cup to him, and he took a sip. He breathed a long breath through his nose and let it out through his mouth. "We need to talk, Claire."

My gut jumped into my chest, and my grip tightened on my mug's wonky handle.

"We do?"

"We do," he replied. Luke sank into a chair at the kitchen table, and I quietly sat beside him as he said, "You know I was like...*worried*, right? You can't fucking disappear on me!"

"I know, I—"

"I mean, I figured you were okay because you were *silencing my calls* and they weren't just going straight to message." Luke had begun to wave his hands about as he spoke angrily, mug now firmly placed on the kitchen table.

"That and the read receipts from the texts, right?" I asked meekly.

I knew, of course, that the function on my phone that shows when I had opened a message from someone was deliberately turned on.

"What the fuck are read receipts?" He returned; his tone still clipped but beginning to thaw.

"How do you not know what read receipts are? Are you *that* techno-logically inept?"

Luke gave me a look that said, '*Yes, you know I am,*' and shook his head, pinching at the bridge of his nose with his thumb and index finger.

"It doesn't even matter, you just can't—you can't ghost me, okay? You freaked me out."

The guilt that I had been feeling was settling in further now, deep within the confines of my chest.

"I'm sorry," I spoke with a cringe.

His eyes darted away from mine, his voice lowering a bit as he said, "Me too." I felt my head tilt to the side as I attempted to understand why Luke would be apologizing to me. I didn't get a chance to ask before he mumbled, "How we slept was...different."

"Oh *fuck.*" I didn't mean to let the profanity slip, but his admission had taken me off guard. I blinked several times in a row. "You, ah—you knew about that?"

"I woke up before you did yesterday." The way he said it sounded like an admission to some sort of crime.

"Oh."

"So, I fell back asleep...and then I woke up a few hours later. You were gone, I had no idea where you went, you didn't text me back at all. You didn't answer my calls, I—I don't understand..."

Rather than respond, I glanced to the floor, my eyes inspecting the pattern of the wood grain by my feet. Luke's touch warmed my cheek and, being a weak-willed individual, I leaned into his palm as I felt the tears begin to sting my eyes. Zoey's words from the night prior rang in my mind yet again, *'You should probably cut that shit off,'* and with that, whatever resolve that was holding my tears back withered away.

I whispered, "This is hard," as Luke's eyes bounced across the streaks of salty residue along my cheeks.

"What's hard? Why are you crying?"

"I don't want to lose you as a friend."

His hand fell from my face with that admission. "A *friend?*"

The harshness of his tone revealed his frustration, and it made me groan.

Without thinking, I blurted out, "This would be *so* much fucking easier if I still thought you were gay."

A short pause spanned between us, Luke's eyes were wide as he stared at me. We had never discussed the interaction that Zoey and I had with the girl at the bar, and I wasn't sure what made me unintentionally spit it out now. I nearly winced under his inquisitive gaze.

"If you still thought I was *what,* now?"

"Um—"

"Why would you think I was gay?"

I exhaled. "There was a rumor mill at Henry's."

Much to my surprise, Luke barked out a loud laugh. *"Still?"*

"You knew about it, then?"

He avoided my gaze then, looking left and right before taking a sip from his mug.

"Yeah," he replied. "I...kind of was the one that started it?"

"Oh?"

"Yeah, ah—it was years ago, I had just moved here from my parent's neck of the woods. I had just left Emma and I just...I dunno. I was getting attention from women that I just...didn't want. Didn't *need...* "

"So, you told some women that you were gay to get them off your back?" I confirmed.

He smiled hesitantly. "Yeah?"

"So, you're not—"

"Very, very not gay," he replied gently, confirming what I already knew.

"Luke," I shook my head and chastised him softly. "That's kind of fucked—"

"I know that's fucked up, I do." His gaze was fixed on the floor. "But it didn't matter to me then if anyone thought that or if they spread that around. I didn't want to be close to anyone then and that helped me with that."

"You didn't want to be close to anyone *then?*" I asked. "You're speaking in the past tense, you know." His eyes widened fractionally, but he said nothing. "Does it matter now, Luke?"

I don't know why I asked. Two conflicting thoughts were occurring in my brain, and I was fighting between both of them. On one hand, I wanted to protect my...I wasn't sure what to call it...anonymity? If Luke and I grew even closer and he knew what kind of life I used to live, I feared that I would lose him altogether. But, on the other hand, the thought of him wanting me in that way at all made a hope blossom in the bottom of my gut that was too strong to suppress. I found myself leaning into the newfound feeling within me rather than my fear, and I leaned toward him, trying to catch his eye.

Luke questioned me with a lowered voice, still staring downward. "You said we're friends?"

"Yeah—you know we're friends," I responded, and he finally looked at me with an emotion that I could only describe as sadness. It was as if he was regretting what he was about to say, his hesitation clear as he opened and closed his mouth a few times without speaking. I pressed him, "What is it, Luke?"

"I don't want that anymore, Claire," he said, and then shook his head as he corrected himself. "I mean...that's not what I mean. I just can't be friends with you...anymore."

It felt like a gut punch. Though distance was what I told myself I needed from Luke and, truthfully, I should have been thankful for his revelation and taken it in stride, I didn't. The less rational side of me reared its ugly head and this entire conversation was suddenly...too much.

"Well, then you should probably fucking *go,*" I demanded, pushing myself up from the dining table so roughly that the chair legs scraped against the floor.

Luke's gaze turned frantic. "Wait, *no.*" I ignored him and began to stomp to my bedroom. "Dammit, Claire, *wait.*" Though I refused to look back or respond, I knew he had gotten up to follow me for I could hear his footsteps against the flooring—could *feel* him staring at the back of my head. "For fucks sake," he nearly growled, *"Claire!"*

I reached for my bedroom door, intending on achieving solace within and slamming it behind me, but by the time my hand was wrapped around the knob, Luke had grasped my wrist and pulled against it. My arms were strung between the door and Luke's grip, and I stared forward.

"You don't want to be friends, Luke?" I spoke. *"Fine.* But you need to leave me the fuck alone if that's the case because I can't do this back and forth."

"Look," he hissed, "I know I'm bad at this and all, but you can't just run away—you have to let me finish!"

I spun around, hair fanning out around me—it probably whipped him in his face, he was standing so closely. I didn't care.

"Why in the world should I let you finish?" I wanted to scream it, but it came out gritty and hoarse instead. "What do you want...do you want closure?"

"What? No, that's not what this is."

"Okay well, you make no sense," I snapped. I tried to free my arm from his grip. His hand was large enough to completely enclose my wrist, and I yanked it this way and that to no avail, groaning loudly. "What do you *want?* You're giving me fucking whiplash over here, Luke!"

If his eyes weren't wide before, they looked damn near crazed now. *"I'm* giving you whiplash?"

His tone reached a volume that I hadn't heard before from him, matching my own voice's raspy intensity.

"Yeah," I retorted, "you are—you act like you enjoy being around me one minute, then you say you don't want to be friends anymore the next, now you're keeping me here trying to explain yourself and I just need you to make up your damn mind!"

"Make up my mind?!" He seethed. "You're the one who needs to make up your mind! You've spent the better part of the last few months eye-fucking me every time you take a shot of tequila." My blush crept up to my cheeks, and he continued, "Yeah, I'm not fucking *blind,* Claire. Not to mention sleeping in my arms, ghosting me afterward, and making sure I know damn well that we're *just* friends." The air around me was beginning to sting my throat, and I realized it was because I had left my mouth open, letting out breaths as if I were panting. "I haven't done this in a long time," Luke murmured, "and you're—my mind is working overtime here. I thought maybe you still wouldn't want to be close to anyone after Colton. You know, like me with Emma."

"I, um," I stammered, "I didn't."

Luke's chest rose and fell several times over. "Didn't?"

"Past tense," I whispered.

"You want to know what I *want,* Claire?" Luke's voice had dropped about an octave, and it sent a jolt right through me. My heart hammered in my rib cage. Before I could even answer, he said clearly, "You. I fucking want *you.* So goddamn badly. So badly that I'm—" He placed a hand on his chest and croaked, "I feel like I'm choking here." He gestured between us. "Please tell me that you feel this too."

I felt myself exhale shakily. "I do."

With one step, Luke closed the distance between us. His forehead rested against mine and he brought his hand to the nape of my neck. My head lolled backward into his touch, and I looked up to see into a storm of grey. Every place that our skin touched was aflame. His breath mingled with mine in the small space between us, and all it would take was a small turn of his head or a squeeze at the base of my neck, and our lips would touch.

He began to ask, "Can I—"

"Yes."

"Oh, thank God," he moaned, and his lips crashed against mine.

I glided my hands up his body, fisting them in his hair. There was nothing soft or slow about it—this kiss was months of pent-up frustration and lost time. It was near feral—tongues tangling and teeth clacking. Short gasps and moans emanated from both of us for a long while until I began to feel a blissful tightening in my lower belly. One of Luke's hands drifted to the small of my back and he pulled me into him, pressing our bodies together as if he could stand the space between us no longer. He gyrated his hips towards me, the evidence of his arousal hard against my hip.

"Ah," I whimpered.

"Yeah?"

"Yeah."

My response came out in a whine, and it caused Luke to release a guttural noise that rumbled into my chest. It was then that I remembered that we were situated directly in front of my bedroom door. I took one of my hands from his hair, grabbed the knob behind me, and twisted it. When the click of my door opening reached his ears, Luke's hold on my lower back tightened, and he slowed our kiss. It morphed into something sweeter and less frenzied. He trailed his lips across my cheek and to my jaw.

"Your door is open," he noted wryly.

"That it is."

His kisses were at my throat now, and I hummed happily. He mimicked my hum, the reverberation going all the way down to my chest.

"Are you taking me for a loose man?" I could feel his smile against me, and I shrugged. He bit the space underneath my earlobe, and I made a sound that was mixed between a yelp and a moan. Luke's body stiffened in return. "Well, that's a sound I'll never forget," he said in my ear. "And...I can't believe I'm saying this but...I should probably go."

"What? *Why?*"

"We don't have to do this now." The way he said it made it sound like he *really* didn't mean it. "I'm worried I'm gonna fuck this up if we go too fast."

Contrary to the way he said the first sentence, I could feel the sincerity dripping from the second.

I sighed. "Do you have to be so gentlemanly?"

I pulled at the material of his sweater underneath my hand and kissed him again, sliding my tongue against his. He made a noise of appreciation, and I moved my hand downward until it landed on his belt buckle. I yanked him forward, and I felt him hard against me once again.

"Ah," he groaned against my lips, and my fingers danced along the denim before me, tracing his length with a gentle pull. *"Ah, fuck."* His mouth jerked away from mine with a smack. "You aren't going to let me leave, are you?" I answered wordlessly with a squeeze of my palm and was rewarded with Luke hissing in a quick breath. His hand that hadn't left my neck pulled me back to him for another, more chaste kiss. "Can we have it on record that I tried to save your virtue?"

"Absolutely," I mewled.

"Welp, I tried," he said rapidly, stepping forward to push us across the threshold to my room.

We stumbled inside, connected at the mouth, and Luke kicked the door closed behind him. He stepped out of his shoes as he walked. We separated briefly for him to pull his sweater off and over his head, leaving him in a white t-shirt. He laid his sweater in a heap in the corner of my bedroom and when he turned back to me, hair wild and eyes dark, I swear it felt like electricity crackling in the confines of my small room. He was back to me in an instant, gave me a single kiss with slow, languid lips, and his fingers touched the skin underneath the hem of my shirt.

"I want to see you," he told me.

I reached down to where his hands were and guided him upwards, pressing his touch into my skin as I pulled my top off.

"Oh my God," he muttered.

The size of my breasts made wearing a bra nearly useless, and today was a braless day. I stood before him, completely topless. He drank me in, his gaze dragging over every inch of my exposed skin, and his eyelids went heavy. He made quick way of his shirt, tossing it to the corner to join his sweater, and grabbed me by the waist, pulling us together to feel skin on skin with a sense of urgency.

I breathed out, "Shit."

The warmth of our skin touching was blissful, but more so was the ability to see and feel Luke's body. To see him shirtless was an experience in itself—he had the build of a runner, and I could take in the sight of his body for days—but hearing him moan as I ran my hands over his chest and abdomen sent a thrill through me.

We began walking to my bed that was situated behind me, and when we both fell onto it, Luke wasted no time. He kissed me deeply once and started working his way down my body with his tongue. If I thought my breathing was erratic before, that was nothing compared to when he reached my breasts. He gave each one a generous squeeze, running a thumb over both of my nipples and whispering a quiet, *"Fuck,"* before giving them the same treatment with his mouth.

My back arched, the sensation of warmth spreading to the apex of my thighs almost overwhelming.

"Luke—*fuck.*"

I tugged at his hair to get him to return to my mouth, wrapping a leg around his hip and pushing with my foot in an attempt to remove his pants.

A low rumble of a laugh sounded from him.

"Oh no, baby," he shook his head, his nose teasing the tip of my right nipple.

I gasped, and he grinned widely at the noise.

"Please," I begged, my voice beginning to sound very unlike my own, warped with desire.

He ignored my plead, nipping at the skin over my ribs, then my waist, then my belly, and easing the pain from each bite with a kiss. I squirmed when he was at the button on my jeans, flicking them open with his thumb and pulling them down gently with my underwear until they were on the floor. He grabbed the backside of each of my knees and tugged me toward him, my calves hanging off my mattress. He stared up at me from between my legs, and I worried for a moment that I would spontaneously combust.

I whimpered his name as he licked up my left thigh until he reached my short mound of pubic hair, and then he started anew with the right.

When he finally reached my pussy, nuzzled the area with his nose, and moaned, I clenched my hands in his hair and shivered. His tongue touched me, and I found myself praying to a deity that I thought I had long forgotten.

"Jesus fucking Christ."

His motions were sensual—soft—and he seemed to derive just as much pleasure as I did from his actions. He groaned when I did, squeezing at my hips to pull me closer before bringing one of his hands down to his belt buckle. I stared as he deftly undid the fastening and the following button and pulled himself out. He was long and thick, and I watched almost hungrily as he gave himself a squeeze, pumping slowly back and forth as he continued his ministrations with his tongue.

The sight of him in combination with everything else was almost my undoing. My legs began to shake, and I felt the beginnings of an orgasm start to build.

"If you don't stop, I'm going to—"

I didn't manage to finish my warning. His mouth was off of me in an instant, halting my imminent release. Luke reached behind himself into his back pocket before kicking off his jeans, revealing a condom. He promptly took the corner of it between his teeth, yanked his head to the side to open it, and spit the wrapper that remained in his mouth on the floor. As he rolled it onto himself and crawled to join me on my bed, I murmured in a wispy tone:

"You're awfully prepared."

He held himself on his forearms, hovering above me as he rested his forehead against mine. He let out a husky chuckle before muttering in return, "Sue me."

His lips patiently pressed against mine, our tongues brushing together softly. I slowly reached between us to position his cock against me, pulling at his backside with my feet. I felt myself stretch, and when he was fully inside me, he exhaled a long, shaking breath.

He groaned, "Oh my *fuck,*" and began to move.

I mewled at his slow, gentle thrusts, arching up to meet him halfway with every movement. He peppered kisses across my cheeks, I dragged my mouth across his neck, and I voiced what I craved.

"More."

I only had to whisper, and he quickened his pace.

"Like that?" He asked in a breath.

I answered with a moan, "Harder."

"Shit," he hissed out, driving into me with a force that caused a light slapping noise to reverberate around the room.

Not after long, my legs began to vibrate again.

"Oh *God,"* I cried out.

"Yeah?"

I couldn't speak. I just threw my head back and moaned again, louder, scrunching my eyes shut.

"Fuck," I heard Luke and then felt his hand at the base of my neck pulling me back to him. "Look at me; open your eyes."

I obeyed, and with that his motions became frantic. The gyrations were short and happening in a staccato now, the regular rhythm lost to an animalistic pleasure. At the moment that Luke stilled and groaned a sound that will be burned into my memory, I was gone. I nearly screamed; the noise muffled by Luke's hand that had moved from my ribcage to my mouth. I spiraled down, and when he looked to be absolutely certain that I was finished, he dropped his hand to the bed.

Luke removed himself from me and fell beside me onto his back, still gasping for breath just as much as I was.

"That was..." he started to try to form a sentence but failed.

"Mmm," was all I could manage.

He let out an audible sigh of contentment followed by a grunt to force himself to sit up, and looked down at me with a lazy smile. He blinked a few times, slowly.

"You," he said, "are just..." Luke hummed what sounded like a praising noise and twisted towards me to kiss my lips.

"Me?" I asked, the word coming out slightly slurred from exhaustion. "I didn't even *do* anything except keep you here."

He laughed softly. "Something about proving to you that I'm not gay gave me some extra determination."

"Well, I'd say you've proved it, but just to be sure..."

"Again? What, *now?*"

I let out a loud, "Ha! No, not now."

Luke wiped a fake bead of sweat off his brow.

"Good, because that's physically impossible for me at the moment. *But* I will definitely be doing that as much as you would like."

He stood, muttering that he was going to the bathroom, and I admired his backside as he walked away from me. When he was no longer in view, my eyes fluttered closed and I felt myself nearly drifting off to sleep. I chose to not bother myself regarding my concerns over becoming even closer to Luke. I couldn't do such a thing at the moment anyway—the exhaustion from my lack of sleep and post-coital bliss left my body feeling like it was buzzing. If I were a cat, I would have been letting out a low, steady purr.

I could have been dreaming. Perhaps I was floating in a bubble—I wouldn't know; the memory didn't stick. I jerked awake suddenly as if my bubble had popped and I was falling, careening towards the ground, waking right as I splat onto the pavement.

"WHAT THE FUCK?!"

I sat bolt upright. It was, without a doubt, Zoey's voice—I would recognize it anywhere. The second voice, shouting just as loudly and somehow more alarmed than the first, was Luke's.

"WHY ARE YOU AWAKE?!"

"Why are you NAKED?!" Zoey screeched back. "OH, my *fucking EYES!"*

I threw my hand over my mouth. Whether it was in shock or to hide my laughter, I didn't know.

Luke stormed back into my room, slamming the door behind him. He stood with his back against it, hands splayed out on either side with the palms flat against the door. It looked as if he had just finished running from a ghost—or perhaps a murderer. His face was sheet white, his eyes wide, his chest heaving with quick breaths, and the condom was still hanging limply off of himself.

Any attempt to contain my laughter was lost now, as I pictured the scene that happened just beyond my door. I imagined Zoey outside with her hands covering her eyes, unable to move due to her questioning whether the living area still contained a very naked Luke.

"So, you didn't make it to the bathroom there, did ya?" I asked with what little oxygen I still had in my lungs.

None-too-pleased with my amusement at the situation, Luke muttered, "Fucking hilarious."

Chapter Eight

"You *whore!*" Zoey screeched at me from the kitchen as I walked out of my bedroom.

"Yeah, yeah, yeah," I grumbled, waving her off.

Luke followed me timidly; messy hair and his tail between his legs.

"This isn't a walk of shame," I said, elbowing him as we made our way to the kitchen table.

"Shame of what we did? No. Of what was witnessed? Yes."

Zoey sat at the kitchen table with a freshly brewed mug of coffee, and I sank into the seat across from her.

"No work today?" I asked her casually.

"After what just happened?" She said, and Luke grumbled incoherently behind me. "Of *course,* not. *So, Lukey—*"

"That's disgusting," he muttered.

"Strutting on out here with a used condom on your cock was a *bold* choice—"

"Why," Luke interjected, "for the love of *God, why*—does this apartment have one bathroom that's shared through a *common area?*"

"Why the fuck did you walk out here naked?" Zoey retorted.

"I don't fuckin' know! I wasn't thinking, it was like my brain got blasted out; I was in this...post-coital haze or something."

"Nice," she quipped quickly.

"Even if I *was* thinking, I would've figured you were asleep; it's early still." he finished.

"I *was* asleep, I was woken up by the sound of Claire, as you just said, orgasming her brains out with you," she returned. "Which, by the way, I thought maybe she was just watching porn or something."

Her comment made Luke's face snap to mine.

"You watch porn?"

"No—I mean yeah," I half-stammered. "Not *lately*, but—"

"But she's had plenty of material to work with since she met you is what she's trying to say."

"Material?" He asked, sitting on the edge of his seat now. "What material?"

"You, big boy," she replied candidly. "You're the material."

Luke's lids fell halfway over his eyes as if he was mesmerized into some sort of trance.

"Oh my God, Zoey, what the fuck," I murmured, feeling the blush creep up to my cheeks.

"Oh *please*," she scoffed. "Embarrassed over jackin' it to the guy you've been boning all morning? Have some pride, I heard *both of you* come with the force of a thousand suns not more than a few minutes ago."

"*Okay*," Luke finally snapped out of whatever reverie he had slipped into. "We're definitely staying at my place from now on."

"Ah, I'm just giving you guys shit—it's too easy," Zoey said. "Don't stress so much."

"So, you didn't hear—"

I began to ask her the inevitable, but she cut me off.

"Oh no, I definitely did. Hot shit. Happy for you guys." Zoey held up her mug in a cheersing motion towards us and took a sip. "I have a more important question for you now, though."

I sighed. "Shoot."

"The guy," she stated bluntly. "The hot ass, bearded, tattooed, long-haired, muscled out guy. Who. The. Fuck. Was *He?*"

"I—who," Luke asked, *"Jay?"*

"Jay?" Zoey and I asked simultaneously.

Luke asked me, "Have I not mentioned him?" I shook my head from side to side, and he spoke to both of us, "I assume he's who you mean; I have no heavily bearded, tattooed friends. Although, I wouldn't describe him as hot, because he's my *fucking brother.*"

He grimaced as he said it, and Zoey shrieked, "You have a *brother?!* Who looks like *that?* What's the situation with him?"

I began to interject, "Zoey," but Luke took over.

"Ah—James is *very* newly separated from his wife."

"So, what, is he down to clown?" She asked.

I admonished her, *"Zoey!"*

"Down to *clown?"* Luke's face pinched in what was either confusion or simply just being horrified.

"D-T-F," she replied with an upward inflection, and then whispered dramatically, "That means down to fuck."

"I know what it means," Luke responded, *"Jesus."* He looked at me with an air of desperation. "Can we go get breakfast or coffee or...*literally anything—*"

"Yes," I returned quickly. "Yes, now, yes, let's go."

We stood, and as we gathered the things that we needed, Zoey muttered, "Fuckin' spoil-sports."

I looked at her in a way of a half-apology, and she smiled a mega-watt smile at me, mouthing, *'Go.'* She held up her right hand, touching the index finger to her thumb, her other fingers splayed wide, and she silently lipped, *'Nice job,'* in the most dramatic fashion possible.

I snorted, waved off her comments with a flick of my wrist, and we were out the door.

As expected, it was snowing again by the time I made my way to Henry's, and I was brushing the thick flakes off of my coat when I stepped into the building. Liam's ever-present body was sitting at the bar, a nearly full beer atop a coaster in front of him. Luke was speaking with patrons on the other side of the room and had yet to notice my arrival.

Liam almost yelled, "Hey, Frecks!"

Over the past few months, Liam had continued calling me *Freckles* like he did the first time he had coffee at my apartment. As time passed, it was shortened to *Frecks*. The first time or two that he whipped out the abbreviation, I disliked it. Okay—I *hated* it. Now, however, it had grown on me. It wasn't that I liked the name—I didn't—it just fit Liam's personality in such a way that I couldn't help but accept it.

I smiled at him. "How are ya, Liam?"

He took a sip of his beer. "I'm great! Hell of a show in the building earlier today, right?"

"I—er—what?"

He couldn't have heard me and Luke—though the walls were paper-thin, Liam's apartment was separated by an entire hallway. I thought that there was no *way* that we were that loud, but I wouldn't have known or cared. My head was in the clouds.

"Oh yeah," he continued. "Went for a walk—"

"In this weather, that early?"

"Yeah, yeah, I know. But I heard something rather…interesting." His thick, blonde brows waggled at me. "It was coming from your apartment. I think you know what I'm talking about."

"I, erm—yeah, I do."

"Don't be shy, who was it, Frecks?"

I chanced a glance at Luke, and our eyes locked. He was still deep in conversation, but he paused for long enough to give me a wide grin and a wave. I waved back and found myself feeling oddly timid. My cheeks reddened, and Liam read the room as if he were a master gossiper.

"I *knew* it!" He exclaimed, his expression beaming with delight. "That was a long time coming, yeah? Been watching you two stare at each other from across the bar for months."

I rubbed the back of my neck. "Yeah, I, ah…I guess so."

"Good, then." He remarked in a very Zoey-like fashion, *"Get it."*

"Thanks?"

He took a long pull from his beer. "Oh yeah, any time."

I rested my elbows on the bar top, my hands holding my jaw as I rested my head and leaned forward. "You got plans for the holidays, Liam?"

"Oh yeah, goin' home next week. Super stoked. Are you headed down too?"

I felt my lips pull down a little at the corners. "I am, yeah. Driving down with Zoey on Wednesday and I'll be back before New Year's."

He cocked his head slightly to the side and narrowed his eyes. "You don't like talking about home, do you?"

I stifled a sarcastic laugh as I replied, "I really don't," and muttered to myself, "Colton made damn sure of that."

Liam made it obvious that he had heard me.

"Oh," he drew out the sound for much longer than necessary. "So the truth comes out!" He waggled his eyebrows at me yet again, and I couldn't suppress my chuckle. "For the record," he tipped his beer towards me, "if he fucked it up with you, he's an idiot."

Luke's voice piped up from behind me. "Who's an idiot, now?"

"Hi," I responded with a smile that I couldn't stop from aching my cheeks.

"Hi," he returned.

"Liam's talking about Colton."

"Oh—ah, not that I don't agree about him being an idiot, but what brings him up?"

"He—"

"Knows," Liam completed my sentence for me with a toothy grin that stretched the scar above his lip. He continued in a voice that emulated Austin Powers. "Oh, I know everything, baby."

"Spilling secrets, are you?" Luke questioned with tight lips and a raised brow.

I rolled my eyes. *"No,* he—"

"Guessed!" Liam finished my response yet again, becoming giddy. "Guessed *correctly.* And heard almost everything."

Luke's eyes squinted at Liam, his distaste for his presence more obvious than usual.

"Would it be an overreaction for me to move?" He asked me without taking his gaze off of Liam. "There's a nice complex down the street. Thicker walls. Somewhere where no one's neighbor has heard you scream and no one's roommate has seen my dick."

"Yes, it would be an overreact—"

"Zoey saw your dick?!"

Liam let out a booming laugh, drawing the attention of the patrons that Luke was talking to earlier. His maniacal giggles danced off the walls for far too long. Long enough for Luke to sigh loudly at Liam's behavior, notice that more customers had wandered through the front door, and turn to leave before saying:

"I'll get them."

Liam finally regained his composure as he watched Luke walk away, and he asked, "He doesn't like me much, does he?"

"I—no, he does—"

"You don't have to lie, Claire, really. He's never liked me."

"I don't think hitting on me when I first moved here helped."

"But that's done and dead now," he replied, waving at the air in front of him. "Doesn't matter, I'll get to him sooner or later—back to Zoey."

"Zoey?"

"Oh yeah," Liam nodded emphatically, his eyes bright. "What's her deal?"

I pursed my lips not in annoyance from his inquiry, but from trying to hold back a grin. Liam was an enthusiastic presence to handle, yes, but playing into this conversation didn't make me concerned for *Zoey*. It made me concerned for *Liam*. Zoey had the ability, nay, the habit, to figuratively eat men alive and spit out their carcasses. She would leave them sated, well-fucked, and praying for more—only, there was *never* an opportunity for more.

"She's single." I began, weighing the odds and figuring that Liam was a big boy—even if he couldn't handle her, he would live. "She likes Fireball if you haven't noticed...and she'll be here in a bit."

He smiled a Cheshire grin. The one that he does when he seems to have a plan in mind, and he's *thrilled* about it. It exaggerated the dimples in his cheeks.

"Another beer?" I asked, pointing at his now empty glass.

"Oh yeah, I'll be here a while."

I made my way to where Luke stood next to the beer taps and went through the motions of getting Liam another drink.

"So," he asked, "How's Liam?"

"Asking about Zoey, of all people."

"Poor Zoey," he said with a chuckle.

"No, no," I pushed the tap back up to its resting position. "Poor *Liam*. You don't have to imagine being on the receiving end of her wrath."

"I don't," he replied, the corner of his lip pulling up.

"I don't know," I spoke, my voice raising in pitch a bit. "They've never really talked before. Maybe they'll hit it off!"

Luke looked at me as if I was speaking gibberish for just a moment, but the emotion seemed to be replaced with a rigid determination within a second.

"Wanna bet?"

"What exactly are we betting?" I asked in curiosity.

"Twenty bucks that he'll repulse her into next week," he said in a cocky voice.

My grin grew across my face.

"Alright, you're on. How about twenty bucks and the loser has to take a shot of that gin that everyone hates."

He shuddered, but a smile remained plastered on his face while he nodded in agreement.

"You're disgusting, I love it."

His light eyes twinkled in the dim bar lighting, and he placed his hand in front of me in a gesture to shake it. I squeezed it, and Luke pulled me toward him only to mutter in my ear:

"I cannot *wait* to see you lose."

His breath tickled the hairs on the back of my neck as he murmured near me, and memories that we had recently shared flooded my brain. I lost my train of thought, and just hummed out what sounded like, *"Mhmm?"*

I wasn't sure if Luke had noticed my moment of weakness at first, but then he began to chuckle as he walked away. I narrowed my eyes at him from afar, though I wasn't truly mad. Instead, an idea of a *second* game for us to play tonight burgeoned within me. I stowed the thought deep in the recesses of my brain and turned back to bring Liam his drink.

Zoey arrived not long after, and it took everything in me not to eavesdrop.

She sat in her usual spot, which was several seats down and around the corner from Liam, and she waved at me. I waved back, pretending to busy myself by cleaning a glass that was spotless while Liam sauntered over to her. He sat, and I cursed softly to myself when I heard his greeting.

"Hey Shortstop, how's it goin'?"

"Come again?"

I could feel her glare, and I wouldn't dare look at the two of them. I was somehow worried that if I paid them any attention right off the bat, I would incriminate myself. I could hear Zoey rattling off a perturbed response, but her words all blended into the mild buzz of bar chatter that surrounded us.

"That glass is mighty clean," Luke whispered in my ear from behind.

I jumped.

"I'm *trying* to listen," I replied, moving to grab yet another clean glass to wash for my ruse.

"She is...annoyed," he narrated. "He is...enjoying that."

I chanced a glance to see Zoey giving Liam an absolute earful. A wide grin was plastered on his face as he looked her up and down pointedly.

"So do I pour that shot for you now, or...?"

I bent forward, pretending to fill the glass I was wiping with ice, purposefully bumping my rear end into Luke's crotch.

"Oops," I announced in his direction. "'Scuse me."

I heard his breath hitch, and he took a step backward. I marked a win in my book for the game that I had created and twisted around to give Luke a wry smile.

He leaned down so close that he nearly brushed his lips against my ear.

"Finished with the ice?"

The deep voice he used was one that I wanted to deem illegal for others' ears, and my face immediately flushed.

I turned to look into his eyes with a raised brow, and replied with a grin, "For now." I moved to where a refrigerator was situated underneath the bar, grabbed a bottle of cider for Zoey, and slid her drink across the counter, offering her a casual, "Hey."

Liam tipped his head towards me. "Hey, Claire," he held two fingers up, "can I get two Fireballs?"

"Who's that second one for there, big guy?" Zoey's counter was quick, succinct, and if nothing else, stern.

I caught Liam winking at her as I grabbed what I needed. Her lips turned into a fine line.

I delivered them their drinks and returned to where Luke stood, not so subtly watching them in an attempt to read the situation. As I approached him, I did the same. Liam had held up his glass to hers and seemed to be saying a few choice words. He was quiet—his voice unable to be picked out of the crowd as he leaned in close to her. Zoey's mouth stretched slowly into a smile and she grabbed her glass, clinking it against his. They simultaneously took their drinks together, and I glanced at Luke with an *I told you so* expression. His mouth had fallen open, his eyes squinted together in confusion as to how Zoey could be smiling at all at this point.

I summoned my sweetest voice, "Night's not over yet," and patted him on his shoulder as I walked past him to tend to more of our customers.

It was three brushes against Luke's crotch, five squeezes of his hands against alternating hips of mine, several whispers in our respective ears, and what was probably hours later that I wondered why Liam and Zoey weren't running out of content to talk about. They spoke animatedly with smiles, laughs, and looks of disbelief smattered on each other's faces throughout their conversing. It was hard to imagine Liam speaking for so long without Zoey putting a fist through him, yet here they were, and she really *did* look intrigued by every word out of his mouth. There was a full shot glass in front of each of them. They were the third ones that I had poured and both glasses had sat there, untouched, for upwards of fifteen minutes. I grabbed a white rag and wiped at the counter, slowly edging my way to their seats until I was within eavesdropping range.

"Let me get this straight," Liam asked, finally grabbing the glass in front of him, tipping it back, and draining it. His face scrunched up from the burn of the liquor. "You used to pitch for a softball team?"

"And why is that so unbelievable?"

The lighting in the bar was dim as usual, but it didn't stop her green eyes from visibly dancing at the opportunity Liam had just handed her.

He paused for a moment and gestured at her. "Well, I mean," he stammered, trying to say the right words. "You're so..."

She finished his thought for him, "Small? Is that where you're going with this?"

He held up his hands in defense.

"That's not what I was going to say at all! I was going to say...delicate?" His voice quickened. "I just can't imagine your hands even fitting around a softball. That's all. I'm just surprised—in a good way!"

Zoey dropped her usual offense and took her shot. Liam watched with intent as she drank and began to mimic her, raising his beer to his lips without looking at the glass. Before it reached his lips, Zoey leaned in towards him. He closed the distance, hunching down to make up for their height difference, and she whispered something in his ear.

He paused in taking his sip, the glass held in mid-air for a beat as he closed his eyes and inhaled. Upon his exhale he set his glass on his coaster, and a wide grin spread across his face. His freckled cheeks flushed red, and he lowered his head to avert his eyes.

Zoey chose that moment to spring out of her seat and skip her way to the bathroom, and Liam cleared his throat, shaking his head.

"Where in the hell did you find that girl?" His voice cracked just slightly on the word *find* as he asked me the question.

"What exactly did she just whisper to you?"

The possibilities were endless, and knowing Zoey, they were all dirty.

"Umm," he hesitated, "I don't want to say...she's—she's a little spicier than I thought she was."

I let out a loud laugh as he shifted a bit in his seat.

"What's wrong?" I pressed him. "Can't handle the heat?"

He smiled as he took a sip of his beer.

"No, no," he said quietly, "that I can handle—I like it."

He looked back toward the bathroom with a shy smile as Zoey was flitting her way back to her seat. I walked halfway down the length of the bar and intercepted her before she returned to him.

"What in the world did you do to him?" I tried to keep my voice low so no one else would hear.

"Why?" She asked with a smile so big that I could see her molars. "What did he say?"

"Well, he asked where I *found you* as if you were like...a Goddess or something."

"I get that a lot, you know."

I snorted. "I'm sure—just one problem though." Zoey squinted her eyes at me in question, and I said, "I think he may actually like you so, you know—careful with that."

"And?"

"And—"

"Claire, you know I've been with men who liked me before—and I've *dealt* with them."

"Yeah," I replied slowly, "and how are you going to *deal* with Liam when he lives across the hall? You won't be able to avoid him forever."

"Oh, you think I'm going to fuck him," she noted.

"Well, if it looks like a duck and it quacks like a duck—"

"Ah, well yeah. Look, he may be fun for me to push around," she said, internally weighing her options as she tilted her head to the side. "He's nice—I surprisingly like talking with him," she continued. "Not to mention he's not bad to look at." I groaned at her and motioned in a circular direction with my hand, hinting at her to make her point. "But," she acquiesced, holding up one of her hands, "I've told you before...I don't fuck where I eat. I'm not touching that with a ten-foot pole."

She bounced away and sat back in her seat, plastering a gigantic grin on her face as she sat next to Liam once more. A deep voice whispered in my ear, derailing my thoughts.

"So, do I need to run to the ATM at some point tonight?"

I turned around with a frown on my face, and Luke's delight was more than apparent.

"*No,*" I replied with a cringe. "She's just...I don't know...messing with him for the fun of it."

"That is the best news I've heard all day!"

"Oh, come on," I retorted, "he looks like he actually likes her...don't you feel a little bad?"

He chortled. "Bad? No, that's not exactly the emotion I'm feeling right now."

"You know he's not, like, a bad guy, right? What's your problem with him?"

Luke sighed. "I'm not trying to sound like a dick, I'm sorry." He continued in a quieter voice. "I just hated it when he was trying to get with you; he just wanted to get in your pants." He shook his head and said offhandedly, "I've seen him be around women before, it's not like he treated you any differently. It just...bothered me when it was with you."

I felt a smile stretch across my lips.

"You were *jealous?*" I accused him.

"Not jealous!" He responded to me in a hushed, almost embarrassed tone. I raised my eyebrows. "Okay, maybe a little jealous," he said as his eyes shot to the floor and he shuffled his feet. "I just thought you deserved a hell of a lot better than that."

I nudged his shuffling feet with mine to get his attention.

"So, what, you kind of like me or somethin'?"

Luke rubbed the back of his neck, and a smile just barely made his lips rise up.

"Yeah," he replied, his eyes locking with mine, "or something."

The rest of the night went as smoothly as possible. By closing time, there were no other customers except Liam and Zoey. Luke and I had silently gone through the motions of closing Henry's, our game withered down to grazing touches at any point that we crossed each other's paths. I wandered to the back room once I was finished, wanting to give Liam and Zoey a moment of privacy. I couldn't help myself though, and I peeked at their interaction from the doorway.

Zoey had shaken her head *no* and seemed to be giving Liam an earful. His eyebrows raised and he sat taller, no doubt taking in every word that she said. I would have said that he was disappointed, but his expression was hard to place. I contemplated it as Zoey continued to speak at him and, eventually, deduced that it didn't look to be disappointment at all. Liam was angry. Pissed, even, but as Zoey finished her spiel with a smug smile on her face, the emotion seemed to devolve into something I could only describe as hurt. He sat quietly for a moment and then finished his beer in one large gulp, turning his head back to her. I couldn't hear what he was saying, try as I might to strain my ears, and I was rendered blind to their conversation completely when Luke appeared in front of me.

"Can you read lips? Because I sure as fuck can't."

I flinched in surprise, reaching a hand to my chest as I gasped.

"Where did you come from?!"

"Saw you spying," he remarked. "You know you're not kidding anyone, right?"

"Yeah, yeah."

He wandered behind me as if to achieve the same angle on the situation that was unfolding in front of both of us. His hands sat on both of my hips, and he swayed me from side to side.

"So," he said, "what exactly do your expert spying skills say is happening with them? My wallet is burning...just like your throat is going to when you take that shot of gin."

I gagged. I was overconfident before when I had added the additional consequence to our bet, and I was certainly regretting it now. It wasn't that I didn't like gin—gin was okay in certain circumstances, especially a good gin. *This gin* had no business being ordered without a substantial amount of mixer to go with it.

"Go pour the goddamn shot," I said without even looking his way. "I want to get this over with."

Luke laughed, and I heard him rub his hands together in a sinister manner before practically skipping past me and off to the bar in glee. I sank myself into a chair next to the grey folding table, and I could barely shift myself to get comfortable before Luke was back, shot in hand.

He set it on the table before me with a flourish and almost sang, "Bottoms up, Buttercup!"

I grumbled at him, staring at the offending liquid in front of me, and Luke danced from foot to foot eagerly. I took it without even smelling it and, to my surprise, it went down smoothly. There was a familiar burn in my chest and the taste of agave lingered in the back of my throat.

"Did you bring me our tequila?" I asked with a disbelieving laugh.

Luke just shrugged, but his grin was all too telling.

I stood to walk over to him and wrapped my arms around his neck. To touch so freely was a welcome change from the silent game that we had created. I leaned into him, burying my head in his chest, and I felt him exhale, wrapping his arms around my waist. His fingers gripped me tightly.

A smile stretched across his face as he looked down at me and he rubbed his nose against mine, leaving a trail of fire in its path.

"You didn't have to bring me tequila, you know," I told him. "I would've gone through with it."

"Oh, I know. You're too damn stubborn to back down."

I hummed in agreement. "I would've made you take the gin."

His soft laugh shook his shoulders. "I wouldn't expect any less." He paused, then said, "You know...there's a good chance that we're alone now."

I didn't even realize that our lips had been inching closer to each other's. When he spoke, his mouth almost brushed against mine, and the playful mood dissipated between us in an instant. We breathed with open mouths, panting—the familiar touch of each other's bodies spurring on our imaginations.

"I've thought of you. Here," he nearly whispered.

"At work?"

He nodded. "*So* many times."

The sound of the front door of the bar closing twice rang throughout the bar. I assumed that it was Liam and Zoey leaving, one after the other, but I couldn't be certain.

"We're closed!" I called out.

There was no response, and Luke leaned down to touch his lips to mine. It was a patient, simmering kiss until our tongues met and I moaned softly. His chest rumbled and that was all it took to quicken our pace to a rolling boil. All I could hear was the deafening sound of our heavy breathing as I laced my hands through his hair. There was no question that both of our minds had wandered to the escalation of our actions as our respective grips on each other shifted from sweet to smoldering—from gentle to groping.

Our lips smacked loudly as Luke pulled away.

"Fuck, I—I don't have a condom—"

I rattled off quickly, "I'm on the pill, got tested after Colt, I'm good—are you?"

His eyes darkened, and he nodded. "Front door," was all he said in a husky breath.

He took my hand, leading me through the bar. It was notably empty. Liam and Zoey's last drinks sat in front of where they were seated—drained, and both holding cash beneath them. It was when we passed their seats that I noticed I wasn't even carrying my belongings.

"Luke, my things—"

"Leave them."

He barely reached the front door when he dropped my hand, slid the deadbolt in the door with a quick flick of his wrist, and was back to me in an instant. His lips were on mine, and he walked me backward. A grunt of sorts escaped me when my lower back hit the wooden molding in the center of the wall, and he pulled away from me rapidly.

"You okay?" He spoke with a single breath and heavy-lidded eyes, looking me up and down.

"Shut the fuck up."

I nearly demanded it, and he laughed as I yanked his head back to mine. Our growing familiarity made the intimate moments better. Our first time was more than memorable, but figuring out each other's preferences and using the knowledge to both of our advantage was becoming one of my favorite pastimes. For example, Luke knew now that when he used his teeth on the soft spots of my neck, I would whimper and grind myself into him. Likewise, I knew that if I were to scrape my nails down his back, his excitement would spur on, and he would curse a string of profanities in my ear.

It was before I knew it that both of our shirts were off and Luke was yanking at the button on my jeans. I did the same, pulling hopelessly at his belt buckle until he made way of it himself and went back to pulling my pants down to my ankles.

When we were together before, we had taken our time as if we had hoped to memorize every crevasse of the other's body. This was different. It was hot, and quick. We didn't bother to undress fully. I had one leg out of my jeans, and Luke's pants had only fallen to just below his buttocks. He pulled me up with a grasp on either of my thighs and sat me on the edge of a cocktail chair that stood next to us, driving himself into me.

He let out a near animalistic growl, and I felt it deep within me. It was a sound that embodied a thirsty man who had finally been given a drink. I understood the sentiment fully and I unintentionally repeated the noise back, feeling my vocal cords grate.

I wouldn't have described his pace as rapid. It was steady—each thrust harder than the last, and the legs of the chair that held me scraped against the floor with every swift movement. Eventually, we had moved so far that the back of the chair hit the wall behind us, and I felt the need to feel him deeper. I raised my left leg, the one that was completely disrobed of my pants, and bent my knee over his shoulder. My calf bounced against his back as he moved, and the sensation of him so deep caused me to moan loudly.

Luke looked at my leg hitched over him as if it were a godsend and bit at the skin behind my knee.

"You're gonna fuckin' kill me," he groaned as he continued on, reaching a relentless tempo.

We quickly reached a point where we were grasping at each other wildly, praying for release. The only noises lingering in the air were the sounds of our moans ricocheting off the walls.

"Come with me," I gasped, feeling my entire body flex with the threat of my impending implosion.

"Oh *fuck,* yes."

When I came—loudly—and my muscles went limp, Luke held me. His fingers squeezed roughly into the skin on my ribcage as he thrust into me three more times and then stopped, releasing a guttural groan into my neck.

I went to move my leg that was draped over him, and he grabbed at it, moving to kiss it briefly before allowing it to drop to the floor. He bent to touch his lips against mine softly.

"Sleep with me tonight?" He asked me in what came across as a soft plead.

"You're still inside of me, and you already want to go again?" I murmured with a wry smile.

Luke chuckled. "Don't be a smart ass. Come home with me—please?"

I nodded and smiled, and we began a slow exit from the bar.

Not long after we left Henry's, I was watching the snow fall outside from the comfort of Luke's bed. I sat in front of him, our bodies turned towards the window to the outside, one of his arms wrapped around my waist. I was content. *More* than content, really—sated was more fitting. Or, perhaps, blissfully happy would have been a better description. It didn't matter how I described the emotion. The only thing of consequence was that I felt...*good.* And it had been a long while since I felt this trouble-free.

"You said you're leaving on Wednesday to go back home?"

I grunted, thinking briefly that my trouble-free moment was short lived, and answered, "Yeah." I tried not to sound bitter about it. I didn't look forward to revisiting home, as I assumed that it would bring back bad memories, but I did so to visit Zoey's parents. They were, in a way, the only family that I had, and I had promised long ago that I would return to see them for Christmas, so there was no going back now. "I'll be back before New Year's, though," I added thoughtfully, not wanting to elaborate on my plans.

"Hmm." I felt his throat rumble behind me, and I hoped that my distaste for the subject had gone unnoticed. It seemed as though it had when he squeezed me tighter and exhaled a quick breath. "I'll miss you," he said quietly, almost nervously.

My chest warmed and my pulse fluttered. I found myself lightly tracing a pattern over his arm for no reason.

I responded back, "I'll miss you, too," and I failed to hide the girlish smile in my voice.

If I were being honest with myself, I didn't care for it. I hadn't heard a tone like that come out of my mouth before and I found it almost...embarrassing. His lips kissed the back of my neck, though, and I decided that I didn't give a shit about how I sounded. I allowed my thoughts to go back to being blissful.

Luke began to fill me in about his plans over the holidays. He had just finished talking up his mother's cooking, insisting that I would *love* it, and didn't skip a beat as he went on about the ambiance of home. A wistful smile spread across my face and I wondered what that must feel like—to *want* to be around family. To relive memories that had passed with a yearning to go back just to do it all over again was a feeling that I've only felt with dear friends and...well...and with Luke. He sighed loudly.

"Anyway, I'm rambling...what are you doing, staying with your parents?"

I had never told Luke about my parents. Of *course*, I hadn't—any time that he had asked general questions, I had skirted them with utmost caution. He never asked for further clarity, and the only mention of my past was touching on the surface of my relationship with Colton. As the conversation turned toward my own plans, I squirmed. I assumed that I played it off as a shimmy to get more comfortable in his arms.

"I'll be at Zoey's."

"Your parents won't want to see you?"

His tone held a hint of sadness to it and based on his description of his happy holiday get-together to be, Luke hadn't considered the possibility of my family being less than such.

"No, I er—I probably won't even see my parents while I'm there."

Probably wasn't the word I should have used. It was a certainty, but I found myself backed into a corner. I could have easily said that they were on vacation—maybe every year they up and take a trip to France.

Maybe Italy.

No...Hawaii. Yes, if I were to lie to Luke, I would have definitely chosen Hawaii.

I couldn't do that, though. I cared for him too deeply, and it felt...wrong. A lie of omission was no better, but it seemed to be my best option.

"I haven't seen my parents in a...while. A really *long* while."

"No?" He asked as if it was an impossibility. "Why not?"

"I know this probably doesn't make much sense to you since you seem to have such a perfect family—"

"Claire." Luke chuckled my name, and though that normally came across as a comfort, it was anything but. "I've had plenty of fights with my family—"

I stopped him by reaching behind me and attempting to place my hand on his mouth. I didn't quite reach where his lips were, but the message was received, and he ceased speaking.

"I may not have left North Carolina just because of Colton." The words came out hushed.

I felt him nod slowly, and I pictured the tension in his gaze. It was replicated in the tone of his voice.

"Is there anything I should know about?" He asked cautiously.

My mind screamed *yes*.

My head shook vigorously from side to side.

I was sure that my eyes were wide and crazed, and I was thankful that I was facing away from Luke. I attempted to sum up anything about my past without being too forthcoming.

"My parents are out of the picture...they split up when I was about 5. Dad's been drunk and more or less MIA since."

There was a silence that I expected, but it didn't make it any less difficult to bear.

"I'm so sorry," he eventually said. "That, er—that explains why you've never mentioned your parents?" I nodded, and he added, "And why you hate talking about home...what about your mom, then?"

I stuttered trying to come up with the appropriate phrasing to explain exactly where my mother was. I'd rather just say that she was dead, but that was too dramatic for my taste, so I just...stated the bare minimum.

"She's been in jail for a few years now...tax fraud."

"Oh," he responded. "When—when did this all happen?"

I could almost witness his mind trying to connect the dots of it all. Though he wasn't facing me, I could *see* his brow furrow. *Feel* his head turn to the side in a combination of curiosity and sympathy.

"When could I tell something was off? I was graduating high school soon, I think. When she went to jail...I dunno, I was 21? 22?"

"That's a lot to take on at that age," he noted somberly.

I wanted to say, *'You don't know the half of it.'* I didn't.

"There's really not much to say about them." *That* was a lie. It was an offhanded one that felt like it had shades of grey mixed into it in such a way that it could be explained off as not *really* a lie...but I knew in my gut that it was. And that nauseated me. I turned in his arms and his silvery gaze was, as expected, tinged with nervousness and worry. I spoke before Luke could think too deeply about what I had said before. "Like I said, they're out of the picture."

His noticeable nervousness seemed to abate only slightly as he nodded to my admission. I kissed him gently on the lips and when I pulled away, I noticed that the only emotion that remained in his eyes was a gentle sadness.

"I didn't realize you had such a rough upbringing," he muttered.

It wasn't pity. I *knew* it wasn't pity—if it were, I would have stopped him right there. It was sympathy, and while I appreciated the sentiment and it tugged at my heartstrings to see Luke expressing it toward me, I didn't want it. Seeing the emotion on his face reminded me of everything I had been through—and what I had told him was only scratching the surface. If he knew the whole of it, I could only imagine how he would act...and that would open Pandora's box.

"Don't worry about me," I reassured him, grabbing his jaw and wiggling it as if I were squishing his cheeks. "I just don't like talking about it."

He nodded back in response, pulling me in against his chest, and silence took over the room. I felt his lips press against my forehead and, not long after, it seemed as though he had drifted off to sleep. His breaths came long and soft, and his grip on my back had loosened to the point that his arms had gone limp.

I was far from sleeping—I was unsure if I would sleep at all after the conversation that Luke and I had. My mind had wandered back to where I so often tried never to venture and as I laid physically comfortable in Luke's arms, mentally I was in turmoil. Mentally, I was transported to years ago—when I was around 19 years old.

The scent of stale smoke and mothballs was one that I had grown accustomed to. I had been staring at myself in a mirror in my bedroom for upwards of an hour, attempting to rattle my brain to the point that it would wake up and take charge, for I had figured that enough was enough when it came to my mother.

She had made the decision to take everything from me—even what I had never begun to obtain—and her actions had dug a hole so deep for me that I worried I would never get out. With the thought of my metaphorical grave running over and over in my mind, I finally willed my legs to move, and I stormed out of my room.

There was a man within view from the staircase who was beginning to exit through the front door. His hand was on the knob and upon hearing me creak down the thinly carpeted stairs, he turned to look at me. I always assumed he was just a few years older than I was, but I had never asked. Dark red hair and a square jaw made up a face that I had unfortunately become familiar with around my home.

"Claire," he attempted to croon, "how are you?"

"Travis," I greeted him coolly. "Dropping off another package for Carla, I'm guessing?"

I used my hands as quotation marks on the word package as I spoke. I wasn't dim. I knew very well what was in those packages and it made it all the worse. It made my veins feel like they ran dry every time I thought of it—of her. My mother, Carla. She was a junkie. I wasn't sure how long she had been like this...there was a point when she was happy and healthy. I just had a hard time remembering when that was.

"You know," he commented, "all in a day's work."

He was so casual. He always was—even in regards to having ruined my mother's life and mine by default—and he definitely knew that he did.

"Sure."

I replied quickly; bluntly. There was no point in arguing with Travis. I wasn't sure if he was legitimately a sociopath or if he just...put himself above all others. All I knew was that I didn't need to waste my time trying to converse with him. Plus, I didn't want to lose all the motivation that I had already worked up.

"I gotta go, Trav."

"No worries, no worries," he said. "Another time."

I felt his eyes rake over my body and I controlled the urge to retch before he turned abruptly to leave. I recaptured my prior momentum and headed straight to our living room.

That was neither the first nor the last time that I had attempted to confront my mother.

Just thinking of Travis again sent an icy chill running through my body. I shuddered, trying to push the memory of him out of my mind, and Luke unconsciously hugged me tighter, looping a leg around my waist. His breathing remained soft and unburdened. I attempted to table my sad trip down memory lane and leaned into his embrace, hearing him hum contentedly and wishing I could relax in the same way.

Try as I might, Luke slept peacefully while I laid awake. Memories of my mother popped into my head hour after hour. When I was young, she looked like me—red haired, blue eyed, freckled yet unblemished skin. As she aged, she became colder. Harder.

The expected wave of guilt washed over me as I thought of her. In her more recent years, she always said that she was in prison because of me. Just because I was the one to turn her in didn't make that statement true—it was my last option.

It started with her getting into my bank accounts. The money I had earned from what little work I did was diminishing faster than it should have and I was naïve. I caught onto her after a while, but it wasn't enough just to tell her to stop. It was to fuel her addiction, and there wasn't much I could do to stop her no matter how hard I tried. Loans and credit cards were taken out in my name and maxed out. In the end, to say I was in debt would have been a massive understatement. It was a pile—a mountain—of around $150,000. It was, to say the least, a shocking amount of money. I would have been happy to tell all of this to Luke, but his response would be obvious.

'What happened afterward?' and, more specifically, *'How in the hell did you get out of debt?'* are questions that, if answered, would bring up the past I had been trying so hard to leave behind.

Chapter Nine

The next morning, I opened the door to my apartment and Zoey greeted me with raised eyebrows from the kitchen table.

"You guys fucked in the bar, didn't you?"

"Good morning, Zoey." I greeted her as I walked through our entrance. "How was your night? Oh, mine was fine, thanks."

"Didn't answer the question," she said, sipping her mug as she normally does at this hour.

"I'm not one to kiss and tell," I quipped.

"But you *should* be. Why the *fuck* wouldn't you? Look at me, Claire."

I turned my eyes to her and sank myself into the chair next to her with as much grace as one who only got an hour or two of sleep could.

"I'm looking."

"I'm in the driest spell of my life," she said bluntly. "It hurts me—it hurts me to my *very core* to admit that I haven't had sex since we left North Carolina."

"Is...is that a long time?"

I did the math in my head and determined that we'd lived here for four months. It was less time than it felt like, especially when considering how close I had gotten to Luke.

"Is it a long *time?!*" She snapped back. "I'm *sorry* that you've gotten laid and forgotten how *dire* the times are when you're in desperate need of dick."

I snorted. The difference between Zoey and me was that Zoey used to have quite a prolific sex life. I wasn't a one-night stand type of girl, so it wasn't uncommon for me to go several months without a sexual partner. Zoey, on the other hand, made it a rule to never spend more than a night or so with a man, and she was rarely lonely up until we moved here.

"And why haven't you relieved your need?"

"Why haven't I ended my dick sabbatical?" She asked.

I chortled and shrugged. "Sure, if you want to call it that."

She seemed to give it a good amount of thought, squinting her eyes and looking to the ceiling.

"Well, at first, I guess I was settling in. New place, you know?"

"Mhm, right."

"Now I'm just," she sighed heavily, "out of my groove. I think I *lost it.*"

"Lost what, exactly?"

"Don't know. My mojo?"

"I'm sure you'll find a nice guy here soon—"

"He doesn't have to be nice," she interrupted me. "Doesn't matter—anyway, are you gonna give me deets from last night so I can live through you?"

"Fine," I said with a roll of my eyes. "Yes, we fucked in the bar."

"Nice."

"Standing up."

"Nice."

"Hard and fast."

"Nice!" Zoey held out a hand in a gesture for me to high five her, and I obliged. She asked, "Then why do you look like shit?"

"I do?"

"Those aren't bags under your eyes, those are *luggage,"* she told me. "What gives?"

I managed a weak grin at her analogy, and upon her mentioning the reason for my insomnia, I slumped in my chair.

"Luke's starting to ask me about my *past.*"

I said the last word as if it were a profanity, hanging my head in my hands.

"That was fast," she noted. "So...what does he know and how did he take it?"

"Just that Carla's in jail and Frank's MIA. Honestly, I don't think I even want to tell Luke the rest...we came here for a reason, right? To leave the past in the past?"

My hopeful thoughts were squashed by the incredulous look on Zoey's face.

"Nah," she replied, shaking her head quickly.

"Oh, come *on,*" I begged.

"I'm not preaching that I'm fit to give relationship advice or anything, but even *I* know that's a terrible idea."

"And if I don't tell him?" I inquired about her opinion on the matter.

Zoey mimed what looked to be a car driving off of a cliff. Her dainty hand representing the car landed on the table between us and metaphorically exploded upon impact. Her fingers writhed on the wood grain to simulate fire.

"Ah fuck, there's blood *everywhere!*" She whisper-yelled, *"I'm burning aliiiiveeee!"*

"Okay, I get it—"

She held up one finger on the hand that wasn't pretending to be an incinerated vehicle.

"Not finished yet," she berated me. "Oh my *God, HELP—fuck,* IS THAT THE GAS TANK LEAKING?!"

"Zoey—"

"WHOOSH!" Her hand flew off the table as high as she could reach and fluttered down slowly. *"Ashes, ashes,"* she murmured as her fingers wiggled back down.

"Are you finished?"

"Did I win my Oscar?"

"Mhm."

"Then yes, I'm finished. You get the picture?"

Her left brow was arched up so high, it disappeared into her short fringe, and my stomach coiled uncomfortably.

"Yes," I said slowly. "You're right...but I don't want to tell him yet."

"You're being an *idiot—*"

I spoke faster in my defense. "I will! Really, I will. I just can't yet—it needs to be the right time. I'll figure it out."

Zoey sang, "Alright," quietly to herself, turning the word into three syllables.

"Speaking of bad decisions," I retorted. "Did you have a good time torturing Liam last night?"

Her know-it-all attitude dissipated slightly.

"Erm...at the beginning, I did. He kind of told me off after it all."

"You *did* dangle a bone in front of his face and then yank it away," I remarked.

Zoey shook her head. "Not why he got mad."

"No?"

It was when she looked to the ceiling and shook her head softly that I noticed how tired she looked. The light purple circles under her eyes marred her normally exquisite complexion. The color could have made the green of her irises seem brighter on a good day. This was clearly *not* one of those days. The fire in her eyes seemed to have been put out, their usual glow diminished significantly.

"You okay, Zoey?"

"Yes," she replied slowly, "and no. Rough night."

"Oh?"

Over the years, I learned that Zoey is kind of like a feral cat. If you wanted its affection, you have to just let it come to you—don't try to trap it in a corner, otherwise you'll get scratched. With that thought in mind, I didn't pry any further.

She inhaled for longer than I thought possible, and upon her exhale breathed out, "Managed to get Liam to talk about himself."

"Oh?"

My curiosity was piqued, of course. It had been months of exchanging conversations with Liam, and I still knew nothing about the man except that he's cocky, enjoys sports, and moved to Virginia from North Carolina when he was 18. Though he was a sunny presence and his happiness seemed to know no bounds, Liam had remained ever-secretive about his life in the now.

"He's in school," she told me.

I asked, "School—*college?*" Zoey nodded, and I felt the need to clarify, "Liam—college?"

"To be a teacher for younger kids of all things—acted all embarrassed when I pulled it out of him."

"Why in the *world* did he say he was *freelancing?*"

Zoey shrugged. "Don't think he's had a hell of a lot of support, or at least that's the impression I got." She shook her head. *"That's* why he was mad at me—I toyed with him and turned him down and of *all things,* he was pissed thinking I was just pretending about giving a shit after he talked about his personal life." She exhaled heavily and glanced at me. "I was a bitch to him. A big bitch. Huge." She sounded exasperated, as if she had been telling herself those same words all night. "And don't even start with me on this one because I *know* you will and I can't handle that right now—"

"Start with what?"

"I have to apologize to him."

"Oh."

That. Yeah, that took me off guard. Zoey was not one for apologies. She'd always been a *take-no-prisoners* type of girl. A bold girl. A *go full steam ahead and never look back at your mistakes* type of girl. A *no-apologies* type of girl. So, hearing her say that she needed to apologize for being a bitch—to a guy, no less—was a shock and a half.

"It's too early to just show up at his place and I don't have his number and I don't want him to think I was up all night thinking about him—"

"Oh?"

"Because I don't do that." She insisted. "I've just been thinking."

"Right."

"That I was mean."

"Mhm."

"And he was...not."

In the spirit of addressing the elephant in the room and getting out of this weird guilt circle that Zoey had created for herself, I told her:

"You know if you like him, you can just tell me."

She laughed a little too loudly for me to be convinced.

"Claire, *oh* Claire. No. That's not it."

She chose that moment to stand up and walk towards her room, effectively cutting off the conversation, and I thought to myself, *'And the cat is feral yet again.'*

I just mimicked her phrasing from earlier, singing quietly to myself, "Alright."

It was so early that the sky was still tinged with pink. Luke stood next to Zoey's car with his arms wrapped around himself from the cold. The time until Zoey and I were leaving to visit her parents for the holidays had passed quickly—*too* quickly. So quickly, in fact, that I hadn't found a single time to speak to Luke about my unsavory previous life. Or, perhaps, that's what I had told myself.

"I told you that you didn't have to walk me out," I spoke softly as I closed the trunk, my voice ringing through the still of morning.

Luke smiled and huffed out a puff of air.

"Nah," he said, shaking his head back and forth quickly. His overgrown hair whipped from side to side, the usual lack of product leaving it messy, and I liked it. "I wanted to see you off," he told me. "You know that."

He wrapped a surprisingly warm arm around my shoulders and pulled me close, the faint smell of him filling my nostrils. I felt him exhale and step back slightly, his hand moving to below my chin, tilting my head up for a short but sweet kiss. I wanted to think that the look in his eyes said that he was going to miss me. We had said it to each other before, after all. But they seemed to say so much more. They seemed warm. Caring. Loving. And though we had never said the words, the thought of him loving me wasn't lost on me. It was something that I thought I would have welcomed with open arms, but seeing the emotion in his eyes scared the piss out of me. Not because it was there, but because I wasn't sure if it would remain after I gained the confidence to tell him everything.

"I'll see you in a week?" He asked. I nodded in response to his question and felt his thumb graze along the side of my jaw. I leaned into his touch and smiled despite my worrisome thoughts. "Call me when you get there, okay?"

Before I could respond, I heard Zoey roll down the window of the car. She had been not so patiently waiting on me from the comfort of the heated inside. She sat behind the wheel bundled with a beanie and mittens, one hand threatening to honk the horn.

She called out, "Yes, she'll call you. Yes, she's going to miss you too. Let's *go*, Claire! Train's leavin'!"

"I don't think I can risk her waking the entire neighborhood."

Luke laughed softly and kissed me once more, saying, "Get out of here, then."

I sat down in the passenger seat, watching him walk away as I closed the door behind me. I ignored the pointed look that Zoey was giving me—I couldn't see it, but I could feel her eyeballs boring into the back of my skull.

"So," she said, "I take it that you didn't talk to him yet considering your oh-so-lovey goodbye."

"So, I take it that you haven't had any coffee yet since you're in such a great mood."

She picked up her insulated mug and brought it to her lips, promptly setting it back down gently into the cup holder.

"First sip of the day, but my mood is perfectly fine," she told me. "Not my fault that you don't want to be called out for not wanting to tell your current boo how you should be in jail with your previous boo because you used to be in a real-life Bonnie and Clyde situationship." She rattled off the run-on sentence as she backed out of the parking space, looking over her shoulder and checking her blind spots effortlessly. She shifted the car into drive, and I made it a point to sigh as loudly as I possibly could. She pressed, "I take it that conversation has still been conveniently avoided?"

"Why, yes. It has." I defended myself quickly to avoid the Spanish Inquisition from Zoey. "The timing wasn't right! Plus, I didn't want to ruin our last few days before I left. Is that such a crime?"

Her emerald eyes shot into orbit, and she pressed her foot on the gas pedal.

"I guess not," she paused, thinking to herself, "but the best time to tell him is long gone by now. You should have told him when he asked you about your past."

I took a sip of my own coffee that had been waiting for me in the second cup holder that sat between us. It was lukewarm.

"I know that. *Obviously.* I just already fucked up and I need to make it...not sound so fucked when I explain it all to him. Does that even make sense?"

"No," Zoey spoke with a sarcasm that only she could throw around. "Of *course,* that makes sense, Claire. The problem is you're thinking about it too much."

My eyebrows scrunched together as I took in her words.

"Beg pardon?"

"You're. Thinking. Too. Much," she reiterated. "Whenever you tell him, it's gonna sound fucked up—no matter how much sugar you try to coat on it." I groaned far too audibly, knowing that she wasn't wrong, and she peeked in my direction as she turned the wheel. "Look, I'm sorry—I don't mean to be so...in your business. It's just that with how chaotic your life used to be, you deserve to be as happy as you look lately."

I thanked her quietly with a quick look and decided to promptly change the topic of discussion.

"Did you talk to Liam?"

The sides of her mouth turned up slightly. "Oh, that?"

I laughed at her attempt to be casual and quipped, "Yes, that. You seemed a little torn up about it before."

"I think that's called sleep deprivation," she retorted, "but yeah, I talked to him. We're good."

The look I gave her almost made her spit up her coffee, and I questioned, "You're *good?*"

"Oh my God, *stop.*" She leaned to the right to elbow me, but I shrugged away out of her reach. "I said we're good, I didn't say I fucked him." I raised an eyebrow extra high, and she reiterated again, "I *didn't.* Liam's...he's been through a lot." Zoey set her coffee down in the space between us. "He said he tends to keep to himself and—look, I know that you know that I don't *do* guy friends, but it's *different,* okay?"

The air of sincerity in her gaze made me halt my incessant questioning. There was a reason that Zoey had remained such a constant presence in my life—and it wasn't because I was earning friend-of-the-year award time and time again. It was because although Zoey was rough around the edges, she was *wildly* protective of those who were in need. I knew that firsthand. It wasn't long after Zoey realized that I could *really* use a friend, not to mention an additional family unit, that she became a constant at my side.

I had been wondering why Zoey had befriended Liam at all. They had spent more time with one another since the night that they spent together at Henry's—that was abundantly clear—and, especially considering her history with men, the idea had become a curiosity to me, to say the least. However, the knowledge that Liam potentially had a dramatic past to tag along with him changed my mindset on the matter immediately. No matter how little time they had spent together, it was clear that, much like me, Liam was another person that Zoey felt the need to bring under her wing. And I didn't question her judgement in that matter one bit.

I simply nodded at her, and she smiled in a silent *thank you.*

Visiting Zoey's parents was always a pleasant experience. They had a gorgeous house in an affluent area, but it wasn't the spacious abode or the 1,000 thread count sheets that allowed me to enjoy myself. It was the one place that I could ever really consider to be a home, and the time passed with ease with little to no drama. Without brothers or sisters to argue with—not to mention having responsible, kind-hearted parents—it was non-existent. Although enjoyable, I found myself longing to go back to Salem after just a few days. I knew it was because of Luke—we had been in constant contact since I left, but it wasn't the same. Spending time with someone for months on end and then suddenly not having them at my side was a foreign feeling that I was none too comfortable with.

Before I had moped for too long, my phone was ringing in my pocket. Zoey and I were watching television, and she sat next to me on the couch in her parents' living room. She glanced my way as I pulled my phone out, and upon seeing a picture that I had taken weeks ago of Luke and me flash on the screen, she grabbed the remote and turned the volume down. Zoey took her own phone out of her pocket and aimlessly swiped at the glass face.

The words *video chat* were written across the screen, and I smiled at the thought of seeing Luke's face. I slid my finger across the green arrow to answer it and was connected with someone who was, decidedly, not Luke.

The man who looked back at me had a chiseled jawline almost completely obscured by dark, short facial hair, and his nose looked like it had been broken a few times in the past. His hair was a lighter brown in color and just long enough to tuck behind his ears. A large, blindingly white grin split across his face, and I settled on a set of strikingly familiar grey eyes.

"Well, hello there, Claire!" He spoke excitedly in a hushed, amused tone.

"I believe you have me at a disadvantage."

"Ah, right, I'm James—the brother," he said, raising his hand and waving at me nonchalantly.

Zoey nearly threw her phone across the room, scrambling to get to my side of the couch. She knew *exactly* who James was. She had only seen him from afar, but she made had made it abundantly clear that she liked what she saw, and I was certain that she wanted to get a better look at him. She crawled on the cushion that separated us like some sort of gremlin, and I kicked in her general direction to keep her at bay.

"Here's the thing, Claire," James said quickly and quietly, "Luke's been talking about you all goddamn week. I'm fairly certain that you've turned him into mush, but that's beside the point." I wasn't sure if my cheeks heated because I was blushing or because I was still kicking at Zoey. James continued speaking, unaware of the attack on my lower legs. "What I'm trying to get to is that I keep telling Luke that I'd like to have a conversation with this mystery woman, but he's been *very* adamant about that not happening...something about me being a pain in the ass, I dunno."

Zoey mouthed, *'What does he look like?'* with flailing arms attempting to get my attention. I didn't answer her, and she smacked my right knee.

I muttered, "Zoey, *stop.*"

"Oh, say hi to your friend for me," James told me nonchalantly.

"James says hi."

She pointed her index finger in the air and spun it in a circle, signifying that I should turn my phone around to give her a better look. I rolled my eyes at her and she sat back, pouting out her lower lip at me.

"She says hi," I replied to him.

A noise must have sounded behind James because he turned his head around. He smiled wickedly and adjusted the view of his phone just slightly enough to show Luke walking around the corner behind him. He seemed to be searching for something, moving papers atop a table and setting them back down. James put a finger to his lips, and I listened intently.

Luke's muffled voice emitted from the background, "Hey, Jay, do you know where I put my phone? I set it down when I was helping Mom with the dishes from lunch and that was like...forever ago."

"Aw, you're such a gentleman," James said sarcastically. "Nope, haven't seen it!" Without even skipping a beat, James said in a loud voice, "So, Claire, tell me about yourself!"

Luke's head whipped to the camera, his eyes wide.

"Oh, fuck me," he said exasperatedly, making his way toward James.

"I knew you had a thing for redheads, bud!" James spoke boisterously.

I tried to hold back my amusement as I saw Luke bound toward James, snatch the phone from him, and center it on his aggravated, stubble-covered face, not yet looking at the screen.

"My phone has a password, Jay, how the hell did you get into it?"

I heard James cackling, saying, "Dude, your password was 1-2-3-4. Amp up your security! It's almost like you *wanted* me to get into it."

I let my laughter go. Seeing Luke so frustrated, it was impossible to hold it back any longer. He turned his face to me, and though the muscles in his jaw were still working as he clenched it in annoyance, his demeanor began to shift. His eyes squinted as he smiled softly.

"Hey, Babe."

I felt my face redden at the endearment, and Zoey made a loud gagging noise from two seat cushions over.

"Y'all nasty," she grumbled to herself.

"You've heard us having sex, and *this* you gag at?" I snapped back.

"Mhm," she retorted, muttering something about cheese that I didn't attempt to decipher.

At some point during her snippy reply, James was still talking in the background of our call, exclaiming, "*Oh*, so she's *Babe* now?!"

Luke winced and muttered, "Please ignore him."

His background shifted as he walked away from James, closing a door behind him. He took a few more steps and flopped down on what I assumed was his bed.

"It's nice to actually see your face," he said. "I didn't think about video chat."

"We've talked about you being technologically inept, yes?" I joked. "Speaking of—1-2-3-4, really? Change your damn password!"

He rubbed the back of his neck. "Yeah, yeah, obviously I will now. So, what are you up to today?"

"Erm...honestly, I have no idea. It's so quiet here, I think I'm going a little stir crazy."

Zoey silently exited the room, phone in hand. I hadn't heard it ring, but she lifted it to her ear and spoke a greeting into it casually.

"I know what you mean," Luke replied. "I think I've reached my James capacity."

"Oh, he doesn't seem that bad," I said, shrugging. "He didn't tell me too many embarrassing things about you."

Luke let out a single bark of a laugh. "Oh, no—I wouldn't be worried about that. I'm an open book; he can tell you whatever he wants."

I shoved my guilty conscience aside for the sake of the conversation and questioned, "So, what then?"

"James is...a *lot.*"

I chuckled. "He *does* seem like a big personality."

Zoey skipped into the room loudly and decided at that very moment to announce from behind me:

"We're going out, bitch! Get yourself together, we're out the door in an hour." She waved at the phone. "Hey, Luke—your brother still around?"

I tilted my phone so he could see her, and he waved at her in response, stating, "Ah, no. In the other room—"

Zoey shook her head. "All good. We'll meet one day; it's on the books, for sure."

"It is *not* on the books." I turned to reply to her and whispered, "You are *not* fucking Luke's brother." Luke stuttered a few *um's* and *ah's* in the background as I continued to talk to Zoey. "And where are we going out?"

"Dunno," she said, "Some place Liam suggested nearby, he was going to meet us there for a few drinks."

I could feel the tension radiating out of my phone, but pushed it out of my mind.

"Isn't Liam a ways away from us?" I remembered the town that he mentioned in which he had moved—Southport. It was upwards of an hour away. "What's he doing up here?"

"I, um," Zoey stammered, "I guess he's just heading home early? He's already on the road, catching a hotel nearby and driving the rest of the way tomorrow."

I felt my eyebrows raise. "Doesn't he love it here? Why's he leaving so soon?"

She muttered, "My thoughts exactly."

Her face twisted up for but a moment before she wiped the expression away, and though her reaction was a curiosity to me that I thoroughly wanted to question, now wasn't the time to do so. Instead, I nodded nonchalantly at her and waved her off so I could finish talking to Luke. She wiggled her fingers in a wave goodbye to me and walked her way out of the room just as quickly as she had come in.

"Going to see Liam, then?" Luke inquired with a clipped tone.

"Thought you were okay with Liam."

"Ah, *no.* He's up to his knees in STDs. It's disgusting."

I snorted. I didn't really *mean* to, but his analogy got to me. Luke narrowed his eyes, and I assumed that he didn't think it was an appropriate time for me to be tickled pink at his phrasing.

"I'm *sorry,*" I replied, "but *up to his knees in STDs?*"

His hardened exterior looked like it was cracking, but only barely, and he exhaled loudly, running a hand through his already messy hair.

"Why did Zoey have to make friends with the *only* guy that I have an issue with?"

"Still don't get your issue," I told him. "So, he's a little promiscuous—"

"He's a hoe, Claire."

"He's *nice.*"

"Nice?" Luke asked with a raised brow.

"Yes, Luke—*nice.* You would know that if you gave him the time of day."

He sighed heavily. "He hit on you a little too much for my taste, okay?"

I laughed a bitter laugh. "Jealousy does *not* become you." He rolled his eyes, and I stated, "Liam hasn't flirted with me in a *long* while, so whatever's going on in your head can just...go away, mmkay? And if you haven't noticed, I'm into *you,* not him—so your jealousy is unwarranted."

His nostrils flared as he breathed out through his nose, and an apologetic smile pulled up his lips. "I'll work on it."

"Okay," I responded, *"Thank you."*

"You're leaving in an hour?"

"Less, probably," I replied. "Knowing Zoey, she set a timer."

He laughed softly; his prior candor seemingly returned. "Well, I should probably let you go then."

I nodded. "I'll talk to you later."

Luke had a look in his eye that said he was about to drag out our goodbye as long as he possibly could. It was a habit of his and, in normal circumstances, I liked it. In this situation, however, I figured a loss of time wouldn't bode well for me.

"Yes, I'll be safe," I said, cutting him off. "Yes, I'll text later."

"Thank you," he murmured, "I miss you."

Brief argument aside, I still felt the emotion in turn—deeply. I looked back at him sheepishly.

"Miss you too, Babe." I returned his earlier endearment.

His smile showed almost every one of his teeth, and he said a quick adieu before ending the call.

***

Right on time, Zoey and I were in her car, preparing for the short drive to the bar that Liam had chosen. She reached to buckle her seatbelt, briefly locking eyes with me, and I couldn't help but notice the worried pinch around them. She diverted her gaze quickly.

"Any idea what's up with Liam heading home early?" I inquired.

Zoey looked at me once again as she shifted the car into drive, and she shrugged. It was clear that she was holding back, but in the traditional fashion that our friendship worked, I let her come to terms with that on her own. I just allowed us to listen to the general whirring of the wheels against the pavement as we drove.

"Actually," Zoey reconsidered her original terseness, "he seemed off."

"Oh?"

"Yeah...okay so we were texting before he called me, right?"

"Mhm."

"He just said he's skipping town early. And I asked him if everything was okay and he said, *'Not really.'*"

"Maybe," I began speaking, trying to make light of the situation, "he just decided that he's in love with you or something."

Zoey let out a very loud laugh. "Trust me, we're on the same page there. Neither of us *do* relationships." She paused, looking melancholy yet again, "Do you know why he moved here?"

I shook my head. "He never said."

"Lots of reasons that are his story to tell," she noted, "but mostly because his mom died."

"Oh."

"I dunno," Zoey shook her head. "I'm just worried. He, ah—his family's an absolute shit show. He doesn't *have* much, you know?"

I nodded. "Sounds familiar."

She looked at me for a beat. "Yeah," she replied. "It does."

The drive to the bar was short. The front of the building dimly lit, a single light was flickering outside as if too many bugs were ensnared within it. The outside walls were built to look as though the structure were a cabin of some sort. Long, wooden panels ran horizontal to the ground and all the way up to the shingles on the roof. There was nothing else that signified the name of the bar—only a sign that hung in a dark window that read *Open*. Upon entering through the front door, the faint smell of stale tobacco and nostalgia washed over me, and I was certain that I had been here before.

The bar was surprisingly sparse. The tables that lined the wall on the way to the counter were empty save for a few older gentlemen who appeared to be regulars. They sat in the seats in the far left corner, smiling as one of them told a tale with an alcohol-induced enthusiasm. The only other patron was a tanned, blonde-haired, troubled-looking man—Liam. He sat at the counter with his back to the entrance, slump-shouldered and swirling a glass of what looked to be at least two fingers of whiskey.

Zoey paused for a moment and muttered to herself a quiet, "Oh."

I didn't *know* Liam. I really didn't, but I *did* act as his bartender and friend for the last several months and Liam was *not* a hard liquor man. I had never—with the exception of the night that he attempted to flirt with Zoey—seen him drink whiskey straight. And I had *definitely* never seen him look so glum.

Zoey pointed toward him and hesitantly said, "I'm gonna, erm—"

"Yes, go, go," I ushered her. "I'll be over there."

I gestured to the opposite end of the wraparound bartop, just beyond where the regulars were seated, and Zoey thanked me silently with a quick glance. My intent was, of course, to give them some space. I didn't know Liam well enough to be barging in on a moment when he was in his feelings. The seat I chose, however, just so happened to give me a perfect view of their interaction. I was able to watch as he gave her a weak smile upon her approach. She sat, gesturing at his whiskey with a raised brow, and he shrugged.

I couldn't tell for sure, but it looked as though Zoey asked what was going on. Liam shook his head, drained half of his drink, and said one brief sentence. Zoey patted his arm in a consoling manner, and I could only make out her single spoken word, *'Sorry.'* I watched them, entranced, as Zoey got her own drink and they spoke quietly amongst themselves. I only managed to tear my gaze away from them when the bartender approached me.

She may have been in her mid-forties. Her long, black hair was peppered with strands of glistening white and looked as though it could have used a good washing about a week ago. Though she looked unkempt, when I met her eyes, they were full of a warmth that told me she most likely played the part of shrink along with bartender on a regular basis. The weathered look of her skin made me assume her to be a pack-a-day smoker, and I expected it to sound like her vocal cords were rubbed raw with sandpaper. I couldn't have been more wrong, though. Her voice poured out smooth like honey.

"What'll it be, sweetie?"

"Vodka soda, please," I responded.

"You know them?"

She asked me the question as she reached below the counter to scoop ice into a short glass.

"Oh, er," I hesitated, wondering if I was too blatant in my observing of Liam and Zoey from afar. "Yeah, that's my friend and her, um—they're both my friends."

She slid my drink to me, and as she glanced my way with an upward raise of her right brow, I commended myself for not telling her more. She had such a trusting face. Her mouth pulled up in a grin, making her look at least ten years younger. It made me wonder if she somehow already knew all of my secrets, and rather than feel the typical nervousness that came with that thought, I felt *relief.* I reached for my drink to keep myself from speaking to the woman who seemed to be a walking truth serum and took a long gulp. I welcomed the warmth that spread through my chest.

"Well," her Southern accent caressed the words, "your friends just bought that for you."

"Oh, er—thank you."

I looked in their direction and the blonde duo were both waving to catch my attention, smiling at me. Their tense moment clearly over, I nodded at the bartender in thanks and sidled my way over to them.

"Hey there!" Liam called out as I was taking a seat beside Zoey.

His mood seemed to have lifted considerably. In fact, he looked to be downright the opposite of what he appeared when we first arrived. His smile stretched so wide that his many freckles elongated across his cheeks. Zoey was all grins for a moment as well, until her expression fell completely as her eyes landed on a point that was situated directly behind me. I knew there was only one person who would evoke such a reaction from Zoey and it was, without a doubt, Colton.

"Claire?"

His surprised, whisper of a voice hit my ears and I flagged down the bartender as she walked past me with a rushed inquiry:

"Could I get a tequila, please?"

Chapter Ten

The bartender must have sensed the urgency in my request for tequila—it was the next thing that she did. The shot glass was pushed toward me in an instant, and I tipped it back. It was a generous pour. So generous that I had to gulp twice to finish it, and the deep burn made me sputter and cough.

"Claire?"

I desperately wished that I could just ignore him, and he would leave. That I could be swallowed up by the floor somehow, or turn back time to before Zoey said that we were going out and suggest *anything* that would have changed the current circumstances that I found myself in. I couldn't do that, though—and Colton was not going anywhere.

I managed to choke out, "Hey," decidedly keeping my eyes on the empty glass in my hand.

"Oh, hey man, you know Claire?" Liam stuck his hand out to shake Colton's. "I'm Li—"

Zoey shoved Liam's hand away, mumbling for him to read the room.

Colton touched a hand to my shoulder, spinning my stool around and forcing me to meet his vivid blue eyes.

"What are you doing here?" He asked.

"Holidays with Zoey's parents," I replied succinctly.

"Oh." He squinted as if that reply was unsatisfactory to him, and his voice lowered. "So, you're still in Virginia?"

I was hyperaware that his hand was still placed on my shoulder and when his fingers squeezed me gently, I swiped at his grip to shoo it away.

"Still living in Virginia? Yes." I replied once his hand was safely back in his pocket.

His gaze darted around nervously, and anyone that knew him would know that it wasn't because of my clear reluctance to this conversation. Colton was not a shy individual by any means. He wouldn't let some-one's feelings about an awkward conversation deter him from getting what he wanted—but, that being said, he was smart. At one point, I may have thought that the way he handled himself was brilliant. I supposed it *was* brilliant, in one way or another. These days, I would rather just call it manipulative and know that I couldn't trust Colton as far as I could throw him, but, hey—to each their own.

"I, um—look, I've been trying to call you," he stated.

I heard Liam whisper loudly to Zoey, "Should we be giving them some privacy, or—"

"No," she hissed back, "ex-boyfriend, *bad* ex-boyfriend."

"Oh—"

"I know you've been avoiding me," Colton said accusatorily.

"Ya *think?"* I retorted.

"Yeah, I do *think.* Why haven't you been picking up your phone?"

"Why would I answer your calls, Colt? I left for a reas—" I cut myself off, redirecting my response. "Actually, that doesn't matter. I haven't been answering your calls because I haven't been getting them, okay? I blocked you."

His head cocked to the side, face scrunched as he said, *"Seriously?"*

"Yeah," I replied quickly. "Of *course,* I did! It's not like I could pick up and start anew with you texting and calling me every five seconds."

"It wasn't every five seconds, but *whatever*. I really need to talk to you about something—"

Liam blurted out, "She's got a boyfriend, guy."

"Liam," Zoey scolded.

"What?" Liam glanced at her. "Is it a secret?"

"Didn't waste any time there, did you?" Colton asked disbelievingly.

"It's new—I, erm—does it even matter?" I stuttered. "I *did* leave you for a reason."

"Yeah, that *reason* is why I've been trying to call." His voice quieted to a murmur, and he leaned in closer to request, "Can we chat outside or something?"

Zoey and Liam both replied, "No," at the same time before I could even think of a response.

"What, do you have cheerleaders now?" Colton asked mockingly. "Zoey, good to see you again—"

"Fuck you," she sneered.

"And is this the guy you're currently fucking?"

I snapped, *"Colton—"* at the same time as Zoey began to retort:

"That's none of your goddamn busine—"

And Liam offhandedly noted with a shrug, "Actually, we're just friend—"

"Cool," Colton cut them both off without allowing them to finish. "Claire—*please*. Outside."

"Colt, I don't have any desire to talk to you, really—"

"Neither of us wants me to bring this up in here, Claire," he stated with a deeper voice.

I held back my groan, but only just. Of course, this meant that he wanted to speak to me about our collective past, and with how insistent he was being, I knew that he wasn't about to take no for an answer.

"We can probably just go, yeah?" Zoey interjected quickly, waving a hand at the bartender.

"Great," said Colton. "Zoey, be a peach and get the tab—Claire, a moment? Outside?"

I sighed loudly. "Fine."

Zoey rapidly murmured to me, "Claire, you don't have to—"

"Just," I met her eyes and saw the anxiety in them, so I softened my tone as I spoke, "meet me outside. Okay?"

She nodded, and Liam pushed himself away from the countertop roughly, his stool scooting across the floor with a grating noise.

"I'll go with you."

He said the words quietly and without flourish, and it made a corner of my mouth pull up. I didn't need protection from Colton by any means, but to receive the offer from someone who was an outsider to our situation was, well, nice. I snapshotted the moment in my brain, filing it away in a folder that resided deep in the recesses of my mind labeled *precious memories.*

Zoey patted him on the forearm.

"It's not like that," she told him reassuringly, digging within her wallet for a method of payment before looking at me. "Go."

I thanked her with a tight smile. As much as I appreciated Liam's gallant offer, I didn't need my past to be exposed to him.

Liam eyed Colton up and down, biting the inside of his cheek as if to stop himself from speaking. He sank back down into his seat, all the while whispering something to Zoey that was so quiet, I couldn't make out the words. She smirked at him, still digging through her purse for a credit card that she had clearly lost, and nodded emphatically.

Colton was already half way to the exit when he called my name out, breaking me from my reverie. When I gave him a smile that was not entirely genuine and made my way to where he waited for me, I saw him take a deep breath. His shoulders heaved with it, and upon his exhale, his forehead pinched together in a rarely seen concerned gesture.

It made my steps falter. My head cocked to the side as I began to approach him, and I squinted inquisitively.

"Colt?"

He opened the door to the exit and decidedly let his gaze fall to the floor.

"Outside, Claire."

I briskly walked to the left side of the patio. My feet patted along the concrete, and my hand skimmed along the wood that covered the siding of the bar. I stopped only when I thought that we would not be overheard and turned to face Colton. My arms crossed, and as I met his gaze, it almost looked like his eyes were pained.

Of everything that I concerned myself with regarding Colt—the life of crime, the manipulation, the list went on and on—the last thing that I ever worried about was him being...jeopardized. And the look that Colton gave me at this very moment looked to be exactly that. One glance in his direction, and I knew that it was either he was in deep shit, or someone had died and he needed to break the news to me. Either way, I felt my chest tighten in preparation for what he had to tell me.

"Jesus, Colt—what is it?"

"I need your help."

"With?"

"Ah—Travis."

"*What?!*"

I was well versed in the subject of Travis. He was always around when my mother was still amongst the public, bringing her various opiates to keep her *just* at the level of strung out that she was accustomed to. The last time that I had seen Travis was when Colton and I had begun to deal with him. It was *not* a time that I remembered fondly, and though I didn't have the best relationship with Colton, I had vehemently hoped that he had stopped involving himself with Travis.

Colton shushed me loudly, holding up an index finger to my face.

I swatted it away.

"You're still dealing with Travis, Colt? *Really?*"

His face twisted in remorse, and he ran a hand over his buzzed head.

"I *know,* okay?" He replied. "I know. I'm an idiot."

"You're not an idiot—"

"Yeah. I am."

"Okay fine, you are." I conceded with little persuasion. "Why do you think I fucking left, Colt?" I questioned him boldly. "We were already skating on thin ice with everything we did, but once we got involved with Travis, I was done. It wasn't fucking worth it."

I saw Liam and Zoey exiting from the front door out of the corner of my eye, and Colton noticed my shift in focus. He took a step closer to close the distance between us, clasping my left bicep with his hand. Only a few inches taller than me, he didn't have to lean down much to speak in my ear.

"I just need you to stay. Please, Claire...I need your help."

His voice was almost hoarse as he pleaded with me, and it sent me back to another time when he had asked me a very similar question.

The adrenaline was still rushing through me, and I wasn't certain whether I liked the feeling or not. It was the third time that we had teamed together for the day to thieve our way through a shopping center, and we were getting to be remarkably good at it.

We would plan our route days in advance, casing out the various locations to observe the higher risk areas that were heavily secured with cameras, and plan our course of attack. On the day of, one of us would divert the attention of those around us, while the other would quickly snag what we could. We stuck with small, easy to grab items. Colton became a master of distraction, and I would play as innocent as I could. It was simple, really.

"This is a lot easier with a partner," he muttered.

Night had fallen, and we had just finished emptying the last of our pockets and my purse into Colton's car. We sat in the front seats of his stationary car, him behind the wheel, when he stretched an arm out to rest his hand on the headrest behind me.

Colton was a confident individual. With what he did to make money, he had to be, but when I looked into his shockingly blue eyes at this moment, they were filled with what I could only describe as uncertainty, or maybe even shyness.

"We, ah...we make a good team, yeah?" He asked with a small smile. I nodded, returning his grin, and as he moved his hand to the space between my shoulder and my neck, I felt my blush creep up to my cheeks. He inquired hesitantly. "Would you stay?"

"Stay?"

His thumb brushed circles along the base of my neck, and the motion sent a shiver running down my spine. Colton was an attractive guy—there was no sense in denying it—and being so close to him while he looked at me with hope in his beautiful eyes made my stomach begin to somersault.

"Yeah," he continued. "Hang with me for a while...you know, get yourself out of debt. Split everything we get down the middle."

Silence hung between us, and his brow pinched as I thought of the gravity of what he offered. The quiet tension couldn't have even been cut with a knife, but it didn't last for long.

"Yes," I replied decisively. "I'd like that."

A beaming smile broke out on his face, and I gasped when he pulled me towards him by the neck. Our lips smashed together, and the tension that had been around us snapped. Our tongues tangled wildly for a moment, drawing out little moans from each of us until we both slowed, and our mouths parted from each other's.

The memory was probably the most wholesome one that I had with Colton, but I still thought back on it with disdain. Thankfully, I had grown over the years, but at the time I was...bitter. I thought that I deserved an easy way out of the hole that my mother had dug for me—life had kicked me around enough in the few years past, after all. It wasn't long after this moment that we graduated from shoplifting to occasional fraud, and from there, it was Colton's idea to begin working alongside Travis. I only withstood involving Travis and all that came with him twice, and after that, I decided to call it quits for good.

Colton knew the risks that came with Travis, but it seemed that the cons were finally starting to outweigh the pros. I felt a pang of sympathy for him at the memory that ran through my mind, and I wondered if the same thoughts flashed through his brain as well. It seemed to be so, as the realization of what he said that had spurred my memory in the first place appeared to have dawned on him. I heard him inhale, and his thumb ran circles along the back of my arm.

I took a large step away from him, pulling my arm from his grip.

"Right," he stated as if reminding himself, "boyfriend."

I exhaled loudly, his vulnerable state combined with the memory of our first kiss making me feel more or less compliant to whatever his request may be.

"What exactly do you need, Colt?" He shifted from foot to foot, as if unsure of how to broach the subject. I ventured to ask, "Should I be asking how *much* you need instead?"

Colton nodded meekly. "Uh huh."

"You owe him money?"

"Ah—I owe several people money," he replied, rubbing at the back of his neck now. "I just happen to owe Travis the most."

My arms hung limply at my sides.

"How much, Colt?"

"Fifty."

"Fifty?" I paused. "As in *thousand?*" He shrugged. "You owe *Travis* fifty thousand dollars?" He nodded, and I croaked, "You're going to get yourself killed."

Colton finally met my eyes, and his were shameful.

"Maybe not if you help me," he said.

"Colt, *no.* I can't, I—"

"Claire—"

"Nope," I replied, "Nuh-uh. Colt, you're in deep shit and I'm sorry—I *really* am—but you're gonna need to find a different way out of this."

His eyes darted across my face, most likely assessing how serious I was, and when he came to his conclusion on that matter, the emotion drained from his expression. It wasn't in a way that suggested he was devastated at my rebuttal, but more as if he was squaring his jaw and cracking his knuckles to prepare for a long, drawn-out fight that he didn't want to have.

"I can't, Claire," he told me. "And I don't have to."

A pit of nervousness bloomed in my gut.

"What the fuck is that supposed to mean, Colton?"

He said nothing in response, he only pulled out his phone and began to swipe through it. The faint blue glow from the screen lit up his features in an oddly sinister manner, and he tapped on the glass face until he found what he was looking for. He placed his phone in my hand without any further word, and when I saw what was on the screen, I inhaled sharply.

"You still have this?"

I tapped the screen to play the video. Sentences that were vaguely familiar came from a slightly younger version of myself, and my stomach twisted. The younger Claire was installing a card skimmer on a gas pump, smiling like she didn't have a care in the world.

I remembered the moment well. I was nearly half of the way through paying off my mother's debt, and Colton and I had been seeing each other officially for a few months. In the video, it was somewhere between late night and early morning, and there were no other people in sight. He held the camera as I went about my business, flirtatiously commenting things that ranged from, *'Oh yeah, just like that, baby,'* to, *'You're sexy when you're serious like that, you know?'* The younger Claire turned to playfully smack his chest, and just as Colton began to let out a boisterous laugh, the video cut off.

I still held the phone in my hand, staring at the frozen screen as if there was more to be seen, though I knew that there wasn't.

I finally spoke, "Why, ah—Colton, why do you still have this?"

I knew the answer, but I had to hear it from him. A lump had formed in my throat in anticipation of what he was bound to say, and I reached my hand forward to give him his phone back.

He took it from me and replied, "Like you said, I'm not fucking dumb."

"Insurance," I uttered under my breath, only just loud enough for him to hear. "That video wasn't just some...cute thing that you randomly filmed. You were getting *insurance* on the off chance that you needed to fucking roll over on me?"

I enunciated each word clearly, choosing each one with care. I wasn't sure how I managed that—my impending rage made it sound like a train was whooshing its way past my ears.

Colton held his hands out, palms facing toward me in a gesture of good will. I, clearly, did *not* take it as such.

"Claire, I don't have a choi—"

"You're fucking *blackmailing* me?!"

"Clai—"

My fist, as if moving independently from the rest of me, swung hard and connected with Colton's face, the sound of flesh on flesh ringing through the deserted parking lot.

A string of profanities left his mouth as he held his left cheek, but they were almost drowned out by the sound of Liam. He stood close to the entrance of the bar with Zoey, eyes alight with entertainment as he yelled:

"Hohohoooo, shit!"

The gravity of the situation was lost on him, obviously, and I couldn't hold that against him. I just redirected my attention to Colton as he stumbled for a step or two, touching his skin gingerly as if to ensure that nothing was broken. I ground my teeth together, wanting desperately to spit in his direction. Perhaps I would have if my attention wasn't shifted to something pulling at my wrist, and then the searing pain that followed.

"Ah, *ah, AH,*" I winced, pulling my arm away from the source of the pain. "Jesus, *fuck.*"

The source of the pain itself, Zoey, grabbed at my waist instead, pulling me away from Colton.

"You *will* tell me everything," she trilled off quickly as she dragged me in the opposite direction, "but for now, let's just get the fuck out of here."

"Claire!"

Colton called to me as Zoey pulled me away, and though I was pleased that it looked like the left side of his face may already have begun to swell, I still attempted to flip him the bird with my right hand.

The finger was immobile, and I was greeted with an additional sharp pain that shot all the way down to my elbow. I gasped, a pained moan escaping my throat.

Zoey tugged harder on my waist.

"You broke something punching him, you idiot," she chastised me. "Work with me here, come on."

I took my chance to use my left hand to raise my middle finger to Colton, and yelled a loud, "Fuck you!" Spit may have even sprayed from my lips with the velocity in which I cursed at him.

"Call me!" He shouted back.

"Like I have a *fucking choice!*"

I fought against Zoey's pull only twice more until she pounded at the space between my shoulder blades. "Use your legs. Walk. Away. Come *on.*"

We were mere steps from her car. When I could see the yellow tint of it in my peripheral vision, I relented in my fight and stomped toward it. I heard Zoey saying a quick goodbye to Liam, apologizing for the rapid end to the night, and she ran the last few steps to the driver's side of the car.

"Claire!" Liam called to me. I didn't respond aloud. I only looked toward him and offered an apologetic cringing smile, waving at him with my injured hand. He pointed to his own and yelled, "Ice your hand!"

I laughed sardonically at his final offer of a goodbye and slid my way into the passenger seat.

"You're gonna have to do a hell of a lot more than ice it," Zoey stated, sitting behind the wheel and gesturing for me to give her my hand. "Let me see."

She clicked on the overhead light, and we both groaned. Only moments after the impact, there were purple and red splotches all around the top of my hand, the base of my thumb, and down to my wrist. Zoey gingerly touched the bruised areas and when she tried to move my thumb, it was as if a hot iron was branding the area.

I shrieked, *"Ah!"*

"I *was* going to say that we could go back to my parents and raid their liquor cabinet, but, ah—doctor first, yeah?"

I slumped my head back on the headrest and replied, "Yeah."

My energy had depleted immensely. The shock of the events of the last hour left me drained, and I wished I could just...sleep. Maybe I could even dream—dream about *anything* other than the shit show that I was just thrust back into. Perhaps I could dream of Luke. The thought made a corner of my lip pull up, but only for what felt like a split second. I had no choice but to tell him everything now, and just the realization that I could no longer happily try to avoid the confrontation with him made me make a sound that could only be described as pained agony.

My eyes were shut tight, and I heard Zoey shift the car into drive.

"Are you going to tell me what the flying fuck happened back there or..."

Zoey allowed her question to trail off until I mustered the gumption to reply.

"Guess who Colton owes money to?"

"Ya know, I should have fucking broken his dick off when I had the chance," Zoey thought aloud as we sat on her bed, cross-legged and resting our backs against her headboard.

My arm was fully casted, two bones having been broken in my hand due to angrily—and incorrectly—throwing a punch. Zoey's parents were still awake when we arrived back, and they didn't *exactly* buy the story that I had broken my hand by tripping and trying to break my fall, but they were gracious enough to not question us any further.

"When, exactly, were you planning on ripping Colt's dick off?" I asked her monotonously.

"Probably after he took you on your first shoplifting spree," she said. "I dunno. I contemplated it a *lot*. He deserved it then and he deserves it *way* more now."

"Well, I did make that choice for myself in the beginning too...but yes. He deserves it."

My phone buzzed, and I angled my body to use my left hand to coax it out of my pocket. A metaphorical knife stabbed and twisted its way through my intestines when I saw that it was Luke.

10:24 P.M.: Hope you're having a good time. Miss you. Xoxo.

"What is it?" Zoey asked.

"Hmm?"

"You're moaning," she pointed out, "and not in the fun, sexy way."

"Ah," I waved my phone at her with my non-dominant hand. "Luke's texting."

"Not gonna say I told you so on this one, I think you've got enough shit going on without the guilt."

I sighed, my head falling back with a soft bang against the white wooden molding at the top of Zoey's bed.

"It's too late to avoid the guilt; it's already there," I told her.

I sent a quick response back to Luke, trying to err on the side of brevity.

10:25 P.M.: Just got back to the house. Miss you too. Xoxo.

"What are you gonna do, Claire?"

My phone pinged with an incoming message, and the preview of what Luke replied with made me groan.

10:26 P.M.: Oh, I figured you guys would be out way later. Have a good night?

I didn't even unlock my phone to mark the message as read. I couldn't yet.

"I have no fucking clue," I replied to her. "Colton's blackmailing me and I can't even *begin* to wrap my head around that. He needs *fifty grand, Zoey—fifty.*"

"Yeah, ya told me."

"You know how long it took us to get me out of debt for three times that?"

"One year and three months," Zoey replied quickly, and I glanced sideways at her with an eyebrow raised up high. "Give or take a few days," she noted. "You're not the only one that kept track. I know it wasn't the same for me, but that year tore me up too."

A bittersweet smile came to my lips, and I threw my casted arm over her shoulder.

"Love ya, too," I told her as I gave her a brief squeeze.

She nudged my ribs with her elbow and muttered, "Yeah, yeah."

"So, I suppose this would only take a third of the time to get the same amount of money if you do the math right—"

Zoey wriggled out from underneath my arm and twisted her entire body to face me, her green eyes wide.

"You aren't seriously considering helping Colton?"

"He's *blackmailing* me, Zoey—"

"Uh, yeah. I'm aware."

"I'd go to *jail* if he turned that video in. Oh my God—"

A thought came to mind that chilled me through, and I sat bolt upright.

"What?" Zoey asked.

Naturally, I knew the jail sentence that one would get for any of the crimes that Colton and I committed. Shoplifting, if over $1,000, could get me up to two years—and we *always* were well over the $1,000 limit to cross over into a felony. Credit card fraud was what we graduated to and, by default, identity theft. That could grant me up to six and a half years in prison and was my current threat as this was what Colton had proof of. From there, with the help of Travis, we moved into drug trafficking. Considering that the drugs we moved were opiates, and the amount that we moved was rather large, I could be locked away for upwards of nineteen years.

This was unsettling in itself, but what was worse was that Colton had evidence of *everything*. He always had little videos—snippets of our life were what I thought they were...and perhaps that's what they really were at the time. Now, however, they served a greater purpose—insurance, as I had called it earlier in the night. I attempted to do the math regarding my potential jail time if I were sentenced for everything I had done, and my head reeled. Multiple counts of this and multiple counts of that rang through my mind, and I suddenly felt as though my chest were rather tight.

It would be a life wasted. I would be old and grey before I was released from prison, if I was to ever be released at all.

"Claire, *what?*" Zoey persisted.

"I—Zoey, this is bad," I stammered, realization finally settling in my bones.

"Yeah, I know—"

"Jail, Zoey," I replied once more. "Like—my life is *gone* jail." I clasped at my chest and breathed loudly in and out, in and out. "If Colt's got proof of it all—and he does—it would be my *life.* And then it's fuck leaving for Salem and fuck having a free life and fuck Luke—*fuck. Luke.*"

"Okay, Claire—" Zoey set a single, dainty palm on my left shoulder. "Breathe, girl. Breathe."

"You can't just tell me to fucking *breathe*, Zoey, that's not how it works—"

"I know, I know, I'm sorry, I—I know it's bad, okay? I know...but you've always landed on your feet. You'll get through this too." I nodded, my breaths evening out after a moment, and Zoey continued, "But you *can't* help him, Claire. What are you going to do, stay here for months on end until he's good to go and then...what...come back home to Virginia?"

"I'm not sure I exactly have a choice—"

"What about your new life? Luke?"

As if on cue, my phone buzzed in my palm to remind me that I had an unopened message from the aforementioned bartender who had started to consume more and more of my life.

"Well...that's kinda shot to hell now, isn't it?" I replied bitterly. "Honestly, I don't even see the point of going back to Salem right now—what am I gonna do, show up and say, *'Hello darling, few things to catch you up on—I used to be a thief so I could pay off the crippling debt that my heroin-addicted mother left me. Oh, and I used to do said thieving with my ex, Colton. OH, and speaking of Colton—he's blackmailing me and if I don't help him, I may go to prison for a lengthy period of my life. So...bye-bye, I guess!'"*

Zoey stared at me, chewing on the side of her cheek. "I mean, you could do it a little less harshly—"

"Oh, *now* you want me to sugar coat my life!" I exclaimed. "Great! That makes total sense."

"I was *joking*, for what it's worth," she muttered.

"Great time for a joke, Zoey." I pointed at my chest with my casted hand dramatically. "My life is in peril."

"I—" Zoey paused. "Your life isn't in peril."

"Fuck if it isn't—"

"Colton turning in whatever videos or evidence or what-not of you incriminates him just as much, no?"

Her brows were peaked up high as if she wasn't believing her own genius.

"I...guess it would, actually," I replied.

Zoey clapped her hands loudly, as if in celebration.

"So, unless Colton's some masochistic fuck that just wants to go to jail then...you're off scot-free, right?"

"He's not a masochistic fuck, but," Zoey began to clap once more and I cut her off with the remainder of my reply, "jail is...probably better for him than facing Travis."

Her clapping ceased, and her hands dropped back to her lap.

"Oh."

"Colton's got three options: jail by turning us both in, paying off Travis by blackmailing me, or death via Travis." I hesitated before deducing aloud, "He'll turn us both in if I don't help him, Zoey. He doesn't have a choice."

Zoey cursed under her breath, and I allowed her to gather her thoughts as I metaphorically faced the music by messaging Luke back.

Claire 10:35 P.M.: Night went to hell, actually.

Luke 10:35 P.M.: Uh oh. Should I ask?

Claire 10:36 P.M.: Ran into Colton.

Luke 10:36 P.M.: Okay?

Claire 10:38 P.M.: I may need to stay here for a while.

Luke 10:38 P.M.: How long is a while?

Tears bit at my eyes. I had no idea how long I would need to be dealing with Colton's situation, and that's what made this so much harder. I had no real answers for anything, and to make matters worse, I couldn't tell Luke about any of it. Not like this, anyway—if I were smarter, I would have told him far earlier about my entire past. I knew that. But it was too late now.

My phone began to buzz, and an incoming call from Luke flashed on the screen.

"Fuck," I cursed aloud.

"Luke?" Zoey asked.

"Yeah, I told him I may need to stay here a while—"

"Fuck if you do." She rattled off as quickly as she could, "Tell Colton he can wait for you to rearrange your entire fucking life before you come back to help him. I don't give a shit what he says or how much he bitches; if he knows you're coming back then he won't turn you both in." The buzzing continued, a loud protrusion into Zoey's monologue. "You're coming home with me—tomorrow—and you'll take a few breaths before you decide your plan. Okay?" I nodded, and Zoey snapped, *"Okay?"* as if I hadn't responded to the best of my ability.

"Yes," I replied hoarsely, patting her wrist with my hand. "Okay."

Her eyes, which had seemed relatively crazed for but a moment, softened, and she whispered, "Thank you. Now answer your damn phone."

I slid my finger across the green arrow on my screen to answer the call and held the phone up to my ear.

"Hello?" My throat was scratchy from my impending tears, and it was apparent in my voice.

"Hey," Luke replied in as consoling a manner as he could. "What's going on, you have to stay for a few more days?"

I quickly pulled the speaker away from my mouth to hide the single sob that escaped my mouth.

"Ah, no—no, I'll be back tomorrow."

"Have you been crying? What—you ran into Colton?"

"Yeah, it's um...it's a long story, honestly—"

"Well, I have loads of time." The line went silent with the exception of my now sniffling nose and Luke's labored breathing until he ushered me yet again, "Claire?"

"When will you be home?"

"Ah," he stammered, "I, er—whenever, I'm not that far. Look, I don't want to be that way but you're...kinda freaking me out."

"Don't—" I couldn't say, *'Don't freak out.'* I couldn't. After all, this was a totally freak-out-worthy conversation that I needed to have with him...and I didn't know what would come of it. "Can we just meet up tomorrow?" I spoke quietly. "Your place, whenever?"

"Yeah." His voice had dipped low, and his insistence had halted. "I'll let you know when I'm back.

Chapter Eleven

W hen I reached Luke's apartment around nightfall, his door was unlocked as it usually was when he was expecting me to come by. I found him sitting on a barstool at his kitchen counter, contemplatively swirling a tumbler filled to the brim with amber liquid, and my steps faltered. He was rather disheveled, donning sweatpants and a t-shirt, though that wasn't what spurred my hesitation. It was his expression and the way he held himself that caught me off guard.

He was focused on his glass as the whiskey swirled, even when the door closed loudly behind me. He took a sip and outwardly appeared to look at the liquid thoughtfully, as if it were an entirely new taste for him. His eyes, however, showed that his mind was elsewhere. He was distant, his sharp jaw arched away from my direction as if he were leaning away from an intrusion, and his gaze was tired.

I had planned on greeting him with a cheery, *'Hello,'* but the moment that I saw him, it seemed inappropriate. It set me on edge, and I stood in his entryway shifting from foot to foot. I spoke first, gaining the courage to walk over to where he sat.

"Hey."

He nodded, only slightly glancing in my direction. If I hadn't been watching him so carefully, I would have missed the slightest of a smile that graced his lips.

"Hi."

We hadn't spoken since the night before when I was beginning to cry from the stress of my life as I now knew it. The lack of communication from him combined with his icy coolness sent a longing through me that wrenched at my chest. I stood next to where he sat, an arms-reach away, and my fingers itched with the desire to touch his stubbled jaw. To cradle his exhausted looking face in my palms and kiss him gently. To not feel...*this*. But I couldn't do that. Not only because it would distract me from the conversation that we so desperately needed to have, but it also seemed that Luke was in no mood to be coddled.

"You seem stressed," I almost whispered.

He set his glass down against the marble carefully, and finally allowed his eyes to lay upon mine. When grey met blue, his shoulders visibly sagged as he exhaled a breath. His brow knit together as if he was preparing to say something long winded.

"You're the one that gave me the dreaded, *'We need to talk,'* line last night," Luke said, his voice quiet.

"I didn't say it exactly like that," I corrected him as casually as I could, giving him a weak grin. "It was more like—"

"Did you fuck Colton?"

Whoa.

The way he asked the question was as if he were spitting out in intrusive thought. A bitter one that left a horrible taste in his mouth. A *nagging* one that just wouldn't let him be. And just like that, his coldness towards me was blatantly obvious.

"What?"

"You ran into your ex at the bar, you're there for a few hours, you tell me that you may not be coming home for a while after you ran into him, and then I call you because," Luke took a breath, anxiety rather than anger etching the corners of his eyes, "because I was *worried.*"

"Luke—"

"And don't get me wrong," he continued, desperate to get out whatever thoughts he had, "I know we never talked about, like, boundaries or any-thing—I mean I never even said I wanted you to be my girlfriend, but that phrase makes it sound like we're five-year-olds and I hate it and I'm sorry, but I *do* want that kind of relationship—" His words were beginning to blur together, and I could feel the nervousness coming off of him in waves. I wanted to interrupt, to tell him that he had absolutely nothing to worry about in that category, but I couldn't bear cutting him off when he needed to air his own concerns. *"Please* tell me you didn't, Claire." His light eyes begged me. "Please tell me that my gut instinct is fucking *wrong,* and I can just apologize for being an asshole and thinking it in the first place."

I did what I so wanted to do before and touched his cheek with my non-casted hand, stroking his five-o-clock shadow that was akin to sand-paper. He leaned into it, his eyes fluttering closed.

"I would never do that to you," I told him. "And for the record, I *also* want that type of relationship—we *do* have that type of relationship."

He exhaled a loud, *"Ah,"* and twisted his face to plant a kiss on my palm. "I, um," Luke paused, and I could feel his smile growing against my hand, "that was dramatic. I'm...embarrassed...and sorry."

"I didn't exactly give you much to ease your worries, did I?" I asked, our text messages and phone call from the night before replaying in my mind.

Luke shook his head, reaching for my right hand and beginning to say, "That's okay, I..." His reply was cut short when he realized that my hand was covered in plaster. "Claire, what did you do?"

"Ah—Colton," I clarified, pressing my lips together in a thin line.

Luke nodded slowly. "I thought that you slept with him and instead..."

"I decked him across the face."

"Oh."

"There's a *long* story to it, I promise," I said.

"Didn't take you for one to resort to violence," he replied with an arched brow, his humor seemingly intact.

"Ah, I'm not—like I said—long story."

"Is it—"

"Broken?" I finished his question for him as he traced the edges of my cast as if to test if it were real. "Very much so."

His expression had morphed into one of amused sympathy, and he sagged his head into my shoulder, wrapping both of his arms around my waist.

I hugged him back, both of my arms thrown over his neck, and I heard him mumble another apology into my hair. I shook my head, pulling back to tell him that an apology wasn't necessary, and when I did, he captured his lips with mine.

We moved slowly against each other, savoring the moment after a week's distance and our brief confrontation. His hands had danced their way under the hem of my sweatshirt and planted on the skin of my back as we shared sweet, soft kisses. It was when he pulled me closer to him, shifting his legs apart so I could stand between them, that he opened his mouth to glide his tongue against mine.

I moaned quietly, and his fingertips flexed against my bare back. I wanted nothing more than to sink against him, fold into his embrace, and give myself to him fully in this very moment, but I couldn't. Not in good conscience, anyway. I pulled my lips away from him, forcing him to emit a whimper that nearly melted my soul.

"We really do need to talk," I muttered.

He sighed, peppering kisses along my cheek and down to my jaw, and finally pulled away.

"Okay," he spoke so softly that I had to read his lips to make out the word. "Whiskey?"

I nodded, pleased with the thought of a *very* strong liquor, and with that, he was up and around his bar top to prepare my drink. It wasn't long before we both sat at the counter on our own stools, our own drinks in hand. I took a tentative sip of the whiskey, hoping that the feel of it burning my esophagus would somehow give me courage.

It didn't.

"Is it my turn to tell you that you look nervous?" Luke asked me. "Because you do."

I chuckled out of sheer anxiety and brought my glass to my lips once more.

"I don't really know where to start," I muttered.

"From the beginning?" He suggested softly.

"Okay," I replied. "Um...Colton and I have a weird history—er—okay, no, I should back up further." Luke brushed his hand against the top of my thigh, squeezing gently in a gesture of comfort. He remained silent, allowing me to say whatever came to my mind. I took a deep breath and decided, as he said, to truly start from the beginning. "My mother is an addict," I said bluntly.

His free hand drifted away from the drink that he had set on the counter and landed atop my other thigh, his fingers tracing the sides of my legs. His expression was thoughtful, but he said nothing. He just nodded; his gaze taught with the anticipation of an upcoming blow.

"I, er—I told you she went to jail for tax fraud. She did. It was just...it was a *lot* more than that. I—I turned her in."

"Oh."

"She had stolen from me—"

"How much?"

I glanced at him, thinking, *'Do you really want to know?'* and his fingertips squeezed the sides of my legs yet again in a comforting manner.

"One hundred and fifty thousand dollars," I told him. "Give or take."

His jaw fell slack, and though he brought a single hand to his glass to sip at his whiskey again, it still seemed that his mouth was dry.

"Ah—how?" He inquired. "I...it's not like you had that much money, right?"

"Technically, it was identity theft," I replied. "I guess that would be the exact term for it—but from skimming my accounts, which she had control of, to taking out credit cards in my name and maxing them out...it just all added up." More hesitant glances of sympathetic understanding were all I received, and I continued. "It took a few years, but I eventually figured out something that she could be charged on and turned her in. That's...about it for my mom, I think. I haven't seen her in years and I don't know—it's not on my mind. That's around when Colt found me, though."

"Found you?" Luke asked, and his body tensed.

"Not as dramatic as it sounds, I promise," I reassured him with a smile that most certainly did not reach my eyes. "I was crying outside of a grocery store, and he just...found me. Right time, right place, I guess? I told him everything because—what the hell else did I have to lose, right?" I paused, awaiting some sort of response. When I was met with nothing but expectant eyes, I stated, "I needed money, and he had ways of making it that—"

"If you tell me that he made you—"

"He didn't *make me* do anything," I corrected Luke quickly. "I could've been coerced because of the situation I was in, but—but Colt never forced me to do anything until—"

"*Until?*"

"Now." I finished my sentence. "Until now."

Luke's words caught in his throat, and a noise sounded from him that was more akin to a growl than anything.

"He's blackmailing me," I confirmed.

Luke promptly grabbed his glass and drained his whiskey, and I decided that it was about time for me to do the same. Fire lined my intestines, but it was for the best.

"For?" Luke inquired.

"Fifty."

"Fifty?" He asked. "Fifty, *what?"*

I breathed in through my nose and out through my mouth, speaking on my exhale, "Thousand."

"Dollars?" He clarified with alarmingly open eyes.

I nodded, and an odd giggle erupted from him—it held a dash of contempt to it that perfectly depicted the disbelief in his expression.

"Who just...has fifty thousand dollars laying around?" He asked in a rhetorical question. "Neither of us do, obviously—what's he expecting?"

"He just...wants me."

"You?" Luke snapped as if the option weren't possible.

"We made a good team—"

He removed the hand that remained on my thigh and stood abruptly, pacing here and there around his kitchen. He finally stood beside his fridge, pinching his nose in frustration.

"And he's suggesting what—that you go back to help him get money by..."

"Shoplifting," I responded. "Credit card fraud. Old specialties of ours."

He looked me up and down, hands falling to rest in the pockets of his sweatpants, and he leaned his shoulder against the refrigerator door.

He muttered, "Would never be able to picture you like that."

"Why do you think we did so well?" I returned. "I'm not exactly suspect number one."

"You paid off *all* your debt by doing that?" He asked quietly, and I nodded. Luke sighed, looking especially tired with the light purple circles that were beginning to show under his eyes. "And he has proof of—"

"Everything," I replied quickly. "I *know* he has everything. It's *bad,* Luke—I'd go to jail for a *long* time."

He ran a hand through his hair, leaving it remarkably disheveled. It oddly matched his eyes that had turned from exhausted to wild.

"What, ah," he blinked several times in a row, leaving his hand gripped just above his forehead, "what's your plan here?"

"Not sure if I have one yet," I returned. "Was going to just stay in North Carolina and Zoey convinced me otherwise."

"Remind me to get her chocolates or something," Luke said offhandedly, rocking back and forth on his heels. "That would have been a particularly painful phone call."

He kept his distance, and I wasn't sure what to make of the way he was holding himself now. He seemed...careful. It was as if he wasn't sure what would be appropriate at this moment.

I wondered if this was the breakup that I was anticipating. Would he say something along the lines of, *'Well, I guess this is goodbye?'* and usher me out the door? The thought shredded me, but because it was only a thought, I simply shook my head in an attempt to erase it.

"I *do* have to go back," I whispered.

He snapped, "Fuck that."

"I don't exactly have a choice, Luke—"

"No," he moved his head from side to side. "Fuck that, and *fuck* Colton, by the way." His face pinched together in disgust. "You finally get a chance to live a normal life, and he does *this?*"

"I'm his best choice."

Luke held up a hand to stop me, saying, "Don't defend him after everything he's done—"

"I'm not," I reassured him, holding up my casted hand in further proof. *"Trust me,* I'm not."

"I..." Luke looked around his apartment and up to the ceiling as if it would give him some sort of divine sign. "I don't really know what to say here, Claire."

His beautiful face still held a tinge of disappointment, and it half way broke me. My throat tightened, and I looked to the floor because I couldn't bear continuing to see his expression contorted in such a way toward me.

I managed to choke out, "I understand if you see me differently now."

There was a pause—a long one. It held a tension to it that made me stand stock still, and I held my breath to hear any sort of response from him...but there was none, and I eventually had to inhale shakily once more. With that noise cutting the air between us, Luke finally spoke.

"I do." His voice was soft. It was as if he didn't want to admit it, doing so reluctantly out of courtesy to me—to what we had. I cleared my throat, not wanting him to see my impending tears. "Of course, I do, Claire," he continued. "How could I *not?* Look at me."

His order made my first sob break through.

"I can't," I told him, my tears obscuring my vision. "I can't look at you. I don't want to see you look at me like that."

"Like what?" He asked quietly. "Look at me, Claire, *please.*"

It was when his voice cracked on the last word that I finally forced myself to look at him. He held my gaze as he walked around his countertop and back to me. His light eyes narrowed at me sympathetically, his head tilting to the side as he sat on his stool next to me.

"I don't want your pity," I whimpered quietly.

Luke shook his head.

"It's not pity. I just...see you."

"I don't know what that *means*," I cried.

"We felt like a fairy tale at first, you know?"

Despite my tears, I snorted, "Yeah, I certainly made sure to ruin that—"

"Fairy tales aren't real, though." He breathed deeply, looking at me in what I could only describe as morbid bemusement, and exhaled heavily. "You. Are a mess." I began to whisper some sort of muddled apology back, but he interrupted me quickly. "Shut up, Claire." He chuckled, tentatively raising a hand to move a lock of my hair behind my left ear. He left his grasp on the base of my neck, and I felt its comfort like none other. He continued, reiterating, "You're messy—and I don't want you to be sorry for it. You just *are*. You're stubborn, flighty when it comes to conflict, and you have a past that I don't think I'll *ever* fully understand but...all of that makes me want you *more.*"

Though my heart went pitter-patter and it seemed briefly that I may have been having an out of body experience, my mind still screamed at me in the worst way possible.

"How could you say that?" I repeated my mind's words aloud.

"You've been dealt a shitty hand at life...but all I know and all I've seen is that you're still standing. You don't just give up, and you try to make the right choice for yourself. Not, ah—not always the *best* choices." I couldn't help but laugh sardonically at that, and Luke grinned, hesitant as it may have been. "You're just...you're strong as hell," he stated, moving his right hand to mimic his left, and cradling my face upward to look at him. "I *love* you. So goddamn much."

I didn't get a chance to respond because his lips were on mine. His words were expressed in the ferocity of his kiss, and I moaned. My reaction wasn't entirely out of pleasure. Though his admission was truly everything

I could have asked for, and it caused a joy to swell throughout the pits of my stomach, it felt impossible. This *situation* felt impossible. The feeling was mutual, and I loved him deeply, but to give in to this chasm of happiness could swallow me whole. I couldn't allow it—not when I knew that I had to go back to my old home. Not when it was unclear when I would be able to return to Salem. For the time being, I had to leave this life behind.

My arms had snaked their way around Luke's neck instinctively, but I moved to settle my hands on his shoulders, pushing him away gently.

"Stop."

The word came out in a hoarse cry. Luke pulled away, holding me by the waist with concern etched across his face as he looked me over. I couldn't hold back my grief any longer, and my cry turned into wracking sobs.

"Claire, no, shhh—it's going to be okay—"

"No," I whined. "No, it's not. I," my lungs interrupted me as my chest heaved, "love you," another gasp, "too." I breathed in and out a few times as slowly as I could. "And I have to leave."

I lost it again on the last word and Luke, who had given me a pained smile for just a moment, was now trying to pull my hands away from my face.

"Claire—I know—I *know* you have to go." He finally wrenched my hands away, and he held them both in his own. "Baby," he tried to assuage me, but it only made me wail louder. "I can't let you go alone."

That did it. That sentence shut me up—and fast. The dry heaves still remained, but other than that, there was a pensive silence between the two of us as I took in the determined look on his face. His eyes were steely stone, and he finally released my hands.

"Okay?" He asked quietly. "I'm going with you."

"Luke, I—" I stammered. *"No—"*

"Did you think I'd let you just go back by yourself? I—"

"I didn't just mean I was leaving Virginia," I sputtered.

"Claire—"

"I meant I'm leaving *you.*"

The breath left his lungs, the scent of Luke and whiskey dancing into my nostrils.

"No, no-no," he groaned.

The sadness in his voice stabbed at me, but I couldn't stop there. I had to push forward.

"I can't let you come with me."

"Yes, you *can.*"

"I *can't,* Luke—"

"Well, why the *fuck* not?!" Luke hissed.

"Because," I replied, "you're too goddamn important."

"I'm *important?"* He repeated back to me, tapping at his chest with his index finger with a thump. *"I'm* important? Claire—"

"What are you going to say, Luke?" I asked him, my voice hoarse. "That you love me again? Because that shit was hard enough. I'm not dragging you through this shit show—"

"You wouldn't be *dragging* me, Claire—I *want* to go, I *want* to help you."

"And I won't *let* you," I told him with a tone of finality. "I can't. I *won't.*"

He looked me up and down slowly, his arms hanging by his sides, his shoulders weighed down as if in defeat as he took in my tone of voice.

"It won't matter what I say, will it?" He questioned me quietly.

I shook my head and whispered, "No."

He pulled me against him, his arms wrapped around my waist, nearly crushing me. Though he was larger than me in stature, the way he held me made him feel fragile somehow. His body curled around mine, shoulders hunched and shaking softly from every uneasy breath he took.

"Stay here tonight," he spoke against my hair.

"Luke—"

"Please." He kissed my temple, then brushed my hair away to reach my cheek and touched his lips to me gently. *"Please."* His mouth drifted to mine, and I noticed that it was damp with tears. The realization made me reach upwards to wipe at them, but there was no use for that. He blinked quickly and the droplets flecked off of his lashes, spraying my face. "Please stay." he requested again in a rough voice.

The tormented look on his face perfectly matched how I felt inside, and I caved. I couldn't help it. This entire conversation had left us both turned inside out and gutted, and we deserved a little slice of happiness—even if only for a little while.

"Okay."

I could barely whisper out my response. Luke attacked me with a passion that rivaled the first night we were together, and I stumbled backward with him away from his kitchen. I buried my hands in his hair, pulling his face to mine. He groaned a strained garble of my name against my mouth and my insides tightened. Our tongues glided against each other's at a quickening pace, the saltiness from our respective tears coating the inside of my mouth in an oddly erotic taste.

He spun me around, a hand cradling my jaw so he could kiss the side of my face down to the back of my neck as he walked me forward. We both stepped languidly toward his bedroom and as we reached the foot of his bed, we sank down together. I pulled my top overhead, tossing it aside. Luke had made quick way of his t-shirt, and he was back behind me in an instant, lowering us both to lay on the mattress as he kissed across my shoulders. His lips trailed down my ribs, back up to between my shoulder blades, and finally to the nape of my neck. He held me tight, the arm trapped beneath me wrapped around my chest and the other splayed across my lower abdomen. His hips flexed, and though I was wearing jeans,

I could feel him hard against me, straining through the material of his sweatpants.

We moaned simultaneously, and I turned my head to the side to capture his mouth with mine once more. Our kisses were slower now. Lazier. With every brush of our tongues together, Luke's erection was pressed into me from behind. I unbuttoned the top of my jeans, pulling the zipper down, and his hand wandered underneath the fabric of my panties, cupping me softly.

"You're wet already," he spoke in a gravelly voice against my ear as he moved his fingers in a circular motion. "Is this for me?"

I hummed, *"Mhm,"* and my breath hitched in my throat as he nipped at my earlobe. He ground himself against me, his fingers moving in the same rhythm as his hips, and he nuzzled my face to urge me to kiss him once more. We continued at this pace, slowly grinding as our tongues mimicked the motion of our lower halves. He slid a finger inside of me, and I moaned against him.

"Oh, *God.*"

His finger moved in and out, my nerve endings aflame. I could feel myself tightening around him with every stroke. My back arched, and I clenched my eyes tight as Luke moved his lips to the back of my neck, sinking his teeth into my shoulder briefly.

I cried out, *"Ah!"*

"Are you going to come on my hand, Claire?" He asked with a guttural groan, slipping a second finger inside of me.

"Fuck."

His movements slowed to a crawl, and he directed me, "Open your eyes, baby—look at me."

I obeyed, locking onto his dark, stormy gaze for but a moment, and he quickened his pace. The sensation of an ache deep inside me made my head roll to the side once more, my eyes drifting closed, and Luke slowed again to a stop.

"What are you—"

"Don't look away from me," he said, his breath coming out in quick gusts. "I want to watch you come. Let me see you."

I nodded, my chest heaving, and his relentless pace continued. I moaned loudly, never taking my eyes off his.

"Just like that," he breathed.

"Yes."

"You want more?"

"*Yes.*"

I begged, my voice a high-pitched whine, and he responded to my plea. His forearm flexed as he moved quicker; the way his palm brushed against my clitoris about to send me into insanity.

He watched me intently, breaking his gaze only to glance down at what was descending me into madness. I squirmed, my release imminent, and my legs began to shake.

"That's it," he cajoled. I called his name in a breathy cry, and he ushered me, "Let go. Come for me, beautiful."

I erupted, an almost pained groan coming from deep inside of me. Luke's eyes went wide, taking in my expression with his mouth agape, drinking it in as he watched me ride out an explosive orgasm. He waited until my body ceased its convulsions and removed his fingers, bringing his hand to the waistband of my jeans to pull them down. I kicked myself free of the fabric, and as I lay naked, Luke pulled his legs from his pants. He kneeled before me, pumping his erection with his fist a few times, slowly, until he moved to lay behind me again, his thick length resting between my legs.

My body had turned to jelly, but that wouldn't have stopped me from instinctively and eagerly bowing my backside into him. As he slid inside of me, an aftershock ran through my body, and I felt myself squeeze around him.

He hissed through his teeth, *"Fuck,"* and planted a hand between my shoulder blades as if to steady himself.

Once he was buried within me, I moaned. It was an exquisite tightness to have him behind me. If I hadn't come once already, the sensation may have been too much. Luke kissed gently at the space between my jaw and my neck and began to move at an excruciatingly slow pace.

"Come here," he murmured, rubbing the spot that he had kissed with his nose.

I obliged, understanding his nuzzling as a plea to kiss him once more. We continued the same motions as we had earlier, the only difference being that his fingers were replaced with his cock. Our tongues at the same speed as the rest of us, we ground lazily against and into each other. Though slow, the intensity of our emotions and longing gazes into each other's eyes built us both up. It wasn't long before I was writhing once more, and Luke's breath had increased to a rapid pant. His tempo remained the same, and I begged him for more.

"Faster."

He hummed a noise that most definitely meant, *'No,'* and I whined an incomprehensible muddle of words.

"I don't want to stop yet," he groaned, pulling me tight against him as he buried his head in my shoulders. *"Fuck."*

My body exhausted, I pleaded with him again and again to no avail. He kept me teetering on the edge of oblivion until we had both developed a thin sheet of sweat on our bodies.

"Luke, *please.*"

"Not," he gasped, "yet."

It was then that I realized that there was a possibility that he had been desperately trying to extend one of our last intimate moments together, and my chest ached terribly. I twisted again to take his mouth in mine, and he whimpered against my lips.

"Luke," I begged between kisses, *"Baby,* please."

He murmured my name back to me and finally grazed his hand along my waist and down my stomach to where our bodies were intertwined. His fingers placed a steady pressure to my clit, and he let out a long, deep, *"Oh,"* as he thrust into me harder.

"Oh. *My. God."*

I cried at each flex of his hips, my voice now a squeal that cut through the thick, moist air like a sharp knife. His fingers circled around and around, and all the muscles in my body tensed. He felt me and quickened to an unsteady, desperate rhythm.

"Yes," he spoke as if it were a plea. "Claire, *fuck."*

I screamed, screwing my face tight as I came with a force I didn't know possible. Luke was quick to follow, moaning loudly and unashamedly into my hair.

And then we were quiet. Silent. Luke brushed his fingertips along my upper arm for a while, and I eventually slid my lower half away from him just enough to free him from me. He clasped at the area he was tracing to still me.

"Don't," he muttered. "Don't move; stay here."

I twisted around to face him and kissed his nose lightly.

"Bathroom," I replied. "I'll be right back."

His expression relaxed, and his eyes fluttered closed as he nodded.

I took my time, wondering how long I should allow my façade of contentment to last. I had decided to leave him for his own good, and the pain of that would only fully settle in once I closed his apartment door behind me. I couldn't give it up yet, knowing how peaceful his arms would feel wrapping around me if I went back to his bed.

When I returned, he had dressed himself in a navy pair of his boxers. He smiled softly at me as I found myself a matching pair and one of his t-shirts in a dresser drawer. I pulled them both on and crawled across the mattress to lay beside him. He greeted me with open arms and kissed my forehead as I laid upon the pillow.

I don't think I could have slept a wink. I hadn't planned to—I only wanted to lay with Luke for a while. I would take his clothing that I dressed myself in as a memento to our last goodbye and stroll out the door once he drifted off—that was the itinerary. After that, I assumed I would mostly cry and pack my things to immediately go back to North Carolina. There was no use in staying here while I carved out my next plan with Colton. That, I could do in a motel room that I would call my home for the next indefinite amount of time.

Every minute that passed as I rested beside him made it infinitely harder to leave. Luke had long fallen asleep, his soft breaths wisping across my face. His grip on me had softened, his arms limp. Normally, I would have turned around by now, fixing his grasp around my waist, and drifted off peacefully. Instead, I just waited, and as the hours passed, the pain clenched further in my chest. Our brief relationship replayed in my head along with the night we just had, and when the tears began to spring to my eyes, I decided that there was no time like the present for me to make my silent adieu.

Luke didn't stir when I left his bed, and only half of me wished that he would. I longed to give him a last, *'I love you,'* or a final kiss, but I figured that would only complicate things even further. I supposed I should be thankful, but I felt anything but. I swiped at the tears that fell down my face and made my way back to my apartment alone.

My brain matter had turned to salt-water taffy—the kind that you can see being pulled this way and that through the window of a candy shop. A worker in the candy store heaves it onto a table to add whatever color and flavor they wish. Only, I didn't have artificial coloring or a flavor to add to my mind. It was just me. And I was just the same as that flavorless salt-water taffy—pale and lacking any vibrancy to my life.

I opened the door to the apartment, fully expecting all the lights to be out and to go straight to bed with myself and my misery-ridden salt-water taffy brain, to see Zoey laying on the couch looking at me with her eyebrows raised. A green blanket was wrapped around her legs up to her waist, her thick rimmed glasses that sat low on her nose and the pillow behind her blonde head signifying that she was ready for sleep. She sighed loudly as if I had bothered her immensely, but the look on her face showed that she was worried.

"It's two in the morning," she remarked casually.

"Uh huh."

That sounded about right, but I didn't have the energy to confirm by checking my phone.

"You've been crying," She muttered. I sniffled as if on cue and nodded. Zoey sat upright, grunting as if she had been laying there for quite a while, and patted the seat cushion next to her. "Want to talk about it?"

To say I had cried before would have been an understatement compared to what came next. It wasn't just slow tears trickling down my freckled cheeks, mourning the loss of a love that had barely even begun. That only belonged in movies, I supposed. Hard, wracking sobs took over my body as I stood in our entryway. I covered my mouth to ease the noise, but it did no good.

"Oh," Zoey said under her breath.

I blindly made my way to the suggested seat next to her and threw myself upon it, arms outstretched as I laid face down on the armrest. I wailed, the heinous noise reverberating off of the walls, but I didn't care. It wasn't like I had to save face in this apartment complex—I would probably be saying goodbye to it forever here soon anyway.

Never being one for outward affection, Zoey patted my back, clearly uncomfortable with my outburst. Her touch was about as comforting as someone tapping me from afar with a broom, anxiously saying, *'There, there.'* The thought of Zoey doing exactly that made me snort in between a few of my sobs, and peals of laughter made their way into my hysterical fit.

"Jesus," Zoey said on an exhale. "Do I need to find you a mental institution?"

I decided not to answer her rhetorical question, but the humor in it distracted me enough to halt my crying for now.

"Figured you would be asleep," I told her, speaking into the fabric of the couch.

"Couldn't sleep," she replied. "Was waiting up for you just in case—you know."

I sighed, sitting up and rubbing at my eyes.

"You didn't have to."

"Based on how you've been the past week or so?" Zoey said, "Yeah. I did have to." And considering that this was Zoey I was talking to, that meant the world to me. She pressed, "So...dare I ask?"

"Well, he thought I fucked Colton for starters."

Zoey let out a loud, *"Ha!"*

"Sure. *Hilarious.*"

"You ended up fucking up his face instead."

"*Ha*—right," I replied slowly. "I told him everything—well, a condensed version of everything."

"And he..." Zoey ushered me with a circular rotation of her wrist.

"Told me he loved me, so that's—"

"He *WHAT?!*"

I flinched at the volume of her voice. "Relax—"

"*Relax?*" She replied as if it was the most ridiculous word to use in this moment. "That's *literally* your best outcome in this situation, no?"

"There wasn't a good outcome for *anything,* Zoey. It was fucking heartbreaking." My breath hitched on the last word, and I held a hand up to my mouth to steady myself. "All our conversation gave me was clarity that I couldn't be with him right now."

Zoey squinted her eyes as if she couldn't see me quite clearly. "What are you saying?"

"I'm saying," my voice turned raspy, "that I broke up with him."

"You *WHAT?!*"

I shoved her—and not in a playful way. "I don't have a choice here—"

"You have a choice to be *happy,*" she cut me off, none too pleased, waggling a chastising finger in my face. "You just did what you've been dreading for weeks, the man confessed that he fucking *loves* you anyway—"

"He also said he would go to North Carolina with me."

"*Jesus,*" she shook her head in exasperation, "that just adds more to my point. He's up there," she pointed to the ceiling to signify his apartment, "wanting to put up with *all,*" Zoey waved her arms in a large circle in front of us, "of your bullshit with Colton because he loves you. Help you through it—be a shoulder to lean on when you need. *And you LEFT him?!*"

"It's not that simple—"

"Fuck if it's not!" She exclaimed. "Let the man go with you, let him *love* you for God's sake, what's the harm in that?"

"Uh—there's *loads* of harm, Zoey. If he comes down there with me and ends up getting hurt in any way, I'd just—I don't know. I have *no* idea what I'd do, it would destroy me." I leaned my head back on the couch. "And I have no idea how long I'll be down there; he would be derailing his whole life—or we would end up doing this stupid long distance thing and I—he—he's an *innocent.* I can't involve him just as much as I can't involve *you.*"

I had made a point to distance Zoey from anything I was involved in over the years. It took a *long* while for me to get her on the same page as me, but she had eventually, and reluctantly, seen things my way in the end.

The side eye that she gave me was glaring, and it was clear that she didn't care for the fact that I was bringing up our old arguments to make my current point.

"Fine," she replied quietly, somberly. "I don't like it—but I get it...and that sucks. I'm sorry." She glanced my way with genuinity in her eyes, and I pressed my lips together in a tight smile as a silent way of thanks for her sympathy. "So," she asked slowly, "what's your plan?"

"I didn't exactly focus on planning tonight."

"Yeah," Zoey stretched out the word. "I may have heard that." I exhaled audibly, and she added gently, "I think the whole neighborhood may have heard that." I yawned, waving away her comments. Zoey groaned, "Sorry—you're tired. I'll let you get to bed...I'll see you in the morning?"

I thought on that long and hard. I knew without a doubt that I needed to leave, and as soon as possible. I wanted desperately to pretend that this was *not* my life, which was why I lingered for several hours at Luke's, but the hard truth was that it *was* my life at the moment. The longer that I waited to make the trip back down to North Carolina, the more bitter it would be—just like when I laid in Luke's arms, tearing myself to pieces earlier tonight as the time went on and on. It would hurt all the same if I were to delay the inevitable, and though my life had been turned on its axis, I knew what I needed to do next.

"I think I need to go tomorrow."

"To—*tomorrow?*" She asked. "No, no. I'll take the day off work; we'll talk about your plans and—"

"Zoey, there aren't any *plans,*" I replied. "There isn't a grand scheme I need to figure out. *Nothing* I can do right now will change my circumstances, and it doesn't matter if I leave first thing in the morning or two weeks from now." I looked into her weary green eyes, nearly begging for her approval. "I have to go—and after my night with Luke, I just...I can't just *sit* here."

Zoey stared off into space for a while, her eyes narrowing every so often as if she were in deep thought. When she finally seemed prepared to speak to me again, she inhaled deeply.

"I wish I could just keep you here," she spoke on her exhale, her voice oddly grating. "Ah—take my car, yeah?" She shook her head and answered her own question. "Yeah, yeah—I don't need it, just take it. When, ah—when do you think?"

My heart panged in my chest. Saying goodbye to Luke—even without technically saying goodbye—was absolute hell. But hearing Zoey of all people sounding torn up over my departure was a whole other element that I hadn't considered.

"Early," I croaked out, my throat betraying me by tightening once more. "You'll probably be asleep—"

Zoey didn't allow me to finish my sentence. Her tiny body was thrown in my direction, her arms wrapped around me in a tight hug. I was so taken aback, mine were still planted at my side. It was over as quickly as it had begun, and Zoey sat back on her heels, swiping at her eyes.

"I'll wake up," she told me. "If I'm not, wake me—seriously. If you don't, I'll be pissed."

I nodded. "Yeah, I'll make sure you're up."

I stood, waving at Zoey as I strolled back to my bedroom, and she called out, "I'll see you in the morning?"

An edge was apparent in her voice—she knew me better than anyone. I was never one for confrontation, and it would have been easier for me to just leave silently before the sun even rose to save myself from all this...additional pain. I nodded anyway though, knowing that Zoey needed to be able to see me off, and went to my room to get just a few hours of sleep.

No amount of sleep would have been enough. Even if I would have gotten a fully rested eight hours, I still would have been exhausted. The stress of the unknown weighed on me heavily—not to mention the knowledge that I was leaving behind a man that I adored who admittedly would have stood by my side, loving me all the way. The latter may have been even worse than the thought of the unknown. I tried not to think about it much.

My goodbye to Zoey was brief. It didn't need to be anything else, and I was grateful for that. Her eyes were only half open when she gave me the keys to her little hatchback, and I ushered her back to bed with an assurance that I would text her any important updates and call her frequently.

I drove silently for the first hour or so, radio off, my thoughts wandering. I cried a bit more about Luke and about leaving my new life that had felt so carefree, but mostly I pondered about what to do next. I needed to speak with Colton and arrange for us to meet up when I got into town, but my cell service was spotty as I drove through the Appalachia's. I had time to kill, and my thoughts over the activities I would have to endure to begrudgingly help Colton went rampant.

I fantasized about escaping to a different, far-off land, perhaps where Colton couldn't find me, but that would just be running away from my problems yet again. Of course, Colton had called me out on that when I first moved away. I ignored his warning, naturally, thinking that he was just being the manipulative person that he was, but Luke had addressed this character flaw of mine as well. It was in an oddly backward way, and he confessed that he loved me directly afterward, but the words still stuck in my brain like glue.

You're flighty when it comes to conflict ran through me over and over until I just couldn't take the thought anymore. I *was*. Luke was right—and so was Colton for that matter. I couldn't run away—not this time—so, I used my quiet time driving through the mountains to consider any way that I could, legitimately, be free of this situation. Not much came to mind until I walked deeper into Colton's shoes instead of my own.

I grabbed my phone that sat in the cup holder extending out from the dashboard. The lack of missed calls or messages from Luke hit me with a hollow pang in my chest, but I moved past it, dialing a number that was burned in my memory.

He answered on the second ring, grunting out, "It's a little early, don't ya think?"

"Right, take all the fun out of you blackmailing me. It's such a fun-laced activity to begin with."

He exhaled a long breath and asked, "What's up, Claire?"

"I'm on my way back down."

He knew that I had gone back to Salem to, as I called it, *'Get my ducks in a row before I come back to save your ass.'*

"Ducks all organized, then?" He asked.

"Mhm."

"When'll you be back in Ogden?"

"Give or take," I stretched out the last word, pondering my exact location, "two hours."

"Where are you staying?"

"Figured the motel off Eighth—"

"Oh *God,*" he replied, and I heard him supposedly sit up on his mattress as it creaked in the background. "That place is fucking—"

"Garbage, I know," I finished his sentence for him. "But it's one of the only ones that I can pay for by the month and I'm *kind of* in limbo here."

"Um," Colton began to speak, and paused for a moment to gather his thoughts, "you know you could stay with—"

"If you even *finish* that sentence, Colt, I swear to *God*—"

"It's not *that* unreasonable," he argued, "you're helping me, so you can stay with me for free."

"I'm not helping you *willingly*," I stated. "Let's get that straight. And no, Colt—I cannot and will not live with you for the time being."

"Because of the boyfriend thing?" He asked, and my sharp, quick inhale made Colton hum something unintelligible. "I see," he deduced quickly. "He's out of the picture?"

"No," I retorted. "It's, ah—complicated. Look, I don't want to talk about Luke with—"

"His name is *Luke?*" He interrupted. "Gross."

"It doesn't *matter* what his name is—"

"Because you broke up?"

"No—er, yes, but that's not really any of your busi—"

"Okay," Colton spoke slowly. "*Now* we're getting somewhere."

"Shut the fuck up, Colt." For once, it seemed that he actually listened. "I'm not talking to you about Luke. I'm hanging by a goddamn *thread* here because of you and, here's the thing, I'm not getting you your fucking money."

"I—wait, *what?* Claire, you can't—"

"I'll text you when I get in town. We'll chat. Bye, Colt."

I hung up my phone and sat it delicately in the cup holder once more, feeling oddly powerful as I took what felt like my first full breath since I had spoken to Luke the night before. My phone buzzed madly with incoming calls from Colton. I ignored them all, deciding to find a decent radio station, and set out for the rest of my trip with my head held high. I would talk to Colton soon after all, but this time it would be on my terms—not his.

When I left Colton in North Carolina months ago, I thought I was taking control of my life. I *was,* but I was naïve. I genuinely didn't look into the loose ends that I would be leaving behind...and Colton wasn't the only loose end in question. I knew for a fact that he wouldn't have chosen to threaten me if he had any choice in the matter, but that aside, it was *Travis* who took that choice away. *Travis* was the other loose end—and it was finally time for me to look the ugliest side of my past in the eye and face it head on.

Chapter Twelve

I was still driving, but not terribly far from the motel I planned on staying at when Zoey inevitably called, greeting me pleasantly with:

"You *bitch,* you said you'd call me!"

"Yes, hello, Zoey—miss you too."

"It's been almost *five hours,* Claire," she chastised me. "For all I know, you could have been dead on the side of the road somewhere—"

"A car crash is not my most relevant threat at the moment," I replied in a chipper voice.

She sighed. "Where are you staying?"

"The motel off Eighth."

"Slumming it, I see," she noted, grimly humorous. "That place is haunted, you know."

"I'm also not concerned about ghosts. More thinking about the drug dealer that my ex owes," I told her with a shrug that she couldn't see. "I'll remember that if it feels like I'm being followed by some dude that fought in the Civil War."

The line was quiet for a moment before Zoey stated, "You seem...not upset. May I ask *why?*"

"Oh, I'm still pissed about my situation with Colton, don't get me wrong." I looked over my right shoulder to check a blind spot before I changed lanes, and then turned off of the highway. "Just deciding to look at this from a different angle."

"Which is?"

"Me *not* helping Colton illegally obtain money to pay off Travis, for one—"

"*Fuck* yeah!" She hollered into the phone, making me hold the speaker away from my ear for a moment. A male voice muttered words of confusion in the background, and Zoey said, "Nothing, Lee—it's all good."

"Liam there with you?"

"Mhm."

"Go ahead and tell him why I'm gone."

"Really?"

"Yeah," I told her. "Figure keeping it from him is a little difficult at this point."

"I mean yeah," she replied, "but I don't mind."

Secrecy was one of Zoey's superpowers, and I appreciated that over the years more than she could ever know. Her discretion kept me sane—and *safe,* for that matter—but with the new theme of my life being owning up to and facing my past, I didn't feel like I needed to hide anymore. *Especially* from someone like Liam, who had grown to be a friend and seemed to have his own demons to hide.

"Yeah, I know," I responded, "but I'm done with the whole *keeping a secret from everyone new in my life* thing."

"Fucking *finally.*"

"Don't go spouting off to anyone, obviously—"

"Well, I'm not dumb, dearest."

I laughed, concluding with, "But Liam's fine."

"Mmkay—so, what's this different angle you're going after?"

I replied simply, "Travis."

The motel was visible now on the right-hand side of the road. The shabby brick building with an orange awning above the entrance had a large sign near the sidewalk that read:

VACANCY NOW.

$89/WEEK.

$279/MO.

The line was silent as I turned into the parking lot, found an empty space, and put the car in park.

"You there, Zoey?"

"Uh...yes," she voiced slowly. "I'm here, you just stunned me into silence for a second there. Quick question for you."

"Yes?"

"Are you out of your goddamn mind?"

She said it casually, as if she were asking me what the weather was like. I pulled the key out of the ignition.

"Why do you say—"

"You said you'd never get involved with Travis again," she scolded me quickly.

"I'm *not* getting involved with him," I reassured her. "I just need to find a way to get him arrested."

"That's even *WORSE!*" Zoey shrieked. "How are you planning on doing that?!"

"Well, I have to talk to Colt first—"

"Oh *good!* You're getting help from *Colton!*" Sarcasm dripped off of her words.

"I mean, I haven't floated the idea by him yet—"

"Claire—"

"Look, I just got to the motel. I have to go get a room, meet up with Colt, all that."

"Claire—"

"I gotta go Zoey, really." I promised, "I'll call you later," and hung up my phone before she could protest against my actions.

I knew Zoey wouldn't take kindly to the idea, but I thought it was my best shot at getting out of this situation once and for all. If Travis were out of the picture, Colton wouldn't need to repay him, and I wouldn't be bound by the threat that Colton gave me. I hadn't thought much further into my plan, but it was the best one I had, and it didn't involve me staying in North Carolina for the unforeseeable future. It gave me a light at the end of this crazy tunnel—and that's all that was keeping me going.

✦✦✦✦✦✦ ✦✦✦✦✦✦

"I fuckin' hate this place," Colton announced, scrunching his nose as he strolled through the front door of my motel room. "It smells like someone shit in a corner and tried to cover it up with my grandma's perfume and a fat cigar."

His description of the scent was oddly accurate. The wallpaper that surrounded us was a faded rose pattern. It was peeling away in several spots, allowing the smoke-tinged manila wall to peek through. As I sat upon the bed, the metal springs complained with a squeaky gusto that made me wince.

"Welcome to my humble abode," I grumbled.

"Hey, you don't get to complain," he stated, pointing an index finger at me as he sat in the rather uncomfortable looking chair that was situated in the corner of the room. "I offered up my place."

"I would rather drink bleach, Colt."

"Nice," he retorted. "Real nice, Claire. Shall we move past the formalities?"

I replied, "By all means."

"Okay—what the fuck did you mean earlier?"

Colton sat hunched over, forearms resting on his thighs as his gaze bored into mine.

"I'm pretty sure you know what I meant—"

"Cut the shit, Claire!" He exclaimed. "You know if you don't help me out here, I have to turn you in—"

"Which turns you in as well—"

"You think I don't know that?!" His eyes were frantic, the lids peeled open in a wide, unblinking stare. "If I don't get Travis money, I'm basically dead—I'd *rather* go to prison." I nodded, my assumption when I was talking this over with Zoey proven true. It wasn't a shock to me—I knew that his threat wouldn't be an empty one. "So," he continued, "what the fuck are you saying?"

"Do you *want* to work with Travis, Colt?"

He exhaled sharply through his nose. "No—I don't. It's been long enough, but it's kinda late now—"

"Let's go at this at a different angle, then...Travis." I started to explain, "Let's put that motherfucker away."

"Put him *away?*" Colton asked me. "What—"

"Jail, Colt—you know after Carla, I had a good relationship with the police—"

"Are you out of your goddamn *mind?!*"

Colton leaped to his feet and began to pace the floor in front of me.

"Obviously," I said monotonously, irritated at how similar his reaction was to Zoey's. "Wouldn't you rather just have all of this over with? The guy's not in the damn mob, Colton. He's not going to send goonies after us or anything. He'll just go to jail and then you don't have to worry about him anymore."

"Claire, you can't just...tell the police that you've been moving H for someone, and you want to turn them in. They'll arrest you—and then I'll," he pointed at himself emphatically, "be in prison *with* him. Do you know how many options I have for penitentiaries in this area? Not fucking many! If he knows that I helped with turning him in, I'll get killed."

"Okay, I know that." I held up a hand in a gesture for him to relax. "I'm not stupid. I was saying to just...lead the police to him. Like a horse to water."

"Isn't the phrase: you *can't* lead a horse to water?"

"Oh my God, whatever," I sighed. "Doesn't matter. My point is, you know Travis. You could figure out where he is and when—"

"You're conveniently forgetting that I owe him money, Claire."

"Okay, then *lie*, say you have his money, I don't care! Between the two of us, we can figure out a way to meet with him...and then we'll call the police and let them know where he is."

Colton's pacing finally stopped, and he tilted his head as he looked at me curiously.

"Your aim is to set up a sting." It was a statement, not a question, and he was right—that *was* my aim. I just nodded. He muttered, "You really are out of your goddamn mind."

I asked impatiently, "Do you want to fix this or not?! You dragged me into all of this before." I paused at the look on Colton's face that said, '*Really?*' and corrected myself with, "Er...I willingly followed you into all of this before, but the point is that we both want to live better lives, no?"

"Are you putting words in my mouth?"

A lopsided smile snuck through his expression.

"I don't know, Colt," I returned, my eyebrows raised, "Am I? I'm going to do it this way with or without you. You tell me."

Just as Colton was sinking his way back into his seat in the corner, a knock sounded at the door.

He asked, "Expecting someone?" I shook my head in response, and Colton announced, "Uh—no housekeeping?"

"Miss Branson?"

The male voice was muffled from beyond the entrance to my room, and I held up a single finger to Colton to signify that I'd be right back.

I walked the few steps that it took to get to the door, unlocked the deadbolt, and yanked it open.

"*Hellooo*, Claire," the man crooned. "I hear you're in a bit of a pickle."

He had the build of an ex-linebacker. Black ink spanned his arms from the sleeves of his t-shirt all the way down to his wrists. He crossed his thick forearms across his chest and looked down at me with grey eyes, chin length brown hair that was tucked behind his ears, a crooked nose, and an amused, yet sympathetic expression.

"James?"

Luke's brother bounded into the threshold of the room and stalked forward as if he owned it—as if he *truly* belonged here, and I stood holding the door open with one hand, staring into the hallway out of mild shock. I let go of the door, assisting it with a shove as it caught itself on the crooked door jamb. I turned to see James standing in front of the bed, looking at Colton in distaste.

"And...you are?" He asked.

"Uh—Colton," Colton replied, holding out his hand.

James shriveled his nose up and ignored Colton's outstretched hand.

"Yeah, that won't be necessary," James murmured. He turned to me then, taking a large step in my direction with a wicked smile on his face, and clapped me on my shoulders hard enough to make my knees buckle. "Nice to officially meet ya, Claire."

All that came out of my dumbfounded mouth was, "I, um...what
—where..."

James strolled away from me and threw himself on the bed, stretching his long legs and crossing his left ankle over his right, his hands
behind his head.

He grunted under his breath, "This place fuckin' sucks," before announcing, "You have questions—I can tell. I'm here to help, obviously.
Yes, Luke's here too. He's in *our* room—112, down the hall. Why is he
not here with me right now? I told him I was getting ice and came to tell
you hello instead." I cocked my head to the side, still speechless. James
spoke for me, "*Oh, James, why would you do that?* I'll tell you *exactly*
why, Claire! Ya see, Luke is a teensy bit sensitive right now considering
how you left and he's still trying to figure out how to, *'Approach the
situation,'* as he calls it."

I finally found my voice. "How did you know where I was, exactly?"

"Oh, your friend Zoey—she is *somethin' else,* by the way—talked to
Luke after you left, he called me, we started to head down here, Zoey
found out where you were staying. The front desk does *not* have issues
with giving out guests' room numbers. Not that hard."

"Ah—James?"

Colton interjected, and James rotated ever so slightly to make reluc-
tant eye contact with him.

"Oh, are we doing this now?" James asked, and Colton furrowed his
brow in confusion. *"Perfect,"* James continued. "Heard all about you,
man—you're a *terrible fucking person.*"

Colton shook his head quickly, mumbling, "Oh—okay?"

"Okay," James continued, *"Miss Branson*—about my brother."

"About him," I replied, placing my hands on my hips in an ineffective
attempt to combat his palpable confidence. "We broke up—"

"*You* broke up with *him,*" He corrected me. "As Luke tells it—correct me if I'm wrong."

"I did—"

"And, may I say, you look *fantastic,*" James said. "Can you sense the sarcasm? Because you and Luke *both* look exhausted and I," he began to sing in a high-pitched tone that *so* did not suit his stature, "*think I know why!*"

I huffed a breath through my nose, and Colton took the chance to interrupt us with:

"Yeah, ah—James?"

"*Oh,* Colton," James sighed, closing his eyes as if his voice grated on his ears. "*Must* you—"

"Yeah," Colton replied, "Claire and I are *kinda* in the middle of something here—"

James laughed with a loud guffaw, and Colton leaned back in his seat with a heavy roll of his eyes.

"Oh, nah," James retorted. "Nope. You are *not* in the middle of anything right now. Right *now*, Claire's gonna come with me to have a chat with her boyfriend that she left in Virginia."

"James—"

"*Claire—*"

"I," I hesitated, wondering how I should begin to phrase what I was thinking at the moment, before I settled on, "you both need to go home."

"Sure." James sat up from the bed, slapping his thighs in a note of finality, and stood. "We'll go. *But* it won't be without you talking with Luke—you're fuckin' *nuts* if you think he's gonna leave without trying to see you and," he pointed at Colton, whispering in a dramatic fashion, "I don't think you want Luke to come in here. *He kinda hates him.*"

I most certainly did not want Luke to barge in while Colton was here. The conglomeration of Luke and my past was not a favorable one, and though I truly thought it was best for both of them to go back to Salem, James was right. If Luke came all this way, he wouldn't simply accept that I didn't want to see him. My best bet would be to face him head on—now—and *definitely* in a room that lacked Colton's presence.

Though I had only left him a few hours ago, my chest ached. I coughed to try to rid myself of the feeling, to no avail, and my stomach sank to the bottom of my gut. I wanted to see Luke—desperately. I hated that he was here and *needed* him to go back home so I didn't worry about him getting involved in this messy situation, but I would be lying if I said my heart didn't flutter when I came to my decision.

I nodded at James, silently telling him that I would go with him to see Luke, and he gave me a small smile, moving to place his hand on my upper back as he ushered me out the door.

"Um," Colton called to me as I exited the room, "I guess I'll just wait here?"

Without even looking behind at Colton, James threw him a very sarcastic thumbs up.

I didn't hear if Colton had responded any further, for the door had closed behind us. James walked with me down the hall to their room, slowing his steps as we began to reach their door.

"It's a good thing that I had the idea to get to you first," he said, reaching into his pocket for the key to his room. "Luke's been...on edge. Not quite sure how he would have treated your scumbag of an ex—not that I care about *him*. I *do* care that Luke doesn't get charged with murder, though." He jammed the key into the doorknob, turned it with a squeeze of his hand, and whispered, "After you."

He walked behind me, a hand on each of my shoulders as we entered the room. Luke was sitting on one of two beds, legs bouncing incessantly, an elbow on each thigh, and his head in his hands. At the sound of the door closing behind us, he looked up at the both of us and froze.

"Jay, what the hell?"

Luke's voice was stripped dry, the hoarse question lingering in the air as his bloodshot eyes stared into his brother's—not mine. *Anywhere* but mine.

"Sorry, man...had a feeling this would be better if she came to you."

James patted both of my shoulders and walked out the door, closing it behind him.

The silence was so heavy that it felt like it weighed on my body. I slouched under its pressure, and though I intended to walk up to the bed across from where Luke was and sit before him, I found myself unable to move my feet. I couldn't even look in his direction. The thought of how he was looking at me—and *if* he was even looking at me—was horrid.

"Not exactly what I intended," Luke finally stated gruffly.

I chanced a glance towards him, and his gaze was focused on his hands that were knit in his lap. At the sound of his words and with much effort, I slowly put one leg in front of the other. I eventually made it to the bed opposite of him and sat, the creaking of the mattress beneath me waking my brain just enough to speak.

"What are you doing here, Luke?"

"Ah—not trying to have James solve my problems for me, that's for sure." He grumbled, "Said he was here for moral support and the first thing he does is go to find you when I said I needed *time.*"

"Time?"

He finally brought his eyes to mine, and they were tired.

233

"Feels like a...delicate situation, no?" He asked. "I rushed down here and even with the five hour drive, I still don't know what to do."

"Delicate?" I responded. "Luke, I—"

"Left me, yeah," he replied firmly, ensuring to hold my gaze as he did. "I know. I *know* that you left me, Claire. We were together for all of five *fucking* seconds, and you up and left me—"

"I had to," I interjected, the hair on the back of my neck bristling at his agitation. "I didn't exactly have a choice, Luke."

Luke's eyes narrowed at me speculatively. "I...I *literally* gave you a choice. I told you I wanted to be here to help you. I—I didn't want you to leave—"

"And I told you that I couldn't let you do that," I told him bluntly, leaning toward him as I spoke. "You shouldn't *be* here, Luke. You need to go home."

"*Fuck* if I do."

And just like that, his agitation that I had judged before had morphed into anger. Perhaps it was anger all along.

"You're *mad?*"

"Mad?" Luke nearly whispered. "You think I'm *mad?*"

My voice quieted to a squeak. "Yes?"

"You left me," he croaked.

"I did—we talked about this."

"I didn't mean the conversation that we had, Claire," he clarified. "I meant...you *literally* left me. I waited as long as I could the next morning—"

"Oh."

"Trying to, I dunno, give you space because I thought we would maybe talk more or something? I didn't," he stammered, "I—I didn't think that you'd just leave—and not just my apartment. The fucking *state.*"

"You were sleeping," I replied quietly. "I didn't want to wake you and go through it all again and—"

"Oh, come on, Claire. I was *not* sleeping."

"I—what?"

Luke exhaled heavily, dragging a hand through his incredibly messy hair and looking to the popcorned, water-stained ceiling.

"I was awake when you left—couldn't sleep. Doesn't matter—"

"Doesn't *matter?!*" I screeched, unable to withhold my emotions any longer. "I fucking *wished* that you woke up—"

"*Why?*" Luke asked with a groan. "Because the way I saw it, you just wiggled out of my arms and up and decided to walk out of my life without a goodbye—"

"I *told* you I was leaving!"

"Not in *fucking HOURS!*" Luke yelled, and I bit my tongue to keep myself from speaking. "I knew you left—I let you go thinking I'd just go talk to you tomorrow, we'd figure out whatever the fuck—whatever. But you weren't *there,* Claire," he stressed. "I came to find you, but you had fucking skipped town already."

My voice fried and raspy, I said, "I *had* to leave—"

"Oh, sure," Luke snapped. "For my *protection.*"

"Well, you didn't exactly fight me much on it—"

Luke slapped his thighs at my words and stood abruptly, waving his hands about as he spoke and walked around the beds aimlessly.

"I *couldn't* fight you on it!" He spoke to the ceiling. "You're the most stubborn fucking person in the *world.* The only option I had was to talk to you once you cooled off—but you had *already fucking left!* So, I had to come here—"

"Did you?" I inquired with a tilt of my head. "Did you, *really?*"

"YES," Luke declared loudly, his pacing halting at the space between the two beds. He stood so close to me that our legs could have touched if we were to shift our weight one way or another. "I *really* had to—"

I felt the need to raise my voice, "Why?!"

"Because I fucking love you!" He exclaimed; his eyes crazed as he looked down at me. "I *still* do—your life is goddamn batshit crazy, and I *still* fucking love you."

"Luke—"

The tightness in my throat increased to a vice, my voice strained beyond belief. His words cut deep into me, for they were exactly what I *wanted* to hear. They were what I wanted—but not what I needed. I *needed* a clean break, but as the tears were beginning to spring to my eyes, it was becoming apparent that a clean break was *not* what was in store for us.

"You're fucking plotting ways on how to steal your ex-boyfriend fifty grand—and I still fucking love you."

"Luke—"

"You left me in Virginia without saying goodbye and," he touched his sternum with his palm, "shredded my heart to *pieces* when you did—and I still fucking love you."

The ever-persisting ache in my chest swelled, and my tears were able to be contained no longer. As soon as they slid down my cheeks, I raised a hand to dash them away.

"Just *stop,* Luke," I whispered. "You shouldn't *be* here."

"I'm not fucking *going anywhere,* Claire!" He blurted, looking me in the eye as he sank himself onto the mattress across from me. "I know you don't want me here and—"

"I *do* want you here," I corrected him firmly. "I want you here *so fucking bad,* Luke. I just—"

"You just *what?*" He asked desperately, his light eyes squinting at me, begging me for an answer.

"I just—"

I hesitated, and it seemed as though our bodies gravitated toward each other. There was no swift movement on either of our ends. No gasps of breath in shock as we lurched toward each other. It was natural—a magnetized pull that drew us closer and closer together until our noses were almost touching. I could taste his breath. *Feel* his warmth without being graced with the touch of his skin.

"I just—um..." My voice turned breathy when I repeated those words, desperate in a *very* different way than they were moments ago, and our unexpected closeness made my will to remove Luke from my current situation begin to crumble away. *"Fuck it."*

With my whispered words, Luke's gaze danced between my eyes and my lips, and I launched myself at him. I sat on his lap, straddling his legs as our mouths smashed into each other's.

"Wha—" Luke's garbled words came out between our lips, and with much effort, he pushed me away. "What do," his brow pinched together as I looked down at him, and he let out the breath he was holding. "What do you mean *fuck it?*"

"I mean *fuck it,*" I reiterated, shaking my head. "Fuck *all* of it. Don't leave. I fucking love you, don't lea—"

And then I was in the air. I saw a brief glimpse of Luke's relieved face breaking into a smile as he held me up by my thighs and placed my back on the bed that I was previously sitting on, and then his lips were on mine. His body pinned me to the bed, capturing me, keeping me close, and when our tongues touched, a conglomeration of appeased moans from either of us graced the room. I scratched my nails slowly from his lower back up to his shoulders and his body flexed from the sensation, pressing an oh-so-apparent firmness into my pubic area.

I smiled against his mouth as he groaned, *"Ah,* fuck," and I reached between us to grasp him.

He chuckled softly, throwing his head back as I pulled at the outline of his cock against his jeans, and I leaned forward to nip the space where his jawline met his neck. His laughing ceased then, and he whimpered as I kissed along his pulse point, his hands drifting upward to grip my neck and pull me closer. I pushed up on an elbow and Luke went with me, shifting himself to sit against the headboard as I straddled him. He reached overhead to pull off his shirt, and I repeated the action, throwing my sweatshirt to the floor. He grabbed me roughly on either side of my face, kissing me deeply, our tongues stroking against each other's for only a brief moment until I pulled away.

I grazed my lips along his neck and chest, shimmied myself to move down to his abdomen, and when I bit at a particularly enticing area just above his navel, he gasped, *"Shit."*

I took as much time as I could, but the elation from having been reunited had worked us both up to the point that we were panting heavily into the air around us. My mouth reached the button fly on his jeans and I yanked at the material with my fingers. Luke angled his hips upwards as I pulled to free his erection and I lowered myself to him, wrapping my mouth around the tip of him as I sucked. The saltiness of his arousal was evident on my tongue, and he groaned long and low, wrapping a hand around the base of my neck to urge me to take more of him in my mouth. I did, and Luke gritted out a strained noise. I bobbed up and down on him with enthusiasm, hearing him come undone by my own doings a pleasure in itself, until he reached down and patted at my back to get my attention.

I looked up at him, cock in mouth, and raised a single eyebrow in silent question.

"Take off your pants," he said in an exhale. "Come here."

I obeyed, kicking off my jeans as quickly as I possibly could, and I crawled up his body. I kneeled on either side of his legs, and before I was able to lower myself onto him, Luke shrank down, leveling himself with the apex of my thighs. He kissed me three times with an open mouth: once on either side where my thighs met my pubic hair, and a last time directly on my clit.

"Ah!"

I gasped as he flattened his tongue and remained there, lazily licking forward and back. His hands squeezed against my buttocks, holding me tight against his mouth as he continued his ministrations. Truthfully, I wanted him elsewhere—but the feeling was too gratifying. Seeing him beneath me, grey eyes flashing up to watch my reactions as he worshipped the most sensitive part of me, was too good a sight to pass up. I let out a quiet moan and gripped his hair, rocking my hips against his face. He smiled against my thighs, returning the noise right back to me, and I pulled on his hair to beckon his head back to me.

I plead, "Come back up here," and he obliged, sliding himself back up until I felt his erection press against my pussy.

I captured his mouth in mine, the taste of myself still present on his tongue. Luke's fingers squeezed on my hips, and I sank down slowly.

"Fuck," he cursed with a groan.

I paused to allow myself to adjust for his size, and he leaned back to look down at where we were joined, grazing his eyes over my body appreciatively. I moved myself up and down with as much patience as I could muster. Luke touched his way up my stomach, gliding his hands along my waist until he reached my breasts and pinched each of my nipples gently.

"Yes."

"You like that?" His voice came out in a husky whisper, and he tugged harder. I gasped, humming out a semblance of approval and he mumbled, "Yeah, I know you do, baby," which only spurred me on to ride him faster.

He pulled my face to his, one hand on the nape of my neck as the other continued to twist my left nipple. He kissed me deeply, matching my movements with thrusts of his hips as he moaned into my mouth. I bounced in time with him, all the muscles below my hips beginning to blissfully tighten.

"Luke, I—*shit.*"

I was going to tell him that I was about to come, but the words were taken from me. Luke's grip had moved from my nipple to my waist and wrapped around me tightly, holding me hovering above him. My movements ceased, my aching thighs thankful, and he began to drive into me relentlessly. I was certain that the resounding *smack, smack, smack* of his motions, not to mention the animalistic noises erupting from our throats, were able to be heard from several rooms over. I didn't care, though. I was lost, and so was he.

We came while shrieking out a garbled semblance of each other's names along with noises that couldn't be comprehended as words. I laid on him for a while after that, my limbs loose and his heart beating rhythmically in my ear.

Eventually, we shifted onto our sides. Still gloriously naked and laying atop the blankets, we embraced each other. I touched my mouth to his chest and collarbone, he kissed along my forehead and down to my cheeks, and we laid as contentedly as we could. There was nothing to be said, as the joyous feeling of being in each other's arms after our oh-so-brief separation was overshadowed by the somber realization of what was potentially to come. And there were no words for that.

It could have been anywhere from five minutes to five hours—I wouldn't have known the difference—when three loud, sudden knocks sounded at the door.

Luke rested his forehead against mine, sighing and kissing the side of my face before calling out, "Dear God, *what?*"

His annoyance made me smile more effortlessly than I had in days.

"Clothe yourselves!" A very distinctive, fairy-like voice rang through the room, and Luke and I sat bolt upright. "I give you ten seconds before we're *all* graced with the sight of your naked bodies."

We scrambled for our clothing, and I yelled, "Zoey?!"

I was dressed with the exception of my jeans when a rustling outside the door grew louder. A deep voice that I recognized as James' chastised Zoey as the key was thrust into the knob and the door swung open.

I jumped, pulling my jeans on over my backside, grumbling, "That was *not* ten seconds," as I fastened the button.

Luke sat on the edge of the bed, pulling his shirt over his head and turning to watch the individuals flood into the room one by one.

Zoey was first, announcing loudly, "She's clothed, guys—relax."

Liam followed closely behind her, beaming at the sight of me and Luke.

"Liam?" I called out curiously.

He waved at the both of us. "Hey, guys."

Luke grumbled just loud enough for me to hear, "Are they a package deal now?"

I sat next to him, nudging him in the ribs with my elbow, admonishing him with a, "Be *nice.*"

Liam exclaimed with a dimpled smile, *"Frecks!* You have a *lot* going on, don't you?"

I inquired, "Why are you here?"

Liam's blonde head tipped to the side as if he were confused as to why I would ask such a question. "You're my friend and you need help," he said plainly. "Do I need another reason?"

His reasoning made me exhale a soft breath through my nose, and I noticed Luke's glare that had been placed on Liam, along with his stiff posture, soften.

Before I had a chance to respond to Liam, James filed in behind him, shooting Luke and me an apologetic glance as he spoke, "They just showed up, she fuckin' barged into our room and stole the key, I *tried* to stop her, she's just—"

I waved him away, and replied, "She's kind of—"

"Unstoppable?" She responded to the entire room rhetorically.

"Unstoppable my *ass,*" James returned. "I should've not been so chivalrous and just tackled you."

Zoey looked James up and down, none-too-subtly, and smiled a Cheshire grin. "I would have *welcomed* that, Jay."

James stood up straighter at her gaze that nearly stripped him bare, and he returned the favor, grazing his eyes from her feet to her head.

"Would you, now?" He asked with a single raised brow.

Liam chastised, *"Zoey!"*

"Right," she shook her head quickly, looking back to Luke and me. "Look, no one is more sorry than I am that I had to barge in here—really. I'm living through your sex life at this point, but you *may* be forgetting that Colton is waiting in your room for you."

"He's *what,* now?" Luke voiced. "Since fucking *when?*"

"Easy, killer," James piped up.

"Zoey," I asked the same question to her as I did to Liam, "why are you even here?"

"Your ex is blackmailing you, sweetie." She told me with an expression of regret, "I should've stepped in a *long* time ago, no matter what you said—y'know, around the time that Colt was trying to make you a drug mule."

"He *what?!*" Luke snapped.

James choked out a surprised, *"Oh,"* his dark eyebrows shooting skyward.

"Ah—finer details of my past that I hadn't gone over. Thanks for that, Zoey," I murmured.

"Claire," Luke inquired, clearly chewing at the sides of his cheeks in agitation, "anything else to clear up?"

"Um...yeah," I spoke slowly. "Er—only got involved with that twice, by the way—that was why I left. Amongst many, many other things." Luke's lips pressed into a thin line, and I said, "Ah—the guy Colton owes money is the same one that we did said mule-ing for?"

I wasn't sure why I said it in a question—it just came out that way.

"Oh?"

That was all Luke managed to say, and I think it was because his mind was running a mile a minute. His grey eyes were so wide that they were threatening to look buggish.

"Er...*yeah.* He may have also been the same dealer that supplied my mother with her drugs of choice?"

"May have?" Luke replied quickly. "Or he *definitely was, and you had some sort of history with said drug dealer?*"

He spoke the last sentence quickly, his neck poking outwards expectantly.

I gritted my teeth and said, "The latter."

Luke groaned loudly, bringing both hands up to his eyes and rubbing them as if it would erase what he was now privy to.

James murmured a nervous, *"Ha*—okay, fuck," as he scratched the back of his neck, and Luke voiced:

"What are you—okay, *no*—are you saying you're going to be involved with this guy—"

"Travis—"

"I don't want to know his fucking name, Claire!" Luke hissed, pulling his hands away from his face.

I heard Zoey whisper to Liam, "This'll be good, I don't think he knows yet."

Liam gasped dramatically. "He *doesn't?"*

"Zoey," I admonished her loudly. *"Liam*—come *on,* guys, what the fuck?"

"Do they *have* to be here?" Luke whined, drawing my attention back to him. "And why does *Liam* know shit before I do?"

"Zoey told me for what it's worth," Liam announced. "You two were broken up at that point, so I'm pretty sure Claire wasn't gonna—"

"Liam, for the love of *God,"* Luke seethed, holding his hands out in front of him and flexing them open and closed. "Stop talking."

"Er—sorry, Luke," Liam spoke quietly, tail seemingly between his legs.

Luke's eyes were closed tightly when he said, "Claire—clue me in, please."

"Er," I hesitated. "Good news, I'm not helping Colton get his money."

Luke exhaled a long breath. "Good," he replied softly, eyes still closed. "That's good."

"Other news," I began, deciding to deem this announcement neither good nor bad.

"Oh no," Luke muttered, wincing at my words as he looked at me cautiously.

"We *may* be trying to get Travis arrested instead," I admitted, and Luke's body froze, forearms resting on his bent knees as his back laid against the wall. Unblinking, he stared at a space just over my left shoulder. I wanted to give him as much time as possible to digest what I had told him, but considering that he seemed to not be breathing, I felt the need to call out to him. "Luke?"

He let out a loud breath once more and then inhaled through his nostrils as he locked his steely eyes with mine.

"This...may sound harsh," he began slowly, "and I mean this in...the *best* possible way." He paused, and I ushered him on:

"Okay?"

"And I'm glad I'm here," Luke enunciated each word carefully. "I love you *dearly,* Claire—I do. But," he gathered himself once more and, as calmly as possible, asked, "Are you out of your goddamn *mind?*"

Chapter Thirteen

It took several minutes to get Luke to breathe correctly again and for everyone in the room to convince me that I actually could use their collective help. I cared for all of them more than I could say and it went against everything in me, but I was somehow *eager* as I walked alongside Luke and all of my friends. We had yet to even begin to wrap up my entire situation in a neat little package, but walking back to the motel room that Colton resided in somehow felt like...closure.

It wasn't closure on the illegal activities of my past—not even close. It was more like closure on being closed off. For years, I separated Zoey completely from my life with Colton, and that directly correlated with how I treated Luke—and everyone else in my new life, for that matter. This feeling of everyone around me being *in-the-know* regarding my entire life was incredibly foreign, but it was exhilarating. Freeing. I was terrified, yet thrilled, to have everyone at my side at this moment—and I couldn't thank *myself* for that. That was all of *them*.

Suddenly I was walking a little bit taller. Feeling a little bit more secure. And it was before I knew it that I was entering the room where Colton resided.

Colton sat in the same corner chair, staring at the ceiling, his hands laced together across his stomach. His buzzed head turned to see all of us standing in the entryway, and a crease formed in his brow.

"Uh—what's up, everyone?"

"It turns out I have some help with me," I said, shrugging.

"I see," he replied, sitting up and scanning each individual that stood with me. "So, by using the process of elimination, I've already met the brother." Colton waggled his index finger at James, moving it to Liam. "This one and Zoey are clearly fucking—"

Liam and Zoey glanced at each other, having somehow just noticed their proximity, and took a single side-step away from each other quickly.

In unison, they said, "We aren't—"

Colton waved them away with an eye roll.

"Don't need to hear the spiel," he noted. "Anyway—that leaves us with...the pretty boy," he deemed Luke as such, laughing to himself. "Really?"

Luke, who stood next to me, narrowed his eyes, crossing his arms as he looked Colton up and down.

"If we just kill him," Luke asked the room, "and hide the body well enough...would that fix all of Claire's problems too?"

James replied, "Maybe...let's call that plan B." He looked to Liam. "You good with a shovel?"

Liam nodded enthusiastically. "Never dug a grave, but you know—first time for everything."

For the first time in, well, *ever*, Luke smiled at Liam. It was a small one, and it was over nearly as soon as it had begun, but it was there, nonetheless.

I chuckled. "Let's not plan a murder, guys."

"Hey, I said that was plan B," James responded with a crooked smile.

Zoey added, "He's a fucking cockroach, guys, he'll just come back to life or some shit."

"You guys are *hilarious*," Colton said with a large roll of his eyes. "*Really* fucking funny. Are you done?"

I felt us all breathe out a collective, quiet sigh, and I led the way as we entered the room. While Luke, James, and I remained standing across from where Colton sat, Zoey strolled past us all, and Liam followed. They both settled themselves on the edge of the bed.

"Zoey," Colton greeted her officially. "Long time no see."

Her face warped itself into an expression of mild disgust. "Bite me, asshole."

"Bitchy as always," Colton noted. "Nice to see you haven't changed."

While Zoey just rolled her eyes, Liam, who had been observing the thin comforter beneath him by pinching the material between his fingers, snapped his head to Colton's at the mention of the word *bitchy.*

Liam demanded, "Hey, watch your fucking mouth."

Since I had gotten to know Liam, and especially after seeing his closer interaction with Zoey, I saw him more and more as a human incarnate of a golden retriever puppy. Flaxen hair. Happy-go-lucky attitude. The one thing that I couldn't possibly picture was Liam being legitimately angry, so his reaction to Colton being outwardly rude to Zoey caught me off guard. I felt my eyebrows raise as I watched their next interactions.

Zoey mouthed, *'It's fine,'* but Liam just shook his head, muttering words under his breath in her direction. She rolled her eyes again, albeit in a more sympathetic way, and patted his arm consolingly like I'd seen her do several times before. He pressed his lips together, seemingly unhappy with her indifferent attitude, but said no more.

Colton shrugged, brushing off the interaction, and said, *"Anyway*—Claire. Where were we?"

"Travis?" I offered.

"Sure you don't want to just run some sort of heist?" Colton was now the picture of amusement as he gestured wildly with his hands around the room. "Looks like you kind of have a team goin' here." Though it was clear that Colton was attempting to tell some sort of a morbid joke, it fell flat upon us all. As far as I could see, everyone's gaze was fixed on Colton—and their expressions varied anywhere on the scale of exasperation to fury. "You guys can lighten up, I'm just joking!" Colton announced brightly. "See, we can joke here. You don't all need to keep giving me murderous looks. It's getting kind of creepy." Silence ensued. "Or keep doing that. You know—whatever works best for ya...back to the topic at hand." He clapped his hands together. "*So*—I was thinking—Travis."

"Yes?" I questioned slowly.

"I'm on board."

"Okay, good—"

"Wait, wait," Luke interjected, holding a hand up as he spoke. "What are you on board with, exactly?"

"Operation: Get Travis Fucked," Colton replied, enthusiastically waving his hands in front of his face for good measure. "It's a go; let's fuckin' do it. So," he looked to me, "where were we—setting him up?"

I nodded. "I figure you can set up a meet with him, tell him you'll have his money, and I can loop the police in and—"

"No, no, no," Colton interrupted. "I can't meet with him myself. Been dodging him for too long for him to not be skeptical when I try to set up a time to meet. I owe him *way* too much and he either gets...stabby or shooty when it comes to matters like that."

James said, "Tell us you have another idea or else *I* will be getting stabby or shooty with *you*."

"Alright, take it easy, Jax Teller—"

"The fuck is that supposed to mean?" James retorted.

"Yeah," Zoey interjected with a sigh. "I totally see it."

"Sons of Anarchy?" Liam asked her, and she nodded. He dragged his eyes over James from his shoulders down to his boots. "Yeah," he shrugged. "I see it."

"I mean, James has more muscle on him," Zoey continued.

"Eh," Liam scrunched his face together. "Does he?"

"Guys." I chastised. "Life in peril. Figuring out solutions. Keep it together for like five minutes, *please.*"

I would have been angry about Zoey's oddly calm demeanor if I didn't know her better. When her nerves got to her, she tended to wear a mask of humor as well as she possibly could. My life would turn on its head and at one moment, she was intensely focused on her worry, and at another, she would joke at the drop of a hat. I had been through this dynamic of Zoey's before though, and my irritation at her distracted, seemingly sarcastic mindset just...dissipated. She cared—I knew she did, so I offered her a timid smile. She returned it with a scrunch of her nose and a down-turn of her lip that stated a silent apology, and I just nodded softly, understanding her along the way.

"Okay," I stated with an exhale. "So then one of us meets with Travis, I guess? Leads him somewhere?"

Colton looked at me with a raised brow. "If by *one of us* you mean *you* meet with him..."

"Why would Claire have to meet with him?" Luke asked abruptly.

"Well, I'd rather not *die,*" Colton told him. "If *I* meet with him and don't have money for him immediately, like I said—stabby or shooty." Colton used his hands on the last words, miming the actions. "None of you guys even know Trav, so that wouldn't make sense. Plus, there are three things that interest Travis most—money, drugs, and..." Colton allowed his voice to trail off as he gestured in my direction.

"The fuck is *that* supposed to mean?" Luke snapped. I gave Colton a warning look, but it was no use. Luke noticed all too quickly and asked, "What? What's that look for?"

"It's...not as bad as it seems," I said slowly.

"Not as bad as it seems?" Luke's eyebrows raised. "He didn't even *say* anything, he just pointed at you."

"I, um—"

I wasn't sure how to explain to Luke that Travis had expressed interest in me in the past—after all, there had been many, many hard truths of mine that were exposed in the last twelve hours or so. I stammered, and Luke waited. I never quite landed on a complete sentence, and his patience quickly wore thin.

He ushered me again, "Claire?" and my voice squeaked, but no actual words were formed. *"Okay."* Luke moved his eyes to Zoey. *"Zoey?"*

She held her hands up in defense. "Don't pull *me* into this, I've never even met the guy."

"God dammit, I didn't want to even have to look at you, but..." Luke turned towards Colton in desperation. "Do me a solid and tell me it's not what I think it is."

Colton sighed. "I don't *know* what you think it is, Luke," he began, "but I'll do you a different solid and tell ya that Travis used to tell me how much he wanted to fuck Claire."

"That is *exactly* what I thought it was," Luke groaned. He turned around abruptly, shouldering past his brother, and began to pace. His footsteps patted toward the bathroom and back again, back and forth.

"I think he's exaggerating!" I called out in Luke's direction.

"I'm not!" Colton announced loudly. "Wasn't exactly fun for me either, guy!"

"Okay—Colt, what are you trying to suggest here?" I asked. "I meet him at a bar or something, lure him in with my tits, and *then* what? Won't the cops need evidence of some sort? I always acted repulsed by everything he did, asking too many questions would be suspicious."

"I mean, you don't need to ask questions," Colt noted. "You just have to get back to his place—"

Luke made noises of unintelligible misery from the hallway.

"Alright," James spoke, stretching out the word, "before Luke has an aneurysm of some sort, maybe let's toy around with the idea that someone should go with Claire?"

"Not sure how that'll work," Colt replied.

"No, no, Jay has a point." Luke was back at our sides, a hand resting on his diaphragm seeming to be an act of comfort. He spoke with determination in his eyes. "You can't set up a sting with nothing, and Claire's not trying to lure him back to his place *alone.* What's she supposed to do, hit on him all night until he's expecting to get laid?" Colton shrugged in response, and Luke retorted, "Absolutely fucking not."

"Okay," Colton rubbed at his eyes, conceding, "okay, we can make this work." After pausing for a moment, he began to speak in drawn out words as if he were putting a thought together piece by piece. "Claire arranges to meet with Trav—one of you is with her—he can't *know* that you came with her because...why would she meet up with Trav *and* bring someone along?"

Luke concluded, "Okay, so I go with her and pretend I don't know her—"

Colton let out a loud, *"Ha!* No. You will not work."

"Why?"

"Ah, *look at you,* man." Colton shook his head, chuckling to himself. "You're about to vibrate out of your skin, I don't think you're gonna be able to keep your cool when Trav's hitting on Claire."

"She doesn't have to lead him on," Luke offered, "it could just be like...*Oh, Travis, it's been a bit, let's catch up—*"

"Yeah, that doesn't sound realistic," I told him. "Not once in my *life* have I said I wanted to catch up with Travis. I'm hard pressed to figure out how to make him believe I want to see him in the first place."

Colton waved off my worries with a hand in the air. "We can figure that out later—but dude—"

"I'm not your *dude,*" Luke sneered.

"Okay, whatever," Colton continued. "We need to get hard evidence on Trav and if it's iffy for Claire to do it, someone else has to...I dunno...act like someone who has a common interest with him. Fucking *sell* him on it."

"Yeah, I'm game," Luke reiterated.

"It's not you, man," Colton stressed. "What are you gonna do, ask him, *'Can you show me your finest drugs please?'* You look too...*pretty* to be asking about that shit."

"Then fucking *brief* me on what I should say—"

"Even if I *do,* you. Won't. Be. Convincing."

"I," Luke stuttered, "I can't just let Claire—" He looked down to me. "I can't let you go alone."

His gaze was pleading, but Colton was right. Luke was just *not* in his element in this world—it was too different from the one he lived in. And as much as it relieved me to take Luke out of the equation, it still pained me to deny his request, so I sighed.

"He's right, Luke—you can't go."

Luke pressed his lips together in a tight line.

"I can," James told his brother. "I'll go."

"Oh yeah," Colton stated, nodding emphatically. *"Way* better."

Luke shook his head, hard. "Nuh uh—*no.* It's bad enough that Claire's in this—"

The look that James gave Luke forced him to stop talking. It was a silent demand to shut up and a promise that everything would be alright all in one, and I heard Luke huff a breath through his nose.

"Okay?" James muttered. Luke nodded reluctantly, and James continued, turning his eyes to Colton. "'Kay, game plan is we get back to Travis' place and...then what?"

"Well, Claire's gonna arrange with the cops—yes?" Colton glanced at me, and I nodded. "So, she can let them know about everything—Claire, can you do that without mentioning my name?"

I could have sworn that I heard Luke's teeth grind together in agitation.

I replied, "Yeah, Colt—I'll figure it out."

"Okay, cool," he shifted to James. "So, then *you.* You're back at his place, make sure some of his shit's out, cops show, bada-bing bada-boo—oh." A thought seemed to appear in Colton's mind, and he mentioned it aloud. "Er—Trav *does* have roommates. Two of them. They'll have to be distracted—"

"This is a bad idea," Liam blurted out from his place on the bed.

Colton glanced Liam's way. "Come again?"

"It's. A bad. Idea," Liam reiterated, glaring at him. "Having the cops bust in on everyone in his house of all places sounds dangerous as hell."

"You got a better one?" Colton asked, annoyed.

"I mean, not really, but—"

Colton cocked his head at him. "You're not very bright, are you?"

"Are you trying to get punched more than once this week?" Zoey interjected, her voice calm but containing a layer of protectiveness that I was intensely familiar with.

Her comment reminded me of the altercation I had with Colton, and I lifted my casted arm to cradle it against my chest. It was an oddly instinctual act and I wasn't certain why it comforted me, but it did.

James' gaze bounced between me and Colton. First, to my injured arm that he clearly hadn't noticed until this moment, and then to Colton's face. He squinted his eyes and pointed at Colton, gesturing towards his lightly purpled left cheek.

James muttered down to me, "You do that?" and I nodded, shrugging.

Liam was looking down at Zoey curiously. He was seemingly unbothered by Colton's attempted insult and wore his signature lopsided smile, dimple on display as he whispered something down to her that I, unfortunately, couldn't hear.

Zoey rolled her eyes heavily, scoffing as she muttered something that, if I could be confident in my ability to read lips, looked like, *'Fucking asshole.'*

"Fine, fine." Colton held up a hand. "Liam, yes?" Liam nodded, and Colt asked, "You were saying?"

Liam sat up a bit straighter and started, "Okay—well, like I said, going back to his place sounds like a fuckin' terrible idea. You're *asking* for a gunfight or some shit—and why the hell aren't *you* involved, Colton?" Liam continued. "Claire's back here to save your ass and—"

"Uh—I'm not involved because I can't be, you sweet peach," Colton responded mockingly. "I'd like to not go to prison or be murdered."

"Well, ya fuckin' *should* be involved," Liam returned. "We're trying to put Travis away, yeah? His biggest interest isn't gonna be some random dude asking to buy whatever the fuck he has, and it's not Claire either—it's fuckin' *you.*"

"How exactly would we—"

Colton, indignified, didn't get a chance to ask how he would possibly become involved in the situation that he had created for me. As Liam was getting through his short monologue, James had stood a little straighter. His hands were placed on his hips as his eyes widened, and he seemed to come to a specific realization just in time to cut Colton off mid-sentence.

James rattled off, "Liam, you're a fuckin' genius," and Liam blinked several times in succession, attempting to absorb the compliment. James continued, "Colt, ya strike me as a guy that screws around a lot. Am I right?" Colton scoffed, and James reiterated, *"Am I right?"*

"Your point?" Colton asked.

"My point," James said, "is that it probably wouldn't be too hard to convince Travis that you owe other people money, too."

"He *does* owe other people money," I interjected. "Right, Colt?"

Colton sighed. "And?"

"Travis may be more inclined to incriminate himself with someone that you *also* owe money to," James concluded. "Enter *me.*"

"So," the lightbulb clicked in my brain, and I picked up where James left off, "I set up a meet with Travis, James just so *happens* to be sitting near us and hears something about Colton, James and Travis can start to *work together* to get what is owed to them, I can get everything recorded on my phone as evidence for the cops and—"

Colton interrupted, "And I—and James, for that matter, look like criminals when you turn in a recording of all of us—"

"You *are* a criminal," Luke remarked snidely.

"And *that* is why I'm meeting with the police to arrange the particulars," I spoke to Colton. "I won't mention you by name, and I'll make sure your safety is a guarantee."

Luke grumbled, clearly unhappy with the notion that Colton would be declared innocent after all he's done, and a slow, wide smile stretched across Colton's face.

"You're the *best,*" he told me.

"Yeah, yeah," I said on an exhale. *"Anyway*—so *then what?* I mention Colt to Travis in passing, James pretends to hear us and says that he's trying to track him down for money, we get Travis to say a few incriminating things on tape, and we walk away and hand the recording to the police?" I paused, waiting for anyone to speak. "Is that it?"

"Prolly not," Colton finally spoke. "I've been through Trav trying to find people that owe him money. You mention me at all, and he's gonna try to use you."

"Use her?" Luke asked. "Elaborate."

James clapped his brother on the shoulder, muttering, "Take a breath, big guy."

"Sounds worse than it is," Colton reassured Luke casually. "He'll probably ask you to call me—seen him do it like a million times. He finds someone who he thinks can get the person's attention—like, Claire to me—and then has that person set up a fake meet."

"So, he'll want Claire to call you and, what...tell you that she's with Travis and he's looking for you or something?" Luke's eyes squinted as he spoke, the gears churning in his head nearly visible.

"No," Colton shook his head, "he won't want her to mention him at all—it's a *fake* meet, right? Like—he'll have Claire call me, set up a time for just the two of us to *catch up,* and then he'll show up in her place to confront me."

"Wait, that's perfect," I spoke, and all heads turned to me. "I'll just play it off like you've been trying to contact me for a while—"

"To be fair, I have," Colton interjected.

I ignored him and continued, "That makes Trav think I'd be able to lure you in...and I can act like I don't want anything to do with you—"

"Which you don't," Luke quipped.

"*Which*," I looked at Luke pointedly at his snarky remark, and then back to Colton, "would make it seem like I'd be willing to call you and set you up for Trav...Trav shows up at the time we planned expecting to trap you into talking about the money you owe him and the cops show up in your place."

Everyone nodded, the plan seemingly coming into place, and a manic smile appeared on Colton's face.

"I believe that's my queue," he announced it quietly, yet it sounded like it rang through the room. "You'll meet with the cops..."

"Tomorrow morning," I stated while Colton stood from his chair.

He nodded, bounding past all of us as he made his way to the front door, and placed a hand on the knob.

"It's been a *pleasure,*" he told us all in a half-mocking voice. "Claire—talk soon."

And then, he was gone—and the room was silent. Until it wasn't, of course. And the only sound in the room had come straight from Liam's mouth.

"So...he's a douchebag."

"Feeling like we established that *long* ago," Luke replied.

"Yeah," Liam responded, his hands back to toying with the thin blanket beneath him. "Claire, how the hell did you stay with him for so long—"

Luke interjected, "Don't—"

"He wasn't like that when we were together," I said. "He was...I dunno. Sweet? Helpful?"

"And not blackmailing you?" Luke finished my response for me and strode to the seat that Colton was once sitting in. He sank down slowly and leaned back, his head hanging back off the edge of the chair. "Shall we address the elephant in the room?"

The only elephant that I could think of was my prior inability to tell Luke all of the pertinent details of my past life and, to say the least, it was a big one. The man drove several hours just to see me after I had broken up with him and fled the state, and he just keeps getting more and more bombs dropped on him. Colton was right, he *was* vibrating out of his skin—I could see it clearly as he stared to the yellowed ceiling. His right ankle was crossed over his left knee, and his foot that was touching the floor bounced ceaselessly with his excess nervous energy. I was surprised that all of this wasn't too much for him—that he hadn't run for the hills after my additional admissions that I had tactfully avoided during our breakup. They were an elephant, indeed—and he deserved to be angry. After all, even love can be defeated by lies, deceit, and a withholding of the truth. The thought made my heart hammer in my chest.

"What's stopping Colt from never blackmailing you again?" Luke asked.

I let out the large breath that I was holding.

"Oh, um—I mean, we *are* fixing his problems for him currently, so...I don't really see him going right back to—"

"You're going to blindly trust him?" Luke spoke the question.

"He said he doesn't want to deal with Travis anymore, he wants an out—"

"Yeah," James began, "an out from *Travis,* not an out from being a generally bad fucking person."

"Thank you, Jay," Luke said in a breath.

James continued, "What, you think he's going to quit everything he's been doing the past few years?"

"I mean, *I* did," I retorted.

"And you get all the props in the *world* for that, Claire." James emphatically waved his hands in front of him. "But ya can't just assume he's going to change—do you see Colt changing his life and deciding to be a fucking shoe salesman or some shit after this?"

"I don't know, I just—"

"Dammit, Claire!" Luke exclaimed, sitting up now as he looked at me with the full intent of his gaze, which was less than warm. "You *have* to stop being so—"

"Being so *what?*" I snapped, not taking kindly to his change of tone.

His head bobbed backward, and he stumbled upon his next words.

"So—I—like you've got this whole—I dunno, fucked up situation and you're acting all—"

"I, ah," Liam quietly spoke, and all heads turned in his direction, "think the word you're looking for is *gullible,* Luke."

Luke sighed heavily. "Yeah," he looked in Liam's direction. "It is—thanks, Liam."

"Gullible?" I inquired softly to Luke. "How the *hell* am I being gullible?"

"Well," Luke stated, "you're assuming he's not just going to get into deep shit *again* and blackmail you for your help *again.*"

I stammered, "I—I just don't see him doing—because he's—"

"Sweet?" Luke threw my own words back to me. "And *helpful.* Downright *courtly—*"

"Okay," Zoey intervened, a single hand raised in the air to tell Luke to stop speaking. *"First of all,* Luke—the last person you should be jealous of right now is Colt. Claire literally went to a different state to get away from that whole mess *and* when he confronted her a few days ago, she fought *so fucking hard* to not even speak to him. *AND* when she did, she ended up giving him a black eye." She gave Luke a look that said, *'You good?'* and he just nodded reluctantly, grinding his teeth. *"Secondly,"* she continued, "Claire, stop being stubborn—you're *totally* acting gullible about Colt."

"Zoey—"

"What?" She retorted back to me. "You *are.* And it's just because you don't want to have to deal with it—you'd rather not get your hands a little dirtier and dig in a *little* deeper because you don't want to be here at *all."*

"Yeah, I *don't* want to be here at all," I hissed at her, my throat feeling oddly tight from the emotions of speaking with Colt, Luke being angry, and now Zoey being...Zoey. "Why the *fuck* would I want to be here?! I just want to go *home—"*

With that last croaked-out sentence leaving my mouth and reaching my ears, it struck me that Zoey was probably right. I was here in an attempt to fix Colton's situation which was, by default, my situation—and I wanted it done as quickly as possible. My haphazard solution with wanting to get Travis arrested was a band-aid, really. It could solve what was creating the clusterfuck at this very moment, but the wound would fester under the surface. Not addressing what Colton had done and what he could continue to do to me would be just that—a wound—and after a *very* pregnant pause, I groaned loudly.

"I...will sleep on what I can do about Colt," I replied to Zoey, and turned to glance at Luke.

He nodded at me solemnly.

An odd tension filled the air as we looked at each other, and Zoey interrupted with a well-placed yawn.

"Is it getting late?" She spoke to the room.

"It's six-o-clock," Liam told her with a confused cock of his head.

"Okay, then I'm hungry, I dunno—we," she gestured at herself, Liam, and James, "should all...figure out room accommodations—"

"Zoey—"

My intention was to tell her that their quick adieu after my strained conversation with Luke was wholly unnecessary, but she was having none of it. She had bounced to her feet and was at my ear in the blink of an eye.

She muttered, "Do us all a favor and fuck the tension out of him, yeah?"

"Yeah, I don't think he's tense because he wants a good lay, Zoey."

She shrugged. "Well, it wouldn't hurt."

I placed both of my hands on her shoulders and pushed her toward the door. James and Liam moved with us, filing their way out of the room before I was able to usher Zoey out of it, and I uttered a quick goodbye in her ear. I closed the door and stared at it, focusing on nothing in particular as I considered how to approach Luke.

"So..."

He spoke first, his voice deep with an emotion that I couldn't decipher without seeing his face. I turned, and upon seeing his jaw tight and his eyes heavy-lidded, verbally took a wild guess at what was going on in his head.

"You're mad."

Luke threw a hand out as if to say, *'Obviously.'*

"Yeah," he replied. "I'm mad."

"I—"

"Actually, no," he interrupted me, thinking aloud in what was now becoming an almost mocking tone. "I'm not *mad*. I'm fucking pissed."

My chest lurched, my internal fears seemingly coming true, and I made my way to the bed to sit across from Luke.

"I know I took a long time to tell you about everything before I left—"

"No, no-no," he brought a hand to his forehead briefly. *"That* could've been better, but I was fine with it—hell, I came down here after you broke up with me, didn't I?"

I nodded, and although the air felt thick around me, I still managed a weak smile as I replied, "You did."

"But—"

"But?" I asked quickly.

"Everything else, Claire," he told me in an exhausted tone. "Everything *fucking* else—who Colt owes money to, to start." His grey eyes bored into me, etched with frustration. "You couldn't mention the specifics of *that?*"

"Travis was irrelevant when I talked with you back home," I said quietly. "I hadn't even thought that I could—"

"Set up a sting for a drug dealer who's known to be violent *and* has historically had the hots for you?" Luke blurted out.

"Look, I know I've had a shitty past, but I can't *control* this, this is all Colton's doing," I retorted, feeling the need to defend myself from his accusatory tone.

"Of *course,* it's his doing and you can't control it!" He exclaimed. "What you *can* control is keeping me in the goddamn loop! I get here to be with you, and it's just bomb after bomb after—"

"When would I have gotten the chance to tell you everything, Luke?" My pulse raced. "After we broke up? Or after everyone barged in on us after we made up?"

"The *problem* is that when the time comes to tell me about anything, I have to fucking," he balled his hands into fists in front of his face and shook them, *"yank* it out of you. It's never the whole story, I just keep getting little snippets of information that someone else accidentally reveals for you, or you *finally* get backed into a corner and you're forced to talk to me. It's like you don't trust me at all."

"I—" My defenses fell to the wayside, guilt settling in its wake. "I *do* trust you." Luke eyed me warily and I reiterated, "I do. More than anything. I just know that this is...a lot."

He nodded. "It is."

"Too much?" I uttered the question quietly.

263

"Yes."

Luke's blunt, rapid response took me off guard, and I inhaled sharply. It was a stab to the gut and when I let my breath out, it faltered. I felt heat flush my face when I attempted to speak again.

"I, um—"

"It's *a lot* that you're in this asinine situation," Luke began to clarify, his gaze intent on mine. "It's *a lot* that James is now inserting himself in my place in this grand...I dunno...*scheme*. What's *too much* is that it feels like you have this—this knee-jerk reaction to hide things from me."

His palpable frustration made my chest constrict because I knew that it was my doing. It gave me a strong urge to crawl into his lap and beg for forgiveness. To wrap my arms around him and drag my lips up his neck and to his mouth in hopes that he would want to do the same and my wrongdoings, along with our argument, would dissipate into the air like smoke. That was what I needed—desperately—but it wouldn't be enough. Not yet, anyway.

"I've done a shitty job at opening up about all of this, haven't I?" I asked, meek.

Luke's eyes softened, but only just. He shook his head and laughed sardonically to himself.

"Uh huh," he agreed.

"I've been so worried about you knowing the, er—finer details of it all," I began, and Luke listened with an intent, albeit tired, expression. "I think my guard's up because what you think means...a lot."

A corner of his lip pulled up, and then sank back down.

"I want to be here."

The way he said it made my stomach feel like lead.

"Why does it sound like you're convincing yourself of that as you say it?"

He chuckled nervously, and it did nothing to help the anxious aura of the room.

"I'm not," he said, looking down at his hands that were knit in his lap. "Really—I *do* want to be here, but—"

For the second time tonight, I repeated back to him, *"But?"*

To say it was unsettling would have been an understatement. Hearing the conjunction insinuated...regret. Just hours ago, I was intent on leaving Luke behind in Salem for his own good, but now, the tables had turned entirely. *Now,* I had a support system in place for my fucked up life that I had never allowed myself to keep before...and it was, for lack of a better word, great. The relief that had engulfed me in the time since I had given in to Luke's request to stay with me was all encompassing. It had come with a few hiccups—okay, a few rather *large* bumps in the road—but I still felt more at ease about my situation now than I ever had. To have that all taken away with a simple *but* was...jarring.

"I'm sorry," I rushed through an apology as quickly as it could form in my brain, my filter effectively turning off. "I'm *really* fucking sorry. I was waiting for the perfect time to tell you everything—" I closed my eyes tightly in an attempt to abate the familiar sting of impending tears. "And I mean fuckin' *everything.* The whole nine yards—my shitty parents, the shitty debt my mom racked up, her shitty fucking drug dealer, my shitty relationship with Colt, and all the *shitty* things we had to do."

Luke's shoulders slouched, his eyes softening with sympathy as I rambled on.

"Claire—"

"But *no,"* I mocked myself, "I waited too fucking long, and everything caught up with me!" I waved my casted arm in front of my face as if it were proof of my wrongdoings. "And then I *had* to tell you—and it was *too fucking fast.* I didn't even get through all the important shit before it hit me in the fucking face that I wanted to leave you so you didn't have to *deal* with me."

"Claire—"

"And *then* you follow me down here!" I exclaimed, my face feeling rather hot; my eyes as wide as they could be for being filled with tears. I laughed disbelievingly. "You fucking perfect, loveable, anxiety-ridden man—you made me feel like everything was okay, so I *caved.* And it felt *so goddamn good.* And *then,* all the shit that I didn't get to tell you yet fucking slapped you in the face and I—" I took a deep breath and shuddered upon my exhale. "It was all wrong. And I don't want you to leave and I'm sorry and..."

Luke stood and sat beside me on the bed, both his quick action to stand and the creaking of the mattress beneath us interrupting my train of thought.

"Relax," he whispered, looking so deeply into my eyes that one would believe he knew the art of hypnotism. "You can breathe, Claire."

"I'm," a sob interrupted my words, *"sorry."*

I felt his arms around me before I saw him move. One hand rested on the nape of my neck and the other around my waist, and he pulled me towards him gently. My face pressed against his chest in such a way that I could hear his heart beating through his shirt, and my breath shook. He shushed me quietly.

"I'm not going anywhere," he murmured reassuringly. "I don't think I could if I tried."

Relief flooded me, and I rasped a quiet, "Really?"

His lips touched the top of my head briefly and he released me, gripping each of his hands on my biceps as if to steady me.

"Yes," he told me on an exhale with the ghost of a smile gracing his mouth, "really. But for the love of *God,* just...*try* to communicate a little better. Otherwise, I'm gonna go fuckin' insane."

I chuckled, swiping at my wet cheeks.

"Deal."

He smiled wider, pulling me in for a brief, sweet kiss.

"Can we just try to...forget about all this for a little?" He asked.

"Yes," I replied as quickly as I realized what he was asking. *"Please."*

"Are you hungry?"

I hadn't realized until he asked that I hadn't eaten all day. The stress of leaving him in Virginia, meeting with Colton, and my plans being completely derailed when Luke, James, Zoey, and Liam arrived had diminished my appetite. Now that I had an opportunity to relax, if but for a moment, my hunger hit me full force.

"Starving."

Chapter Fourteen

The alarm sounded at 7:30 A.M., far too loud. The unfamiliar clang of the motel room's clock grated on my ears, and I groaned. I slapped blindly in the direction of it, and on the third attempt, hit a button that switched the obnoxious alarm noise to radio. Hispanic music blared through the speakers, screaming at me to, *'Dame más gasolina.'*

"Ah, no-no," I whined, opening my eyes and sitting up to silence the old contraption.

I felt Luke's body vibrate behind me in quiet laughter, and he wrapped an arm around my naked waist as I poked and prodded at the clock.

"My favorite song, you shouldn't have," he murmured. "It's about," he yawned, "this girl who loves gasoline. Can't get enough of it—wants more of it. Great story."

The radio was silenced, and I fell back to the bed with a thud and a squeak. I grumbled at my oddly sore muscles as I stretched my arms this way and that. Luke planted a kiss between my shoulder blades.

He crooned, "Mornin', Jesse James."

"You're chipper this morning," I muttered with a smile.

"This is *far* better than how I woke up yesterday, so...yeah," he deduced happily, "chipper."

I smiled a bittersweet smile, knowing that he was referencing waking up to my absence.

"I'm sore," I told him in an accusatory voice. "What did you do to me?"

It went without saying that our pent-up frustration from the situation that we were in went to good use the night before. I was honestly shocked that the wonky bed frame was still standing on all four legs, though I was certain that I had heard it scoot across the carpet a few times after a well-timed thrust.

The scruff on his face scratched at my bare back, and he rotated his hips pointedly into my backside, erection ever-present.

"Maybe I didn't do enough," he said gruffly.

Oh, help me.

I turned around in his embrace to face him, and his eyes were sleep-filled and carefree. I hated to take that away from him, but it was time to suck it up and face reality. I kissed him lightly, pulling away when he began to lean in for more.

"Tempting," I simpered, "but we have to get going."

He pouted out his lower lip but didn't stop me as I climbed out of bed. His gaze followed me around the room as I walked to my suitcase, and he rested his hands behind his head.

He asked, "Is it possible that if we never leave this room, all your problems will just...disappear?" I shook my head, laughing, and he further pondered, "Or we could just move out of the country. Would you like Canada? I feel like you would like Canada. You like winter, right?"

"I *do* like winter," I responded. "Congratulations, you know me *so* well." I grabbed Luke's duffel bag off the floor and tossed it at him. "Even Canada can't fix my problems, though. Now, get up!"

He sighed loudly, asking, "It was worth a shot though, right?"

"Of course, it was, baby," I cooed at him as I waltzed into the bathroom with a fresh outfit in hand.

We dressed in a comfortable silence. We brushed our teeth at the same time and as I leaned over to spit, Luke patted me on my rear. He fussed with his hair while I slowly detangled mine, and when we locked eyes in the mirror, we gave each other a soft smile. Save for the fact that we were in a low-rent motel due to my haggard past, it was unextraordinary—and at this moment, I was *craving* unextraordinary. I didn't think either of us were ready to face what was to come today, but truthfully, we had no choice.

It was 7:59 when the rap of Zoey's knuckles on the front door met our ears.

"Hey there," she said, eyeing me up and down. "Have a nice night?"

I ignored her tell-tale, *'I know what you did,'* look and just nodded, responding, "Oh yeah. You?"

"Mhm," she replied, "uneventful. Ready?"

The drive to the station was interesting, to say the least, and I was under the inclination that Zoey's night was not, as she had said, *uneventful.*

All of us squeezed into Zoey's little hatchback; one could say that we were well over capacity. Liam, being the largest of the three men, graciously took the passenger seat while Zoey was sandwiched between Luke and James in the back. Us being packed into the little vehicle as if we were ready to don clown attire wasn't what intrigued me, though. What piqued my interest most was the near constant attempt at eye contact that James was throwing Zoey's way. It was difficult for me to keep my eyes on the road as every adjustment of his body and shift of his gaze seemed deliberate. By the time we arrived, even *I* felt flustered.

Vehicle safely in park, Zoey exited as if she were struggling for breath, and I failed to hold back a snort of laughter. Her normally golden skin was ashen, and I could see more of the whites of her eyes than I typically could.

If I weren't right next to them, I wouldn't have heard Liam ask her quietly, "You okay, Zo'?"

She nodded quickly, resting a hand on her upper stomach as if she were feeling ill.

"Just a little car sick," she mumbled.

Zoey had never been car sick in her life. I was forced to hide my smirk at her lie as I allowed the men to walk ahead of us and pinched at the fabric of Zoey's green blouse to keep her behind.

She turned to me, and I asked, "Car sick, eh?"

"Mhm," Zoey hummed back.

"Something happen last night, I take it?" I pressed.

"Er—yes?" She spoke the statement as a question.

"What?"

"No—"

"Well, *which is it?*"

"Look, you have a *lot* going on right now, Claire," she remarked. "It's nothing. Really."

"Well, *obviously* it's something, look at you."

"Fine," she hissed. "Fucking *James.*"

"Yes, I assumed that it was about him."

She unnecessarily tucked her blonde hair behind both of her ears. "He's being all...*flirty.*"

I joked, "What, you can't handle flirty? What have you become?"

Zoey held up a hand between us. "I can *handle* flirty. The problem is that he wants to *date.*"

"Date?" I responded. "He *asked you out?*"

She wore a grimace on her face. "It was more of an...*after all this blows over, do you want to grab a drink with me...*type thing."

"Doesn't he have a whole *wife?*"

Zoey shook her head. "Nah, they've been separated for a few months. Divorce proceedings take a long time, yada yada."

"Hmm—so he asked you out and you said…"

"That if he wanted a dirty, back-alley fuck, I'd be *happy* to oblige…" I laughed at her comment that was so very Zoey-like in nature, and she continued, "but, I don't *do* dates—and he was *very* uninterested in the one-time sexcapade that I had in mind."

"Darn." I chuckled, peeking behind her to see Luke, Liam, and James peering at us curiously. "So, what's the plan, then?"

"Well," she started, "he's a little…*intense*…if you haven't noticed."

"I have."

"Makes things a bit difficult for me since I *want* his tattooed ass, but I can't do anything about it." She sighed heavily. "I am up to my fucking *ears* in sexual tension, and I haven't gotten laid in *months.*"

I laughed softly at her dramatic misery and ushered her, "So…"

"Er—step one, avoidance," she responded. "We are currently in step one, if you haven't noticed."

"I have—go on."

"Step two…rub one out in a bathroom again."

"Again?"

"I've had a long night, Claire," she rattled off quickly. "Step *three,* once this is all over—distance."

"You guys coming?" Luke called out to us from the front doors of the precinct.

We yelled in unison, "Yeah!"

"Forget about me," Zoey demanded as we began to move our feet once more. "You've got enough happening at the moment—let's go fix your life, yeah?"

I replied, "Yeah, let's go," bringing thoughts on greeting those who I hadn't in years to the forefront of my mind.

The building was just as I remembered it: small, and grey. The familiarity of a rural town apparent in the chatter of close-knit voices hummed throughout the room. Though it was only roughly 8:30 in the morning, the scent of coffee in the air was stale.

I made my way to the counter, everyone congregating behind me as I walked through the nostalgia wave that encompassed me.

"Hi, I was hoping to—"

"Claire?!"

A loud voice came from far beyond the counter, the body it belonged to soon following to greet me. He had a stocky build, his frame struggling to hold onto the muscle that he had obtained decades ago when he first started working with the force. His blonde hair was cut in what one could call a typical cop fashion, flat across the top and practically shaved clean on the sides.

"Hey, Paul," I replied, smiling.

I would have been surprised that he recognized me, but with this being such a small town, I supposed that I was probably one of the more high-profile cases that he'd had. When I was turning in my mother, I talked almost exclusively with Paul. He helped me through everything, really. Though he was just another reminder of my colorful past, seeing Paul was more of a relief than anything. A familiar face in all of this—one I could trust, even—was welcomed.

He made his way over, clapping me on the side of my left arm, squeezing it briefly. He glanced down at my opposite casted side with his blue eyes curiously, but didn't inquire about it further. He glanced around, scanning the faces that stood behind me.

"Claire and friends?" I nodded hesitantly and he squinted at me. "You're not just here for a social call, I take it?" I shook my head. He sighed, his smile fading. "Alright, come on back then." He pointed at our group. "Coffees?"

It tasted like dirt. Maybe I had just gotten used to the coffee house that Luke and I frequented back home, but...man, this *really* tasted like dirt. We gathered in Paul's office, practically shoulder to shoulder from lack of room. Liam, standing directly behind me and next to Zoey, lifted a styrofoam cup to his mouth and stifled a disgruntled noise.

He leaned down almost to Zoey's level, whispering, "Will they be offended if I don't drink this?"

She exhaled through her nose quickly, amused, mumbling, "Coffee snob."

"Seriously," he continued softly, and I strained my ears to listen. "This is even worse than *your* coffee, and I don't know how that's possible."

"Pour it in the plant," she muttered, tipping her head towards what looked like a Ficus that stood next to Liam.

"What?" He whisper-hissed. "No—it'll *die,* Zo'! I can't have a plant's death on my hands!"

She let out a louder chortle, her breath catching in her throat, but quieted herself as Paul strode into what I assumed was his office and closed the door behind him. His desk was littered with various papers; a computer monitor angled towards his chair only partially visible from where I stood displayed a digital collage of his family and friends.

Paul sat in his black desk chair and rapped his fingers on the wooden counter with knuckles.

"Okay, Claire—what can I do ya for?"

If the nostalgia that hit me when I entered the precinct was a wave, this would have been a tsunami. With that one sentence, I was flooded with a dejavú of my first time there.

"What can I do ya for?"

Paul looked at me with light, yet concerned eyes.

He couldn't understand the gravity of my situation—of course, he couldn't. To him, I was just a young girl. A college student, perhaps. All he knew was that I had something to discuss with any police officer that would give me the time of day. And I really, really did not know where to even begin.

"It's my mother."

I opened my mouth a few times, closing it promptly afterward, and Paul waited patiently.

"Take your time," he told me reassuringly, cocking his head to the right as he asked, "Is she okay?"

"Not, uh—not exactly. My mother, er—hasn't been okay for a while, to be honest, but this isn't really about that."

"What do you mean?"

"My mother's not a...a bad person," I prefaced, attempting not to stammer as I gathered my thoughts.

"Of course, not."

"I mean she wasn't," I corrected my statement. "She's dug herself a bit of a hole—erm, she uses. A lot. I tried to help, but now everything is affecting me, and I can't—"

"It's Claire, right?" I nodded sheepishly, and I could feel the sympathy in his ocean-colored eyes. "I can tell you're nervous," he said slowly. "Don't worry—you're trying to protect your mother; we can help you with that. We can give you information on rehab centers—"

"Ah," I hesitated with my interruption. I could tell that Paul wanted to help me however he could, but I didn't need the spiel about getting her into rehab. I had gone down that avenue already—several times, in fact, and it was to the point that that option was as exhausted as I was. "No...I am trying

to help her," I stressed. "She just," I paused momentarily, "she's been stealing from me."

Paul's thick eyebrows raised. "Oh?"

"That would be putting it lightly," I said.

"Putting it lightly...how?"

"Well, for one, I went to apply for a loan for a car. The credit check came back and there were all these loans...credit cards I had never seen before, too, and I asked her about it—"

"Hold on a minute." Paul leaned across his desk toward me. "She took loans out in your name?" I hummed in acknowledgment. "Claire, that's identity theft—that's not just stealing."

"Yes," I agreed. "She said she would get it all back. I believed her, but it just keeps happening."

He bobbed his head up and down and took a breath.

"Now, I'm not saying I don't believe you—I do." Paul's gold wedding band reflected a small bit of light as he held up a single hand. "But you do need to have proof of everything if—well, I should ask—you're trying to make a report of this?"

I nodded emphatically, replying, "I know what she skimmed off my accounts in the past few years and the loans—er, there are several debt collectors that call me non-stop, you could talk to any of them."

"No, no—a credit report will do," Paul stated blandly, opening a drawer to grab a notepad and a pen. He clicked it several times. "You said she skimmed your accounts?"

"Since I was 16," I confirmed. "I'm, er—I'm 21 now."

He jotted down a few notes on his yellow pad.

"Five years, huh? And these were your accounts? How did she—"

"Some, she had control over," I answered his question before he could finish it. "For others—credit cards and such—fake driver's license. My name. Her face."

"Creative," he murmured, nose to paper. "And how much has she taken, including the loans?"

"Ah," I paused. "I can't even—"

"Ballpark," Paul stated. "It's okay if it's not exact, we can figure that out once we have your records of it all."

It was a dreaded question—I knew it would come up in this meeting, but I still didn't like answering it. Not necessarily because it was embarrassing per se, but more because of the low likelihood of someone believing the large number.

I told him, "Upwards of one hundred and fifty grand."

And with that, Paul's scribbling stopped. He glanced up with an inquisitive expression and held it, his eyes scanning my face as if he were attempting to see the lie that I had just told written across it.

"Come again?"

Memory lane sucked. I looked back into Paul's blue eyes as they crinkled at the corners with a familiar, yet knowing, concern, and I figured that there was no reason to beat around the bush. In the several meetings that I had with Paul after the initial one that I relived in my dejavú flashback, Travis' name had come up more than a handful of times. I had made it known that he was my mother's dealer, and though Paul was well aware of his reputation *and* his occupation, there was no proof of his wrongdoings to speak of. And, in Paul's words, Travis was *slippery*.

"I think we can help you get Travis," I said.

Paul's brows rose quickly, wrinkling his forehead. "Oh."

James muttered, "Well, that was quick and to the point."

Paul started to ask, "How—"

"We have a reason to believe that someone owes him money. Or drugs, either way. We want to lead him somewhere and make him think that he'll be confronting this someone...we can record any of our meetings as proof and, well...that's where you come in."

Paul crossed his arms across his chest. "Someone, eh?"

I pursed my lips together. "I—" I was unsure how to respond, as I needed to protect Colton's name. "Yes."

"I take it I'm not going to get that out of you?"

"Ah, no," I replied quietly. "I need to, erm—guarantee their safety...in exchange for getting Travis."

"Listen, Claire," Paul offered me an apologetic glance. "I—even if I *could* grant this... whomever immunity with the exception that we're able to put Travis behind bars, this is—" He fumbled on his words as if he were unsure of how he should approach the remainder of our conversation. "This is...unorthodox. Our force is small—you know that. Travis knows each and every one of us here at the precinct, and I can't offer anyone to go undercover, I—" He paused again. "A sting arranged by civilians is—"

To my surprise, it was Luke who spoke next. "Exactly what you need."

I squeezed his hand in a silent thanks, and he looked down at me to give me a slight smile.

"I was going to say, '*dangerous,*'" Paul clarified.

"It *is* exactly what you need, though," I repeated Luke's words. "Travis knows all of you here at the precinct, so none of you are viable. *We* know how to draw him in, and he only knows me."

Paul's fingers thrummed on his desk rhythmically as he thought to himself, his expression somber and pensive. Once his drumming stopped, he sighed heavily and asked:

"What exactly is your plan?"

Chapter Fifteen

L uke exclaimed, "Is that really fucking necessary?!"

He gestured at me wildly; the floor of the hotel room yet again taking a beating against his relentless walking back and forth.

I glanced down at my body and asked, "Is what necessary?"

I knew exactly what Luke was referencing, though. It had been months since I had worn this outfit. It was the first day that I worked at Henry's, and I had conveniently missed the way that his eyes raked over my body. I wrote it off as judgement rather than attraction and since Henry's was more of a casual place than anything, I had since decided to maintain my typical more modest attire. I was more comfortable that way, anyway.

Today, however, Zoey had used double-sided tape and sheer force of will to position my breasts in the most favorable fashion underneath the tight green halter top. With my rapidly upcoming meeting with Travis, it was best that I appeared to be a woman who had a significant interest in him—and that effort had not gone unnoticed.

"You know exactly what I'm talking about, Claire!" Luke spoke, his voice muffled as he was obscured from my view, pacing in the hallway. "Do you have to look so..."

"Hot?" Zoey finished his sentence for him. "Yeah, she kind of does—she's supposed to look like she *wants* to see Travis, right?"

Luke strode up to us and flopped himself hopelessly into the chair that resided in the corner of the room. A grimace marred his beautiful face, scrunching his nose.

"Yeah, I get the impression that she *wants* to see me when we're together too, and she normally just wears a regular shirt with jeans and converse so *riddle-me-fucking-that,*" he rattled off to her.

"Okay," Zoey retorted quickly, accepting the challenge without even taking a breath and holding up her index finger. "I will *riddle-you-fucking-that.* First night she worked with you, she wore—"

"This exact fucking outfit, I know," Luke grumbled, running a hand through his hair in frustration.

"You remember what I wore on one day half a year ago?" I asked gently.

"You looked..." Luke tried to find the words, shaking his head softly.

Zoey finished his thought with, "Amazing. I know she did. You're tellin' me that the *second* she strolled into that bar that you didn't wonder if she dressed that way for you?"

"No, I—"

"*Lukey—*"

He whined, "Gah, do you have to call me that?" Zoey smirked and raised her eyebrows in silent challenge. "And *no,*" he replied in a slightly higher pitch than his voice typically is.

"Even for a little bit?" Zoey pressed.

"*No—*"

She interrupted with a singsong two-syllabled, "Lu-uke."

"Okay *fine,*" he relented. "*Yes.* For like a split-fucking-second, I wondered if she wanted me, okay? How could I *not* when she was looking like *that?*" My cheeks flushed at Luke's admission, and his grey eyes shot to the ceiling for a moment before he gestured at Zoey with a flick of his wrist. "You happy? You like being right?"

Her emerald eyes sparkled, and her grin widened to show off her teeth. "Thrilled, Lukey."

Luke looked at me, exasperated, and I offered him a brief smile. I hoped to convey that I wished that we were absolutely anywhere but here, and he returned a soft grin to me. His jaw was tight and the smile didn't quite reach his eyes, but his understanding of my intent was conveyed. Our silent exchange was over once the door clicked open behind me, and Liam and James walked in.

"Hello, ladies," James announced his entrance, and Liam closed the door behind them. "Luke, you're included in that."

Luke rolled his eyes at this brother. *"Thanks,"* he sneered.

"Sorry, man—you are a *touch* whiney right now."

I noticed a corner of Zoey's lip pull up in a smile that she attempted to hide.

"Do ya fuckin' *blame me* for that?" Luke retorted. "I still think I should be going with all of you."

As we had discussed earlier, we all decided that it was in our best interests if Luke kept himself separated from the group. Though everyone was truly emotionally invested, Luke was anxiety incarnate—and we knew that he wouldn't be able to keep a level head.

"And we all still think that's a bad idea, so you're not," James quipped.

Luke tossed his head backward and groaned. "Tell me again why—"

"Brother," James began, but Luke bit back and cut him off.

"No, *really,* because this is *insane.* We can't think for a few more god-damn minutes to make a plan other than, *'Oh, right—Travis looooooves Claire! Let's use her as bait!'?"*

"To be fair," Zoey interjected, "Travis doesn't *love* Claire. From what I heard, he just wanted to fuck her—"

I hissed, *"Zoey!"*

"Makin' my point *for me* Zoey, thank you," Luke replied through gritted teeth. "I don't think *Trav,*" he said his name as if the mere presence of it felt oily in his mouth, "is going to care a whole lot about consent if it comes to it—"

"He's not gonna be able to actually *do* anything," James reiterated for what seemed like the umpteenth time.

"Oh, good, so Claire will only experience the trauma of the *beginnings* of an assault," Luke countered sardonically, his eyes narrowed in James' direction. *"Great."*

"Brother," he repeated, this time with more gusto, "I will be there. It's gonna be *fine.*"

"You rushing to defend Claire from Travis would make no sense if you're pretending to be on his side, and you know that," Luke retorted.

"Not to, ah," Liam paused as he spoke, "interrupt or anything, but I'll be there too." He inhaled a long breath that puffed out his chest in a manner that I couldn't decipher as proud or cocky. "In the background." He sighed loudly. "Awaiting any trouble that arises. Here to serve and protect—"

"We *got* it, Liam," Luke complained.

Liam rested a hand on his sternum and continued to speak, "As the largest, loudest, and proudest of three men here, I think it's important to consider that I'll be ready to kick some ass, that's all."

"This is, like—*serious,*" Luke told him in a quick reprimand. "You know that, right? Shit goes wrong and I don't—I don't even know..."

Luke's concern seeped through his words, and my chest constricted. I was certain that one of the many emotions he was feeling was hopelessness, and I truly hated that. I wished that I could change the inevitable or determine the future somehow, but none of us could—and Luke had even less say in that matter.

"I—sorry, I'm sorry," Liam replied rapidly with a shake of his head. "I don't do serious very well, sometimes it all gets all," he waved one of his hands around his forehead, "...drowned out, I dunno. I *am* here to help. Really."

Luke exhaled heavily, rubbing at his eyes, conceding with, "I know, man—I know."

"Okay, ah—can you guys give me and Luke a few minutes here? I'll meet you all in your room in a bit."

Zoey noted, "We don't have that much time, Claire—"

"I won't be long," I told her.

Liam, Zoey, and James all nodded, each making their silent descent.

Upon the closing of the door, I nearly whispered, "You seem stressed," as I walked back to him and sat on the edge of the bed.

"Stressed?" Luke questioned my choice of words, his light eyes piercing into mine. "I—no, I'm fine."

It was a lie, clearly, and I understood his intention. We had no idea how the next few hours would go, and with me putting myself directly in the line of fire and him being forced to bow out, I could tell that Luke didn't feel that his stress was warranted.

"You are not *fine,* Luke," I spoke softly. "You can tell me how you're feeling, you don't need to do that."

He sighed. "*Stressed* wouldn't even begin to cover it, Claire. *Stressed* is a busy night at Henry's with no one to help cover me—and I power right through normal stress. I don't give a shit about stress. *This,*" he waved a hand about, "is not stress."

I used to think of Luke as carefree—a sunny presence that could brighten my day in an instant. That Luke wasn't here now, though. He was replaced with a version of himself that was panicked, and he was right—the word *stress* didn't cover his emotions at the moment. And that truly made me ache.

"I know," I replied, my voice hoarse. "I'm sorry this is so—"

"I don't—you don't need to be sorry," he told me. "You shouldn't be sorry; I just need you to—" He cut himself off and shook his head.

I ushered him, "What?"

His head turned side to side once more. "No, I don't—"

"Luke—"

"I just *need-you-to-be-okay,"* he quickly trilled. "Okay?" He let out a quick breath. *"Please?"*

The ache in my chest grew. I stood and took the few steps to where Luke sat and he straightened, his posture rigid until I stood between his legs and took his jaw in my left hand, angling his face up to meet my gaze. His eyes softened, if only slightly, and I felt his hands reach up to brush against the back of my thighs softly.

"It's going to be—"

"Don't say it's going to be fine, Claire," he told me quietly. "I appreciate it, but none of this is fine."

I nodded somberly. "I know."

I leaned down to touch my lips to his, and his fingers flexed against my thighs to pull me closer.

Luke spoke again, "How are you feeling about all this?"

I rested my forehead against his and used the dreaded word once more. "Fine."

His thumbs traced patterns along the back of my jeans as he asked, "How?"

Somehow, that question felt loaded. I supposed that my gut's initial answer to that was...*familiarity.* I had been put in plenty of precarious positions via Colton in the past, and this felt no different. It was never until

I was fully separated from the dangers of...well...*everything* that realization would dawn on me and I would metaphorically implode. This was different, though. I had an entire support system behind me, and that was so very, very foreign. Before, I had to lift myself above it all to keep myself from drowning, and now...well, it only settled into my brain at this very moment that I didn't need to tread water anymore.

I blinked rapidly, my eyes suddenly burning with tears that I had no chance of keeping at bay.

"I'm not, actually," I deduced aloud, quietly, retracting my previous statement. "I'm not fine."

Luke's touch moved up to my lower back, and I straddled his lap as his hands splayed behind me, pulling me into an embrace. I cried silently into his shirt for an unknown amount of time, his touch grazing my back slowly, up and down in a comforting gesture. Once my tears slowed and my breath stopped shaking, he quietly voiced:

"We're going to get you out of this."

His vocal confidence was unwavering, the comfort in his words knowing no bounds, and it made me smile softly. Moments ago, I had felt the need to ensure *him* that everything was going to be alright. Now, the weight of the emotional burden of it all had shifted as Luke was stoic and I felt like I was about to crumble to pieces. We couldn't break down at the same time, after all—the give and take of our now-relationship made it so we wanted to put each other back together. And that made me love him all the more.

I pushed myself up and away from his chest, and kissed him slowly. Softly. Luke only began to pull back when we could both tell that we were about to lose ourselves in each other and, instead of following through with his silent suggestion, I pressed my lips against his more insistently. When I ran my tongue along his lower lip and bit it gently, he let out a deep, gravelly hum.

It was our mutual understanding, I think, that this was what I needed. What *we* needed, really. And that was an opportunity to take a break from all of this, if only for a moment. To express our love for each other. And, for the love of God, to not think about what the next couple of hours could entail.

He kissed me back eagerly, moving his hands to the back of my head and cradling it along with two fistfuls of my hair. Our breaths entwined in the space between us, leaving the air hot as we gasped into each other's mouths. It was no time at all before Luke's hands were delving underneath my top with an air of desperation. He pulled it over my head quickly and as it fluttered to the floor, he laid his eyes upon the mess before him.

Several strips of clear tape were used to pull everything—and I mean *everything*—up as high as could be mustered. The matte finish of it spanned across each of my breasts, and Luke scowled at it.

He hissed under his breath, "Fuck this shit," and his hands moved to the ends of the silicone-like texture of the tape on either side of me, ripping it from my skin in one swift motion.

The act wasn't painless by any means, but whatever discomfort I felt from it was quickly soothed with his mouth. He was damn near everywhere, cupping my freed breasts towards him to kiss at the skin that had turned pink from the brisk removal of the tape. My head lolled back at the sensation, and I laced my hands in his hair to angle his head this way and that. I began to grind myself onto him, his erection hard and straining against the zipper of his jeans. He moaned as I moved, his tongue never stopping the relentless motions against my chest, and I raked my nails along his back to grasp at his shirt.

I pulled it over his head and before it even hit the floor, the sound of the door opening reached both of our ears, and a string of curse words left Luke's mouth.

Zoey screeched, "Are you guys fucking *kidding* me?!" Luke pulled me to him tightly in an attempt to disguise my naked torso, and I felt rather than saw his glare in Zoey's direction. "Okay, *sorry*, Luke, Jesus—Claire, we *really* have to go."

"On my way," I told her, my head buried in Luke's neck.

Luke whispered quietly in my ear, "I swear to *God,* if anything happens to you..."

I cut off his tension-laced words by pushing myself up ever-so-slightly, pressing my mouth to his.

"I'll be fine," I replied.

It was a lie, of course, and it was overusing that same damned word. I could tell that Luke didn't care for my response, but he mustered on anyway, huffing out a breath and pulling up a corner of his lip in the smallest of smiles.

"If shit goes sideways on you guys, I'm dragging you out of wherever you are and taking you to Canada."

I nodded solemnly. Of course, if anything were to go wrong in this situation, Luke probably wouldn't be able to do a damn thing about it. He knew that; he wasn't a stupid man. So, there was no need to correct him—and there was no need for anything else to be said either.

I peeked backward to see that Zoey had made herself scarce, the door just barely cracked to give us a last moment of privacy, and I stood to redress myself for the unknown events ahead.

"Did he *really* have to ruin my masterpiece?"

Zoey groaned as if she were a child and Luke had up and stomped on a diorama that she had spent days meticulously creating. I rolled my eyes, though I couldn't hide the snort that came through my nose.

We, of course, had not even attempted to re-affix the tape to pull my cleavage upwards, and I had no intention of doing so. We were driving in Zoey's little hatchback, Luke left behind from our upcoming grand endeavors.

"They're just tits, Zoey," I told her.

"Just tits?" She asked me, swerving slightly as she drove along the nearly deserted highway and peered at me through slitted eyes in the rear-view mirror. She repeated, "Just. Tits?"

Liam, though he was clearly amused at Zoey's reaction, had splayed his hands across the window and the center console, effectively securing his bulky body in the passenger seat beside her.

He pleaded, "Could you pay attention to the road, Zo'?"

"Yeah, yeah," she grumbled, easing up on the gas pedal. "That was God's work I did, Claire," she continued to berate me. "And you just—"

"Let Luke rip it off me?" I countered. "Yeah. I did. I liked it, too."

"Kudos," James muttered from my left.

Zoey shot me an almost apologetic glance—*almost.* "You could have at least let me fix you back up."

I grimaced. "Didn't really care for the thought of Trav ogling me, anyway."

She pressed her lips into a fine line. "Yeah, okay."

We were pulling off the highway then, and as I saw the dim lighting of the bar in the distance, I sat a little straighter.

"Park down by York."

"York?" Zoey questioned. "That's like two blocks away."

"And it would be totally inconvenient if Trav saw us all pull up together," I reminded her.

"Right," she murmured, passing the building entirely and turning on the street I requested. "York."

She parked along the street, headlights dimming as she turned off the engine, and there was a stretch of time where no words were said. The absence of the hum of the engine left the space eerily quiet, and the tension in the air grew thick as we all sat in the dark. I could only assume that no one wanted to be the person to say that it was time to face the metaphorical music, but once Liam began to shift in his seat and Zoey's keys clinked together as she pulled her keys out of the ignition, James bit the bullet for all of us.

"So, uh—"

"Yeah," I voiced quickly, reaching for the handle to my right, opening the door and triggering the lights above us to automatically illuminate. The nerves bloomed in my gut as it felt as though I were walking straight into fire, and I twisted to face James. His expression was somber, the overhead lights casting long shadows across his face, and I asked, "Are you good, Jay?"

A large part of our plan was, of course, based on James selling himself as a man that Travis could relate to. Earlier in the day, Colton had briefed James on his prior misdemeanors with men similar to Travis, the intention being that James could use the detailed plot as his own. I could only use my imagination regarding the actions Colton had described. I had watched James' face contort in disgust as he held his phone against his ear, his crooked nose scrunching as he replied with occasional sardonic phrases like, *'Lovely,'* and, *'Oh, is that all?'.*

James nodded regarding my inquisition, and I further pressed, "Did Colt give you enough to—"

He held up a hand to silence me, for I had asked the question repeatedly already.

"Colton told me so much that I want to scrub my brain with a memory-loss detergent," he replied in a consoling tone, giving me a soft smile. "I've got this; don't worry about me."

"Okay," I murmured, and James ushered me with a tip of his head to the outside:

"Go."

"Yeah," I whispered. "See you guys in a bit."

I walked out into the damp night air. The amount of time that it took to reach the front door of the establishment was undeniably short, my nerves not even allowing my mind to wander as I placed one foot in front of the other. All I focused on as I walked was the light in the distance that was situated on the patio of the bar, calling me towards it with every flicker as it toggled on and off.

Arranging my get together with Travis was easier than I had anticipated. A handful of text messages back and forth were all that was needed to pique his interest. Naturally, he was curious as to why I wanted to see him at all, but upon saying that we could chat when we met in person, he was all too eager to meet up. The bar that he had chosen was the same one that had gotten us all into this mess. It felt like I had oddly come full circle as I passed the space on the patio where Colton had confronted me, and where my fist had subsequently come into contact with his face.

When I entered, the dim, nostalgic atmosphere hit me in the same fashion as it had when Zoey and I were here less than a week ago. The feeling combined with seeing Travis sitting around the corner of the bar, eyes on me the second my heel clacked on the flooring in front of the entrance, shot a chill down my spine.

He was lifting a short glass partly filled with a dark liquor toward his face, but stopped halfway when he noticed me. Truthfully, he was an attractive man. His hair was a dark auburn, long enough to just barely tuck behind his ears. The strands held a natural soft curl to them, most noticeable at the nape of his neck and in the tendrils that fell across his forehead. His jaw was square, only slightly obscured by ginger stubble, and his dark eyes crinkled at the corners as he smiled in my direction.

His looks could have invited anyone in. They *did* invite any-one—everyone—in. I was certain, in fact, that several women had fallen into the trope of, *'Oh, I can fix him,'* only to be sorely mistaken because Travis was *not* a nice man underneath it all. I didn't know him terribly well, but I knew enough to confidently say that his narcis-sism knew no bounds. That, along with his violent tendencies and a fondness for drugs—not to mention his connections to my estranged mother—made my legs almost lock up as I strolled my way toward his seat.

That wasn't an option, though. Instead, I bit the inside of my cheek to prevent myself from scowling—hard enough that I briefly tasted the coppery tang of blood. Then, I mimicked his smile back to him the best I could.

"Claire," he crooned as I took the seat beside him. "You're a sight for sore eyes."

"Travis." I did my best to trail my line of sight over his figure down to his feet and back to his head again, grazing past his boots and jeans and lingering on the threads of his fall themed flannel. "You look good."

Saying the words out loud felt...greasy.

"I look good? Shit," his Southern accent peaked through on the profane word, and his smile grew to bare his teeth, "the hell did I do to gain your approval?"

Somehow, I managed a soft laugh and a shrug of my shoulders. "A lot of self-reflection," I deduced, vaguely. "Separation from Colt helped."

"Ah, right," he replied. "Shit bag of an...ex, now?"

"Mhm," I hummed in confirmation, "I *did* leave Colt, yeah. Skipped town for a bit."

"I noticed. Where'd you take off to?"

One eye on the man behind the bar in a desperate attempt to get his attention so I could soothe my nerves with alcohol, I asked, "Colt didn't tell you?"

"Nah." He followed my darting gaze. "You want a drink?"

"Guilty," I admitted with what I could only hope came across as a coy grin.

The bartender noticed me then and I gave him a small wave. He looked like he had been at a bar for half of his life—and not necessarily just behind the counter. Puffy, red circles lined his eyes and his belly was distended, though he didn't look like he had much weight on him elsewhere. I asked for a shot of tequila and he nodded, his thinning hair practically blowing in the breeze from the movement.

"So, where've you been?" Travis pressed me as he took a sip from his glass.

"Ah, Virginia." A shot glass was slid in front of me at the most fortunate time, giving me an acceptable reason to not elaborate on my exact living accommodations. I grabbed it, clinked my glass against Travis' that he still held in his hand, and said, "Cheers."

Warmth flooded my veins almost as soon as I chugged it, and Travis raised an eyebrow at me, his smile widening as I set the empty glass on the counter before us.

"Look at *you.*"

His muttering was drowned out by my internal thoughts desperately wishing that James would arrive sooner rather than later. Thankfully, it wasn't long after a shrug and yet another forced smile that I felt the humid breeze from the front door wisp across my face. I couldn't make eye contact with James for fear of it becoming obvious that we were well acquainted, and I didn't have the chance to do so. Travis had thoroughly distracted me, placing a hand on my upper thigh and squeezing, murmuring something in my ear about getting me another drink if I'd like one.

I resisted the urge to cringe, wince, flinch, or anything of the like. Instead, against every instinct I had, I leaned in toward his words so closely that I could feel his breath on my ear. His grip remained on my leg, only tightening as I angled myself in his direction, and I fought like hell to maintain the slight smile on my lips.

James sat beside me, leaving one stool between us for good measure, and ordered himself a beer as the bartender walked by. Not long after, Liam and Zoey came through the entrance, another gust of air reaching us as the front door opened and closed yet again, and they sat at a booth that was just barely within eyeshot.

"Virginia, huh?" Travis asked me, bringing our conversation back full circle.

"Yep—not too far," I lied.

"Close enough for visits, I take it."

"Definitely close enough for visits."

"You like it there?"

I shrugged, not wanting to be overly-emphatic about my love for my new living situation.

"Yeah," I told him. "It's nice."

"Why'd you leave, anyway?"

The chance to mention Colton while James was within earshot was too easy to pass up, and I took it. I huffed out a loud breath.

"Why do you think? Damn town's too small—I'd run into Colton wherever I went if I stayed."

James, playing the part, held his bottle of beer in mid-air as if he were going to take a sip and paused at the mention of Colton's name. I felt his eyes on me, looking me up and down as if he were trying to place me, and he set the bottle down with a purpose.

Travis began to ask, "Rough split—"

"Sorry, I—not to interrupt," James spoke in our direction, and I twisted my body toward his voice. "Do I know you?"

"I don't think so, guy," Travis said offhandedly, fingers flexing on my leg to pull my attention back to him.

"No, no," James said, waving Travis off and gesturing towards me. "You, I swear you look familiar."

"Um," I squinted my eyes and shook my head, "I don't *think* so."

"I'm James," he said, grinning at me in a lopsided manner and sticking out a hand for me to shake.

"Claire."

I stretched my arm over the chair between us and shook it.

"Claire," James spoke my name as if he were testing it. "You from around here or what?"

"Used to live kinda nearby...moved a while back to—"

"Look, man," Travis announced over my shoulder to James, "we're in the middle of something here, okay?"

"Ah, sure." James held out an index finger. "Just one question, and it's probably a stretch—guy I used to work with dated a Claire..." His outstretched finger gestured at my hair. "Think she was a red." Travis let out an exasperated sigh, his annoyance with James ever apparent until

James said, "You're not Colton's Claire, are you? Buzz cut, icy blue eyes that could cut through you, total douchebag?"

I didn't have to see Travis to notice that his demeanor changed entirely. His posture straightened, and his touch on my thigh finally subsided until he released me entirely.

"Langdon?" I said Colton's last name as a clarification point, and James nodded. "Ah, no—*not* Colton's Claire anymore. I agree with you on the douchebag front, though."

"You got a problem with Colton?"

Travis spoke now, his voice holding a note of curiosity, and James snorted.

"A problem isn't exactly what I'd call it. Fucker owes me."

The ink on James' arms flexed as he lifted his beer bottle to his lips, taking a large gulp. Travis hummed to himself.

"We may have started off on the wrong foot," he said thoughtfully, thrusting a hand across my body towards James. "Travis." James shook his hand as Travis noted, "I think we have something in common, James."

"Yeah?" James' eyebrows lifted as he took Travis in.

"Yeah," Travis confirmed. He looked like he was pondering something to himself for a moment before finishing his drink in a single swig. He set the heavy glass on the bar top, clunking the wood counter, and asked James, "You wanna walk with me? I could use a smoke." James shrugged noncommittally, and Travis' hand was once again on my thigh, his other hand flagging down the bartender. "You want another drink? I'll be back in a bit."

I nodded, telling him that a vodka soda would be fine. A small voice inside of me somewhere screamed that having another drink when I needed to keep my wits about me was a terrible idea, but I quashed the thought quickly. After all, I was the one who messaged Travis to meet up for drinks...it would be odd for me to refuse one at this point.

The man behind the counter made my drink quickly, setting it down closer to Travis than myself in his haste to tend to other patrons who were awaiting his attention at the opposite end of the bar. Travis grabbed the short glass, fingers along the rim and palm facing down to the clear liquid, and slid it towards me.

"I'll be back," he muttered down to me as he stood. "Don't you go anywhere."

I watched them leave, absentmindedly bringing my glass to my lips and taking a tentative sip as they exited through the front door. Zoey caught my eye then, mouthing, *'You okay?'* from across the room. I gave her a reassuring smile and Liam, who was sitting beside her on the same side of the booth, leaned down slightly to say something in her ear. She broke her eye contact with me, nodding at whatever he had said.

I tried to keep my mind blissfully empty while James and Travis were gone, but that was an impossibility. Realistically, it was somewhere between ten and fifteen minutes that they were outside speaking to Colton's wrongdoings, but the time dragged on and it felt like hours. I mostly thought of James and if he was successfully convincing Travis that he had been duped by Colton as well. The idea of what their conversation was like at this very moment made me feel damn near twitchy with anticipation, and it wasn't long before my drink was drained. The ice clinked together as I sat the empty glass down on the counter, and the front doors opened yet again to reveal a Travis whose wide, Cheshire-like grin was stretching across his face.

He strode up and stood behind me, wrapping an arm around my front to give me a very brief, tight squeeze before he let me go. I twisted around to face both him and James and upon witnessing Travis' palpable giddiness, relief flooded my veins.

"Claire," he inquired. "Have you heard from Colt lately?"

I shook my head. "We're not exactly on good terms. He tries to reach out pretty often, but I never respond."

James flashed a wide, toothy smile, and he muttered, "Lovely."

"You think he'd answer if you called?" Travis asked.

I scoffed, throwing in a roll of my eyes for good measure.

"Yeah, no question there. Been ignoring him since I moved, but he's been *kinda* relentless with trying to get in touch."

"*Oh,* Claire," Travis cooed at me. "We have *lots* to chat about."

"Do we?" I asked, my voice going up an octave. Travis quickly pulled out his wallet, placing a few bills on the countertop that would have sufficiently covered our tab and James did the same. "Oh—are you leaving?"

"Just thinking we," Travis gestured towards the three of us, "could chat outside."

I asked the both of them, "I—er, what does this have to do with Colt?"

Travis extended a hand to me and as I took it, he pulled me upright.

"Let's go." He insisted. "It's...*loud* in here, no?"

I don't think anyone would have described the atmosphere in the bar as *loud.* It was clear that Travis simply did not want to be heard, so I just shrugged and began to walk behind him and James, all the while trying to calm my rapidly beating heart. As we approached the door, Zoey cast me a fleeting look that questioned how things were going once again. Both her and Liam's eyes told me that they were anticipating this entire situation to go downhill, so I shook my head and gave them a slight smile as I walked past.

The air hit my face and before the door even closed behind me, Travis was in the process of lighting himself another cigarette. He sparked the lighter three times with this thumb before it was able to hold a flame and brought it to the cigarette he held between his lips, inhaling deeply. I followed both James and Travis to a burnt orange truck situated in the middle of the parking lot that I could only assume belonged to Travis. As Travis leaned back against the vehicle's tailgate, he took the cigarette in between two fingers and pulled it away from his face, exhaling a cloud of smoke into the night sky.

"Your *lovely* ex," he spoke to me, "owes me and James a fair bit of money. Colt's been radio silent for weeks—the only person I've talked to lately that's heard from him at all is you."

I took a breath to steady myself, for I couldn't be outwardly excited about how everything was occurring according to plan, nor too eager to get in contact with Colt.

I stammered in question, "Oh, um—okay?"

"I," Travis began, gesturing between himself and James, "*we* need you to call Colton and—"

"*Ah,*" I groaned and shuffled my feet, "look...I do *not* want to talk to Colt. I've been avoiding him for half a year for good reason."

"Well," Travis replied, "I would be...*very* grateful." I sighed audibly, crossing my arms over my chest, and he pressed, "One call—five minutes or less. I'll snag the phone from you and do most of the talking, even."

Unbeknownst to Travis, James flashed me a quick, questioning glance as our expected arrangement deviated slightly. I recalled how certain Colton sounded when he told us all that Travis wouldn't want to make himself known in this situation—the expectation from Travis' point of view being that he fooled Colton back into his untrustworthy arms. Travis' casual mention that he would do most of the talking insinuated otherwise, and because I couldn't outwardly express that I was grasping at straws regarding Travis' intention, I shrugged in an attempt to show James that I was as confused as he was.

"I dunno, Trav, what would I even *say?*" I tried to get any sort of intel on Travis' inner thoughts. "I don't even want to hear his voice—"

"I'll take care of it," Travis noted with a casual flick of his wrist. "Just act like you're trying to catch up and I'll take it from there—he's gonna get what's coming to him, Claire, I just need you to do me this *one* solid."

For just a moment, I froze—and I was certain that James did as well. It was clear that at this point, we were going in blind. It set my nerves on edge to think so, but because it felt necessary, I powered forward with what scraps of our plan remained.

I muttered, "Alright," and pulled my phone from my pocket, tapping the glass face a few times, and holding it up to my ear.

I only had to wait for a ring and a half for Colton to answer eagerly. "Claire?"

"Colton."

"You're with Travis? How's it going over there?"

It was so subtle that I could have imagined it, but I could have sworn that Colton's voice quavered on the second sentence. He was nervous, understandably, and hearing that emotion from him of all people shot a shiver down my spine that I had to play off as a reaction to the light breeze that blew my hair across my face.

"Yeah, I'm in town." I pretended to have not spoken with him in months. "It's...fine." I paused for just a split second before saying, "Virginia, yeah, it's—"

"Is this supposed to be a convincing conversation?" Colton mocked; his nervousness seemingly abated for just a moment.

"Ah," I took the chance to interject my emotions of how this night was going whilst being as vague as possible, "yes and no. Not what I was expecting."

Travis cocked his head to the side, brows pinched together as I continued to speak into my phone, extending a hand in question as if to say, *'Ready for me to take over?'*. I held up an index finger in silent response to his questioning, showing him that I needed a minute.

"Erm," Colton asked, "why not?"

"Haven't quite figured out what's going on here," I admitted.

"Okay, *be careful with your wording, Claire,*" Colton warned me. "Trav gets skeptical *real* easy these days—"

My heart hammered twice against my rib cage, and I quickly added, "With *us?*" Colton sighed audibly, his breath shaking as I continued a false one-sided conversation. "I meant what's going on with my *life,* there is no *us,* Colt, *Christ.*"

"You're a fucking terrible actress," he rattled off, "and if he believes you then *great,* but Claire, I *really* need you to listen to me. What we talked about before—Trav telling you to call me and set up a fake meet—that's not happening?"

"No."

"James good, Trav believes him?"

"Yeah."

"Uh...ok, er—" Colton stammered as the gears in his brain churned in an attempt to figure out what was going on in Travis' head. "You're with Trav, right? He's watching you talk to me right now?"

"Mhm."

"And he told you to call me?"

"Yes."

"Did he say to...to tell me anything at all?"

"No, not at all." The line was silent for long enough that I questioned if he had hung up. "Colt?"

"He told you he wanted to grab the phone to talk to me himself at some point, didn't he?" Colton asked, his voice dropping an octave.

"Mhm," I confirmed. "Currently waiting for that."

"Leave."

"What?"

"Leave, Claire. I've seen him play this card before, he—"

"Colt, you of *all* people—"

Colton screamed, "NOW!"

I unintentionally flinched away from the word, my blood running cold at the panic in his voice, and Travis pushed away from his tailgate, standing to his full height as he snatched the phone away from my ear.

"Colton," he said menacingly. "Long time no talk." He ashed his cigarette by flicking his fingers and took another drag. "Yeah, I'm *sure* you were just about to get back in touch with me. Look—you know the drill, man." Travis fully blew out the puff of smoke that had been slowly escaping his mouth with every word, and he shook his head at whatever Colton was saying on the other end of the line. "I skipped *right* over that option, bud. Just—no—Colt, *no*—we're past that, man. We're past it. Okay?"

Travis had maintained his close proximity with me from when he retrieved my phone, close enough that he managed to reach his hand down to enclose my casted wrist. From the appearance of an innocent bystander, his grip could have been perceived as friendly or even romantic. I could tell, however, that it was anything but. Regret filled the pit of my stomach as I realized that my time to run, as Colton had urged, was long gone.

James peered at us curiously, his eyes shifting from Travis' grip on my cast to me. He saw something in my gaze that caused his expression to drop, if only for a moment, but he recovered swiftly.

"Trav," he asked, "we good, man?"

He nodded, taking a last drag before throwing his cigarette to the concrete, stepping on it, and saying:

"Talk soon, Colt." Colton's voice rambled out of my phone with rapid words that I couldn't decipher as Travis ended the call with his free hand. He tossed my phone to James, and after bobbling it for a beat, he caught it. "Claire," Travis crooned down to me, "you're going to come with us."

James squinted, considering Travis' statement, and placed my phone in his pocket as he asked, "We going somewhere?"

"Oh yeah man, I got a spot," Travis replied offhandedly.

"Oh." I tugged my wrist slightly to wriggle out of his grip, and his fingers tightened. "Ah," I let out a nervous laugh. "Trav, what is this?"

"Listen," he spoke down to me with a lopsided smile, "this whole night has become far more...*fruitful* than I anticipated. Colt cares about you and I'm just using that to my—*our,*" he gestured towards James, "benefit."

"Wait," I blinked several times trying to understand Travis' intent, "what?"

"Fill me in, Trav." James insisted.

"You're gonna make me actually *say* it, man?" Travis whined. *"Fine. Colton is fish. Claire is bait."*

If I weren't so intently focused on James' reaction, I wouldn't have noticed him inhale deeply through his nose and out his mouth.

He began to ask, "Are you saying—"

"Bad analogy." Travis interrupted, correcting himself. "Colton is fish. Claire is fish's loved one—"

"Are you trying to fucking *kidnap me?*" I spoke in a breath upwards to Travis, again attempting to free my arm from his grip. James' eyes went wide as I yanked my arm this way and that to no avail, and Travis moved to embrace me from behind, his arms catching me in a vice. My voice came out breathless and panicked then, as I jerked my body to either side. *"Travis?!"*

"Ah, Trav," James tried to speak quickly, "I don't—"

"Kidnapping's a misleading term," Travis told both me and James. "One, you're *clearly* a woman." His grasp on me tightened briefly, "Two, I prefer the phrase *holding for ransom.*"

I took calculated breaths, halting my struggle as I considered Travis' motives.

"I—what—Colton doesn't care about me as much as you think he does," I stated, unconcerned that our plan had come apart at the seams and more focused on my potential escape. "I don't really think I'm a good, um—bait."

"He'll come," Travis said, none too convincingly.

He began to take steps, pushing me along toward his truck. I dug my heels into the ground, the soles of my shoes scraping against the concrete as I tried, and failed, to gain any traction.

"How do you know that?" James spoke now, hands held up in a *wait a minute* gesture, clearly attempting to dismantle this escalating situation. "What if she's right and he doesn't show, I'm not gonna hold a girl for ransom for nothing."

"James—" Travis grunted against my movements and took another step while I kicked my legs out frantically in each direction. *"Stop it, Claire!* James, just fucking *help me* before anyone sees us—"

"Travis, I don't know if I like—"

James had begun to speak but was cut off by a voice in the distance. *"Hey!"*

Though I couldn't see him through my struggle, I knew it was Liam. His heavy footsteps pounded the pavement as he rushed towards us, yelling at Travis to stop what he was doing.

"Everyone has to be a fucking hero," Travis grumbled. "James, you take her."

James was at my side in an instant, taking Travis' place, saying, "Not exactly on board with this, man—"

Travis spat, *"This is happening with or without you, James!* Are you along for the ride or not?"

James relented, nodding, and Travis jogged to confront Liam.

From that moment until I made it into Travis' truck, all I could hear was James' heavy breathing. It replicated mine: short, shuddering breaths that only could represent panic. He muttered reassuring words in my ear as he guided me into the vehicle, phrases like, *'You're fine,'* and, *'We'll fix this,'* falling on my lost ears. He slipped into the back seat along with me and shut the back passenger door closed with a slam.

"Fuck!"

James gritted out the expletive, running his hands through his hair the same way that Luke does when he's frustrated beyond belief. He exhaled sharply, placing a hand on his upper stomach as he took a few large breaths.

"We're gonna figure this out, I promise," he told me, resolve in his voice. "He's not gonna hurt you, you don't have to worry about that."

I shook my head but immediately regretted that decision. I was lightheaded—extremely so—and I assumed that adrenaline was still pumping rapidly through my system, leaving me spinning. I absent-mindedly thought about how I should have eaten something before we left, leaning my head back against the headrest behind me.

"You don't know him, Jay," I whispered, thinking back to Travis knowingly ruining lives with zero regard for them. "Guy's a psychopath, honestly."

James cocked his head to the side. "Are you okay?"

I blinked, my eyelids heavy and my head still spinning from our last encounter.

"'M'fine—call Colton. Call Luke," I said slowly. "I have my phone; I can still try to keep in touch with you guys—"

"Do you really think I'm *leaving* you right now?!" James looked at me incredulously, though his eyes darted to witness anything unfolding in the parking lot behind me. "Don't be an idiot, I'm going with you guys. Liam and Zoey—they'll get back to Luke, they can call Colton, Paul, or whoever the fuck—*fuck.*" On a final flicker of his gaze over my shoulder, James' face fell. "Fantastic."

Instead of asking what he saw, I turned my entire body to look. My head sat atop my shoulders, bobbling as I continued to try to come to terms with my dizziness. It looked like Zoey had been pushed to the ground, but she was seemingly unscathed. Travis was striding towards Liam, one hand clutching his left jaw.

"I—what did I miss; did Liam punch him?!"

James monotonously replied, "Yup," watching the rest of this go down with his brow knit together in concern.

Travis swung back at Liam, making contact with his jaw. As Liam was knocked back, Travis reached behind himself for something tucked into the waistband of his pants. Even I could tell that whatever Travis was reaching for was hard and vaguely in the shape of an *L*. James quickly grabbed at the car door, mumbling an incoherent string of curse words, and I smacked his hand away from the handle.

"You can't go out there!" I reprimanded him. "You're supposed to be watching *me*, right?"

James' words came out in a flurry. "He has. A fucking. Gun, Claire. I'll play it off somehow, just let me go before one of them gets shot!"

It was then that the fog settled on my brain. It had been building and building—for how long, I wasn't sure, but I knew for certain that something felt wrong. I thought to myself that I should be concerned. Liam, not to mention *Zoey,* were both in what seemed to be imminent danger of some sort, but I couldn't focus on them. Their bodies, yes, but their actions, no—it was as if my mind just simply could not keep up.

I kept a hand on James' arm, silently telling him to stay as he watched Zoey scurry to her feet. I saw her mouth calling out to Liam frantically as she ran to him. Liam continued to stalk back to Travis, ignoring Zoey's pleas until Travis pulled his gun out and pointed it directly toward Liam's chest.

Liam froze. Even James, as convinced as he was to run out into the night before, stayed glued in place. The only movements outside for a beat were Liam and Travis' shoulders as they collectively breathed large huffs of air, in and out, as they stared at each other. I would have thought that life as I knew it had paused if it weren't for Zoey running smack into Liam, trying to pull him backward by wrapping her tiny arms around his waist. She yanked on him as hard as she could manage until he relented, backing away slowly without turning around.

I thought that I saw Travis lower his weapon. I *thought* that I felt James' entire body next to mine sag in relief, but I couldn't be sure. The fog that had fallen over me moments ago had become too much to bear. I tried to watch Zoey and Liam walk away, but they became blurrier by the second. My head spun more aggressively, and I clutched at both the door handle and James' arm in support, feeling myself weave violently forwards, and then back again.

My tongue, now suddenly seeming too big for my mouth, caused me to fumble over the shape of James' name in my mouth.

"Claire?" He questioned me, and then turned his entire body my way, grasping at either of my shoulders. *"Claire?!"*

It was no use—my mind was stuffed with cotton, and my world faded to black.

Chapter Sixteen

My body buzzed and I was fairly certain that while I was uncon-
scious, my mouth had been filled with sand and then promptly
emptied. My neck was angled sharply downward, chin to chest, and I
could tell that I hadn't been moved from this position in quite some
time with the way that my body ached. The muscles pulled in my neck
painfully as I raised my head. I tentatively opened my eyes and as I fully
came to, I realized that I couldn't move. I was bound to a chair at each
of my elbows and above my knees.

"Good morning."

I turned my head to the familiar voice and took in the room before
me. I was seated in a kitchen, just out of reach from a circular wooden
table. The entire room, including what areas I could see around it, was
drab. My gaze followed the dingy white tile where I sat, past the hon-
ey-colored cabinets that I was certain were crafted in the seventies, and
through a doorway to floors covered in a peeling vinyl that matched
the kitchen's cupboards. Scanning back to the voice that had originally
greeted me, there were brown boots and long, jean-clad legs that sat
beneath a broad body and a silently apologetic face. James raised a
coffee mug to his mouth, taking a tentative sip.

"What, um—" I grimaced, my throat dry and scratchy. "What happened?"

He set his mug down, face pinched together as if he were pained to remember it.

"Well, Travis drugged you, for one."

My mind spun, proving that I was still partially under whatever effects had been forced upon me.

"Did he?"

"Spiked your vodka soda." James clarified, grabbing his mug by the rim with his fingertips, palm facing down, in the same way that I remembered Travis grabbing my glass. "Slip of the wrist, as he called it."

I looked behind me to see nothing but a screen door to the outside world.

"Where is he?"

"Dinner run—should be back soon."

"How long was I out?"

"Three hours, give or take."

"And where are we?"

James clenched his jaw. "I—um—I don't know."

I blinked a few times, allowing that to sink in, and returned, "You don't *know?*"

"One of Travis' places, obviously—"

"You don't know where we are?!"

If possible, I felt my mouth go drier than it already was, and James closed his eyes for a long moment.

"I looked for landmarks, I kept track of exit signs while we drove, but Claire, we're in the middle of fucking *nowhere.*" He admitted, "There's no cell service; the closest house is like a mile away and I'm pretty sure it's abandoned—"

"So," whatever was left of the withered gears in my brain cranked away as I spoke, "I was drugged."

"Yes."

"Am currently being held for ransom, I remember that."

"Yes."

"For Colton, who cannot physically show up because he doesn't have any of Travis' money or drugs or whatever-the-fuck—"

"Yes," James replied yet again, this time holding his head in his hands as he rested his elbows on the table in front of him.

"At what looks like a fucking murder cabin in the middle-of-fuck-ing-nowhere—and we have no service."

"Mhm."

"And Luke, Zoey, Liam—*Paul?* What do they know?"

"Nothing."

The word came out as a guilt-ridden murmur, and I screeched back, *"Nothing?!"*

"Nothing from me, it was too fucking risky!" He exclaimed, pulling his hands away to show wide, familiar grey eyes. "I was in the seat next to him while we drove, I couldn't just whip out my phone and text anyone our status; he would've seen or gotten suspicious or something. Claire, I'm sorry—I'm *so* fucking sorry."

"I...um..."

I faltered on my words several times more, shock settling into my bones at the state of our current affairs. It wasn't James' fault. We should have run when we had the chance—sprinted for escape the moment that Colton had instructed me to leave—but we didn't, and there was no changing that. James couldn't have known that he would have no means to contact anyone that could help us. I didn't get to tell him that I didn't blame him for how unhinged our situation had become, though, because it was then that Travis strolled in behind me.

James' demeanor changed entirely, the only exception being the tinge of pure anxiety that remained in his eyes.

"Sleeping beauty!"

Travis greeted me as he rounded the table and placed a plastic bag of gas station burritos atop it, lowering himself into the chair beside James.

"Took ya long enough," James told him. "I'm starving."

"You." I seethed at Travis. "You fucking *drugged me?* Are you fucking *insane?!"*

"It was just Xanax—all in good business, Claire," he responded as he reached for a burrito after James helped himself. "Don't take it personally."

"Were you gonna fucking rape me too?"

James paused mid-chew of his first bite and seemed to have to force himself to swallow.

"No, Claire—I was not *planning* on raping you. And again, it was *Xanax,* not a fucking roofie—it's not like I needed you passed out for the whole night—"

"The fuck does, *'I was not planning on it,'* mean, Trav?" I asked with more than an edge to my voice.

He chewed through a large bite and once he was finished, said, "Look, if Colt doesn't want to see you hurt, then you don't have to worry—"

"You're not fucking raping her," James interjected, his eyes a steely grey and his jaw set tight as he stared Travis down.

"What, did you two get well acquainted while I was out?" Travis mocked James, a wry smile on his lips. "You got a little crush there, James?"

"Nah, but I'm not down for that—*fuck* that."

Travis nodded, holding up a hand as if acquiescing to James' demands, and leaned in to speak a few words to him in a low voice that I couldn't make out. James sat up straighter then, his face paling in complexion, and I noticed his Adam's apple bob as he swallowed.

"Burrito, Claire?" Travis bypassed the subject of my potential torture as if it were a trivial issue.

"You know, I'm just not hungry for some reason," I snapped back.

"Fine," he ate the last bit of his dinner in a rushed manner. "We have business to take care of anyway."

"Business?" I asked, unable to keep my tone of voice from rising.

"Yeah—like why isn't Colton here yet, Claire?"

I shrugged, replying, "I told you—not sure I was great bait."

"It's been," Travis rotated his wrist to look at a watch that was hidden under his flannel, "three hours. He hasn't even reached out."

"Ah," James spoke, "not to be the bearer of bad news, but even if he wanted to, he couldn't. No service here, man. Should we be at a more accessible loc—"

Travis pulled a large, block of a phone out of his pocket and waved it about James' face, the chunky antenna nearly brushing his cheek.

"—ation." James finished speaking the word. "Erm—what is that?"

"Sat phone," Travis replied. "Colt knows how to reach it *and* there's been no missed calls."

James' eyebrows flew upwards. "You've had a fucking satellite phone this entire time and you didn't tell me?!"

"You got someone you need to get in touch with that bad?" Travis inquired with a cock of his head.

"Ah—girlfriend." James blurted out the lie. "Been out of contact for a bit here and—"

"Girlfriend, huh? What's she like?"

"Short, blonde, sassy as all hell," James replied in an instant. "And she'll have my ass if I don't get back to her soon."

A grin stretched across Travis' face.

"Y'know, I don't get the whole domestic thing, but how about we get some work done first and then it's all yours."

"What are you suggesting?" James questioned.

"Call Colt and give him a little reminder."

I suspected that I was the only one that noticed, but James let out a small exhale that appeared to be in relief.

"Yeah, yeah—that I can do."

"Alright," Travis began dialing numbers that he knew by heart on the phone, "let's get this show on the road, shall we?"

Loud, individual beeps rang through the room with every press of a button and then the ringing began, the speaker emitting the noise loud enough for us all to hear as the phone sat on the table.

"Hello?" Colton answered, hesitant.

"Colt!" Travis' voice boomed, and I had to refrain from flinching. "We—and by *we,* I mean Claire and me—oh and James too...did I mention your buddy James is here too? We all have been wondering where in the *world* you are."

He eerily spoke in an upbeat manner.

"James is there too," Colt muttered seemingly more to himself than into the phone. "Am I on speaker? Claire?"

"Right here, Colt," I replied solemnly.

Colton sighed loudly. "Travis, what the fuck are you doing, man?"

"I think the question is more: What the fuck are *you* doing, Colt?" Travis returned. "Been a while. Been *quite* a while. You know how this works—"

"How what works?" James inquired quickly, but Travis didn't answer him.

Colton rattled, "No, no, no Trav, listen—I'm coming, okay? I'll be there—"

"Will you?" Travis replied, his voice now beginning to rise. "I'm starting to doubt that; you didn't even reach back out when you knew I took your girl—"

"She's not my girl—"

"I don't *give a fuck*, Colt! Instead of taking this seriously, you're just sitting on your ass—"

"I thought maybe she got away," Colton admitted in what I was certain was a lie. His words were beginning to run together with the velocity in which they were leaving his mouth. "She's sneaky, you fuckin' know that, Trav, I thought she ran—I thought she fuckin' bolted!"

"Well, she didn't—"

"Look, Trav, I'll be there, okay? I will, you just gotta give me a little time—"

"How," Travis paused, "Colt, how are you supposed to get here if you don't know where we are?"

Colton stammered, "I, um—I figured you were at the, ah, your place north of town."

Ominous silence spanned between us all, and Travis glanced at James. James shrugged, and Travis stood, the legs of his chair whining against the tile as he scooted it back. He walked to the kitchen, opening drawers, rummaging through them, and then shutting them loudly. He returned to us all shortly, announcing:

"Not where we are, bud! Not where we are at all, and I don't think you were planning on asking. I don't think you're very *motivated.* "

"Motivated? I'm plenty motivated, you've gotta trust me here," Colton retorted.

"I don't have any reason to trust you right now, Colt," Travis spoke, moving his hands animatedly as he enunciated each word with care and paced slowly between James and me. "Especially after everything you've lost me, I'm feeling like I need to light a fire under your ass."

James squeaked, "Is there a need for fire, really?"

"Come on, Trav, you don't have to do this," Colton argued.

"Do what?" I asked.

"See, the thing is," Travis said, "I do."

"What do you *have* to do, Travis?" I pressed again.

James' eyes were bouncing between us, taking in the conversation until Travis halted in front of him, his back to me at such an angle that I couldn't see what he was doing.

Travis shifted on his feet, grabbing something from either the waistband of his pants or his pocket—I couldn't be sure which—and James stood from his chair abruptly.

"Dude, what the fuck?!"

"I told you not to get attached," Travis snapped.

He turned around and pointed at me with the tip of a knife that was so large that it looked like it could have been used to skin a deer.

My breath caught in my throat. My heart hit my ribs like a sledgehammer and I half expected to see it rolling away from me, having jumped out of my chest, leaving a bloody trail along the white tile.

"Hey, um," I stuttered, feeling my hands begin to shake behind me, "Colton, there's a *very* large knife being pointed at me, care to chime in?"

"God dammit," Colton spat. "Travis, this is *not. Fucking. Necessary.* I'll meet you soon, okay? I'll get you whatever the fuck you want! You don't have to do this."

James' wide eyes jumped from me to Travis, his breaths coming out in short bursts. "He said he's coming, Trav." He stepped his way toward Travis slowly. "You can put the fucking knife down, yeah?"

Travis looked behind himself at James. "Can you shut the *fuck* up? How are you so fuckin' *soft* for this girl, I swear—"

"I—not, I'm not," James stammered back. "That doesn't mean I want to see her get hurt, I just wanted to get my money, man—"

"Listen to Jay, Trav." Colton's voice rang out again. "You don't have to do anything to her."

"Are you two buddyin' up?" Travis called over his shoulder, "James, why are you even *here* if you aren't willing to—"

"I don't want to see a girl get *fucking stabbed, Trav!*"

"Well, *I have to!*" Travis hissed, spinning on his heel to turn to James, who held up his hands, palms forward in an act of defense. "Get with the fucking program or get out." Travis turned back to me, taking a step to close the distance between us. I leaned away from him as much as I could whilst still being bound, but he was so close to me now that I could smell stale mentholated cigarettes on his breath. "This ensures that Colt'll actually show up," Travis continued to speak quietly, tilting his head to the side.

As Travis began to move his hand which wielded the knife swiftly, James lurched forward. He wrapped one of his arms around Travis' neck, pulling him back with a few stumbling steps. Travis jerked his body in an attempt to free himself, and when he swung the knife behind him and toward James, James cursed loudly and twisted to dodge it. The scuffle caused James' grip on Travis to loosen just enough for Travis to raise his elbow, hitting James square in the nose.

James' head whipped back quickly, his steps faltered, and Travis wrenched himself free. As Travis stomped his way back to me, James yelled in protest. He reached out in desperation, but his grip found nothing, and with a grunt erupting from his mouth, Travis thrust the blade into my thigh.

I didn't feel it at first. I even wondered idly if he had missed my leg completely and driven the knife into the wood of the chair, but it hit me soon enough. A blinding, burning pain shot through the wound and throbbed through what felt like the entire bottom half of my body. A blood curdling scream that I vaguely recognized as my own pierced my ears. The conglomeration of voices yelling at each other was lost to me for a moment as all I could focus on was the knife driven into my leg to the hilt.

"Alrighty!" Travis clapped his hands together once with gusto. The room fell silent once again, save for my heavy breathing. "Colt—just to get you in the loop here, Claire has approximately five inches of knife embedded into her thigh. Good news is, I'm gonna leave it in there for a while. She's barely even bleeding, really." He was right, there wasn't much blood to speak of, but I had a feeling that wouldn't last long. My thought process being practically spoken aloud, Travis remarked, "She *might* bleed out...if I decide to pull the knife out, that is...but that'll be a ways away from now. If you get here soon enough, you can drive her to the hospital yourself instead of having me put her out of her misery."

"Jesus, Trav," Colton spoke with a grit, "how soon is soon?"

"I'm not a fuckin' doctor, Colt, I dunno." He looked at my leg curiously, as if it were a science project. "A while?" Travis continued, "Just forget about the money, forget about the product. I'm starting to care less and less about what you owe us—I really just want to see your pretty little face. I'm sure we can come to some sort of...agreement."

James, who had been staring at the knife in almost as much shock as I was as he stood with helpless, limp limbs, shook his head to break himself out of the tension of the moment, remembering what persona he was supposed to have.

"Hey," his voice quavered, but he pushed past it and continued to exclaim, "that is *not* what we talked about! I'll wait as long as I need to, but I'm not fucking leaving here until I get what I need."

Travis rolled his head around to look at him again, his dark eyes squinting.

"We can talk about that with Colt once he gets here, can't we?" He paused. "Because now that I did *what I had to—you're fucking welcome,*

James—Colt'll be here." He pointed a finger at James, and James took a single step back, eyeing him from head to toe as Travis said gravely, "You pull a stunt like that again, and I'll bury you in the goddamn ground." James exhaled heavily, nodding several times, and Travis spoke to the phone on the counter, "Colton! Where are ya?"

"Um—I'm at my house."

"Then you're about an hour east of me; you know the place."

"I—yeah, I do, but...ah, there's no way I'm gonna be there that soon, I—"

"Why the *fuck* not?"

James grumbled, "Colton, you've gotta be fuckin' kidding me."

There wasn't a definitive reason that came from the phone's speaker. Colton continued to attempt to put a coherent sentence together to explain his absence, but it was no use.

Travis looked to James and me, his head turning between the two of us. Succinct and to the point, he gruffly stated, "Get him here," to both of us, and walked out the back door, calling to James that he was going to have a cigarette.

The screen shut behind him with a smack, and a second door followed. I heard him shove it closed with excessive force, the sound of the latch clicking shut the only thing that gave us any sense to speak freely.

"FUCK!" James yelled out from the depths of his diaphragm.

"Claire," Colton questioned rapidly, "are you okay?"

"She's not *fucking okay*, Colton, SHE'S BEEN STABBED!"

"Okay, I know, I know, I-know, *I-know,*" he rambled back, his breath now coming out ragged and static through the phone.

"Jesus *fucking* Christ—Claire," James said to me, "I—I'm so fucking sorry, I tried to stop him." I just nodded at his apology and squeezed my eyes shut, moaning as the radiating pain continued on, and on. "Shit, okay—look, we don't have much time with him out there," James told the both of us in a rushed voice. "Colton, do you know the address of this place?" Colton did, and he rattled it off immediately. James responded, "Stay put unless we call you, you fucking piece of—"

James allowed his profane phrasing to be cut off as he jammed the *end call* button with his index finger. He pulled out his own useless phone, his fingers swiping quickly until he seemingly found what he needed, and pressed numbers one by one into the sat phone, his head bouncing back and forth between the two as he dialed. This time, he held it to his ear, keeping the conversation private, and he walked away from me to what I assumed would be considered the living room.

I could still see him to my left, walking aimlessly in circles across the vinyl. A hand was holding his hair away from his forehead, elbow pointed skyward.

He anxiously murmured, "Liam—it's James."

Before we all went on our way earlier in the day, James had exchanged phone numbers with everyone in the group—Liam and Zoey included—to ensure that we could all keep in touch. It wasn't lost on me why he chose to call Liam of all people. We were friends, certainly, but out of Luke, Liam, and Zoey, Liam was bound to be the one who would react in the most level-headed way. In response to Liam clearly asking where we were, James told him the same address that Colton had given him moments ago.

"You all need to fucking get here, man—no, it's *not* good—Claire's been stabbed—in the leg—*shut-up-and-stop-asking-questions!*" James' words came out in a flurry. "I don't have time—just get here, bring everyone, call Paul—okay, good—no, don't tell Luke about Claire. *No*, do *not* put him on the phone—Liam—*Liam do not put Luke on the pho*—hey, brother..." James' tone of voice shifted, almost raising an octave, and he glanced at me. "Um—she's fine—"

"James?" I called to him, and he looked over tentatively, walking back to the kitchen to peek out of the window behind me to find Travis taking his time with his cigarette. "Give me the phone," I demanded. He tried to shake his head at my inquiry, but upon me bitterly saying, "Let me talk to Luke before I fucking *die here, Jay,*" he relented and cautiously put the phone to my ear. I shrugged my shoulder upward to hold it in place, and James moved to keep an eye on Travis through the window in the back door all the while.

I breathed, "Luke?"

"Claire, thank God." He exhaled heavily. "We're on our way as fast as we can—" He paused, no doubt paying extra attention to any sound coming from my end of the phone. "Why are you breathing so hard, what's going on?"

I could have said it was adrenaline—I had plenty coursing through me at the moment. I could have said I was scared—could have started crying—could have said *anything* to protect Luke from the panic of what this situation was. None of those statements would technically be lying, and it was true that I considered saying them all for the briefest of seconds.

I didn't, though.

"He fucking drugged me, Luke."

Luke's voice came out in a low, angry pitch.

"He *what?*"

I wasn't sure how to break the rest to him—that Travis called Colton, assumed he wasn't going to show, and decided that some form of torture until he arrived would be the best tactic. It all was too long-winded, and I didn't have the breath in me to say it all anyway. I looked down at the blade, blood beginning to ooze out around it and soak my jeans.

"There's a knife," I inhaled, "in my leg." Exhale. "He stabbed me—I'm not—it's not good."

There was silence then again, save for the faint background noise of an engine whining against the force of a gas pedal being pressed to the floor.

"You are going to be fine," Luke told me, each word punctuated definitively. "We're coming to get you, you'll get all fixed up, and I—" He paused. "This'll all be over and I'm taking you home. Okay?"

"Okay."

The word came out meek; quieter than I intended.

"I lov—"

Creaking sounded behind me, no doubt the sound of Travis returning. Before I could hear either the remainder of Luke's words or Travis' footsteps into the kitchen, the phone was ripped away from my ear and James stepped away from me leisurely. He paced as if he had simply been walking past me, and spoke into the phone himself.

"I *know* it's late, baby," he feigned his conversation and vaguely answered inquiries from Luke. "Yeah—mhm—no, no, no—I'll see you soon, I *promise*—okay, bye."

Travis slid back into the seat he once sat in, eyeing James with a casual amusement. James ended the call, and Travis held out his hand expectantly. Once the phone was back in his possession, he asked:

"How'd that go, lover boy?"

James huffed out a breath and pushed his hair out of his face once more, striding back and falling into his chair with a loud grunt.

"She is *not* happy with me."

Travis' lips pulled up in a wry smirk, the expression causing wrinkles to appear at the edges of his smile and the corners of his dark eyes.

"We'll get out of here soon, man."

Travis told him that in a reassuring manner, but the sentence was anything but. James' jaw clenched at the insinuation, and Travis chuckled, his misunderstanding of James' agitation likely our only saving grace.

Chapter Seventeen

N one of us spoke much in the meantime. I tried to focus on happy memories to keep myself calm and failed miserably. The lack of distraction combined with nonstop radiating pain caused the time to pass excruciatingly slow. I couldn't stop myself from flinching when a knock sounded at the door, finally breaking the silence. The movement made the blade move in my wound and I cursed loudly.

Travis, fully ignoring any noises I made, traipsed through the living area and turned a corner out of my view. The knocking continued from the direction that Travis walked, I assumed from a front door that I couldn't see from where I was bound.

Travis spoke, "Sounds like it's your knight in shining—mother *fucker.*"

James, who was previously resting his head on his forearms on the table, was now at full attention, back ramrod straight as he glanced at me nervously.

"What is it?" He asked.

Travis stomped back to us, his expression grim. He seethed, blowing out a long breath through his nose as he angrily grabbed the satellite phone off of the table.

"I don't know," he said as he hit a previously dialed selection and held the phone to his ear, "but that's *not* Colt out there—*Colton.*" Travis shifted his focus from James to the phone. "Do you have any idea who this preppy fuck is that's outside my house?" James and I stiffened. I strained my ears to hear Colton's response from the other end of the line, but the banging against the front door resonated throughout the room and rendered my attempt useless. Travis sneered, "Tell me why I should believe that you're still coming here."

"Maybe because you have me hostage and you *fucking stabbed me*?"

The combination of blood loss, anxiety, and relentless pain shooting through my lower limb had left me in a state where I could no longer hold my tongue. James gave me a fleeting warning look, eyes wide.

Travis held the phone's speaker against his chest, tilting his head at me in curiosity.

"I'm sorry," he remarked sarcastically, "was stabbing you not *enough*? Do you have a suicide mission?" I chuckled sardonically, deciding not to respond, and Travis brought the phone back to his ear, complaining to Colton, "She's getting...*lippy*. It's annoying—it's fifteen past the hour, Colt...it seems oddly convenient that someone else is here instead of you." He paused and weighed his options internally, bobbing his head from side to side. "Fifteen more minutes. Max."

He threw the phone back on the kitchen table as if it had offended him and the door was smacked yet again, this time so hard that it rattled against the hinges.

A muffled voice that I recognized as Luke's spoke from behind it, and my heart jumped in my chest.

"Hey, I'm sorry to bother you, but my car broke down up the road—"

Travis laughed disbelievingly. "Is this guy serious—"

"You're the first house I found in a ways," Luke continued. "I have the cables; I just need a jump."

"Go somewhere else, guy!" Travis yelled.

"I don't have anywhere else to go," Luke complained. "I'll be walking for miles—"

"God dammit," Travis whined. *"Fine,* just give me a second!" He looked at James exasperatedly. "Colt says he's close, but I don't know if I buy it. Let me get this guy out of here—something doesn't feel right. Keep a fucking eye out, yeah?"

James hummed in agreement as Travis turned on his heel to leave the house. Neither of us could make out the muttering voices once the door shut behind him, leaving us alone.

"What are you doing, Luke?"

James murmured the sentence to himself rhetorically when the creaking of the screen door behind us brought both of our attention to Liam and Zoey. Their eyes simultaneously widened as they took in my appearance along with the blood that had begun to spatter the floor below me.

Zoey uttered a quiet, *"Fuck,"* and had seemingly frozen in place.

Liam shook his head after a quick glance at Zoey and ordered, "Scissors, Jay—anything to cut her loose, we're parked out back."

James was up and yanking cupboards open frantically before Liam even finished speaking, finding a pair of red-handled scissors in the third drawer that he rifled through. He handed them to Liam and quickly rushed to the front door and out of sight.

"How the fuck did you guys get here so quietly?" James asked from around the corner as Liam snipped the zip ties at my elbows. "The dirt road to get down here is loud as hell when you drive on it."

"Did some off-roading; got creative," Liam replied.

"What's Luke doing?" I asked as the bindings were cut from my legs, and I took in a sharp breath from the minuscule movement.

"Distracting Trav; Luke's the only one he hasn't seen before...we don't have long, Paul's just a few minutes behind—"

"Yeah," James interjected. "Liam, you carry her to the car. I'll stay and keep a lookout for—*fuck.*"

"Fuck? What fuck?" Liam had asked the question as quickly as he could, but there was no need for James to respond. Liam's dark eyes widened in horror as he saw James running back to the kitchen. The puzzle pieces fit together quickly in his mind as he demanded James, "Take Zoey—*go!*"

James grabbed a shocked Zoey by the wrist, pulling her toward the back door that was still ajar.

She fought against him, worriedly calling out, "Liam?"

Liam had an arm gingerly wrapped underneath my useless legs. As he stood to pick me up and I exhaled through the pain at the movement, there was a loud rustling from around the corner. It was not visible to us, but the conglomeration of Luke and Travis' angry voices combined with the clear sound of a vicious brawl made Liam hiss to Zoey:

"Fucking go!"

At his words, James was finally able to yank her out of sight and Liam began to move, rushing as carefully as he could toward the back door. One eye behind Liam's shoulder, I saw Travis bounding towards us with Luke not far behind.

Travis' gaze darted around the room, and he yelled, "God fucking dammit!"

Luke, eyes crazed as he saw us, screamed so loudly that his vocal cords began to grate. *"FUCKING RUN, LIAM!"*

Luke attempted to tackle Travis from behind, his arms wrapping around Travis' chest and yanking him backward. Travis jerked, elbowing Luke in the ribs to free himself briefly.

Liam repeated a mantra of, "Fuck, fuck, fuck," as he ran us through the back door, onto the wooden patio, and down the two creaky steps that lead us into an open, grassy area.

Illuminated by the light on the back porch, Travis reached behind himself and aimed the same gun that I saw earlier tonight toward Liam and me. I tucked my head into Liam's chest.

I yelled, *"Gun, Liam, gun!"*

I barely heard him begin to shout out a reaction of his own to my declaration before a loud bang rang out, shaking the air around me with its blaring force. The left side of Liam's body jutted forward, throwing us off balance. He dropped my legs, his arm suddenly inept, and we both tumbled to the ground. White hot pain shot through me as I landed almost directly on my wounded leg, and I shrieked in agony for what felt like the millionth time.

Liam landed a few steps away from me, letting out a guttural, pained noise that bordered on animalistic. He screamed until it seemed that all the breath was out of his lungs, gasped for air, and then began again.

Zoey screeched from a distance, "LIAM!"

I craned my neck to see her struggling against James' embrace mere steps away from her car, wriggling with all her might to escape. Liam looked around frantically, his gaze finally landing on Zoey.

"Zoey," he called back, fear lacing his tone. He cursed, cradling his left shoulder tightly as if his grip was the only thing holding it to his body. "Get in the car, *now!*"

She fought against James, and I could see him pleading with her as she kicked her legs out to try to free herself. James managed two steps toward the car before her legs reached the door that was left open, and she kicked it shut.

She begged, "Let me *go!*"

"Zoey, what are you doing, get in the—" I had begun to yell, but Liam's voice powered over mine.

"Get in the *FUCKING CAR, ZOEY!*"

He used an abrasive voice that I didn't realize he was capable of. It was clear that the tone itself stemmed from sheer panic, and he watched her as he rushed to get to his feet.

She deflated against James, and her squirming against his embrace ceased. She nodded vigorously, whimpering in agreement as James murmured something in her ear. Liam let out a long breath when she reluctantly disappeared into the vehicle, and James filed in behind her.

Liam jogged the two steps to get to my side, asking, "Where are they?"

He was asking the question that I was wondering—where are Travis and Luke? Travis had shot at us from the house, but he most certainly had never left it, and Luke had been right behind him.

"I—" I whipped my head all around us, finding nothing as Liam offered me his blood-soaked right hand to help me stand. "I don't know, I—" I took his hand and he pulled me upward, all my weight going to my good leg. I slung my arm up to grasp at his non-wounded shoulder, and we tried to continue our escape to Zoey's car.

It was then that a gunshot rang out, muffled by the walls of the house.

We both flinched, breathing through our respective pain, and Liam tried to coax me to hop along faster.

"Claire, we need to move—"

"No, no, no-no," I groaned, fighting to turn back, and another bang reached our ears.

This time, however, it was immediately followed by a gritty shout that could only represent agony. I shrieked at the insinuation that the noise represented, and Liam continued to yank me forward instead of allowing me to go back.

The only thing that distracted him from pulling me all the way to safety was the sound of a vehicle throttling down the long driveway toward us. The police car had its lights illuminated, flashing blue and red throughout the dark night, and it skidded sideways, gravel shooting this way and that. Once the wheels stopped moving, Paul exited quickly, running his way to me and Liam.

"Paul—HOUSE!" I yelled at him, shooing him away from us with a wave and directing him to the porch.

He made his way as quickly as he could, reaching absentmindedly towards his radio to speak a few code terms that I couldn't even begin to decipher, but stopped when Travis stepped outside and onto the wooden porch.

His auburn hair was wild as if someone had attempted to yank it from his scalp, and blood dripped out of a corner of his lip. He pushed along an equally bruised looking Luke, holding him in front of himself with one arm around his neck and the other loosely holding his pistol by his side.

Liam and I had both long forgotten about the concept of escape, frozen to the spot as we both had turned to witness the stalemate that was occurring in front of us. Paul held his gun out toward Travis in warning.

"Let him go, Travis," he told him in as calm of a voice as he could muster.

Luke spat blood onto the porch beneath them, gritting his teeth, almost snarling as Travis pulled his arm tighter around his neck.

"What is he to you?!" Travis called out to me, dark eyes crazed as he gestured my way with the gun in his left hand.

Liam muttered a string of profanities under his breath, and I desperately tried to contain my rapid breathing.

"I—" I began to respond with some sort of a lie, but it all came out in a nervous sputtering. "I don't—who—no, I don't—"

"I can see it on your *GODDAMN FACE!*" Travis shouted. "Was this all part of a fucking *plan?*"

He motioned at Paul with his free hand that held his weapon, and Paul announced, "Put the gun *down,* Travis, let him go and step *aside!*"

"Oh, I'm already *getting a fucking life sentence, Paul,*" Travis whined, throwing his head back. "It's *over,* I get it—what's the *fucking difference* if I feel more justified going into it, huh?"

"Claire, *go!*" Luke begged me, sputtering blood as he spoke and wriggled against Travis' chokehold.

My voice strained, tears falling down my face as I cried his name back.

"Do I shoot him again?" Travis asked the rhetorical question, and I noticed that Luke was cradling the right side of his abdomen. Travis lifted the gun towards Luke's cheek, pressing the metal against his skin and angling his gaze away from us. He looked directly at me and stated quietly, "You deserve it, you know? You've always been *fucking worthless.*"

The combination of hysteria and dread that ran through me at that very moment was something that I wouldn't wish on anyone. Bile rushed to the back of my throat. My breathing, previously a heavy pant due to the wound on my left leg, was now constricted to the point that it sounded as if I were choking. My hands and feet prickled, and then turned numb.

I didn't have to feel that way for long, though, because that was when Paul took his shot.

It was a very brief moment when Travis twisted his body, and it happened in less than a blink of an eye. My ears rang for what I hoped—no, *needed*—to be the last time of the night, and Travis lay in a heap on the patio.

Luke had fallen as Travis did, and he scrambled to kick himself away from Travis' presence. He finally stopped, sitting against the siding of the house, moaning and clutching at his ribcage.

Paul, weapon still at the ready, paced his way up to where they both laid and tentatively looked at Travis. He breathed, just for a beat as he stood over him, and then lowered two fingers to the side of his neck. He coughed in a gruff manner and brought his radio to his lips.

"10-54; down by lethal force," he croaked. "10-52; 10-52."

"Is he—" I began to ask but was unable to finish the sentence.

"I—I think he's dead," Liam answered for me.

Calm seemed to settle over the meadow-like area that we resided in, and I heard the door to Zoey's car open in the distance.

James rushed to his brother, and Zoey ran smack into Liam.

He grunted as she figuratively tried to squeeze the life out of him and he noted weakly, "I'm fine, Zo'. Get off; I'm all bloody."

Zoey hissed, "You are *NOT* fine!" and stepped away from us, grabbing at the hem of her cotton shirt. She horizontally ripped the material with a surprising amount of ease, yanking away the bottom few inches of her shirt. *"Both of you,"* she ordered, "sit the fuck down."

I stammered, "I—I need to see Luke, I—"

Zoey exclaimed, "James!"

We all looked toward them and found James crouched by Luke, the white of the skin on his back glowing in the moonlight a stark contrast to his inked arms. He pressed his bundled t-shirt to Luke's ribs.

I heard him tell Luke, "You were only grazed, thank *fuck,"* as he looked back to Zoey.

She called out, "Is he good?"

James gave her a distracted thumbs up as he continued to say choice words to his brother, and the breath that I had been holding was let out of me in a hoarse sob.

"Can you fucking sit now?" Zoey begged me, and I nodded, allowing Liam to assist me to the ground. I winced as she moved my leg to slip the scrap of material from her shirt underneath it. She wriggled the fabric to just above the knife, and as she tied it off in a tight tourniquet, I yelped in pain. She then looked up to Liam, who was still standing and observing her as he clutched at his shoulder. "The *fuck* are you doing, Liam, I said *sit!"*

"I'm fine, Zo—"

"You're pale as shit; you're fucking bleeding out, Liam, *SIT.*"

Zoey stood, shoving him in his good shoulder, and he finally obliged, kneeling on the ground. She reached for the bottom of his shirt, and as she pulled it past his shoulders and over his head, he gritted out a very loud:

"AH, FUCK, Zoey!"

A sheen of sweat glinted off of him, the blood that continually oozed out of his wound staining the smattering of blonde hair on his chest.

Zoey rested Liam's shirt over his shoulder and muttered, "Brace yourself."

Before Liam could comprehend the words that she said, she lifted his arm to string the shirt underneath it.

Liam yelled, *"JESUS,* Zoey, I need more warning than that!"

Zoey tied either end of the shirt together, red rapidly seeping into white. She affixed it as some sort of a makeshift bandage and she admonished, "Shut up—lay down—put pressure on it."

Liam obeyed, and Zoey finally sat back, legs bent in front of her and her hands over her eyes.

I saw her shoulders begin to shake, and I asked, "Zoey, are you good?"

"Oh, *shut the fuck up, Claire!"* She groaned back to me, her glassy eyes looking at me as her hands fell away and she questioned, "Are *you* good? Jesus *Christ."*

I nodded vigorously, freely crying now. It was slow, singular streaks streaming down my face until I heard Luke call out:

"Claire!"

Then, I was bawling. Hard, wracking sobs took over my body as I looked over to where I heard his voice, though I couldn't see—my vision was obscured by my tears. I felt rather than saw him as he leaned down and gently touched his hands on either side of my arms, the blurred outline of him looking me up and down thoroughly. I wiped at my eyes and saw Luke's shirt bunched up above James', which had been tied around his waist. A tight knot secured it to him in a similar fashion to the way Zoey had bandaged Liam, and I reached out to touch the fabric tentatively.

I choked out, "Are you okay?"

"You're asking if *I'm* okay?" Luke returned, mouth agape at my question.

The crunch of gravel rumbled in our ears, becoming louder and louder as two ambulances raced down the driveway toward us all, and I nodded at his question. He just shook his head and pulled me into him, my head in his chest as he clutched at my back and we awaited the help that we all so desperately needed.

❧❧❧❧❧ ❦❦❦❦❦

The medication I was given when we arrived at the hospital knocked me out for quite a while. I woke to the blaringly white surroundings of a hospital room, squinting as my eyes adjusted to the brightness. I noted that the knife had been removed from my leg as I reached down to inspect my limb and when I tried to move it, I gasped loudly.

"Well, it's not gonna be healed instantly, ya goof." James sat in the chair next to me, a thin white bed sheet wrapped around his bare shoulders, grey eyes lit up at his own joke.

"You're hilarious," I responded monotonously, groaning a bit from the pain of the stitches. "Where's your shirt?"

"Ah, blood-soaked," he replied. "Totally unwearable. I blame—"

"Me," Luke strode into the room wearing a magenta nurse's scrub shirt, a lopsided smile on his face. "He blames me. I'm *so* sorry that I bled through your shirt, brother. I'll buy you a new one."

James sat up a bit taller, taking in his brother's appearance and gesturing at his top.

"Did the nurse give you that?"

Luke nodded. "Go to the front desk in a few minutes and ask Liz for one—*not Rhonda*. Rhonda is *not* a fan of us."

"Liz, not Rhonda," James murmured. "Got it."

Luke quickly reached my bedside and placed a hand on either side of my face, angling me upward to kiss me briefly. His grey eyes nearly twinkled as he looked down at me, and I felt my head loll into his touch. He whispered, "Hi, Baby."

James let out a loud giggle. "Y'all are cheesy, *damn.*"

Luke's eyes rolled to the ceiling, he leaned in to touch his lips against mine once more, and he released me. He stepped back, hands in his pockets as he asked, "How's the leg?"

"Sore," I murmured, turning my head to examine the room. A light blue cloth separator hanging from the ceiling was pushed aside to reveal an empty hospital bed to my left. I wondered if it was previously occupied by someone, or if it was called for in the near future, and I gestured to it in question. "Is this yours? How's your—"

I was going to ask about the wound on his ribcage when James snorted. "He was *grazed.*"

"I was still *shot,*" Luke retorted, pulling up the nurse's shirt to reveal the gash along his ribs that had been closed with several stitches. "See?"

"Yeah, but you don't need a bed," James argued.

"I was discharged," Luke told me. "Quickly. I'm good."

A timid Zoey poked her head into the room, her eyes seeming to brighten only slightly when she looked my way.

"Oh, you're awake—you okay?"

Her gaze was worried, and I reassured her quickly.

"Yeah, yeah, I'm good."

Zoey knotted her hands in front of her, playing with her fingers. Though she wasn't crying, her eyes were red-rimmed and her face was puffy as if she had just recently stopped. Her smile at my response was genuine, but it was apparent that her mind was elsewhere.

"What's wrong?"

"Nothing's wrong," she said.

"You look terrible."

"Claire, I'm fi—"

"Liam's still in surgery."

James spoke now, looking straight at Zoey with anxious eyes. She kept her gaze downcast and Luke, silently observing their interaction, squirmed uncomfortably. I pushed myself up as much as I could to sit at attention.

"Shit, have they said anything?"

"He's going to be fine," James told me confidently, still trying to catch Zoey's attention. "He got hit in the shoulder; they're just figuring out... mechanics."

"They said his collarbone was shattered." Zoey finally looked at James. "That's a little more than *mechanics*...and they said he lost a lot of blood."

"Zoey," James spoke to her in a calming voice, "a bullet went completely through him. Of *course,* he lost a lot of blood. But he's here now. He's gonna be fine."

She relaxed a bit at his words and as she nodded, I felt as though I were intruding on a personal moment. They seemed unable to unlock their eyes on each other's until James cleared his throat and looked to the floor.

I leaned my head back against my pillow, my eyelids heavy as the grogginess from whatever medication I had been given weighed me down.

"Tired?" Luke asked me quietly, and I hummed in affirmation as I rolled my head to glance at him, struggling to keep my eyes open. One slow, long blink later, I saw him give me a soft grin. "Sleep," he told me. "We'll be here."

I nodded, not needing to be instructed any further, and closed my eyes. Despite the pain in my leg and the after-effects of whatever they gave me to knock me out, I felt...normal. Well, as normal as I could have felt. Mostly, my mind was exhausted, and I drifted off to a heavy, burdenless sleep.

That's what I thought I did, at least.

My eyes snapped open once again to the sound of several yelling voices. At first, I was unsure if I had simply blinked or if several hours had passed. My question was answered when I saw Liam laying in the bed beside me, arm in a sling and just about as worked up as those who stood in the hallway.

I called out to him, loud enough to interject above the surrounding noise, "Liam?"

He immediately ceased his yelling, looking at me with a smile that was almost carefree.

"Hey," he said, waving his good arm at me.

"Are you okay?!"

He bobbed his right shoulder up and down quickly. "Can't complain."

Not wanting to continually raise my voice, I mouthed, "I'm so sorry!"

He rolled his eyes comically, waving me off with a hand.

"'M'fine. Really," he told me, and I gave him a pointed look that questioned that statement entirely. He reiterated, *"Really."*

I nodded, relenting. Though it was a small curiosity, I neither knew nor truly cared if he ended up on the bed beside me by pure chance or by request from our group. I considered questioning him on the subject, but as the indecipherable voices from the hallway grew louder, I dropped the thought entirely.

I glanced toward the noise and back at him, asking, "What gives?"

Liam looked at me, timid, and called out, "Um...guys?" There was no response. He exclaimed louder, "Guys!"

Zoey and James' heads each poked into the room, realizing I was awake and giving them a questioning look. Luke, however, was nowhere to be found.

James stepped through the threshold, now wearing a teal nurse's scrub shirt. His tattoos stretched as he reached behind his head to rub at the back of his neck. He spoke to me in an uncharacteristically high voice, "Oh—hey, Claire."

"Where's Luke?"

"Uh..." James faltered, looking to Zoey for guidance.

She shook her head from side to side, hard, walking to sit in one of two chairs situated between me and Liam, saying nothing. James followed her, mimicking her actions as he took the chair closest to me.

I looked at her, inquiring, "Zoey?"

She avoided my gaze completely, humming to herself quietly.

I turned my head to Liam, smiling at him sweetly.

I cooed, *"Liam?"*

He broke immediately, blurting out, "Colton's here; Luke's pissed."

Zoey and James both gave him a scalding look, chastising him with a simultaneous, "Liam!"

He argued, "What, like she wouldn't find out anyway?"

Zoey softened first, a gentle grin appearing on her lips. James seemed more perturbed, holding his annoyed glare at Liam until Zoey smacked his arm, scolding him under her breath.

I closed my eyes, sighing loudly at the thought of Luke getting into an altercation with Colton.

"Erm," Liam spoke through the silence, "if they *were* going to try to beat each other up, this would be the place to do it though, right?" He shrugged his right shoulder optimistically, smiling a lopsided smile at the entire room. James rolled his eyes heavily and Zoey bit her bottom lip to keep from laughing, but the room remained quiet in response to Liam's statement. He trailed off, mumbling, "You know...because...hospital."

I questioned James, "Why in the world didn't you try to stop him?"

"You think I didn't?" I squinted my eyes at him skeptically, and he noted, "Okay, fine, I didn't try *that* hard—what?!" He responded to the look I shot at him. "Colt had it coming to him, don't tell me you're trying to defend him."

"I'm not—what I'm worried about is Luke getting hurt since his ribs are all jacked up already!"

James chuckled. "He'll be fine."

As if right on cue, Luke calmly walked into the room, whistling to himself quietly. The only visible injuries he had were the ones that he had sustained earlier in his violent scuffle with Travis.

"Oh, hey," he remarked as if seeing me awake was a surprise. "You get a good nap in?"

"What did you do?!"

"Ah—Colt sends his best."

"Luke."

"He said he wished he could have stayed for longer—"

"*Luke.*"

"We   had   a   really   good chat—I-told-him-that-if-he-ever-pulls-that-shit-again-we'll-frame-him-for-your-kidnapping-and-more," he spoke so quickly that I had to pause to allow the words to fully sink in.

I eventually replied, "We don't have enough evidence for that—"

James boomed out a laugh and stated, "Oh, *yes we do.*"

"Oh—I," I hesitated, and then dropped the subject, figuring that there was much that James had yet to tell me regarding anything that he had secretly recorded whilst having conversations with Travis. I redirected my focus to Luke. "Okay, er—good, thank you. That doesn't answer my question from before, though; what did you *do?*"

"Is it really that important?"

"Luke!"

"I...kindly escorted Colton to the parking lot after he asked to see you. And *then,* I punched him in his other eye, okay? A few times." He glanced at James with a smirk on his face. "I feel *much* better now."

I decided not to dignify that with a response. I took a better look at Luke's appearance from head to toe, almost leaning out of my bed to do so. His faded, distressed jeans had a new smattering of red on them that was notably absent before.

"Is that blood on your pants?!"

His eyebrows knit together as he looked down at his legs, grumbling as if the stain were a minor intrusion.

"Uh," he paused, "It's not *my* blood on my pants. Does that make it better?"

Liam let out a cackling laugh from the other side of the room. I glared at him, and he smacked his hand over his mouth to try to silence himself.

"I'm sorry, I can't—"

He continued laughing until Zoey chuckled out, *"Lee!"*

"What? *It's funny.* Sorry, Claire." I rolled my eyes at him as he began to speak to Luke. "Hey, he'll never call you a pretty boy again, so you got that goin' for ya."

Luke let out a hearty laugh, joining Liam in his amusement.

"I wouldn't plan on any of us ever seeing him again, but thanks, bud."

Epilogue

I t was a quiet New Year's Eve night—and I don't think anyone minded that in the least.

Luke and I were tangled in each other's arms as we sat on the couch in my apartment. We had finally managed to finagle a position where the pain of our respective injuries weren't exacerbated. I laid on my right side, twisted toward Luke with my left leg *very carefully* rested over his hip. Luke was angled to me, his hand casually grazing back and forth over the side of my upper thigh.

Liam was snoozing two cushions over, his legs outstretched on the coffee table. A large, black sling encompassed his left shoulder all the way down to his arm. Though my own recovery was bound to be an absolute *bitch*, Liam's was projected to be even worse due to the nature in which his clavicle was broken. His strict regimen of prescribed medication to keep his pain at bay would regularly leave him exhausted, and none of us could bear to wake him.

Beyond Liam, Zoey and James sat at the kitchen table across from each other, playfully bickering about something that I couldn't bring myself to focus on. I exhaled softly, genuine happiness running through my veins as the quiet noise from the television signified that the clock had struck midnight, the ball in New York City had dropped, and *Auld Lang Syne* began to play.

"Happy New Year," Luke whispered into my hair.

We shifted just enough to look into each other's eyes, and I replied, "Happy New Year."

Our lips brushed together, and we both hummed contentedly.

There's no telling the intention of the word *escape*. Had I escaped *from* North Carolina those many months ago? Or was I trying to escape *to* something greater? At the beginning of my journey, I would have said the former. Now, however, as I was surrounded by those that I truly loved, I found myself believing in the latter. Though I never truly thought it was something I could obtain, I knew that all of us had evolved into a semblance of a family. The thought made me breathe a sigh of contentment as I folded myself back against Luke's chest.

His heartbeat rhythmically thrummed in my ear and I smiled, for I knew that I had found my own definition of the word that had daunted me so long ago.

Dear Reader

Thank you so much for reading *Thinly Veiled!*

I hope you've enjoyed coming to know the characters in the little world I've created. It has been a thrilling adventure cultivating the plot of these characters' lives, and Claire's story is the first of many to be coming out of Salem. *Veiled in Brick,* the sequel to *Thinly Veiled,* explores Zoey's story and has a release date of August 18, 2023! Find my Amazon author page or website below to learn more.

I would love to hear from you, so feel free to drop me a message on my website or you can follow me on Facebook, Instagram, Twitter or TikTok under the user handle elizamodiste. I also would thoroughly appreciate a quick review if you are so inclined to do so!

Thank you, again—and happy reading.

Eliza

Universal Link to *Veiled in Brick* – https://mybook.to/jjNfi

www.elizamodiste.com

Made in United States
North Haven, CT
13 July 2023

38912442R00211